LIGHTBRINGER

LIGHTBRINGER

GUARDIANS DUOLOGY BOOK 1

RACHEL TERRY

PHARUS PRESS

For information, contact: https://www.rachel-terry.com

Cover art by Coco Merwild

www.cjmerwild.com

Cover design by Rena Violet

www.coversbyviolet.com

Map made with Inkarnate

ISBN: 978-1-960519-00-9

10 9 8 7 6 5 4 3 2 1

To my mom, with whom I shared Wysteria first.

Thank you for stepping through that Gate with me

and for being there every step of the way since.

Because of your encouragement,

the Gates are now open to everyone.

It's been a long time coming.

I hope you enjoy the journey.

Wysteria

The Green Sea

Water Gate
Grasslands
Lightning Gate
The Necropolis
The Swamps of Malenwar
The Briarwood

Ice Gate
Arctic Bay
Iceland
Ice Palace
The Glowing Gate
Flame Gate
Enchanted Forest
The Great Desert
Khae
Wind Gate

COMMON ELEMENTS

FIRE

EARTH

WATER

AIR

UNCOMMON ELEMENTS

LIGHTNING

ICE

RARE ELEMENTS

LIGHT

DARKNESS*

*According to the chronicles of Lumyn, darkness is considered a corruption of one of the other elements, caused by the practice of dark magic, and not an element in and of itself. Due to the forbidden nature of dark magic, it is therefore a rare occurrence.

1

Flames seared Felix's back, their light flickering before him, illuminating the night. The heat was so close, it was painful but he dared not move. His mother's last words to him echoed in his mind, telling him to run and not look back. He had run but he hadn't made it far before the noise had stopped him in his tracks, forcing him to turn.

Why couldn't he have just listened? Why had he stared, unable to look away? Young as he was, he knew the images would haunt him forever—if he didn't have so little time left to live.

Embers flew through the air, smoke nearly choking him as it whipped through the village, obscuring his view. They were still out there, looking for him. He could have run. Maybe he should have. The river wasn't too far away. Would it be enough to quench their flames?

He could run to the Flame Gate and find Damaris. That would have been his best chance. But there was no way he could outrun a fire wolf. Nor could he hide. With their sense of smell and acute hearing, it was only a matter of time.

A moan to his left nearly made Felix jump and he glanced over at the pale arm lying in the grass, refusing to allow his eyes to rise any further and take in the rest of it. The fingers twitched, as though reaching for him. Still alive, then.

For a moment, his heart surged. It wasn't too late. He could find a healer and—

No. No one could survive wounds like that.

The smoke cleared briefly and he could see them. The pack of wolves stood in the middle of the village, their fur ranging from bright orange to dark crimson red. The largest one's blue eyes seemed to glow in the firelight, his over-long fangs stained.

Felix imagined those fangs tearing into him, the way they had his mother, and he shuddered.

"I know you're here, little one. Come out." The wolf's voice was guttural, but also strangely soft. "We'll find you sooner or later. Why not save us both the trouble? We won't hurt you. You're no threat to us."

Felix didn't believe the creature for a second. But he could feel his heart thudding in his ribcage, so hard he felt lightheaded from it. His nose was filled with smoke, charred wood and the tangy, coppery scent of blood. He could feel his resolve slipping, the urge to run seizing him.

His muscles were trembling, unable to remain still as he crouched behind the corner of what had been his home— before it had been set ablaze. He should have picked a better hiding spot. He should have kept running. He shouldn't have looked—

He looked up to see the wolf's ice blue eyes fixed on him and knew he'd been found.

"There you are," the wolf hissed, striding forward.

The beast was in no hurry, but he didn't have to be. Felix's limbs, so eager to flee only moments before, had frozen in place. He took a deep breath. He would be brave. He wouldn't cry. He could do that much.

A flash of movement behind the approaching wolves snared his attention. One moment the unicorn wasn't there and the next, she had coalesced out of the smoke like a ghost. White was her coat, black her mane, tail, hooves, and the horn spiraling from her forehead. Her eyes glowed a solid red, unlike all the other times Felix had seen her.

She looked like a demon stepping through the smoke, a creature of fire and ash, but the fear that Felix had felt melted away as he stared at her. He wanted to call out to her, but he dared not. The wolves seemed oblivious of her presence.

But his mind called out the name, anyway, as if she could hear him.

Damaris.

The alpha wolf seemed to realize something else had captured Felix's attention. One of his long ears snapped backward and he glanced over his shoulder, muscles tensing as he saw the Guardian.

Damaris's lips peeled back, revealing her fangs. For a moment, no one moved. Then a gust of wind swept through the village, smoke once more obscuring Felix's view. He cowered behind the corner of the house, arms thrown protectively over his head, listening to the snarls and yelps of pain that rang out.

One of the fire wolves melted out of the smoke, flying through the air to land only a few feet away with a bone-crunching thud. Felix flinched, but it did not move. He shut his eyes so tightly they hurt. Part of the roof collapsed, landing behind him in a shower of sparks that stung his skin, but still he did not move.

The sounds of the skirmish faded around him. He lay there, shaking.

Waiting.

And then she spoke. "Felix."

Felix gasped, his eyes flying open in time to see his room illuminated for a split second by the streak of lightning, the crash of thunder following immediately, shaking the palace walls around him.

For a moment, he lay still, trying to get his bearings, breathing heavily. His skin was glistening with a thin layer of cold sweat and the bedsheets were tangled around his legs. He was in his room at the palace. There was no wolf, no fire. No Damaris.

He sighed, taking a deep breath, and sat up in bed. He was safe here, safer than anywhere else he could possibly be. The Glowing Gate would keep any threats from entering the palace grounds.

Felix stood, bare feet sinking into the plush carpet, and walked to the bathroom that was attached to his bedroom. He picked up a pitcher of water and poured it into the basin, cupping his hands and splashing the liquid over his face and neck.

He refused to glance up at the mirror, knowing all too well what he would see. It would only remind him of that night long ago.

The nightmares were always the same, or some variation of each other. Felix had relived it all too many times to count, but he never got used to it. He went to bed every night, half afraid, wondering if this night would be peaceful or if they'd come for him again. In the past, dread had sometimes kept him from seeking sleep and he would put it off until exhaustion overtook him.

But that didn't make for a very effective soldier. People were counting on him. Their lives depended on his ability to act when necessary. His certainly did. If and when the time ever came to face that creature from his past, he had to be ready. He would likely only get one chance.

So he had eventually learned to simply surrender to sleep, hope that the nightmares left him alone for one more night, and if not, then to deal with it.

The worse ones were where Damaris never arrived and his imagination filled in what would have happened had she not been there that night. But she had come. He was living proof of it. That night, she had been more than merely the Guardian of the Flame Gate. She had been his Guardian as well.

Felix turned, walking back into the bedroom, making his way over to the doors that led out onto the balcony. They were open, allowing a slight breeze to wash over him, chilling his skin. Despite the warmth of the Wysterian summer night, he shivered. He leaned his arms on the stone railing and looked out at the sight before him.

The Enchanted Forest was vast and he surveyed the dark silhouettes of the trees, thunder rumbling in the distance. The worst of the storm had not yet reached the palace, but it would soon enough; Felix could see the lightning flickering in the clouds above and felt the first raindrops caress his skin. Below, he could just make out the tiny, distant golden glowing lights that floated about the forest, flickering every now and then like fireflies.

He turned to look out over the courtyard, at the flowers, sculptures and the large fountain in the middle, its water silvery in the moonlight. The lanterns were lit around the palace fence, positioned at regular intervals. Even at night, there was a warm glow to the place.

His eyes went to the Glowing Gate itself that marked the entrance to the palace. It was a massive, tall structure, gently pulsing with white light, tinged with gold.

Felix was about to go inside and attempt to sleep when he heard it. A deep, eerie howl rang out, long and low.

Gooseflesh crawled up his arms as the hair on the back of his neck stood up.

It was too deep to belong to an ordinary wolf. He knew what it was. He'd just seen the creatures in his dream. Only this was no dream.

He leaned over the railing, frantically searching the grounds below, but could see nothing, no cause for alarm. The howl had been in the distance, though far closer than he'd heard in years. In fact, he couldn't remember the last time.

Some believed they had simply faded away when Galatea had left and that they no longer existed.

Felix didn't believe it. For one thing, he knew it wasn't true, but he also couldn't *afford* to believe it. He knew they were waiting, somewhere out there, just as he was, biding their time, but that their paths would cross again.

The howl came once more, both chilling and an immense relief. As much as he loathed them, he needed them to still be alive. At least one of them.

He waited, but the world remained silent except for the wind whispering through the trees and the occasional soft tinkling of windchimes. The sound drifted down from Lylla's quarters at the top of the palace. She loved her windchimes. Listening to them, he felt some of the tension leave him.

But it didn't last long. There were fire wolves out there somewhere. Why were they active now after years of silence, without so much as a sighting? Did it mean something or was he merely reading too much into it out of desperation?

He had to restrain the urge to rush out there right now and hunt them down. He wanted nothing more. But that would be foolish in the extreme and he was reminded of what happened the last time he tried such a thing every time he looked in the mirror.

Felix reached up absently with one hand, running his fingers over the scars that marred the left side of his face, the flesh puckered, jagged lines across his skin, red and angry.

The scars weren't burning, so either the wolf was too far away or it wasn't him. Or both.

A sudden surge of anger spiked through him and in that moment, he didn't much care what had brought the wolves back. There was only one thing that mattered. If the wolves had returned, Felix was determined to find them.

And kill one.

2

It was dead.

Sara knew that, but she was startled to find the eyeless, desiccated fox leering at her as Mrs. Miley leaned over the counter. Sara considered it to be something found along the roadside rather than draped around an old woman's neck, but Mrs. Miley was of the generation that over-dressed whenever leaving the house—even if only for a trip to the library.

She liked Mrs. Miley well enough, but today it was an effort to return her smile.

"Can I help you with anything?"

"Oh, no, thank you, dear. I'm just looking."

Mrs. Miley turned to face the rest of the room and Sara exhaled. She was the only one in the library at this hour, which wasn't surprising in such a small town, and knew she could expect several more hours of dull monotony.

Still, it was an enjoyable enough job. She'd had it for only a few months and it didn't pay very well, but she wasn't doing it for the money.

Sara was simply grateful to have something to do during the summer months, to take her mind off the one thing she didn't want to think about. The one thing she couldn't seem to escape.

"Interesting collection you've got here," Mrs. Miley remarked, interrupting Sara's thoughts.

The old woman had moved to the center of the room, where several large glass display cases stood, regarding the items contained within.

Sara's gaze flicked over to it and she swallowed. The collection of curious items had been added to over the years, donations streaming in from the townspeople. Her mother had been one of them, but that would have been too difficult to explain.

"That's Professor Lawrence's," Sara said instead. "He's the library's director." *And something of a curator, too.*

"Will he be in today?"

"I'm afraid not."

The older woman pressed her lips together. "Pity. I'd have liked to ask him about it. Do you know anything about them?" She gave Sara an odd look, her eyes narrowing slightly.

Sara looked up at her again, feeling slightly uncomfortable under the woman's sudden scrutiny. She found herself wondering, not for the first time, just how old Mrs. Miley was. She looked at least eighty, but Sara had found she was terrible at guessing people's ages.

"I'm afraid I don't," she lied.

She wished Professor Lawrence were there even more than Mrs. Miley did, so he could explain. The old woman had eyed the items with interest during previous visits—it would be hard not to—but she'd never asked Sara about them.

Sara's mom had loaned some of the items to the local college and upon her death, they'd been bequeathed to

Professor Lawrence, who had since displayed them here at the library.

But Sara didn't feel like explaining that to Mrs. Miley, or to anyone for that matter. It was a subject that was still too raw.

She'd looked at the collection when she'd first been hired and occasionally found herself drawn to the items beneath the glass whenever she was bored. There seemed to be no rhyme or reason to it, other than perhaps she felt a connection to her mother in a way. A piece of her that still remained.

There was an antique dagger; a purple gemstone; a hand mirror; something that vaguely resembled a piece of jewelry, fashioned in a circle out of crystals with strings of more crystal beading hanging down; vases; small statues; antique cups, and many more items that Sara didn't know the significance of.

But being a library, the thing that had interested her most of all was a thick tome. The cover and spine were cracked with age and the ends of the pages were yellow and uneven. It had been set to one side, half-buried beneath old medicine bottles and other useless bric-a-brac.

Sara looked down at the necklace dangling over her chest and picked up the smooth green stone, running a finger over it. It, too, had been yet another item once belonging to her mother. Another painful reminder that she couldn't quite part with.

She suddenly found that she couldn't stand to look at it a moment longer and shoved it beneath her shirt, out of sight. She glanced up to find the old woman watching her.

"Anyway," Sara said quickly. "Are you sure I can't help you find anything?"

"Actually, yes." Mrs. Miley set a small slip of paper down on the counter, a book title scrawled in pencil across its folded surface. "Do you have this in large print? My eyes aren't what they used to be."

It was the work of only a moment to locate the book Mrs. Miley desired. Sara scanned the book, stamped the due date, and handed it to her.

"There you are."

Mrs. Miley thanked her, taking the book in her small hands. As she turned to leave, Sara bid her a good day and watched as the woman's diminutive figure tottered toward the door.

It was only after she had gone that Sara realized Mrs. Miley hadn't told her to have a good day as well. It would have been unremarkable except the woman said the same thing each time, always responding with, "You do the same."

Sara shook the thought away. Perhaps she wasn't the only one having a bad day. It shouldn't have bothered her.

But it did.

***

The library was dark and quiet as Galatea approached, her feet silent on the stone steps. She had waited long after the last light had flicked off, the doors locked for the night, and the girl hurrying toward home. It would not pay to be too hasty. She hadn't achieved all she had by being impatient.

But she had waited too long for this. She didn't know why any human would still be here this time of night, alone in the dark, but if there happened to be anyone inside, it didn't matter now. Nothing was going to stop her.

She stopped, placing her palms flat against the heavy double doors. This was by far a less sophisticated method, but she didn't have the luxury of picking a lock. Loud, but efficient, it would be the work of only a moment.

Galatea summoned the wind, air pressure building up between her palms and the doors until they burst forward with such force they cracked against the walls on either side. Without hesitation, she stepped inside, flitting like a shadow.

Moonlight streaming through the far window illuminated the library enough for her to see. There was no one behind the counter.

She was alone.

Now that she was inside, she forced herself to keep her posture stooped, her movements slow, steps shuffling across the carpet, as an old woman would. Soon, she would be able to abandon Mrs. Miley's guise, but not yet.

Galatea chuckled to herself as she thought of both how easy it had been and what she had been reduced to. It had been so simple to convince Mrs. Miley to open her door and then she hadn't stood a chance.

Glamours could change one's appearance, but Galatea couldn't take on the guise of someone living. Small town though it may have been, she could hardly go traipsing around Mayfair looking like her real self and risk possibly being recognized. She'd solved that problem quickly, Mrs. Miley proving to be the perfect solution.

Conscious of the noise she'd made breaking in and time slipping away, Galatea made her way across the floor.

If she'd still had access to her attribute, or main element, it would have been easy. She could have simply manipulated the lock and walked in the front door.

But alas. It would do no good lamenting the loss of her former element. She had gained something far more powerful in return.

If the night's efforts proved successful, she would finally be able to leave this realm behind. Earth was a fractured shell of its former grandeur. It had once been vibrant and flowing with magic just as much as Wysteria, but now it was dead and lifeless, sapping her power the longer she lingered. And she had lingered a long time.

At least she could still manage to conjure a convincing glamour to disguise her appearance. After fifty years stuck on Earth, it was quite an impressive feat. *Especially considering that the girl hadn't seen through it.*

Galatea stopped before the glass display cases, tapping a fingernail against the surface.

This was another instance in which her main element would have come in handy. Glass was made from sand, which was part of the earth, and thus she would have been able to manipulate it without a problem, causing it to crack and shatter at a mere touch.

Those back home who weren't earth attributes had often looked down on her element and found it to be less useful than their own. Damaris would have been in agreement. Why manipulate plants when you could just incinerate them?

Galatea's lip curled. How wrong they were. Earth was far more useful and dangerous than they gave it credit for and she liked to think they had realized it before the end. But she had sacrificed it for something even better.

Any element would have provided a more elegant solution, but where Galatea had magic, Mrs. Miley did not. Brute force would have to do.

She picked up one of the library chairs, pretending to struggle as she lifted it, and tossed it against the glass. It shattered, shards tinkling down like rain.

Mindful of the jagged glass ringing the opening, she reached through the hole. A contemptuous flick of her hand scattered the cups and glass bottles resting atop the worn, thick book in the corner. Wrapping her fingers around its spine, she lifted it out.

To call it a book wasn't really fair. The proper term was grimoire. The cover was faded leather, absent of any ornamentation.

Galatea cracked the grimoire open and began leafing idly through some of the pages. Faded black ink greeted her on some, but, perplexingly, some of the pages remained blank. Was it because they had never been written on in the first place or was the text somehow hidden from her sight?

She frowned. It would warrant looking into later. For now, all that mattered was that she actually held the tome in her hand. The girl had told her the collection belonged to Professor Lawrence. She could always confront him about the blank pages if it came to that.

But not yet. Not in the state she was in.

She may be able to summon wind and maintain a glamour, but that was a world away from taking on a fellow Guardian.

Galatea reached back through the hole she had made, snatching the purple stone. The instant her fingers touched it, her nerves tingled as if her arm had fallen asleep.

She inhaled deeply as the magic prickled, like pinched nerves coming back to life. Well, the night was far from a loss. She had the grimoire and she had just acquired an Echo Stone, which would amplify her magic. She could use more, perform more complicated techniques, at less cost to her energy.

The glamoured elf tucked the stone into a pocket. She had heard of Echo Stones before, but never seen one in person. They were very rare—for good reason—and highly sought after—mostly for the wrong reasons.

Glancing at the case once more, Galatea snatched up the antique dagger. She didn't know how far she could strain her depleted magic, but if she was forced to resort to less dignified means of defending herself, at least she would have a weapon.

For good measure, she stuffed a few cups, medicine bottles, and antique silverware in her other pockets. One couldn't be too obvious, after all.

She turned and headed for the door, having completed what she'd come for. Galatea touched one hand to the doorframe as she passed, igniting it instantly.

Damaris did have one thing right. Sometimes all one needed was a little fire.

She'd already blended into the night by the time the fire alarm went off.

Mayfair had a volunteer fire department and they were not always on duty at the station. It would take some time for them to arrive and by then, she'd be long gone. *All according to plan.*

The time had come for her to leave Earth for the time being and her heart quickened at the prospect.

But for that, she needed a Gate.

There were three in Mayfair to choose from, some more appealing than others.

She could take the Ice Gate, but not only would she have to deal with the Guardians on both sides, she'd end up in Iceland and in her current condition, she wasn't strong enough to withstand its biting cold.

She could choose the Lighting Gate, but if she managed to get past the Earth-side Guardian, she'd still have to face Wanderer and she wasn't strong enough for that, either.

That left only the Wind Gate. Professor Lawrence's own Gate, which seemed somehow fitting.

He shouldn't be a problem. He'd be asleep in his house and the Gate was a few acres behind his home, hidden within the woods. Usually, Guardians did not like to be so far away from their Gates, but having a hidden one had its advantages.

That was one reason why Damaris could leave hers for such a long period of time. It had made her indispensable to the queen. Not even Galatea knew where the Flame Gate was—much to her annoyance.

The last thing Professor Lawrence would expect was her sneaking through his Gate in the middle of the night after she'd just stolen his grimoire. The thought gave her distinct pleasure.

But she would still have to face Wysteria's Guardian once on the other side. Kadir was not always at his Gate—being the chieftain of the desert elves often meant he was in the city of Khae.

If he was at the Gate, she would just have to deal with it as best she could. She did have one advantage over him, one element he could not use.

Even if he wasn't there, he left guards posted at the temple that housed the Wind Gate. She would have to face them at the very least.

But they were no Guardians.

Galatea made her way through the town and into the countryside. Most of the windows in the houses she passed were dark and only streetlamps illuminated the road. She wasn't worried about late-night drivers spotting her—there was no one on the road and if any were to approach, she could summon a quick glamour.

A stray cat eyed her from across the street, but kept its distance. Somewhere nearby, a dog barked. There were no other signs of life.

The streetlamps ended along the road out of town, just past the church, and she was gradually plunged into darkness. The truck route went down a small hill, with two small fields on either side. The trees that ringed the road seemed to encircle it and made the darkness feel closer still.

Galatea dropped her glamour. She felt no difference physically—it was only an illusion after all—but she much preferred her true form. She was an elf, six feet tall, with unnaturally pale skin and black hair down to the middle of her back. Her long black dress swished over the grass along the side of the road.

After about two miles of walking from the library, Galatea reached the farm field beside Lawrence's home and turned off the road, heading straight back to where the field met the woods.

And there it was, hidden amongst the thick leaves.

The Wind Gate wasn't much to look at on this side. Just an old, red metal gate that was badly rusting. But Galatea knew what she would see on the other side and smiled to herself.

There was no one to be seen—the only sound a symphony of frogs at a nearby pond—and no one attempted to stop her as she raised a hand and compelled the Gate to open, thankful she still had enough magic to accomplish the task.

The Gate swung open, the only sound a slight hissing as the bottom scraped against the fallen leaves. Stretching out ahead was more of the same woods, but Galatea knew better.

She stepped forward and the instant she walked through, her surroundings changed. She found herself enclosed in the back of an enormous building, its walls made of gold.

Gone was the humid summer night of Mayfair, replaced with the chilly air of the desert at night. She shivered involuntarily and turned to close the Gate behind her. On this side, it appeared as the back wall of the temple, which had a gaping hole in it for the moment, the tiles having peeled back, but it closed at her command to become solid once more.

Galatea took a deep breath, her earlier bravado somewhat fading. Now, she had to pray that Kadir had not chosen this night to spend at the temple. This wasn't the day of their annual festival, was it?

She couldn't remember. Although time passed on Earth the same way as it did in Wysteria, the seasons didn't—at least not in the Midwest—and it had confused her.

There was only one way to find out.

She strode forward, feeling grains of sand beneath her bare feet. The front of the temple was open and years of wind had strewn sand across the temple floor.

Galatea paused next to the massive statue of Azuma, the spirit of the Eastern Wind, an enormous dragon that would resemble an Eastern dragon if not for the two vast feathered wings. She crouched next to his talons for a moment, peering out of the tall entrance.

She did not see Kadir's familiar figure, but she could make out the silhouettes of two guards, the moonlight gleaming on their white hair.

She breathed out a silent sigh of relief. It seemed luck was on her side. She fingered the dagger tucked into her belt, tugging it free. The element of surprise would be enough for the first, and she felt confident that her magic could take care of the second.

Treading on silent feet, she crept up behind the first guard, dagger in hand. In one fluid motion, she brought it around in front of him and slashed his throat.

He staggered away from her, one hand reaching up in a futile attempt to staunch the flow of blood pouring from his neck, eyes wide in horror.

His companion turned toward her and she knew he recognized her. In his shock, he foolishly scrambled to free his sword instead of attempting a magical defense.

The delay was all she needed.

Galatea thrust her hand forward, lightning springing from her fingertips. It lanced toward the remaining guard and struck. He cried out briefly, dropping his weapon onto the sand with a muffled *thump*, his muscles seizing up as electricity coursed through him.

A moment later, he joined his companion and slumped lifeless to the ground, the lightning having stopped his heart.

Galatea regarded them both without sympathy. Their deaths could have been much more unpleasant.

But to use darkness against them would have raised eyebrows even further. They would probably all suspect her to be behind the attack as it was, but why give them undeniable proof?

Anyone could have murdered two guards with lightning and a dagger.

Galatea turned away and surveyed her surroundings. Sand stretched in each direction for miles, where it would eventually meet the sea. In the far distance, she could see the trees of the Enchanted Forest and the snow-capped mountains of Iceland. The city of Khae lay to the east, alight even at this late hour.

She had done it.

For the first time since stepping through the Gate, Galatea allowed herself to relax. She could feel her magic returning already, strengthening by the second. After fifty long years, she was back where she belonged.

She was home.

She tilted her head back to look up at the sky, where stars were visible between whisps of cloud. In that moment, it was the most beautiful sight she had ever seen.

Galatea closed her eyes, the wind stirring her hair.

I'm coming, Jack.

3

T he sharp *ding* of a text message jerked Sara out of sleep. She groaned, silently cursing herself that she hadn't remembered to silence her phone before going to bed, and rolled over, blindly groping for it on the desk. Her fingers wrapped around it and she tapped on the screen.

She hissed as it came to life, blinding her in the darkness, and she stabbed at the brightness meter, lowering it all the way down. Squinting, she peered at the screen. It was well past midnight. The text, from her friend, Nadia, read:

Something's going on at the library. There are fire trucks and the police are here.

A stab of alarm shot through Sara. The police? It had to be something serious. And Nadia would know. She lived only a few houses down from the library.

Her phone pinged again as Nadia sent another text, adding:

Thought I saw smoke but couldn't be sure.

Sara threw the covers off and hastily changed out of her pajamas. Part of her knew she should simply go back to bed. There was nothing she could do. But getting back to sleep would be impossible. She'd worry about what was going on until she knew.

And even then, there was no guarantee that she wouldn't continue worrying.

Her hair had begun to come out of the braid she'd put it in, but that would have to wait. She shoved her phone in her bra—upset, and not for the first time, that women's clothes had a disturbing lack of pockets—and headed for the door.

The house was dark and quiet. Sara winced, freezing in place, as one of the stairs creaked beneath her weight. But her dad would be sound asleep as he always was after a long day at work and the house remained quiet. She let out a sigh of relief.

In the kitchen, Sara snatched up her keys from the bowl on the counter, keeping them pressed together so they wouldn't jangle, and hurried to her car in the garage. She lived about a mile from the library and so getting there would take no time at all.

The library parking lot was lit up when Sara arrived. The lights on the main fire truck were flashing and, true to her word, the police Nadia had mentioned were there, too, parked by the door. Instinctively, Sara looked up through the windshield, searching for smoke. She found none, but the library entrance was blackened and charred and her throat tightened at the sight.

She parked on the far side of the lot, out of the way of any emergency vehicles, and stepped out into the muggy summer night. She'd expected to see Nadia, but she wasn't in sight.

A policeman was standing in front of the door and held out a hand to deter her as she approached.

"Sorry, miss. This is an active crime scene. I'm going to have to ask you not to come any closer."

"Crime scene?" Sara demanded, feeling her pulse spike. "What's happened? Is anyone hurt?" She glanced around but didn't see an ambulance.

"Seems to be a robbery. Now, if you'll step back—"

"A robbery?" Sara repeated. It looked more like there'd been a fire. "What was taken?"

"Some items out of the museum collection."

That could only mean one thing. Professor Lawrence would be devastated. Sara wondered if the thief had taken any of the items that had once belonged to her mother. She felt anger beginning to boil up, causing heat to wash over her skin.

That heat was immediately doused in ice, anger swallowed by cold fear. Her eyes flicked once more to the blackened entrance. What if there was nothing left at all?

"What about the fire—"

"It was contained to the front lobby," the policeman assured her.

Sara let out a slow breath. A robbery and fire both on the same night was no coincidence and a nasty word came to mind. Arson.

Who would do something like this?

Sara shook her head. "Where's Professor Lawrence?"

"He's inside, speaking to the sheriff. He'll be out shortly—hey!"

Sara had ducked past him and charged for the door, hardly knowing what she was doing. "I have to see him. Now!"

She had to make sure that he was all right and find out if there was anything she could do to help. The robbery would upset him and she hated seeing him unhappy. He had been kind to her when she needed kindness and she was determined to do all she could to repay that.

But even more than that, she had to see what had been taken. She had to know.

The entryway smelled heavily of smoke and burnt wood as she ducked inside, coughing at the lingering fumes. The walls had taken damage from both the flames and water, but it could have been far worse. The fire department had responded quickly.

She found Professor Lawrence, standing in the middle of the library, speaking to the county sheriff, Harris. "Professor?"

Professor Lawrence turned to her, looking surprised. He was in his seventies—at least Sara thought so—with wiry white hair and a beard to match. Thick wire-framed glasses perched on his nose.

Sheriff Harris pursed his lips. "Miss Montgomery."

"What's happened? What's been taken?"

"It's all right," Professor Lawrence said to the sheriff, before turning back to her. He gestured to the glass display case.

She gasped as her eyes fell upon the gaping hole, glass shards spilled out across the floor. Several items had been knocked from their places and there were bare spots on the shelves.

"I've checked my records and tried to make sense out of the chaos as best I can," the professor replied. "So far as I can tell, we're missing a book, an antique dagger, a purple gemstone, and a few of the porcelain cups and glass bottles."

"Worth anything?" the sheriff asked, his tone making it clear what he thought of such items being stored in a library.

The professor shrugged. "They're worth a great deal to the people who donated them, certainly. But they don't have much monetary value."

"They were there when I left for the day," Sara blurted, hoping neither of them would suspect her of taking anything.

"I'm sure they were," Professor Lawrence assured her.

"Did you see anyone suspicious yesterday, Miss Montgomery? Maybe someone you hadn't seen before or who showed undue interest in the collection?"

She turned to the sheriff and swallowed. He was a large man, probably approaching middle age, with a few wisps of hair clinging to the top of his head.

"I—no. It was a slow day." *Like usual.*

The sheriff turned back to the professor. "Do you have any security cameras?"

"Yes, I do."

"We'll need a list of all the people who came in yesterday and withdrew material." The sheriff turned to the Professor. "And of course, we'll check the security camera footage."

Sara glanced at Professor Lawrence, fidgeting, wishing she could be of more help. "Do you think the fire was deliberately set?"

"That would be for the fire marshal to determine, but let's just say it certainly looks suspicious."

"How did they get in?"

"Fire department got here first," the sheriff replied. "They reported the double doors were wide open, engulfed in flames." He shook his head and hitched his belt higher. "Well, we'll keep an eye out for any shady characters in the area. I'm sure it'll be the usual. Someone needing beer money or some quick cash for their next fix."

"Thank you, sheriff."

"Is there anything I can do to help?" Sara asked, eyeing the broken glass.

Professor Lawrence smiled at her but it didn't quite reach his eyes. "That's very kind of you, my dear, but I'll see to it. Obviously, the library will have to close for the time being until the damage can be repaired, so don't worry about work."

She followed the two men back outside. The policeman was still at his post and upon seeing the sheriff, he began to apologize.

"I'm sorry, sir," he said, glancing in her direction. "I tried to stop her—"

But Harris silenced him with a wave of his hand.

Not knowing what else to do, Sara made her way over to her car without looking back. Fumbling with her keys, she manually unlocked the door, wishing she had an automatic key fob. She sank down into the driver's seat and sighed, leaning her head back against the headrest.

Her earlier anger resurfaced with a vengeance and she clenched the steering wheel with her fingers until they ached. She didn't think any of her mother's items had been taken, but she couldn't be sure. But either way...

How dare someone take something so important from someone else?

Sheriff Harris was probably right. Most likely it was some lowlife who had seen something that looked shiny and valuable and taken it without sparing so much as a thought for the pain it would cause Sara.

There wasn't a lot of crime in the area, but what there was always happened for the same reasons. She hoped bitterly that Sheriff Harris caught the culprit.

The car needed gas and not yet willing to return home, Sara pulled out of the library parking lot, heading for the gas station at the edge of town. It was just across the road from the Country Corner diner where she, Nadia, and Max always hung out. Max's sister worked there as a part-time waitress.

There was a light shining from within the convenience store, if one could call it that. It looked more like it was out of the fifties or something, untouched by time, and still full service. If she so wished, Hank, the proprietor, would come out and pump gas for her or clean her windshield.

There was no need for that now and Sara stepped out, thankful that the place at least accepted credit cards. She looked up as the store door swung open and Hank meandered over to her. She smiled to herself. He'd likely recognized her car with its peeling paint. Lord knew she'd come here often enough.

"Bit late for you, isn't it, Miss Sara?" Hank inquired, leaning an elbow on the top of her car.

As usual, he was dressed in a flannel shirt, undone at the collar. His blue jeans were paint-splattered, his work boots scuffed. His dark brown hair stuck out from under his newsboy-style cap and his jaw was covered in prickly stubble. He looked to be in his forties.

She smiled, reaching for the pump. "Yeah. Nadia texted me, saying there was something going on at the library. Fire trucks and police."

Hank intercepted her, pumping gas for her instead. It seemed to come naturally to him and she didn't mind. "I saw the fire trucks go past a while ago. Didn't know where they were headin'. Is everything okay?"

Sara leaned against the car, crossing her arms. There was no one else about this time of night except for the two of them. "The fire didn't spread much, so that's good. But someone had broken in and stolen some of Professor Lawrence's antiques."

Hank looked up at her sharply, the humor fading from his green eyes. "The police know who did it?"

She shook her head. "They're gonna check the security cameras. And the library is closed until further notice. He didn't show it, but I think Professor Lawrence is really upset."

Hank gave her a look that told her that he knew she was upset as well. He replaced the pump in its holder and Sara collected the receipt. "You be careful, lass. This type of stuff don't happen 'round here. I don't want you getting hurt."

Sara gave him a funny look. "I doubt I'm in any danger. The thief took what they were after. I don't think they'll be back."

"Still. You see any strange folk, unfamiliar, you steer clear of 'em. And if you ever need help, you know where to find me."

She let out a nervous laugh. "Of course I do."

Hank was starting to scare her. But he was probably just concerned for her because he knew she worked at the library and that happened to be where the crime had taken place. He wouldn't be acting this way if the bank had been robbed.

Hank smiled, crow's feet appearing around his eyes. "Atta girl. Well, I'd better let you get back home or wherever it is you're off to." He winked as though she'd just let him in on a secret and it was safe with him.

Sara rolled her eyes. "I'm a good girl, Hank. No sneaking around after hours for me."

He chuckled. "I know you are, sweetheart. Oh, before I forget." He reached into a pocket in his shirt and withdrew a Snickers bar, handing it to her.

She grinned. He'd given her free candy bars from the time she was 'knee high to a grasshopper'. "People will start to think you play favorites, Hank Marshal."

He shrugged. "Maybe I do. You be careful going home." He stepped past her, heading back toward the door and waved as she drove off.

Sara waved back. Hank didn't have to worry about going home. His house was connected to the back of the gas station. She sighed, pausing at the four-way stop to unwrap and take a bite of the Snickers bar.

She'd known Hank for most of her life. He'd been good friends with her mom and she knew that he was trying to help her, in his own way, just like Professor Lawrence.

She took her time on the short drive back home, mulling over what had happened, glancing at the dilapidated, neglected buildings of the town she called home and felt a pang in her chest. It felt like sadness and disgust, both mixed into one emotion if that were possible.

The town really was a dump. There was no other way to put it and she was tired of it.

Once she graduated high school next year, there would be nothing for her in this place. Nothing to keep her here, other than the few people she knew. There had to be something more to life than this sleepy little town where nothing ever happened.

Well, nothing until tonight.

Her dad had told her stories of growing up in this town and how it used to have so much more. Multiple car dealerships, a lumberyard, a barbershop, a meat market, a grocery store…

Looking at it now, she just couldn't imagine it.

Once upon a time, Sara had seen college as her ticket out of here, to a successful photography career, perhaps traveling the world as a photo journalist. But she still had one more year of high school to slog through. And after her mom died, any such ambitions had seemed to die with her. Photography had always been something they'd done together, a passion her mother had encouraged, and now it lacked its former appeal. The thought of picking up her camera was more than she could bear.

It was all she'd wanted to do with her life and she had no back-up plan. Sometimes she felt adrift, like a boat with sails but no rudder. Winds were blowing, taking her along with it, but she had no way to steer.

Sara pushed the thoughts away and the emotions they threatened to bring with them. She just had to be patient, that's all. Eventually, she'd make it out of this town and find a place that was meant for her.

With a sigh, Sara pulled into her driveway. Once inside, she made her way back up the stairs and collapsed into bed without bothering to change out of her clothes.

The next morning, she met Nadia and Max at the Country Corner diner for breakfast. It was an appropriate name, considering it was situated on the corner. The outside was painted to look like a white barn and the inside reflected that as well.

Sara slid into the seat opposite Nadia and Max in their usual booth. She liked to be able to face the black cat clock on the far wall.

"There you are!" Nadia exclaimed. "We've already ordered. Sorry. I told Max to wait but he wouldn't hear it."

"I'm hungry," Max grumbled, shoving his glasses further up his nose.

He was heavyset, with dark, shaggy hair while Nadia was thin as a rail, with long blonde hair she usually wore in a ponytail.

"It's fine," Sara replied. "Sorry. I meant to be here sooner, but I overslept."

Conversation momentarily stalled as the waitress came over and took her order: a coffee and two pancakes. Before coming to the diner for the first time, Sara would have thought that two pancakes wouldn't have been enough to feed anyone, but her mind had been changed for her. Oftentimes it was all she could do to finish both of them, they were so big.

The diner had a reputation for having greasy food, but at least you couldn't say they skimped on the portion sizes.

"So spill!" Nadia said as soon as the waitress had left. "Are you going to tell us what happened at the library last night? Or am I going to have to wait to read about it in the paper? You know I don't read that. Although, in this case, I might. Still, it won't come out until Tuesday and today's Friday!"

Sara obligingly filled them in on the details and by the time she finished, her food had arrived and she dug in hungrily.

Nadia gasped. "I can't believe it! A real-life robbery, right here in Mayfair! That's the kind of thing you see on the news, not here. I mean, this type of thing just doesn't happen around here."

"So people keep saying," Sara remarked, aware of the irony. How many times had she wished for more excitement around here? Now she'd gotten some, but it was far from what she'd had in mind.

"That's not true," Max protested around a mouthful of burger. Sara could barely understand him. He gulped it down and continued. "What about the bank robbery of '79?"

Nadia rolled her eyes. "He never even robbed the bank! The bank president knocked the gun out of his hands and held him down until the police arrived. He's dead now anyway, I think, so it couldn't have been him."

"I wasn't suggesting it was," Max retorted. Nothing made him happy like a good debate and it was on now. "Well, what about that creepy green van?"

Nadia shook a pink sugar packet, ripped it open, and dumped it into her coffee. "What creepy green van?"

"You know, the creepy green van that was seen around town a year ago and supposedly broke into someone's house."

"*Supposedly*, Max," Nadia said, reaching for a second sugar packet. "Supposedly."

Sara shrugged. "My grandparents' house was broken into a long time ago. Someone took some knives." But that had been a *long* time ago. Long before she'd been born.

"See," Max said. "Stuff like that does happen around here."

"Okay, so we're not completely crime-free. But it doesn't happen like *this*."

Max glanced out the window. "And then there was the incident with the clowns last Halloween…"

"Ugh, Max. You don't actually believe that, do you?"

"Of course I do!" Max replied, feigning offense. "They lived in that old abandoned school bus in the field."

Nadia launched into a rant about how clowns, or anyone for that matter, couldn't possibly have lived in that bus, saying that the windows had long since been removed and they would have frozen to death in the winter, not to mention having to compete with racoons for living space. It was all just a stupid rumor someone had made up, thinking themselves clever, but when you really looked at it, it fell apart. And besides, the only people who used that bus were hunters, not clowns, Max!

Sara kept silent, listening in amusement.

Max really would believe anything.

4

The bodies of the two elven guards outside the temple were discovered shortly before dawn, when two other guards arrived to relieve them. Kadir, the desert elf chieftain and the Wind Guardian, was sent for at once.

He rode out to the scene on the back of a white steed and dismounted to stand in front of the fallen soldiers, a faint breeze stirring his long white hair. He wanted nothing more than to be able to move the bodies out of the sun, which would become blazing within a few hours, and take them somewhere respectable where they could be prepared for a proper burial.

But he knew he could not. Whomever the queen sent to deal with this would want to see the bodies as they had been found. And he thought he had a pretty good idea as to who it would be.

In spite of the situation which would bring about such a result, he found his spirits lifted by the thought. It would be good to see her again.

But then his eyes alighted on the bodies and his momentary gladness vanished, replaced by a profound sense of guilt.

He, Kadir, was the Guardian of this Gate and therefore its protection fell to him. It was his responsibility. And where had he been last night? Safe and sound within the city walls, in his lush house.

Whatever had attacked these guards should have fallen to him to face, but they had been the ones to pay for it.

He shook the thought away. No Guardian, however responsible or powerful, could be expected to be at their Gate at all hours. It wasn't physically possible. And the Gates had been safe for many years.

There hadn't been an incident since the Cataclysm.

But that was no excuse for negligence or leniency. The situation would have to be dealt with.

Kadir turned to his captain, who had accompanied him. "Have your soldiers search the surrounding desert in all directions for any tracks leading away from the temple."

The man carried out his orders, but reported that they had found nothing. It wasn't surprising. It had been a fool's errand, a desperate hope. Any tracks that may have been left in the sand had been blown away in the desert winds.

There was only one option left to him now.

****

"Kadir is in the reception hall."

Lylla turned from her desk, brushing her long turquoise braid over her shoulder, and faced Felix. His face was expressionless, giving nothing away.

He was dressed entirely in black, save for a little silver trim, and stood at attention although there really was no need. But he took his role as one of her Shadows very seriously.

The light streaming through the tall, thin windows landed on his crimson hair and turned it scarlet in places. It also fell upon the scars raking down the left side of his face, but she was used to them and met his green eyes instead.

"Very well," she said, putting down her quill and rising, the bottom of her white dress pooling around her feet. "Is it serious?"

He fell into step beside her, his height even with hers. "He didn't enlighten me as to the details but I imagine so. I can't think of anything that would bring him here if not a grave situation."

The two separated as they reached the reception hall, a large circular room off the foyer of the palace, supported by tall columns. Felix went to stand motionless by one of the columns, enough out of the way to not be intrusive, but close enough to hear every word and leap into action at a moment's notice should there prove to be any threat.

Somewhere in the room, Colin was likewise positioned. Another of her Shadows.

Lylla knew the moment she glimpsed Kadir that Felix had been right in thinking something was wrong. His long white hair was unbound and traveling at speed had left it untidy and bedraggled. He was dressed in fine blue silk, trimmed in gold, but it was crumpled, and his expression was grave. Anyone who did not know him might miss it, but the subtle signs were there in the tension in his jaw, the pinched skin around his pale blue eyes.

Kadir bowed. "Your Highness."

"Kadir." Lylla nodded to him, coming to a halt. "To what do I owe the pleasure?"

The elf grimaced. "No pleasure, I'm afraid." He took a deep, pained breath. "The matter is rather urgent. This morning, the bodies of the two guards posted outside the Wind Gate were discovered. One's throat had been cut and the other we believe to have been electrocuted, based on the burns found on his skin."

In spite of the morning sun, Lylla felt herself go cold. "The Gate has been breached." She could have made it a question, denying the obvious and prolonging the inevitable, but there was no point.

"We believe so, but whether whoever attacked the guards *came* through the Gate or *went* through is unknown."

"I see. And you would like me to send someone to get to the bottom of it?"

"That is what I would like to request, Your Highness."

Lylla inhaled slowly. There was only one person she could think of that could be responsible, unless one of her human Guardians had suddenly gone rogue and that did not bear thinking of.

But neither did the alternative. It would be so much worse. She had hoped that she'd died in the Cataclysm, as so many believed.

But you don't really believe that. They never found a body.

"Very well," she said aloud, summoning what she hoped was a small, but reassuring smile. "I will send Damaris and she can travel back with you."

Damaris would take care of whoever was responsible. Even if it was *her*.

***

Damaris was pleased at the prospect of returning to the desert, even if the circumstances were less than ideal. She had arrived at the palace within an hour of receiving the news, though she hadn't been far away.

It seemed she rarely was, these days.

Lylla had briefly apprised her of the situation and she'd set off with Kadir. Thus far, the chieftain hadn't been one for conversation, which was unlike him, but Damaris wasn't surprised. And conversation was hardly practical, with both of them flying on the back of one of the red desert dragons, the only means of transportation that could bring them to the desert in a reasonable amount of time.

The creature was more than large enough to carry both of them at once, occasionally beating the air with massive leathery wings. Its scales gleamed scarlet in the sunlight, two silver horns curving back from its head. Its claws were also silver and its tail ended in a sharp spear point.

They were sentient beings, answerable to no one save the queen herself, but the desert elves had maintained a good relationship with the dragons for centuries and they were known to assist the chieftains in their time of need.

It never hurt to have a Guardian in one's debt either.

They reached the Great Desert in the afternoon and headed straight for the Golden Temple where the Wind Gate was housed. It was a massive structure, whose function was also to serve as a shrine for the wind spirit, Azuma. The entire building was made completely of gold and shone in the desert sun, visible for miles.

Kadir glanced at her. "I would be grateful for any assistance you can provide, *kirena*."

Damaris dismounted after him and after a brief hesitation, decided to remain in her human form, which had been necessary for the ride. She much preferred her true form, but it tended to intimidate people.

As a human, she was tall for a woman, with brown skin and black hair that she kept in two short braids, each reaching only to her collarbone.

She nodded an acknowledgement to Kadir and then her eyes went to the bodies lying in the sand. "Are these the ones? Have you moved them at all?" She knelt down for a closer look.

Kadir shook his head, his eyes saddening as he looked down at his fallen guards. "No. I wanted to, but I knew you'd want to view them as they were."

Lylla had already told her how each had died. Both were now partially buried beneath the sand, blown in by the wind.

Damaris's eyes narrowed, both in anger at the crime and in puzzlement. "Seems odd, don't you think? The manner of death, I mean. Why attack one with a physical weapon when you can use a magical one?"

"The thought had crossed my mind," Kadir admitted.

"Unless there was more than one attacker."

He blanched. "I hope not."

In spite of the unlikely nature of the suggestion, Damaris found she could believe it. The guards Kadir chose to protect the Gate in his absence would have been highly trained, with magical skill of their own. It was impossible to say whether either of them had put up a fight of any kind, but if they had mortally injured their opponent or opponents, there was no sign of any other bodies.

And any trace of blood would have long since vanished.

Damaris straightened up, crossing her arms. "And you have no idea if someone came through or went through? No tracks leading away, or perhaps a body if their attacker walked away but later succumbed to an injury?"

"We looked. If there were, the wind has erased them."

Of course it has, Damaris thought, the wind tugging at one of her braids.

"Well I suppose I'll have to speak to the Guardian on the other side. I'll be sure to let you know what I find out."

Kadir nodded to her. "Thank you, *kirena.*"

To him, she had always been *kirena.* Elvish for 'my friend'. She thought to herself that if he ever called her by her real name, it would feel strange.

Venturing into Earth was not something she found appealing, even if only for a few minutes. But with the only other people who knew the truth lying on the ground dead, there was no other option. She had to speak to the Wind Gate's other Guardian.

"You can take the bodies away now," she said softly. "They died protecting the Gate and they will be avenged."

She stepped into the cool shade of the temple and began heading for the back. Even after so many years, her human form still felt alien to her. She would never get used to standing on two legs instead of four, or at such shorter height.

Hands did come in useful, though.

With a flick of one hand, she commanded the Gate to open and the back wall peeled away in response. She stepped through and found herself standing in the woods, overlooking a field, in which soybeans had been planted this year. The air, though warm, was instantly cooler than the desert heat and muggy enough to be unpleasant.

She inhaled deeply and began walking along the edge of the field, hoping Professor Lawrence would be at home, or else she'd have to walk all the way to the library. Her sandals crunched on the rock driveway. She rang the doorbell and stepped back.

Out here it was unlikely that anyone would see her, but even if they did, she thought her choice of clothing—a red halter top and black shorts—looked ordinary enough.

There was a glimpse of movement through the window and then, after a moment's struggle with it, the door swung open to reveal Professor Lawrence.

Her first thought was that he looked exactly as she remembered. The differences, if there were any, were subtle. Perhaps he was a bit thinner, his skin a little looser. It made her heart hurt to think of him growing older, but humans didn't live forever.

But then, neither would she.

His eyes were round as saucers. "Damaris!"

She found herself smiling at his expression. "It's been awhile."

"You haven't aged a day. Come in." He moved aside to allow her to step up into the house.

"Thank you," she accepted, stepping up into the small foyer. The floor here was wood, but it transitioned to green carpet as it met the living room.

She followed him over to a low coffee table next to the fireplace. On one side sat an ugly, but comfortable-looking brown recliner, and on the other an even uglier floral-patterned armchair.

"Make yourself comfortable. I can make some tea, if you'd like. Or perhaps something stronger?"

Damaris grinned. "You know me too well."

"Whiskey?"

"Of course." She settled herself in the ugly floral chair, crossing her legs. "You may need it after what I'm about to tell you."

"That good, is it?"

Five minutes later, Professor Lawrence was seated across from her, with his own glass in hand. "Well I suppose you'd best get it over with. What is it?"

Damaris took a sip of her whiskey, savoring the way it burned as it went down. "Last night, two guards standing watch outside the Wind Gate were killed. It seems likely that someone breached the Gate. Do you know what side they may have crossed over from?"

Lawrence had turned an alarming shade of white, the skin under his eyes appearing gray. He swallowed a large gulp of his drink. "I had no idea," he breathed.

"So you…didn't see anything?"

He shook his head. "I must have been asleep. Or maybe I was at the library."

Damaris set her glass down on the coffee table. "I thought the library closed at five."

"It does. But there was a break-in last night. Someone stole some of the artifacts."

Damaris tensed in her chair, her entire body going rigid. "What was stolen?"

"An antique dagger, the Echo Stone, and the grimoire of spells. The rest of it was of no importance."

"What do the police say?"

"Oh, the usual. No money in the till and they saw something shiny so they took it."

"And the very same night, someone crosses through *your* Gate and kills two guards. I think, given that knowledge, that it's safe to say they crossed over from Earth."

"I didn't know about the guards," Lawrence murmured. "I'm so sorry."

He looked positively wretched and Damaris felt a prick of sympathy for him. She was suddenly aware of how fortunate her position was. The ability to leave her Gate unattended for long periods of time simply because it was hidden. It had made her invaluable to Lylla. But not everyone was so lucky.

"You've nothing to be sorry for," she said briskly, getting to her feet. "But I think you should be careful. If this person has stolen some of the artifacts, they may very well return for the rest."

"But who would do such a thing?" Lawrence demanded, leaning forward in his chair, whiskey forgotten.

"I can think of someone."

"Who?"

"I don't want to speculate before we have facts, but..."

"You think it's *her*, don't you?" Lawrence's voice was a mere whisper, as if speaking her name would bring the house down upon them. He had turned his head in a way that made the light reflect off his glasses and she couldn't see his eyes.

"I don't know," Damaris answered truthfully. She couldn't lie to him. "I've been to Malenwar. I've seen the destruction. It's a city of the dead. I don't know how anyone could have survived the explosion."

"But you think she did. And what's more, there's a part of you that hopes she survived."

Damaris looked up in surprise. The old man was more perceptive than she'd expected. It was almost as if he could see through her.

"I can see the anger in your eyes," he added.

She smiled, but it was self-mocking. "Yes, but no." She shrugged as if that explained everything. "*If* it's her, she'll wish she died that day. I'm not finished with her yet."

Part of her knew it was foolish to hope that Galatea had survived, knowing how much destruction she had inflicted on both worlds—and could inflict again—but she couldn't help it. It was a vengeful, destructive part of herself that she was not proud of—and in the past had been frightened by.

"Nor, it seems, is she finished with us, if your suspicions prove correct."

Having delivered her unexpected news and receiving some, Damaris soon left Professor Lawrence's house, after bidding him farewell and reminding him to be careful. She had the information she'd come for, but there were others she needed to visit.

If it were possible that Galatea had returned, they needed to be warned.

The gas station was busy when she arrived, much to her annoyance. She walked straight past the motorists and into the store, grabbing the first thing she saw—a pack of powdered donuts—and plopped them onto the counter when it was her turn. At least it would appear like she had a legitimate—human—reason for being at the counter.

Hank looked up in surprise, his eyes meeting hers as he rang up the donuts.

"I didn't think you'd come all this way to satisfy your sweet tooth," he murmured, voice pitched low so as few people as possible could hear.

"I didn't," she replied, smirking. "Although I have to admit, you people have it good in some ways." She gestured to the snack. "Anyway, I heard about the robbery."

He nodded. "Last night."

"That's not the only thing last night," she said darkly, jerking her head toward the door to signify that he should meet her out there as soon as he had the chance, where they could talk more privately. "And you can keep the donuts."

"You don't want them?"

"I do," she confessed. "But I haven't any money."

Hank shook his head. "Keep 'em. They're on the house."

"Honestly, Hank. It's a wonder you stay in business."

He grinned. "Well, as you can see, business is pretty good."

Damaris knew she was holding up the line, so she snatched the donuts and hurried outside. Being on Earth did have its perks, she supposed, leaning against the wall. And she hadn't had breakfast this morning, either. The whiskey hardly counted.

She tore into the plastic packaging and was on her third donut when Hank came back out. "I've only got a few minutes, so what's up?"

"Last night—the same night that some of Lawrence's artifacts happen to take a walk, mind you—two guards outside the Wind Gate on the Wysterian side were killed. Given what Professor Lawrence told me, I'm left to conclude that whoever stole his items breached the Gate and crossed over."

"That's the fear, anyway," Hank said, staring at her with his brow furrowed.

Damaris nodded. "That's the fear, anyway. So I'm here to tell you to be careful."

He smiled. "I can take care of myself."

"I know you can," Damaris retorted, popping another donut in her mouth. "But whoever is responsible may do it again. And they've already killed twice."

"I'll keep an eye out," he promised, sobering. "But who's going to tell you to be careful?"

She gave him a look, momentarily letting part of her glamour drop, revealing her true eye colors, crimson irises and amber sclera. No words were necessary. Hank looked away first.

"Now I suppose I'd better go warn the Reverend."

"I'd offer to do it myself, but as you can see, I'm a bit busy."

"You need an assistant," Damaris remarked, brushing her hands together to dislodge the powder.

"You volunteering?" Hank teased.

"I already have a job and I like it very much."

"I usually have one of the local high school students help out but apparently he decided not to show up today."

"Want me to track him down for you? It's probably on my way."

"That won't be necessary. No need for you to put the fear of God into the lad. But you should probably wipe that off before you go." He pointed to his mouth.

Damaris licked the powder off her lips and glared at him. "Well I'm off."

"Bit far to walk."

"Ah, but not to run."

As soon as she was away from the town and headed down the road that would take her back to Professor Lawrence's house, Damaris shifted to her true form and set off at a gallop, taking care to stay well back from the road.

If anyone did happen to see her, they would see an ordinary white horse rather than a unicorn, courtesy of a glamour. It felt exhilarating to be able to stretch her legs after being confined in a human form, the ground rushing past her hooves, the wind whipping through her mane.

Cutting across the woods and fields brought her to the small church and cemetery that housed the Ice Gate. Behind the church stood a small house, home to Reverend Pierce, its Guardian.

Luckily, there was no one around at this hour and she shifted back into her human form, rapping on the house's door with her knuckles.

It opened to reveal a young, thin man with dark hair. For a moment he stood there in the doorway, gaping at her. "D—Damaris!"

"The one and only."

"Well it must be serious if they've sent you. Uh, come in, come in."

"Thank you." She stepped over the threshold. "I won't take up much of your time, so I'll be brief."

She'd already spent too long here. It was too early to feel the effect of Earth's drain on her magic, but she'd start to feel it if she planned on taking an extended vacation here. And if she were right in her suspicions, Galatea was loose in Wysteria!

As quickly as she could, she relayed the information she'd learned, including that of the robbery, a fact he'd been ignorant of until now.

"Good Lord! That's awful."

Damaris nodded. "I'm just here to make you aware of the situation and to remind you to be cautious. This person is dangerous and could try again."

"I'll certainly keep my eyes open."

"Good. Now I'm afraid I have to go and update the queen." She glanced out the window at the cemetery. "I would take your Gate back, but I don't fancy a trip through Iceland. I guess I'll have to impose upon Hank again."

"I don't blame you. Godspeed."

As she stepped back outside into the warm summer sun, Damaris paused, turning to gaze up at the small white church. There was a steeple and a small group of stairs led up to the front door. The sun had bleached the siding and the weather over time had worn it in places, giving it a rustic appearance.

The tree to the left stood out from the others, nearer to the building, and tall. It would have been a perfect place to hang a swing.

The graves were on the other side of the church, to the right, stretching out across a gently sloping open patch of grass. The newest stones were closest to her, the old ones the farthest away, pressing up against the barbed wire fence so closely they nearly melded into the trees.

"It's beautiful, isn't it?" the Reverend asked, snapping her out of her reverie. He had followed her and was standing in the doorway.

"Yes," Damaris said softly, thinking back to another place that had once been beautiful and was no longer. "Yes, it is."

She was tempted to ask the Reverend if he was all right out here on his own. There was nothing but trees all around the church. And the dead, who wouldn't be much help if something happened.

Professor Lawrence and Hank were only about two—three at the most—miles apart, but the Reverend was closer to ten miles away from both of them.

But she kept the question to herself. She knew better than to offend a fellow Guardian by questioning their abilities.

They were Guardians. They were meant to be all right and capable on their own.

She left him there and approached the fencing. There was a small gap between it and a white shed that likely housed equipment used in the upkeep of the cemetery. She squeezed past and emerged among the stones.

Damaris could feel the Reverend's eyes on her even though he had not followed her. She ignored him and walked slowly among the rows, careful not to tread on any headstones that might be flat and even with the ground.

Near the end, among the older stones, there were elaborate statues and even a few mausoleums—one of which housed the Ice Gate—but she didn't approach them.

She stopped halfway, where the new section met the old. A carved angel adorned this particular grave, wings curling at her sides as she peered down as though reading the inscription.

There were no flowers left at the base or standing on either side in small vases. No one had likely put flowers here in a long time.

She glanced down, eyes roaming over the inscribed name.

It meant nothing to her.

Somewhere in this quiet little cemetery was a dark secret.

But she didn't know where.

***

As soon as she returned to the palace, Lylla rushed out to meet her. Her blue eyes narrowed, filling with concern as Damaris related everything she had learned.

"We don't have proof that it's her," Lylla warned.

"No, but I think we have to hope that it isn't and prepare as though it is."

"Yes. And whoever it is, they're here in Wysteria. I'll have patrols doubled. We must be vigilant."

"If there's nothing else you need me to do, I think I'll go check on my Gate."

"A wise decision." Lylla paused, looking down at her hands. "Damaris? What do you think she could be planning?"

Damaris glanced over her shoulder, meeting the queen's gaze, and spoke with certainty. "If it's her, nothing good."

***

The destruction of Malenwar took Galatea by surprise, even though she knew it shouldn't. In those first few months on Earth, she had thought back to that fateful night and wondered if she had imagined the devastation incorrectly. If perhaps somehow, she had overexaggerated it.

But it was exactly as she had pictured, the desolation utter and complete.

For a moment, she could only stand there on the precipice of the ruins, swamp water stretching out before her.

She had done this. But instead of the knowledge settling on her heart like a stone, she felt a strange sense of glee.

I did this.

It was a testament, undeniable, of what she could do. And now she was capable of so much more.

Gripping the stolen grimoire in one hand, she started forward, walking along the cracked cobblestone path that had somehow—mostly—survived. All around her was swamp water, glowing a sickly shade of green from the floating algae. The smell of it was repugnant, but Galatea scarcely noticed.

Huge chunks of stone protruded from the water like headstones, the ruins of a once-great city. The air hung thick and muggy. Twisted black trunks of trees were interspersed within the ruins. The borders of the swamp were ringed with similar trees, lifeless and gnarled, their crooked branches reaching out.

It was perfect in every way.

During her journey here, in moments when she'd had to stop and rest, Galatea had studied the spells written within the grimoire.

It was the Chronicles of Lumyn, the first Lightbringer, just as she'd thought. It was a record of all known spells that had ever been cast throughout history, added to over the years. And there had been a lot of spells. This couldn't possibly be all of them. The pages that were blank and stubbornly refused to give up their secrets were far from merely empty. There was something hidden on them, something forbidden. No doubt Lumyn wouldn't have approved of some of them, and so they'd been concealed.

They must be terrible spells, indeed, and that only piqued her curiosity further.

But they could wait. She had found the spell she wanted, the reason she had stolen the book in the first place. Now all she had to do was put it into action.

Yes, the swamps of Malenwar truly were the perfect place.

The water was murky and difficult to see through, but if she concentrated, Galatea could make out various things. There was an overturned cart, with one wheel missing. Barrels and crates, shattered pottery, clothing, armor, weapons, pieces of broken furniture.

Remnants of a city, suddenly and violently interrupted.

But that wasn't all the water held.

There were bodies, both of elves and horses, and a few other animals, frozen in time. The swamp water had perfectly preserved them and they appeared just as they had fifty years ago. There was no current, but their hair seemed to drift slightly as Galatea passed. It had been bleached of all color, just like their pale skin.

This was as good a place to stop as any. If this worked, she could continue further into the city, to the Necropolis. But these corpses were better, perfect as they were.

Galatea cracked open the grimoire and flipped to the spell she wanted. Her fingers were clumsy as she turned the pages, hands trembling.

This had been a mere dream once. She'd been unsure if she'd ever make it a reality. Before the Cataclysm, she had felt such rage, the likes of which she had never experienced before. It coursed through her veins and burned away all other emotion, regret, or desire.

She had vowed revenge, screamed at them all that she would have vengeance.

But that had faded when she had fled to Earth, the fire dying down to dwindling coals. She couldn't possibly go back to Wysteria after that. She had no allies left, save for her faithful wolves.

Her wolves… She'd had to leave them behind. She didn't know if they were even still alive.

She had forgotten about them, too. Just like she had forgotten her revenge for a time. It had seemed so pointless. He was gone and she was trapped in an unfamiliar, hostile world.

But it was a world he had grown up in. Wysteria was nearly as foreign to him as Earth was to her. He had given it up, for her. She owed it to him to try and understand and perhaps even appreciate this strange world. His world. It was the least she could do.

So Galatea had resolved to live on Earth and tried to let go of her sentiments of vengeance. It was a hopeless, unrealistic venture anyway.

Until she had stepped into that library and seen the grimoire. That grimoire had represented possibilities previously only dreamt of and given her hope. She didn't have a chance at revenge on her own.

But she didn't have to be on her own.

Galatea raised a hand and began reciting the spell. The text lit up a bright green and so did the water around her. The spell itself wasn't a difficult one—it was what came after that would require more of her. Only a short time ago, she wouldn't have dared attempt it. But the little time she had spent back in Wysteria had revived her magic and although it still wasn't completely restored to its full strength, it didn't have to be.

She was a Guardian, after all.

The spell finished and Galatea looked up, studying the body closest to her. For a long moment, nothing happened. Then its eyes flew open, glowing the same solid green as the text had been.

One by one, the bodies of the swamp raised themselves out of the water and came to stand around her.

Galatea surveyed them, with their lank, damp hair and tattered clothes. They looked eerie enough, but they'd need to be proper soldiers if they were to be of any use.

Some of them, those who had been soldiers in life and on-duty during the blast, were wearing armor and carrying weapons. But those who were ordinary citizens were not.

"Those of you who do not already have them, fetch armor and weapons for yourselves," Galatea commanded, not convinced they would obey.

But the unarmored elves turned away to do as she said, fishing gleaming pieces of armor and weapons out of the swamp water. They moved with uncanny and alarming grace for being dead, likely due to a combination of them still having muscles and flesh on their bones and her magic keeping them upright, sustaining their "life force", such as it was.

They obeyed her without question. They could not feel fear or anger or pain, being dead. They would be the perfect soldiers if not for one disadvantage.

Being dead, they no longer had access to magic, which was only gifted to living beings and even then, some more than others. They could only utilize their physical weapons: swords, daggers, bows and arrows, maces, and shields. Not that those weren't efficient, but to use most of them, one had to get close. And getting close to an opponent who *could* use magic was difficult. Even arrows were no guarantee.

She would need more. Lots more. And Malenwar, due to the tragedy that had befallen it, was the perfect place to find corpses. She would overwhelm her enemies with sheer numbers.

Any that fell and whose bodies were not completely destroyed, she could reanimate. And any of her enemies who fell would rise again to join her ranks and turn on their former comrades.

The thought gave her distinct pleasure. She could imagine the look of horror on Lylla's face—on all their faces—as their friends and family turned on them.

She allowed herself a moment to picture the look there would be on Cassius's face when his sister, Cyren, turned on him. He would be forced to destroy her or be killed by her. It would be a fate crueler than if she had merely been killed.

But first, Galatea would have to put her soldiers to the test. Seamlessly following orders was of no use if they were ineffectual in real combat.

Galatea turned at the sound of movement behind her, raising a hand to ward off any would-be assailant, but she froze as she saw who it was.

Several large wolves were sauntering toward her. The males were a deep red, the females a dark orange. In the lead was a particularly large male, his ice blue eyes glowing faintly in the dim light of the swamp.

He stopped in front of her and spoke in a deep, gravelly voice. "Mistress. We had sensed you returned, yet we hardly dared to hope."

Galatea smiled, overjoyed to see him. She would have thrown her arms around his neck if it wouldn't have been so undignified for such a noble creature.

"My dear Venryk. I have not only returned, I have come to finish what I began." She spread her arms wide to indicate the surrounding undead.

The wolf's lips peeled back in a feral grin, a baring of teeth. "It's only a matter of time now."

Like all fire wolves, he was heavily built, more like a lion than a wolf, and as large as one too. His ears were long and pointed and his upper fangs were overly long, protruding from his mouth similar to a saber-toothed cat's, but not as thick.

The spell had worked and her wolves had returned. They had survived without her and waited for her return.

Yes, it was only a matter of time before her vengeance was fulfilled.

And she *would* have her vengeance.

5

True to the Professor's word, the library did not reopen the day following the theft. But he called Sara, asking her to meet him there anyway, instructing her to use one of the side entrances, which he had left unlocked. The main entrance was barricaded by caution tape, orange signs warning people to stay away.

"Ah, Sara, good," he said, looking up at her arrival, and then gesturing to the glass display case before him. "I've been giving it some thought and I think it would be best if the rest of the items were moved someplace else for the time being."

"You think they'll be targeted again?"

He shrugged. "I don't know, but better to be safe than sorry. Would you mind helping me box them up? We can take them back to my house until I figure out what to do with them."

"I'd be happy to," she replied.

He sent her outside to fetch several carboard boxes from the trunk of his car.

What he didn't tell her was that Damaris's warning had rattled him. The one thing they knew for certain was that the thief hadn't been an ordinary human criminal—not if they had crossed through a Gate afterward. The thief knew, at least marginally, the significance of the things they had stolen and there was no telling if they would return.

Undoubtedly, they had left behind some valuable items, whether they realized that or not. He had to admit to himself that he didn't even know what half the things did, only that it was important for them not to fall into the wrong hands.

Not that he could tell Sara any of this, he reflected ruefully.

But was the thief *her?* Damaris seemed to think it could be, but why? She hadn't been seen or heard from for fifty years. Perhaps it was merely because there was no one else the Flame Guardian could think of who might be responsible. The idea that another Guardian had gone rogue was too horrible to contemplate.

There was a flash of movement in the corner of his eye and Lawrence looked up, expecting to see Sara had returned. Instead, Sheriff Harris stood there, his expression pinched, gaze troubled.

"Sheriff. Any news?"

"We've analyzed the security camera footage," he murmured. "The thief appears to have been Mrs. Miley."

"What?" Lawrence exclaimed. He'd known Mary Miley for over forty years and couldn't imagine such a kind woman being behind something like this. "Impossible."

"That's what I thought," the sheriff said, shaking his head. "But the footage doesn't lie. It was very clearly her."

"Have you spoken to her? What does she have to say for herself?"

Could this possibly get any stranger? Mrs. Miley couldn't be behind the crime, he reminded himself. Not if the thief had crossed over into Wysteria and killed two guards in the process.

"That's just it," Harris said, mouth tightening. "We went to speak to her first thing this morning, only we found her dead."

"*Dead?* What happened? A—a heart attack, perhaps, or—?"

"Preliminary investigation would suggest blunt force trauma, but that's for the coroner to figure out, obviously."

"Did she fall or—?"

"I would say it's unlikely."

So Mrs. Miley had broken into the library and then someone killed her shortly thereafter? Had she been coerced somehow into helping the real thief? That was a possibility Lawrence found more likely, but why Mrs. Miley?

Harris leaned closer, lowering his voice. "This stays between the two of us, Professor. The last thing I need is for this to be plastered all over the papers. I don't know what the hell happened last night, but it couldn't have been Mrs. Miley we saw on the security footage."

"Why not?" Now Lawrence was thoroughly confused. "You just said it was her!"

"It looks like her," Harris agreed, "but it can't have been. Like I said, we found Mrs. Miley dead in the basement of her home and—I'm no pathologist, mind— but she'd clearly been dead for some time."

Behind Harris, standing in the shadow of the entrance, Sara let out a gasp.

***

Sara knew she shouldn't have been eavesdropping. She'd gone to fetch the boxes like Professor Lawrence had asked, but as she was getting them out of the trunk, she saw the sheriff's car pull up. By the time she followed

Harris inside, the two men were already engrossed in a conversation. Once she'd heard Mrs. Miley's name and knew they were discussing the robbery, she couldn't help but listen.

She had hoped that the police had learned something, even though it was still early in the investigation. But nothing could have prepared her for what came next.

The sheriff whirled around, lips flattening as he saw her.

"Sara's helping me," Professor Lawrence explained before Harris could say anything, waving to her.

She crossed over to him, setting the boxes down next to the glass case.

"How is that even possible?" she demanded. "Even if she didn't break into the library, I just saw Mrs. Miley earlier that day."

"I don't know," Harris said unhappily. "This is above my pay grade. In my twenty years on the force, I've never had anything like this. Either the woman we found in Mrs. Miley's house is her or else looks convincingly like her. I don't know, but you can be sure we're going to get to the bottom of this. In the meantime, Miss Montgomery, I don't think I need to tell you not to breathe a word of this to anyone."

"I won't," she said, reflexively, because what else was there to say?

The sheriff nodded once, sharply, looking slightly happier now that he had passed on the news. "Right. I'll leave you to it, then. Let me know if you learn anything else."

The two of them watched him go and then Sara whirled on Professor Lawrence. "But how is that possible? What is going on?" Was the dead woman the real Mrs. Miley or a fake? Had the woman Sara interacted with yesterday been the real thing or had that been false as well?

Suddenly, she remembered the misgivings she'd had about Mrs. Miley leaving without bidding her a good day. But what did that prove? Surely it couldn't mean anything…

Professor Lawrence let out a heavy breath. "I don't know what's going on, Sara, and I'm sorry. I know that's not the answer you want to hear, but I think this only serves to reinforce what we're doing." He nodded to the cardboard boxes. "The collection can't stay here. Let's get to it."

Sara wanted to pursue the matter, not the least bit satisfied, but what could he say? He likely didn't understand it any better than she did.

Taking a key from his pocket, Professor Lawrence unlocked the case and together, the two of them carefully began removing the various antiques, one by one, and placing them into boxes, wrapping them in newspaper and bubble wrap.

They worked in silence. Sara forced herself to focus solely on the task at hand, treating each item as if it were made of the most delicate porcelain. The last thing she wanted was to accidentally drop one and break it.

But out of the corner of her eye, she noticed a tension in Professor Lawrence and wondered if he was still thinking about Mrs. Miley. His hands shook slightly and his eyes were cloudy, unfocused as he stared at the antiques.

"Your mother loved this stuff," he said softly.

She picked up the small hand mirror, placing it face-down on the bubble wrap and looked up to see him lifting the strange crystal headdress. It really was far too big for a human to wear. She wondered if she'd been wrong about it being a headdress, although she thought that's what her mother had told her it was, all those years ago. Maybe she remembered incorrectly.

"Do you know where she got most of this stuff?" Sara asked, feeling a small twinge of unhappiness that her mother had never explained it to her. She wasn't sure if this topic was any safer to explore than that of Mrs. Miley, but it was too late now.

"I believe it's been in the family for years," he replied absently.

Sara was tempted to ask why it was that Professor Lawrence had inherited the items if they'd always been in her family, but she didn't. It didn't matter now. He had been one of her mother's professors at the college once upon a time and had become a personal friend. A mentor of sorts, in a way.

Clearly, she had trusted him and wanted him to have the items and that was good enough for Sara. It would have to be. Besides, she couldn't imagine what she would do with them all.

When a box had been filled, Sara closed it up and carried it back to his car until there were no more. Not wanting to leave him with the burden of carrying the boxes into his house alone, she offered to come with him, driving along behind.

She'd been to Professor Lawrence's house before when she had mowed his lawn the previous summer, but she had never set foot inside. Whenever he had come outside to offer her lemonade, they had always enjoyed it on the porch.

Sara carried the first box inside while he held the door open for her, gazing around at the décor.

"Just set it on the coffee table for now," he instructed. "I'll go through them all later and decide where I want to put them."

There was an African mask hanging above the fireplace, two spears crossed beneath it. Everywhere she looked there seemed to be little curios. A clay statuette on the sideboard, an oriental rug on the floor. There was a globe beside the television, an antique sword on the wall hanging next to a large tapestry. It reminded her more of a museum than a house.

Bringing her attention back to the matter at hand, Sara bent to place the box on the table and went to fetch the others. Twenty minutes later, all the boxes had been brought inside and placed on or around the table.

Sara straightened, wiping sweat off her forehead. "Are you sure you don't want any help unpacking?"

He smiled warmly at her. "No, I've imposed upon you long enough. I can manage. Thank you for the help."

"Anytime. Let me know if you need anything else." She wanted to ask if he had any idea when the library might open again, but it was much too soon for that.

In the meantime, she was out of a job.

***

Under the cover of darkness, Galatea led her new soldiers out of the swamps of Malenwar and into the Briarwood. They followed without question and moved with a surprising amount of stealth, their eyes glowing faintly in the darkness. Venryk padded beside her. She had chosen to leave the rest of her wolves behind in the swamp, but she wanted her alpha by her side, unwilling to part with him after so many years.

The Enchanted Forest was rarely ever completely dark, even in places where the tree canopy was so thick moonlight struggled to penetrate. It gave off a natural light of its own, emanating from the plants and trees, a faint green or blue. And then there were the golden glowing lights that twinkled, always seeming just out of reach.

But here, in the Briarwood, there were no such lights. The trees here were not as gnarled as those in the swamp, but their trunks were dark and they were tall, towering high above their heads.

The Briarwood had been on the border of Malenwar and had been just spared the destruction that the city had suffered. Still, it was different from the rest of the forest. It had an air about it that had always struck Galatea as darker.

Huge briars were interspersed with the trees, coiling up and around their trunks, the moonlight shining on the large thorns. It was this feature that had given this part of the forest its name.

If I still had my attribute, I could make good use of all those thorns, Galatea thought wistfully. But she could control the earth and its plants no longer.

But this outing wasn't about her abilities. She had brought her undead soldiers here because she knew, unless things had changed since she had last been in Wysteria, that there was a small fort on the border of the Briarwood and the Enchanted Forest.

Such forts and watchtowers were scattered throughout the land. It was a place where patrols could swap, travelers from a great distance could substitute tired horses for fresh ones. There were food and supplies at each, along with a small barracks area for guards to rest in between their watches.

Galatea had found herself stationed at this very fort many, many years ago, before she had been assigned as Guardian of the Earth Gate. Things had been very different then. She'd been nothing more than a wide-eyed recruit, with enough training for a lookout position, but little else.

And then her magic had awakened and everything changed.

As they approached the border, Galatea cloaked herself and her soldiers under a cover of darkness. She did not think it likely that they would be detected, but she was taking no chances. Damaris had a habit of roaming the forest and running into her was the last thing they needed. Her undead wouldn't stand a chance and her plan would be over before it had even begun.

If Damaris is even still alive, she thought suddenly. She dared not hope that the Flame Guardian might have died in the years she had been gone, but Galatea realized she didn't truly know for certain who the Guardians were anymore.

She hadn't seen Kadir at the Wind Gate, but was that because he'd been staying in the city or because he had died? If the latter were the case and they hadn't found a Guardian to replace him, they would be forced to put guards on the Gate every night.

That was a situation she could use to her advantage. Although she knew better than to think it could possibly be true. Elves were immortal. They didn't just die and the odds that something drastic had happened to bring about Kadir's death were not high.

They halted amongst the trees and briars of the Briarwood, peering out through the darkness. Galatea could see the fort, its walls made of sturdy stone. The gate was open and there was a fire glowing in the middle. She could make out three soldiers sitting around it and at least two more walking around within the fire's glow.

Venryk let out a low growl, but stayed where he was. He knew this task was not for him.

"Take the fort," Galatea instructed her soldiers, without taking her eyes from the fort and its inhabitants. "Leave no one alive."

The undead shuffled forward, armor clanking as they increased their pace, and Galatea and Venryk settled back to wait. Another elf might have wanted to get closer to survey the handiwork of the undead, but Galatea could see quite well from her vantage point, even through the darkness.

The soldiers headed straight for the open gate. A shout went up from within as they stepped into the light and were spotted. Light flared—fire, judging by the orange color— as magic was summoned, but the soldiers within the fort had been caught off-guard.

A scream rang out, though from pain or sheer horror at seeing the undead soldiers, Galatea couldn't tell. The undead mass scrambled up the stairs to where lookouts were posted along the walls, swarming over the fort. The soldiers stationed there would soon be overrun.

She watched as one cornered lookout summoned lightning to his fingertips and launched it at the undead surrounding him. But they no longer had nervous systems or beating hearts to be affected by the electricity, and though their flesh began smoking from the heat, it did nothing to stop them.

The nearest sword plunged into the lookout's body and he went down, the wall behind him stained red. But the fire attribute was having more luck and wouldn't go down so easily. With a wave of his hand, he set the nearest undead on fire, the flames eagerly eating away at the flesh and sinew, even while leaving the armor untouched.

A few of her soldiers had been cut down and Galatea willed them to rise again. They stirred, limbs coming to life.

The fire attribute took notice and set them ablaze, willing the fire to burn hotter and faster.

The downed undead collapsed as their limbs seared away and after a moment, all that was left was a set of empty armor and ash.

Galatea felt a prick of anger, but not of surprise. She'd known that fire was one of the few elements that could destroy the body, leaving nothing left to rise again. It was the only way her new soldiers could truly be stopped. Or if she ran out of the energy and strength to maintain and control them. But with the Echo Stone amplifying her magic, that wasn't likely to happen any time soon.

Not unless she found herself in a direct confrontation with a powerful opponent. Unbidden, Lylla's image flashed in her mind and Galatea shoved it away, focusing back on the battle unfolding before her.

Fire may have been an effective weapon, but the soldier had overexerted himself, forcing the flames to burn so quickly in order to completely destroy the fallen undead.

He slumped against the wall, panting, too exhausted to summon another attack or even a paltry defense. He fell to join his comrades on the ground.

The undead, their task finished, gathered in the middle around the campfire.

Galatea glanced at Venryk. "Let's see the fruits of our labor, shall we?"

Dropping the shroud of darkness, she strode forward, out of the cover of the trees, her wolf beside her. If any within happened to still be alive, despite her efforts, she would deal with them herself.

The forest was still and eerily quiet, except for the crackle of the fire. The ground of the fort was littered with the bodies of fallen undead and the fort's own soldiers. Galatea turned in a slow circle, but nothing moved. With the wounds visible on the bodies, there was little possibility that any of them were playing dead.

She held out a hand and commanded not only her fallen warriors to rise, but those they had slain as well. Within moments, there were no dead bodies left lying on the ground. They had all joined her ranks.

Galatea smiled to herself in satisfaction. It worked better than she'd hoped. They hadn't even had time to light the signal fires to let one of the other forts or watchtowers know they were in trouble.

"Mistress!" Venryk barked sharply.

She turned. The wolf was standing over by the stairs that led both up onto the outer walls and down into the barracks below. Slowly, she walked down the stairs, coming to a stop at the bottom and peering down at a young shadow elf, cowering beneath the stairs.

The only survivor.

She didn't know how he'd managed to survive, but survive he had. And he might have lived to tell the tale if Venryk hadn't scented him.

"Come out," Galatea said softly.

The elf stayed where he was. "Pl—please don't kill me."

"Come *out*," she repeated, harsher than before.

Realizing his fate was sealed either way, he extricated himself from under the stairs and came to cower before her. Unlike most shadow elves, such as herself, he wore his black hair cropped short. It barely reached his pointed ears, which curved slightly as they went upward. His eyes were the amber color of all shadow elves, save for Galatea herself, and they were wide and filled with fear.

"Please," he whispered.

"Shall I kill him?" Venryk growled.

Galatea held up a hand, signaling him to wait. "Do you know who I am?" she addressed the shadow elf.

Wordlessly, he shook his head.

She sighed. "Forgotten so quickly. What do they call you?"

"N—Noraak, ma'am," he replied.

"Well, Noraak, perhaps you can help me. I find myself in need of information." She thought back to her earlier realizations, that she didn't even know for certain who the Guardians were anymore or who the queen was for that matter. Had any of the other Gates been destroyed since she'd left? She could suspect the answers but that was no substitute for the truth. "How many Gates are there?"

Noraak swallowed. "Five."

She nodded. It was one less than there had originally been at the beginning of all things, but that much hadn't changed since she'd left.

"Name them and tell me who is the Guardian of each."

He gave her a funny look but did as she asked. "Cassius protects the Water Gate, Cyren the Ice, Wanderer the Lightning, Kadir the Air, and Damaris the Flame."

Nothing had changed. It was all exactly the same as when she had left. But instead of feeling disappointed that none of her enemies had died, she felt strangely pleased. If they were dead, they only would have robbed her of her revenge.

"And who sits on the throne at the Glowing Gate?"

Now Noraak's expression became one of incredulity. "Queen Lylla the Lightbringer. Everyone knows that."

"Well I have been gone for a while," Galatea said dryly.

His eyes widened, flicking rapidly between her and Venryk. "Wait…you're her, aren't you? You're Galatea." He shrank away from her, but there was a wall at his back.

She smiled. "We have a winner."

Noraak threw himself at her feet. "Please, don't kill me!"

The smile vanished. "I'm not going to kill you."

He blinked. "Y—you're not?"

"No… I find myself in need of an assistant and you've proven yourself useful. Your reward is your life. If you should prove loyal and competent, the rewards will increase."

"I will," Noraak vowed, still looking as though he was in awe of her. "I will do all that you ask of me."

Galatea gave him a curt nod. If he changed his mind, she could easily get rid of him. "What is your attribute, Noraak?"

"Earth."

It was what she had secretly hoped for. Ordinary elementalists had access to only one attribute and were therefore typically stationed somewhere their element would be most useful. The Briarwood was notorious for earth attributes. And it made him doubly useful to her, able to use the element she had lost.

"Good. Come, Venryk, Noraak. We have work to do."

Obediently, the two turned and followed her back up the stairs. The ranks of undead fell into place behind as they made their way toward the swamp. It was only a matter of time before the destruction at the fort was discovered and the news reached the queen's ears.

This outing had been a success, but the fire worried Galatea. This one had been a weak fire attribute at best, but Damaris was the Flame Guardian. Galatea knew what she was capable of. She had fought alongside her once upon a time and thought to herself that she would not want to be on the receiving end of her flames—which she now would be.

She needed a soldier that could defend itself against magical assault. She glanced at Venryk, thinking of a possible solution.

Noraak sucked in a sharp intake of breath as they stepped back into the swamp, but he said nothing. Undoubtedly, he had never seen the desolation of Malenwar before. No one likely ventured in here.

Galatea led them over to the pools of swamp water that she had raised her soldiers from. Aside from the various debris, all it contained now were the bodies of horses and other animals.

Malenwar had been famous for its sleek black horses, creatures long used in war. If the resurrection spell worked for elves, why not their horses?

Galatea withdrew the grimoire from the pocket of her dress and opened it to the correct page. Venryk and Noraak observed silently.

Like their elven counterparts, the horses had been perfectly preserved in the water and when the spell had finished, they rose up to join them.

But Galatea wasn't finished with them. When she had first begun studying dark magic, she had used it to mutate the fire wolves and imbued them with fire, giving them the uncanny ability to self-combust.

For the horses, she chose a different element. Darkness itself. It wasn't corporeal, but insubstantial and ethereal. Darkness wasn't solid; it could be stepped and moved through. She wanted her horses to be able to shift into a second form at will, one of darkness, of mist. Any magical or physical attack would simply go straight through them.

And, like the fire wolves, she also chose to modify their appearances.

When she was done, Galatea surveyed the creature standing before her.

Its eyes glowed solid white, its mane and tail made of darkness that pooled and flowed like ink. There were spurs above each hoof and its ribs were visible, pressing up against the skin. It opened its mouth to reveal rows of sharp teeth and a long, slimy tongue snaked out.

"What is it?" Noraak whispered, recoiling.

"They're my Nightmares," Galatea answered, shutting the grimoire with a snap, feeling rather pleased with herself. *Not bad for one day's work.* She turned to face him. "And now, Noraak, I have a job for you."

6

Felix urged his horse, Tempest, into a trot as the Briarwood's fort came into view. It was customary for patrols to stop and check in with any outposts or watchtowers they encountered along the way, to see if they might have spotted something that patrol had not.

Colin hurried along behind him on a horse of his own, the rest of the patrol following. It felt good to be able to be out in the early morning air. A faint covering of mist had begun to evaporate in the sun, the rays of light slanting down through the forest canopy and landing on Felix's back, warm and reassuring.

He had been relieved when Lylla had chosen him and Colin to lead this patrol. There had been a time when he hadn't been sure she would ever trust him again. But Colin was there and so were the others. It wasn't the same as being on his own.

The fort's gates came into view, gaping wide open.

Felix turned to one of the riders behind him. "Wait here for us and keep an eye out."

Colin accompanying him on his own mount, Felix nudged Tempest, a large Friesian stallion, through the open gates, feeling a frisson of unease. Why were the gates open? Maybe the soldiers stationed here had been lax in their security. After all, there wasn't much to worry about out here.

But still, one could never be too careful.

Tempest snorted, pawing at the earth and Felix knew his unease was justified.

"What's that?" Colin asked softly, pointing. "Blood?"

Dark stains littered the grass, spattered on the stone walls. Felix swallowed; there was no doubt it was blood. He slung his bow from his back, nocking an arrow, fingers loose on the string.

The fire in the middle of the fort had burned down to smoldering coals, but there was no sign of any life. No sign that there had ever been any life at the fort at all aside from the ominous blood stains.

"Where is everyone?" Colin asked. "What happened?"

"Check the barracks," Felix called to Colin. His friend nodded and dismounted, disappearing down the stairs, sword drawn.

Felix slipped from the saddle and walked over to the blood on the wall. He ran his fingers over it, but it was dry. Not an extremely recent attack, then. He frowned, looking around. There were crates and barrels still stacked along the walls. If the soldiers had suddenly decided, for whatever reason, to pack up and move, they would have taken their supplies along with them.

Colin reemerged from downstairs. "Nothing."

Felix felt a chill settle over him, as if something wicked had touched him between the shoulder blades. "This isn't right," he muttered. "If they were attacked, then where are all the bodies?" *Of both the soldiers and their attackers.*

But there were no corpses from either side, not even any wounded.

He glanced down at one of the dried pools of blood, a piece of metal catching his eye. Brow furrowing, he bent down and picked it up, hissing as it touched his bare fingertips. It was iron and iron burned if it came into contact with bare skin, one of the few ways to defend against magic.

Felix flipped it into the palm of his fingerless gloves and the burning sensation ceased. The piece of metal was curved, the tip pointed. The broken end was jagged. The shattered tip of a sword. Likely meaningless, but he slipped it into his pocket anyway.

"Find something?" he asked Colin. His friend had knelt down, studying something in the grass.

"Piece of cloth," Colin answered, straightening and holding it out to him. It was pale and slightly muddy, as though it had been trod into the ground. "There's a symbol on it, but I can't make it out."

Felix took it and the chill that had stolen over him earlier made his blood run cold. "It's the symbol for Malenwar."

"Are you sure?"

A sword surrounded on either side by twisting tree branches. "Yes, I'm sure."

"How would you know? Malenwar fell fifty years ago."

"I've seen it in a book in the library."

Colin shook his head. "You and those books. What's a scrap of cloth from Malenwar doing out here?"

"You know, for having all the questions, Colin, you don't seem to have many answers," Felix said, trying for a light, teasing tone to hide his unease.

He didn't have an answer for Colin's question either. It made no sense. The cloth had clearly seen better days. How could it have ended up in a fort in the Briarwood? A fort whose soldiers had mysteriously gone missing.

"We should look for tracks," he heard himself saying.

The piece of cloth could have come from anywhere, he told himself. Not everyone who had lived in Malenwar died in the Cataclysm. Perhaps one of the soldiers stationed at the fort had once lived there or had family who did and kept the cloth with them to remind them of the city.

Felix might have believed that if it hadn't been for the eerie silence hanging over the fort. Where had the soldiers gone? Their disappearance, combined with the fort's proximity to the swamp made it hard for him to believe so innocent an explanation.

If ever there were a place where ghosts lingered, haunting the earth, it was Malenwar.

Felix pushed the thought away. It was the living who could hurt you, not the dead. He turned, slipping the scrap of cloth into his pocket with the sword tip, and followed Colin back outside.

One of their scouts called, "The horses are still out back!"

So whoever had attacked the fort hadn't bothered to take its horses. *If only those horses could talk.*

"There are tracks," Colin shouted, "leading towards the swamp and back!"

Felix followed him, peering at the ground closely. Both he and Colin had been taught from an early age, as had all soldiers, how to search for tracks. To look for the smallest detail or hint. Crushed blades of grass, broken sticks, mud that may have been stepped in, or a piece of cloth snagged on nearby branches—anything that would leave a visible mark.

There were plenty of signs to look for. Whoever had walked through here had made no attempt at stealth.

He froze. There was one print that had been captured perfectly in the mud and it didn't belong to any elf.

The massive fire wolf print seemed to stare back up at him. The claw-marks and pads were clearly visible, pressed into the wet ground by the weight of the animal. It was at least eight inches across.

Felix tore his eyes away and looked up. The gnarled trees of the swamp were mere yards away, marking the boundary between the Briarwood and Malenwar. He hadn't realized he'd walked so far, searching for tracks and absorbed in his own thoughts.

The fire wolf print pointed towards the swamp. Felix had never been so close to the ruins of Malenwar before and the piece of cloth seemed to burn a hole in his pocket. It was a relic of destruction, a reminder of evil.

He shivered. Where had the sun gone? It no longer filtered down through the trees.

"Hey," Colin caught up with him. "You look like you've seen a ghost."

"I have," he murmured, nodding down to the wolf print.

Colin looked down, his eyes widening. "Is that—?"

He had been fortunate enough never to see an actual fire wolf. He had every right to believe they were a myth or that they were all dead now. But he had believed, for Felix's sake. He had never doubted his word.

Felix nodded tersely.

"I thought I heard them howl the other night," Colin whispered. He raised his gaze toward the swamp. "The tracks lead that way but we can't go in there."

I don't want *to go in there,* Felix thought, but didn't say.

Once upon a time, he'd have leapt at the possibility of a fire wolf being in there, but now caution prevailed. He had learned the painful price of being reckless.

He sighed. "No. We'd better report this."

Felix turned and headed back to where Tempest was waiting without another glance at the swamp, but he did not feel warm again until the Glowing Gate was in sight.

The horses were left in the care of the rest of the patrol while he and Colin stepped through the massive double doors of the palace and began the search for Lylla. They were informed by a passing servant that she was in her private quarters at the very top and hurried up the spiral staircases.

The way to Lylla's rooms were blocked by two heavy oak doors. Felix rapped on one briskly.

"Come in," called a familiar voice from within. She didn't ask who it was; she didn't need to. She knew him by his knock.

The doors swung open to reveal the queen sitting on one of the carpets on the floor. A scroll was spread out before her, but she folded it and rose to her feet as they entered.

Half of the back wall of this room was open, supported by stone columns, allowing light and air to flow through. Windchimes hung from the ceiling, tinkling softly as the breeze stirred them. Bookshelves lined one wall, with a desk and chair nearby. Cushions and plush rugs lined the marble floor. Colorful drapes hung from the ceiling above their heads. A fountain bubbled quietly in the corner, the water overflowing into a small stone basin set in the floor. Paintings of various landscapes of Wysteria decorated the walls, including a few pieces Felix suspected were from Earth.

It was warm in the room and with the combination of the gentle wind, windchimes, and the fountain, it had always been one of Felix's favorites. It instilled a sense of peace and comfort that even the chill of Malenwar could not penetrate. His previous fears seemed almost silly here, but he knew he must report them anyway.

Lylla herself was dressed in a yellow gown that looped around her neck and left her shoulders bare. The skirt was long, trailing behind her and reaching the ground, but it became sheer as it passed below her knees. Her skin was tanned as though she spent a lot of time in the sun, her blue eyes framed by long, dark lashes. Her turquoise hair tumbled down her back to her waist and seemed to shimmer as she moved, like small jewels catching the sun.

But Felix knew better. It was her element. Her hair always glittered in the light and sometimes in the dark too, almost as though she were made of light itself.

"What is it?" she asked, approaching. "What's happened?"

Felix and Colin took turns explaining what they had found at the fort, the lack of bodies of any kind, the tracks that went to and from the swamp, and lastly, Felix pulled the sword shard and piece of cloth out of his pocket and held them out in the middle of his palm.

"We found these," he said softly. "The cloth bears the mark of Malenwar."

Concern flared within the depths of her turquoise eyes, but she said nothing, reaching out first for the piece of metal. The nails on her slender fingers were silver. Her bare fingers picked it up and brought it closer.

Felix knew direct contact with the iron must have hurt her, but she gave no outward sign of it. A piece that small would be a mere sting for one of her power.

She took the cloth next. "That is indeed the mark of Malenwar," she said, wrapping the sword tip in the cloth.

"What does it mean?" Colin asked.

"I do not know," Lylla answered. "I know that is not the answer you'd like, but it is the truth. We need to know what's going on in the swamp before we can be sure."

"I'll go!" Colin volunteered eagerly. "I've always wanted to see what the Cataclysm did. It can't be that dangerous, can it? Everyone who was there died."

"Not everyone, idiot," Felix said, not unkindly.

Lylla smiled. "I appreciate the offer, Colin, but I need you both here. *Something* attacked my soldiers and then retreated into Malenwar. I intend to find out who. But this could be a dangerous mission. Clearly, they've used violence before. I'll send a message for Damaris. In the meantime, I'd like you to hold onto this for me, Felix." She handed him the cloth back, with the shard wrapped inside. "You've done well, both of you."

He took it back from her, he and Colin giving quick salutes before accepting their dismissal.

Felix was slightly disappointed that he wouldn't be accompanying Damaris. There was a morbid part of his curiosity that agreed with Colin. He would like to see what Malenwar looked like now. He'd seen drawings and paintings. It had once been a grand city, the center of trade in Wysteria, enough to rival Khae. But that had all changed in the span of one night.

Wysteria had lost not only a city but a Gate that night, as well as countless lives.

But Lylla was right that the mission could be dangerous. No one really knew what lurked within the swamps now.

He had seen a fire wolf print. That didn't prove anything other than a fire wolf had been there. But he hadn't forgotten who had created the fire wolves and if her reaction was anything to judge by, Lylla hadn't either.

***

Unlike most, Damaris had not only set foot in the swamp before, she had lived to tell about it. At least that's what she told people whenever they asked.

In truth, the only things to fear in the swamp were mosquitoes and the noxious fumes of the swamp water. One had to be cautious walking along the stone pathways and any platforms that remained. The rocks could fall out from under you or collapsing ruins could crush you from above.

But nothing was going to leap out and attack you. There was nothing left living to worry about.

Damaris knew something was wrong the moment she stepped past the first gnarled trees. The parameters had changed. This was not the same as it had been when she'd last set foot here.

The sky had darkened, turning a deep bluish-green, and a sense of unease washed over her, sending her heart fluttering. But the queen had sent her here for this mission, chosen out of all possibilities, because she could handle whatever may be lurking in the shadows.

She was the Flame Guardian, after all.

Keeping her ears perked, Damaris started forward, swishing her long tail at the mosquitoes and wincing as it trailed into some of the water. At least the glowing algae gave off enough light to see by.

The air was muggy and oppressive, but the heat didn't bother her. No sound reached her ears, other than that of her legs and tail swishing through the water or the squelch of mud as her hooves sank into the muck. But each sound she made seemed amplified in the stillness.

She was relieved when she could climb up onto the stone walkway that led deeper into the ruins stretching ahead. There were blue lights visible in the distance. *Must be some wisps.*

Will-o-the-wisps were a common occurrence in both the swamp and the Enchanted Forest. Sometimes they could be helpful, guiding lost travelers in the right direction, but Damaris wouldn't trust any that appeared here, likely hoping to lure the unwary into deeper water that would suck them down and commit their bones to the depths.

But as she drew closer, she realized they were not wisps at all, but two lit torches set on either side of an archway. The top of the arch had long since been broken off, leaving a gaping hole.

There had never been lit torches before.

Frowning, Damaris willed the torches to go out and the blue flames extinguished. A moment later, however, they sprang back to life unbidden.

Whatever had caused this was powerful magic and Damaris didn't think it friendly.

She stepped through the archway and continued onward.

A sudden splash sounded behind her and she whirled, but it was only a stone that had fallen to land in the water below.

Damaris exhaled between her teeth. This place was setting her on edge. The sooner she could find something conclusive, the sooner she could leave.

The ruins were more intact in this area, but the further along she went, the worse they became. Those closer to the blast had suffered more damage, the shockwave radiating outward.

The stone was interspersed with trees and more water, shallow in some places and deeper in others. Some pools were deep enough to submerge wreckage. She had seen it before. The wreckage was still there—carts, barrels, crates, clothing, shattered pottery and toys, all sorts.

But not the bodies.

The corpses of farm animals remained and pets, but not the horses or elves of Malenwar.

Damaris walked on, checking other bodies of water, but there were no elven corpses to be found. And there were more blue torches spread throughout the ruins.

She looked up. White figures were flitting through the ruins. The distant ones were too far away to make out much detail, but the ones closest to her bore remarkably clear features. They were elves: men, women, and children, both civilians in ordinary dress and soldiers in armor. All captured exactly as they had been the moment the Earth Gate was destroyed, creating an explosion and sending out a shockwave that decimated a city and its people.

At least it had been quick for those closest to the blast. Others had tried to flee only to be crushed by falling debris or trampled.

Damaris could make out the trees and ruins behind the pale figures' translucent forms. Their eyes were solid white and expressionless. They did not seem aggressive in any way as they wandered the ruins. If anything, she thought they looked lost and a little sad.

From somewhere came the quiet sound of weeping, echoing as though in a deep tunnel underground. One of the figures approached and before Damaris could move, passed *through* her, leaving her chilled like she'd just stepped into Iceland and all the warmth had fled her bones.

She shuddered convulsively.

She was looking at the ghosts of Malenwar.

The ruins were haunted, the stories said. With so many dead, murdered in one night, how could they not be?

Well, they weren't until tonight!

Damaris looked down as something slithered out from between the cracks in the stone pathway. White grubs were pushing their way to the surface, as though trying to get away from the ghosts and whatever influence was riling them up. She recoiled, teeth bared in disgust, fighting the urge to burn the disgusting creatures.

Whether the ghosts were truly restless spirits trapped, unable to move on to the next life, or whether they were merely illusions—something had disturbed the dead. The bodies were missing from the swamp just as they'd been missing from the attacked fort.

There were only so many possible explanations as to where the bodies may have gone and what happened to them and Damaris did not think it because someone had moved them in order to give them a proper burial.

No, this spoke of something darker. She had spent enough time here and needed to report back. The sound of weeping came again and somewhere far in the distance, someone screamed.

Damaris wanted to turn and run, to carry herself out of here as quickly as possible, away from its corrupting influence. But she was the Flame Guardian. She did not run from a fight and she certainly would not run from something that posed no danger.

She turned and walked out of the swamp, feeling that something watched her the whole way.

***

The news was alarming enough for Lylla to call an emergency council meeting. Each of the Guardians held a seat on the council and their presence was requested since they and their Gates could very well be in grave danger.

The meetings were held in a large circular room whose ceiling was a dome high above their heads. Ringing the upper tier were massive stone statues of various past Guardians and heroes.

Felix craned his neck back to look up at them as he passed. There was Lysander, Lylla's father and previous ruler, who had led his people to safety in the Exodus centuries ago. Rehan, the hero of the desert elves, who had tamed three of the four winds. Lumyn, the first Lightbringer. Yehara, the first Flame Guardian. Most of the rest he didn't recognize, but he wondered if hundreds of years from now whether or not Damaris and Lylla would be given their own places among Wysteria's heroes.

Lylla was already at the platform designated for her, the white banner unfurled behind her. It proudly displayed a yellow sun, with pinpricks of light spearing out from its center. The colors and symbol for light, her element. Each Guardian had a platform and banner representing their element at the Gate they protected.

Felix and Colin took their positions on either side of her, standing straight, arms behind their backs, and waited for the others to arrive.

Damaris was already there, in her human form for the sake of convenience. Felix would never get used to seeing her as a human.

Her hair was black, the same color her mane and tail were as a unicorn, and styled into two short braids, one on each side, hanging down to just below her collarbone. On anyone else, the hairstyle might have given her a young, girlish appearance, but not on Damaris.

Her lips were red, the fingernails on her hands black like her hooves. There was a dark beauty mark beneath her left eye, but it was those eyes that ensured everyone recognized her no matter what form she assumed.

The irises were crimson red, but the whites of her eyes were not white at all, but amber yellow, ringed by thick, dark lashes.

It was said that these unusual eyes were what struck fear into the hearts of her enemies and Felix could well believe it.

Wanderer, the Lightning Guardian, arrived next, because her Gate was the closest to the palace. Felix tried unsuccessfully to hide a smile as she entered.

In many ways, Wanderer was the exact opposite of Damaris. She had pale skin and her black-and-white striped hair was always disheveled. She wore a bright green kimono and her feet were bare. Two large white wolf ears protruded from atop her head and a white, black-tipped tail swished behind her.

Felix knew them to be illusions, part of her glamour. She was a wood elf, the same as he and Colin. One rumor claimed she was raised by wolves and she maintained the glamour as homage to them, but he didn't know if he believed that. She liked her eccentricity.

Wanderer waved at Damaris and skipped right up to Lylla, her teal-colored eyes wide. "What's with the sense of urgency? Must be something big."

"It is," Lylla agreed. "But I'm afraid I can't discuss the details until the others arrive."

Wanderer pouted, crossing her arms in a theatrical manner. "That's not fair. I bet Damaris already knows."

From her seat on her platform, Damaris smirked good-naturedly at the Lightning Guardian.

"Yes, she knows," Lylla answered, "because I sent her to investigate."

"You could have sent me," Wanderer pointed out. "I'd love a little excitement."

"Excitement can be a dangerous thing to wish for," Lylla cautioned gently. "And you have a Gate to protect. A Gate—" she added quickly when Wanderer opened her mouth to protest—"whose location is common knowledge."

Wanderer sighed. "Yeah, I know. I'm just giving you crap." A wicked grin spread across her face. "I bet Felix would tell me what's going on."

Felix smiled at her. "Nice try, Wanderer. My lips are sealed."

"Aww, come on. You'd tell your old pal, right?" She leaned an arm on his shoulder, crossing her ankles. "There might be something in it for you. I could get you one of those bags of nacho-flavored chips from Hank."

"I'd like some," Colin admitted. "And maybe some bottles of that fizzy liquid?"

"Ah, see, Archer? Colin'll take the deal if you won't."

Lylla chuckled softly to herself and shook her head. "Sit down, Wanderer, and stop harassing my Shadows."

Wanderer shrugged, looking at Felix and Colin. "Your loss."

Cassius and Cyren arrived together, which was unsurprising since they seemed to be attached at the hip. Cassius was the Water Guardian and his sister the Ice Guardian. Some thought they were twins, but it was impossible to say. They both had long black hair and amber eyes, as did all shadow elves.

Felix stiffened as Cassius stepped into the room, but the Water Guardian's attention was focused on Damaris.

"Well, this is a surprise. The Flame Guardian is here early for once," he remarked.

"Fashionably," Damaris retorted.

Cassius grunted and took his place next to Cyren on the other side of the room. Wanderer had taken her position by Damaris.

"As usual," Cyren murmured, "Kadir is the last to arrive."

"He does have a long way to go," Damaris pointed out.

"Well I hope he arrives soon," Cassius said. "Some of us *do* have Gates to protect."

Damaris audibly snorted, rolling her eyes.

"Like you know anything about that," he added.

"Fortunately, unlike you, I don't have to spend my every waking hour stuck inside a little cottage on a cliff. I'd suggest you get out more, Cassius, but we both know that would never happen and I don't think it would make a difference even if it did."

Cassius was robbed of his retort by the arrival of Kadir, the Wind Guardian. The chieftain of the desert elves had snow-white hair, as all desert elves did, and light blue eyes. His skin was brown and unlike most elves, he had facial hair—a small beard on his chin.

Felix reached up absently, scratching at the whiskers on his own chin, though a few whiskers was all they were.

Lylla rose to her feet as Kadir took his place beneath the air banner, and all the others did likewise. "I understand that you all have duties to perform, so I will keep this meeting as brief as possible." The others listened with rapt attention as she went on to describe the situation at the fort and then Damaris's report of the ghosts in the swamp, the lack of corpses, as well as the recent Earth-side robbery, the artifacts that were stolen, and the two guards slain at the Wind Gate.

When asked, Felix produced the piece of cloth she'd asked him to keep safe. It was passed among the Guardians, one by one, except for Damaris, who had already seen it.

After the news had been delivered, a heavy silence fell over the room.

It was Cyren who spoke first, surveying the cloth in her hands. "It is the mark of Malenwar, there is no question."

She handed it to her brother. "This proves nothing," he scoffed. "I know what you're thinking so I'll come out and say it if you won't. You think Galatea is behind this."

Felix found his gaze drawn to the empty chair in the room, where one other Guardian should have stood. But the chair beneath the earth banner remained empty. There was no Earth Gate anymore and they all knew why.

"That's impossible," Kadir protested. "She died in the Cataclysm."

"Exactly," Cassius nodded, passing the cloth to him. "No one could have survived that blast."

"*You* did," Damaris pointed out, her two-toned eyes roaming over him and Cyren.

"That was only because I realized that she was about to destroy her own Gate and was able to summon an ice wall to shield us from the blast," Cyren countered. "It absorbed most of the force, but still shattered. We were both injured and lucky to be alive. Galatea had no such luxury."

"Her body was never found," Damaris pressed. "She probably went through the Gate while you two were cowering behind your ice wall and destroyed the Gate from the other side."

"She's dead," Cassius said firmly. "I know you'd like her to be alive, Damaris, so you can get back at her for…" He gestured in Felix's direction and he felt his face burn. "Well, you know, since you can't get back at Venryk, now can you? But she's dead and unless someone has seen her, here in Wysteria, I refuse to believe otherwise."

"Who else could it be?" Damaris snapped. "Unless you mean to suggest one of our human Guardians has suddenly gone rogue, stolen artifacts, crossed over, killed two guards, and attacked a fort?"

"Why not?" Cassius shouted, his voice rising to match hers. "Humans aren't to be trusted and anyone who thinks differently needs to re-read an account of the Exodus. I'm sure Her Majesty has a copy in the library she'd be more than willing to let you borrow."

"I was at the Exodus. I don't need to read about something I've lived through."

"Ah, yes, sometimes I forget just how ancient you really are."

"Humans have crossed over before," Kadir said hurriedly, eager to change the subject.

Damaris dismissed the idea with a wave of her hand. "Not for a long time."

"Why now?" Wanderer asked, taking the cloth from Kadir. "I mean, if it is Galatea, she's been on Earth for fifty years. Why now? What is it that she wants?"

"Oh, I think we can all guess what she wants," Damaris muttered darkly, raking the siblings with her gaze. To Felix's satisfaction, Cassius had to look away. "I can see how you two wouldn't want to believe it's really her. I wouldn't either, if I'd done what you did."

"We did what we had to," Cassius growled, the venom unmistakable in his voice.

"We won't discuss that now," Lylla interrupted, a hint of uncharacteristic anger in her own voice. "Someone stole several of Professor Lawrence's artifacts and came through the Wind Gate, killing two guards. A fort was attacked last night with no evidence of any bodies, and tracks leading into the swamp, where ghosts have been spotted and corpses are mysteriously missing. We must decide on a course of action."

"What would you have us do?" Cassius exclaimed. "Charge into the heart of the swamp?"

"Something's stirring in there," Damaris retorted. "You didn't see what I saw."

"I don't see the point," Kadir said, more quietly. "We have no proof that it's her and no reason to think so other than speculation."

"But whoever did this is dangerous," Wanderer pointed out. "They could strike again until they're stopped."

"Still, I don't think launching a full-scale offensive into the swamp is the best course of action."

"I have already doubled patrols," Lylla spoke up. "And they will continue."

"I think our collective talents would be best utilized by continuing to protect the Gates, being extra cautious, of course."

"Aren't you the least bit alarmed that the grimoire of spells was stolen?" Damaris challenged. "If it is Galatea, she's already demonstrated that she's willing to destroy her own Gate. Imagine what kind of destruction she could wreak with every known spell in existence at her fingertips."

Cyren held up a hand. "With all due respect, what does it matter if Galatea has stolen the grimoire? The only spells written in there are common ones that everyone knows or has heard of. Hardly earth-shattering knowledge. She can't read the rest of it. No one can—if there's anything even written there at all."

"There's nothing else we can do," Cassius agreed, then gestured to Damaris, his words directed to Lylla. "Send your executioner to find the culprit, if you wish."

Lylla sighed. "Very well. You may all return to your Gates. I will think over what has been said and decide on the best course of action. Be vigilant."

The Guardians stepped off their platforms and began to file out the door. Wanderer hesitated at the doorway, glancing over her shoulder, and then she was gone. Within moments, only Damaris and Lylla remained, Felix and Colin beside her.

Damaris stepped down and moved to the center of the room, returning to her true form, a white unicorn with a black mane, tail, and horn. "Why didn't you order them to do something? You're the queen."

Lylla sighed. "You and I both know there's a higher chance of the stars falling from the sky than getting the Guardians to agree."

"I suppose that's why you're queen and I'm not. Cassius is a fool," Damaris spat. "He wouldn't admit it was Galatea if she walked up and slapped him between the eyes."

"They're frightened, Ris. If Galatea really has returned, they're scared of what that might mean. She's been gone so long, they likely believed it to be over, dead and buried with Jack. They'd rather believe a lie than accept the horrible possibility that she may not be finished with us."

"And what if she isn't? What if it's not over?"

"We still don't have any proof that it *is* Galatea."

"No," Damaris admitted unhappily. "But if it is her, she won't stay quiet for long."

***

Whatever the others may have thought, Kadir had decided to take the threat seriously. That was, after all, what they had taken an oath to do, was it not? And it was his guards that had been killed, not theirs.

Upon returning to the Wind Gate, he dismissed the guards he had posted—two more than usual—and took over for them. The sun was beginning to set, turning the dunes golden-orange. The city of Khae glittered in the distance.

The sun had almost completely sunk beneath the horizon when he first heard the footsteps approaching and turned to see a tall shadow elf walking in his direction, accompanied by a large red wolf.

Kadir stiffened, clenching his fists, hardly daring to believe his own eyes, and torn between the instinct to stand his ground or to flee. He told himself he wasn't in any danger. Two of his guards had been killed, yes, but perhaps they had engaged her and provoked a response. She wouldn't harm a friend.

But they had been friends in the past and all it took was one look at her to realize that the Galatea standing before him was not the Galatea he had known. That Galatea had been the Earth Guardian, before she went through her Gate onto Earth, returned with a human, angered the entire council, and in the end, destroyed her own Gate, unleashing the Cataclysm that destroyed Malenwar. Yes, that Galatea seemed to be gone.

Her hair was still long and black, but her skin, which had once merely been pale, now had a white, almost gray, tinge to it. The irises of her eyes, which had been yellow like all shadow elves, were now solid black, so dark he couldn't make out the pupils.

Galatea halted in front of him, her wolf circling behind her legs, and regarded him with those black eyes. Her long black dress fluttered in the wind. Always black, always mourning, never forgetting.

"So it was you," Kadir murmured. His earlier unease was clamoring at the back of his mind, but all he could feel at the moment was shock. He really had wanted to believe she'd died in the explosion. "You were the one who came through the Gate. And killed two of my guards."

Her black lips turned upwards at the corners. "An unfortunate, but necessary, occurrence. They were soldiers, Kadir. They knew the cost of serving."

"That doesn't matter. They had families—" He broke off, forcing himself to swallow his anger. He was displeased at the loss of his soldiers, but knew that she was right about them being aware of the potential cost of their profession. They had not agreed to protect the Gate in his absence naively believing it to be a safe undertaking.

But it has been. Until now.

He put his arms behind his back, hoping to appear nonthreatening, to signify he wasn't looking for a fight. "Damaris and Lylla seem to think it was you, but the others are more of the opinion you're dead."

"Cassius and Cyren *would* think that."

"I didn't believe it either."

"Well, they say seeing is believing."

Kadir looked at her, feeling suddenly tired. If she was here, it meant that she was likely responsible for the attack on the Briarwood fort and whatever was happening in the swamp. He thought back to a question Wanderer had raised at the meeting.

"What do you want, Galatea?" he asked wearily. "Why come back now? It's been fifty years."

Her arched eyebrows drew slightly together. It was hard to read emotion in those solid black irises, but he thought she looked sad. "Why do you think I'm here?" she asked softly.

Damaris had been right, too. She hadn't said it in so many words, but she'd been right.

"It's over, Galatea. Malenwar is destroyed. Jack is dead. Let it go."

A spark of anger flared within the dark depths. "'Let it go'? That's easy for you to say. They didn't murder the one you loved!" She pointed an accusing finger at him.

Kadir held up his hands. "I advised caution and compassion. I didn't want him dead any more than you did."

Her eyes softened again. "I know you didn't. You wouldn't. You understood, in a way that no one else could."

"But it's over. What do you hope to accomplish?"

"What if there was an artifact that could change all that?"

It was wishful thinking and Kadir said as much. "There isn't one."

Galatea reached into a pocket of her long black dress and withdrew a thick grimoire. "Oh, but I think there is."

He exhaled heavily. "So you were behind that, too."

Galatea wasn't listening. She was leafing through the book, flipping to a page that was blank. She turned it around so that it faced him. "Some of the pages are blank and I can't read them. I don't suppose you know how?"

"I'm afraid not. I don't even know what most of those artifacts do. It was a bit before my time."

"Pity." She closed the grimoire. "I guess I'll have to figure it out on my own."

"You can't honestly hope to go through with this… It's bad enough that you've stolen that thing, but you shouldn't use it. You don't know what half of those spells do."

"And why shouldn't I use it?" she challenged. "Do you know where I found this grimoire? In a dusty old display case in a cramped little library in a forgotten town in the middle of nowhere! This—these artifacts—are our legacy, our inheritance. They belong to us! We, who know how to use them. Why should the humans keep them in their world?"

"By the queen's light, Galatea, you can't bring someone back from the dead!"

"I intend to try," she said in a low voice. "And I would advise you not to try and stop me. I expected you to understand, Kadir. You know what it is to love a human. Don't tell me you wouldn't do anything for her. Because you did."

Kadir didn't have the words to deny it. They would have been lies.

"I'm not asking you to go with me," Galatea added. "I'm just asking you not to get in my way. We were friends once, Kadir, before all this. We're both Guardians. We don't have to be enemies. But don't think I won't remove any obstacles that get in my way." Her voice sank to barely a whisper. "You have far more to lose than *I* do."

Kadir thought immediately of Emily, dead now. Lylla had given him the news a few months ago. He thought that he'd let her go, but nothing could have prepared him for the searing grief her death caused—and she hadn't even been killed by another the way Jack had. He couldn't imagine Galatea's own pain.

He'd already lost Emily. He couldn't lose her again. And his wife had died long ago. But he loved his city—his people. Kadir turned to look at the city of Khae in the distance. He would do anything for them.

Galatea could destroy all of Khae if it came down to it. She had destroyed a city once before. Their lives were not something he was willing to gamble with. Galatea could kill him, but she wouldn't, not even if he defied her. She would only kill him in a different way. If he could ensure the safety of his people, as their chieftain, he had a responsibility to do that.

Yes, he had sworn an oath to protect the Gate to which he had been assigned, but also to protect Wysteria itself and all its citizens. What was Wysteria without its people?

He could not fight her, he knew that. She was more powerful than he was, he could sense it. She wore an air of power around her like a cloak. Power and the threat of violence.

Perhaps he could help reunite her with Jack and that would be an end to it. After all, was that so wrong?

His voice was hoarse when he next spoke. "What do you need me to do?"

"Right now, I need you to step aside."

She wants to go through my Gate.

Of course. She would have come out directly at the cemetery if she'd taken the Ice Gate, but it was guarded by Cyren and there was not a chance she would let Galatea through. She needed someone else, someone who would understand.

It was forbidden for a Wysterian to cross through a Gate and into Earth unless they were on official business or visiting one of the human Guardians. It was possible that was what she intended, but if so, it wouldn't be for anything good. Kadir knew that, but what choice did he have?

Refusing wasn't worth risking all of Khae.

And if he were honest with himself, there was a small part of him that wanted Galatea to succeed. To be reunited with her lover and have the future that was stolen from the both of them. A future that he himself had been denied.

He looked up at Galatea, meeting her eyes, and wordlessly stepped aside.

7

The woods were dark and quiet when Galatea stepped through the Gate, Venryk beside her. Kadir had let her through. He hadn't tried to stop her. She'd figured she could appeal to him, as a friend, and as someone who understood the pain of loving a mortal. She hadn't wanted to threaten him, but she had come too far to let him stand in her way. She had secured his loyalty for the time being.

But was loyalty truly loyalty if it was coerced?

Golden light shown in one of the windows of Professor Lawrence's house, but Galatea wasn't concerned. He couldn't see her and Venryk from here and it wasn't him she'd come to see.

The two of them were forced to walk the remainder of the distance to the cemetery, but it was less ground to cover than if they'd trekked through Iceland only to come out in the cemetery itself.

The graveyard was deserted when they arrived, as she'd expected. The windows of the small church and house behind were dark. An owl hooted to their left, somewhere in the trees. The sky was clear, stars winking overhead. There was enough moonlight to illuminate the way.

The small gap between the fence and the shed had been closed off for the night and Galatea began climbing over the fence, mindful of the wire. She grimaced as the iron burned where it met her bare skin.

She should have worn gloves…and shoes.

Venryk edged back a few paces and took a running leap over the fence. "Which one is his?"

Galatea didn't answer, setting down on the grass on the other side. She straightened her dress and strode forward. "It's unmarked."

She wouldn't have known which grave belonged to Jack at all if she hadn't hidden and watched the burial itself. At first, she'd been surprised that the others would bother to bury him at all, but she supposed they hadn't wanted to bury a human in Wysteria. It had been a hurried affair, without rites or ceremony, aided by the man who had been the Ice Guardian before the current Reverend.

Letting the moonlight guide her, Galatea stole between the rows of headstones until she came to the one she wanted. It was plain and slightly crooked. Lichens had grown up over the surface of the stone and it looked as though it could pass for much older than it was.

She stole a glance at one of the mausoleums standing at the far side, but it remained quiet. No one had any reason to come through the Ice Gate tonight and she hoped it stayed that way.

"Keep an eye out," she hissed to Venryk as she cracked open the grimoire and began to recite the spell.

There was no flash of light or hum in the air. Nothing to signify the spell was working. But a moment later, the ground trembled and shifted beneath her feet. A pale hand burst to the surface, clawing and tearing at the grass as it fought to free itself.

Galatea clutched the grimoire to her chest and watched in a mixture of horror and fascination, hardly daring to breathe, as Jack clawed his way free of his grave until at last, he stood before her.

Time had not been kind to him. He no longer resembled the young man she had known, now more bone than flesh after fifty years left to rot in the earth. Galatea felt tears spring to her eyes as she looked at him. There was still hair attached to the skull and she reached out to brush away the loose dirt. His eye sockets glowed a solid green.

"Oh, Jack, what have they done to you?" she whispered. "Jack? It's me. It's Galatea."

There was no flicker of recognition, no response to indicate he'd heard.

"Jack, say something."

The corpse's mouth opened as though he wanted to speak, but all that came out was a quiet, rattling sigh.

Galatea's shoulders slumped and she turned away. "I knew it was too good to be true."

Her love was nothing but a mindless thrall like the others she'd resurrected. That wasn't her Jack. It was an empty shell, ready to do her bidding. A wave of emotion washed over her, carrying her along with it whether she wanted to go or not.

Galatea threw the grimoire at the nearest headstone, digging her fingers into her scalp. She tried her best to stifle the sob she felt rising in her throat, but it slipped out anyway.

Venryk came up behind her, nudging her side and Galatea sank to her knees, wrapping her arms around his neck and burying her face in his thick fur.

How could the world be so cruel? How could she have come so far only to fail yet again? Jack was supposed to be different. The spell was supposed to bring him back fully.

"We've got company," Venryk murmured.

Galatea lifted her head. A light had clicked on inside the house.

"Damn it," she hissed. "He must have heard something." *Or perhaps he'd sensed the spell.*

She'd been hoping to avoid any confrontation with Earth's Ice Guardian, but now it seemed unavoidable.

"Jack, stay there," she ordered, hoping at least that he would listen the way her soldiers did. "Venryk." She hurriedly moved to stand behind a nearby headstone, motioning for him to follow. The wolf bounded to her side and she summoned darkness to cloak them from view.

The small house door swung open to reveal the Reverend dressed in striped pajamas, a bathrobe hurriedly thrown on. His hair was ruffled as though he'd just been roused from sleep. He gripped a flashlight in one hand and clicked it on, shining it around the cemetery.

"Who's there?" he called.

The beam settled on the form of Jack, standing where Galatea had left him. He hadn't moved and he gave no response to the posed question.

"Hello?" the Reverend called, starting forward, unable to see Jack clearly from a distance. "I'm afraid we're closed. Visiting hours are over."

Galatea tracked his progress as he approached Jack, pulling the stolen antique dagger out of her belt. Carefully, still concealed by the cloak of darkness, she crept closer.

"Are you all right?" the Reverend asked. "Hello?" He'd nearly reached Jack, stumbling to a halt as the flashlight beam revealed the decomposed flesh, glowing eyes, and dirt-speckled clothing. Galatea could no longer see his expression, but she could hear the horror in his voice. "Oh, God!"

Quick as a viper, Galatea darted out from behind the stone, fingers clenched around the dagger, and slammed the pommel against the Reverend's temple. He dropped like a stone, falling limply to the ground. The flashlight slipped out of his hand, landing softly on the grass.

She dropped the cloak of darkness and Venryk trotted up to them, bending down to sniff the motionless man. "I think you killed him."

The side of his temple, where she had struck him, was caved in as though the skull had fractured from the force.

Galatea let out a shaky breath. "Maybe. But I'm not taking any chances."

She bent down, grabbing ahold of the man's collar and set off toward the house, dragging his dead weight behind her. "Venryk, bring the flashlight."

The wolf gripped the flashlight between his teeth and trotted after her, the beam dancing wildly. Galatea dumped her burden unceremoniously at the top of the stairs, near the door. The door, unlocked, stood slightly open, but she gave it a fierce kick anyway, as an intruder would have done, sending it crashing back. Venryk deposited the flashlight beside the body as Galatea knelt and slashed the dagger's blade across the unconscious man's throat. She stepped into the house, just inside the doorway, and summoned wind. It roared through the house, tearing drawers out of cabinets, overturning furniture, and ripping paintings off the walls.

"There," she muttered, stepping back outside. "It'll look like he was fending off a robbery. Come on."

Wiping the blade on the grass, she tucked it back into her belt and made her way over to Jack.

"What are you going to do about *him?*" Venryk asked, jerking his muzzle at the risen human.

"Take him with us," Galatea replied, snatching up the grimoire from where she'd thrown it. "There has to be a spell in here that will bring him back as he once was. I know it! I just have to find it. Jack, follow me."

They began the long walk back to Professor Lawrence's Gate, moving in silence. Galatea retreated deep into her own thoughts, emotions a tumult inside her.

She refused to believe that this was a hopeless task she'd set for herself. It was clear that the resurrection spell she currently knew would not be enough. There had to be another one. There just had to be.

But now a second matter weighed more heavily on her.

She had killed a Guardian, which was tantamount to a declaration of war. They'd be after her now. And yet, she wasn't nearly as frightened as she knew she ought to be. Perhaps it was the lingering anger over her failure tonight. But she had soldiers and allies of her own now. She would hardly be fighting alone.

This was what she had intended all along. Revenge. The Reverend may not have even been born when Jack had been killed and she'd destroyed her own Gate, unleashing destruction upon Malenwar, but he was still one of them. And they would all pay for what they had done or allowed to happen.

It was only after the successful attack on the fort, when she had seen her undead warriors in action, that the idea had fully been realized in her mind. Initially, her sole focus had been bringing Jack back, but now that she had soldiers of her own, why shouldn't she move ahead with the only other thing she wanted? To make those that were guilty of his death answer for it? And why shouldn't he be there to witness the culmination of her revenge with her?

But it was no good if he were only a shell of his former self, just another mindless thrall.

Kadir was still waiting outside the temple when they crossed back over into Wysteria. He blanched at the sight of Jack's corpse shambling behind her and Venryk.

"You really went through with it. Look at him, Galatea. I told you—you can't bring someone back from the dead."

"Yes," she snarled, whirling on him in sudden anger. "You told me."

She had come so close and risked so much, all for potentially nothing. She had known that there was the possibility it might not work, considering all the others she had raised were nothing more than empty shells themselves. But she had hoped, believed that Jack would be different. The others had been commoners and soldiers—nobodies. And Jack had been so vibrant, so full of life when she'd known him. Not at first, perhaps, but she had shown him how to live again—that there was something worth living for. Something of the man he'd been had to remain. But it hadn't made a difference.

"There are spells in here that I can't read!" she went on, holding up the grimoire. "I know the spell I need is in here. *I know it!* But I can't read it."

Kadir rubbed his chin in an agitated manner. "There might be a book in the queen's library that would tell you what you needed to know, but other than that, I can't think of anything."

"Oh, and how do you think that would go?" Galatea sneered. "Marching up to the palace and demanding a tome. 'Excuse me, Lylla, but I need access to your library so I can bring my dead lover back to life—you know, the one you murdered.' Please! No, I stole this from Professor Lawrence. If anyone knows, it's *him.*"

Kadir frowned. "I suppose you'll be asking to go through my Gate again, then, when the time comes."

"Oh, I'm not asking," Galatea assured him.

"You can't keep this a secret forever," Kadir said, exasperated. "There's only so many Gates and sooner or later, someone's bound to wonder where exactly our security breach is, how you keep coming through. What am I going to tell them?"

"You'll tell them that you tried to stop me, but were injured in the process."

"Injured?"

Lightning sprang from Galatea's fingertips and Kadir fell to his knees, unprepared for the attack, as the electricity coursed through him. She lowered her hand and before Kadir could attempt to rise, Venryk lunged, his long claws piercing clothing and skin.

Kadir cried out, writhing, trying to shove the wolf off of him but he was too heavy. It was amazing how helpless even the most powerful Guardian could be rendered when they were panicking.

Galatea slammed her dagger's pommel into Kadir's head, much the same as she had the Reverend, only this time, taking care not to kill her victim. Silence fell over the desert.

Kadir might not understand her reasons for attacking him, but it would help them both out in the long run. There was simply no way to provide him with an excuse that would sound reasonable without wounding him sufficiently.

"It's for your own good," Galatea informed him, even though he could no longer hear her.

***

Early the next morning, Sara met Nadia and Max at the diner again for breakfast. She ordered her two pancakes and coffee as usual. Max ordered another burger and Nadia chose French toast.

"How're things going at the library?" Nadia asked after they'd all ordered and the waitress had left. "Have the police found who robbed the place yet?"

"Not yet," Sara replied glumly. She didn't like thinking about it.

She had gotten little sleep the previous night, wondering again about Mrs. Miley and how such a thing could even be possible. Sara desperately wanted to share what she had overheard with her friends, but she had promised the sheriff she would tell no one.

The more she thought about it, the more frightened she became and still no closer to an answer. Nadia and Max might be able to suggest a solution—Max especially—but with Nadia's love of social media and Max's penchant for conspiracy theories, the news would be all over town before the day was out.

She knew a bit about forensics from watching true crime documentaries. If the body in the basement really was Mrs. Miley, they would be able to identify her.

And then what? How long could they possibly keep this a secret? Sooner or later, word would get out. In the meantime, Sara kept the knowledge to herself, feeling all the while like she was harboring some terrible secret.

"I heard a crew was called out to assess the fire damage, though," she added. It was all she could tell them, but it did little to assuage her guilt.

"At least there haven't been any more break-ins," Nadia said brightly.

"No," Max agreed, "but there was a murder last night."

Sara paused mid-sip, the coffee going down the wrong way. A murder, *here*, in Mayfair? It was unthinkable!

But then, she recalled in further detail what the sheriff had said about the body they'd found in Mrs. Miley's basement. Blunt-force trauma. Could that, too, have been a murder or had she simply slipped and hit her head on something?

"What?" Nadia exclaimed, her brown eyes widening as she turned to him. "Who was killed?"

"That Reverend out by that small church about ten miles out of town. Pierce, I think his last name was."

"My family used to go to that church about five years ago! Who would want to kill him?"

Max shrugged. "Beats me. He was found by one of his parishioners coming over early this morning to talk to him about something. They think it was a robbery. The door to the house was open and the inside had been trashed."

"How do you know all this?" Sara asked, finding her voice again. "I hadn't heard anything about it."

Max gave her a pointed look. "It's a small town. People talk. Besides, the radio reported it early this morning."

It's a small town. People talk. All the more reason why she had to keep her mouth shut.

"I don't listen to the radio." Sara gripped her cup unnecessarily hard. "What's happening to our town? First a robbery and now this."

"I know," Nadia agreed, her expression turning more serious. "Killed in a robbery. Seems like such a waste. He'd have given them whatever they wanted."

Another robbery.

"Somehow, I can't see our library burglar being behind this one," Max remarked.

"Really? You'd be the first person I'd expect to suspect them for both crimes," Nadia said. "With all your conspiracy theories."

"But if it's not connected, that means that there's two separate people running around town committing crimes," Sara argued. That was a frightening thought.

Max shrugged. "Could be. But I think the library thief is probably long gone by now."

Sara thought again of interreacting with Mrs. Miley the day before the break-in. Mrs. Miley, who was found long-dead in her basement.

Suddenly, she found she had no appetite for the food she had ordered and pushed up from her seat. "I gotta go."

***

As it does in small towns, gossip spread like wildfire and it was only a matter of time before word of the murder reached Hank's ears. He was appropriately appalled, but also was able to draw conclusions the police could not.

Reverend Pierce had been a Guardian. Valuable relics had been stolen from Professor Lawrence, who was also a Guardian. Damaris had paid all three of them a visit, warning them to be cautious. And now one of them was dead.

It couldn't be a coincidence. The police could believe whatever they liked, that the Reverend had been killed in a robbery, but he didn't believe it. They would waste their time searching for a human culprit on this side of the Gates and never find them.

The others had to be told. They'd have no other way of learning of the tragedy otherwise. Without explanation, Hank flipped the sign on the door of the convenience store to read *Closed* and made his way to the back of the store where the restroom was located.

It was a single, unisex room, which had caused no shortage of problems in the past when a lot of people required its use and there was only one. It seemed like a silly place for a Gate, but no one had asked him.

He opened the door and stepped inside, moving over to the far wall. He laid his hand on it and the Gate opened at his command, the bricks of the wall fading. Hank stepped through, the walls of the gas station vanishing, replaced by the trees of the Enchanted Forest.

Wanderer was sitting underneath a large tree trunk, but she sprang to her feet as she saw him, her false ears perking. "Hank!" she cried, grinning, but she stopped short, noticing his expression. Her ears dropped. "What's wrong?"

***

Damaris was finding herself spending more and more time on Earth, she thought, as she galloped through the farm fields that would take her to the Ice Gate. It was ridiculous, but something had to be done.

The run did nothing to lift her spirits this time around. The knowledge that one of her fellow Guardians had been killed weighed heavily on her. This was more than just a robbery. The theft of a few artifacts was bad enough, but this… The others would have to take the threat seriously now, whether they believed Galatea was the culprit or not.

The Reverend's body would have long since been removed from the scene, so she couldn't hope to glean any clues from it, but Hank had reported that he'd supposedly had his throat slashed and his skull fractured.

It struck her as overly violent, in a way. *Why would they hit him on the head and then slit his throat?* It made no sense, and it definitely didn't make any sense for the attacker to do the opposite.

The attack spoke of hatred, almost. Of a passion, a rage so intense that they felt compelled to fracture the man's skull—which probably killed him by itself—and then slash his neck open afterward.

A mere thief would be unlikely to do that.

Damaris slowed well before she reached the church, reverting back to her human form and then walking on, following the unlined road that would take her there.

There was yellow police tape ringing the church and house, but Damaris wouldn't have been able to take a look and ascertain whether or not anything had been stolen regardless. Instead, she paused outside the wire fence, arms crossed.

Why would Galatea kill the Reverend? There must have been a reason. Perhaps he'd gotten in her way—the way of what? If he'd tried to stop her, what was he trying to stop?

A sense of foreboding gripped her and Damaris didn't think that she'd find whatever she'd come here to find in the church or the house.

With a quick glance at the church, she slipped through the fence and into the cemetery. She didn't know which grave was Jack's, only that he'd been buried here. She could rule out the stones which obviously weren't his. A flow of meaningless names scrolled past, each one as helpful as the last. Some of the inscriptions on the older stones were so weathered they were unreadable. But they couldn't be the one she was looking for—they were too old.

Damaris stopped. A grave in the next row looked as though it had recently been disturbed. The grass was torn, the earth overturned. It was unmarked.

Apprehension growing, she approached it. Either someone had come in the middle of the night to perform an illegal, hurried burial or they had come for whoever was buried here.

She shot another glance at the church, but no one was watching. Still, she must be quick.

Damaris thrust a hand forward, willing the earth to move. Within moments, she had emptied the grave of its dirt, piled neatly on either side. She hadn't expected it to be completely empty and it wasn't.

A wooden coffin lay within the hole. Its lid had shifted to one side, revealing the interior.

It was empty.

Damaris huffed and piled the earth back on top of the grave. The others could no longer deny the significance of this. Galatea was back. And she had killed a Guardian.

It was time she left the cemetery. She couldn't be seen here. She was a stranger and the last thing she needed was for people to blame her for what had happened.

There was no answer when she knocked at Professor Lawrence's door, much to her annoyance. She found him at the library, surveying repairs that were being done to the front of the building. Beside him stood a teenaged girl whose brown hair was styled in a long braid. The girl looked up at her with some surprise, obviously never having seen her before. Professor Lawrence merely looked resigned. No doubt he'd already heard the news.

Lawrence turned to the girl. "Sara, this woman is from the insurance company. She's here to talk to me about the stolen items."

Damaris shot him a quick glare. If she'd known this was the excuse he was going to give, she would have modified her appearance to suit the role he assigned her. As it was, she had no briefcase and doubted she looked much like an insurance agent, dressed in a halter top and shorts.

"Yes," she said smoothly., schooling her expression. "Do you have someplace private where we could talk?"

"We can use the office. It's this way," Lawrence replied, then added to the girl, "It'll only take a moment."

Damaris followed Lawrence further inside to a small back room, with windows set into the wall. Lawrence shut the door behind them and took a seat at the wooden table.

Keeping up appearances, and mindful that others who might be passing could see them through the windows, she sat down instead of standing.

"How go repairs?" she asked.

"The damage was minimal. We should be up and running before long."

She nodded, then got down to business. "I assume you know?"

Wordlessly, he nodded, confirming her suspicions.

"They've got the church cordoned off," she began. "But I had a look around the churchyard. You helped bury the man, I believe. Where in the cemetery is Jack's grave located?"

"Near the southwest corner."

"Mm. That's what I thought. I checked it out. The ground had been disturbed around it and there was nothing in the coffin."

Lawrence suddenly looked decades older. "So it really is her, then."

"And not only that, she's taken up necromancy as well as sorcery."

He folded his hands together on the table. "Poor Pierce. He didn't deserve that."

"I'm going to be sending some soldiers to help you protect your Gate."

He looked up at her sharply and she thought she saw a flash of annoyance in his eyes. "What? Just how many strangers do you think will go unnoticed in a town like this? It's not like I have visitors regularly. They'll not go unseen."

"They will," Damaris insisted. "The queen's Shadows specialize in remaining unseen." She smiled. "That's why they're called Shadows." Her amusement faded and she jabbed a finger into the table. "Lawrence, I'm not going to tell you how to do your job, and I know, as a Guardian myself, how much this must rankle. I wouldn't appreciate being told that I needed help guarding my own Gate either. But we *know* for a fact who we're dealing with now and she's already killed one Guardian. She stole some of your relics and has raised at least one person from the dead." She reached across, laying a hand on his wrinkled and liver-spotted one. "We can't risk losing anyone else. It's too dangerous."

Lawrence sighed. "I will do whatever the queen asks of me. And I will do all I can to stop Galatea."

"As will I." Damaris gave his hand a gentle squeeze and then let go. "I have to go. I can't stay."

"I know. Thank you."

She rose to leave.

"Damaris."

She froze. "Yes?"

He looked directly at her. "How did Galatea get through? Once I can understand—we were caught off-guard. But how was she able to get through a second time? Whose Gate did she use?"

Damaris felt worry begin to worm its way around her stomach, cinching tight. If Galatea had killed one Guardian, why not two? Was that how she had crossed over again so quickly? Had they already lost more than one?

"I have to go," she said tersely and yanked the door open.

***

Sara watched the unfamiliar woman leave, walking briskly, her sandals thumping down the steps. She stuck out like a sore thumb. Her clothing—just a simple crimson halter top and black shorts—seemed an odd choice for an insurance agent. But beyond that, she was unusually tall and her bare arms were well-muscled.

The woman strode out without another word and Sara watched her go. She stopped at the base of the stairs and looked back over her shoulder as if aware she was being watched, her eyes meeting Sara's. Her gaze, strangely intense, made Sara uncomfortable.

In that brief moment, the woman's eyes were no longer dark brown, but crimson, with yellow whites. Sara drew back a step, blinking rapidly.

The woman's eyes were once again brown.

She turned and walked away.

***

Jack's grave was in the cemetery that housed the Ice Gate, so the logical conclusion was that Galatea had used the Ice Gate to cross over. It would not have been Damaris's first choice, but rather her last.

To reach Cyren and her Gate, there was nothing for it but to brave a trek through Iceland. The snow first began in the farthest reaches of the Enchanted Forest, but as one continued, the forest fell behind and was slowly replaced by the slopes and mountains. In places, there were lodges where some elves lived, where one could stop and warm themselves, but they were few and far between.

Deep within Iceland, set amidst the mountains, was the ice palace where the Icelandic mountain dragons were supposed to live, but they were too busy fighting amongst themselves. The civil war had started shortly after the Exodus, when Wysterians had fled Earth. They'd been fighting ever since over who the true ruler was.

Rumor had it that a dragon named Icicle, who claimed to be the true Empress, had recently recaptured the ice palace and was currently holding it.

But that's not who Damaris was going to see. Cyren's Gate was deep in Iceland as well, set by the cliffs that overlooked the sea.

She chose to avoid the long trek by returning to the cemetery and going through the Ice Gate itself, hidden within one of the mausoleums. She stepped through as a unicorn, but her white fur did little to keep out the chill that instantly shocked her system. It seemed to bite into her bones and within moments, she was sure she'd never be warm again. While she may have been immune to heat, she seemed hyper-sensitive to the cold.

Why anyone would want to live in this godforsaken wasteland is beyond me! Damaris thought, trudging through the snow toward Cyren's lodge, the icy wind lashing her mane. She rapped on the door with one hoof.

It opened a moment later to reveal Cyren. Damaris felt a rush of relief. At least she hadn't been killed like she'd feared.

"Damaris," Cyren exclaimed, opening the door wide. "Come in."

The unicorn gratefully stepped into the room, out of the biting cold. Cyren shut the door, cutting off the screaming wind. There was no fire in the hearth, but Damaris lit one, for her own comfort more than Cyren's. Just as she was immune to heat, Cyren was immune to cold. She could go traipsing in the snow completely naked and it wouldn't bother her any.

The lodge resembled a log cabin, built entirely out of wood. The hard floor was covered with thick pelts, mostly snow stag, but Damaris thought one orange pelt must have been from a fire wolf.

Cyren sat in an uncomfortable-looking chair, fur draped over it. "What's happened?"

Damaris explained the newest development. Cyren gaped at her in horror to learn that her Earth-side counterpart had been killed.

"It's just me now at this Gate," she murmured, hugging her arms to her chest.

"Lylla has ordered that extra guards be placed at all of the Gates," Damaris said softly. "Cyren, we can no longer deny that it's Galatea. I went to the cemetery. I saw the grave. Jack's gone."

The shadow elf nodded numbly. "I guess she survived after all. And now she's resurrected Jack. We killed him once; we'll have to kill him again."

Damaris flattened her ears. *Have you learned nothing?* she wanted to scream, but swallowed back her anger, shifting her weight from one hoof to the other. She didn't want to ask, but it had to be done. Galatea had managed to cross over somehow.

"Cyren…has anyone gone through your Gate?"

The elf's head snapped toward her, her yellow eyes narrowing dangerously.

To suggest that a Guardian was incompetent or incapable of doing their job, or that they might need help, was a grave offense, widely understood and respected. One did not suggest such things, especially not one Guardian to another.

They were *Guardians* after all, gifted with the ability to control more than one element. It was what set them apart. They were supposed to be fine on their own, protecting their Gates without assistance. It was what they had sworn an oath to do.

"Why do you ask?"

Damaris had expected an outright denial, but she could tell that Cyren was keeping her temper in check with difficulty.

"Because," she replied, keeping her voice level, "Galatea has managed to cross over somehow. It seems too easy. Unless she killed a Guardian, snuck through, or was let through, she would have been stopped."

"No one's gone through my Gate," Cyren said, with a hint of ice in her tone. "I've been here ever since the meeting. I haven't left, not for a moment."

Damaris wasn't sure she believed her. Cyren had been of the belief that Galatea was dead and so she might not have taken the threat seriously. If she had been careless with her security, believing it couldn't possibly have been Galatea, she may not have been as vigilant as she claimed. Galatea may have had an opportunity to sneak through in Cyren's carelessness.

Galatea couldn't have gone through Damaris's own Gate. She didn't know where it was. Only Damaris herself and Lylla knew. Besides, it wouldn't have helped Galatea any if her goal was to reach Jack. The Flame Gate came out on the other side of the world.

The Earth Gate had been destroyed and was no longer functional.

That left only the Water, Lightning, and Wind Gates. Lightning was unlikely. Galatea would have had to go through both Wanderer and Hank and even if one should have been away, the other would not have. That's why there were Guardians on both sides.

Professor Lawrence may well not have known if someone had gone through his Gate. He hadn't known the first time. *All the more reason to post extra guards at his Gate.*

Kadir had not been present at the Gate the first time Galatea had crossed through—his guards had and they had paid the price. But surely after the meeting, he knew to take the threat seriously. Or did he?

He hadn't believed Galatea had survived the Cataclysm either. But it wouldn't be like him to be so irresponsible. He would have been at the Gate himself and he wouldn't have let Galatea through.

Unless she killed him.

As soon as it had appeared, the horrible thought would not leave Damaris alone. It was certainly possible. She had to check and make sure he was all right. She would not be able to rest until she had seen him, safe, with her own eyes.

"You got that far away look in your eyes," Cyren said, breaking into her thoughts. "You don't believe me, do you?"

"I believe you," Damaris replied, still unsure if she did. "I have to check on the others."

Cyren nodded slowly. "I'll keep an eye out for the extra guards. Though I feel sorry for whoever gets posted here." She waved a hand at the snow whipping past the window outside.

So do I, Damaris thought.

***

That evening, Sara's dad came home early from work and surprised her by offering to cook dinner. Knowing that he was notoriously bad at cooking, she volunteered to help him, pleased that they could do something together the way a normal family would.

The dish was a simple homemade pizza that they managed not to burn, but it tasted especially delicious to Sara. She wished she saw more of her dad.

She didn't get to spend as much time with him as she would have liked. There weren't many job opportunities in Mayfair and those there were often did not pay well. Her dad commuted around two hours a day to and from work and he was often too tired at the end of the day to do anything but rest.

She felt closer to him since her mom had died, but they still seldom got to see each other.

Sara glanced across the table. Her father was looking troubled, his hands clasped together, elbows propped on the table, a piece of pizza lying untouched in his plate.

"Is something wrong?" she ventured.

He sighed, lowering his hands. "I need to talk to you about something."

For a split second, Sara thought he was going to bring up the recent robbery and murder that everyone seemed to be talking about. But then she realized what it was before he put it into words. Her sense of happiness vanished, dread settling in her stomach like a stone. *Here it comes.*

"Have you given any more thought to that scholarship offer?"

The local college had offered her a scholarship that would cut the tuition cost in half, making it far more affordable. This wasn't the first time her father had brought up the subject of college. She knew he desperately wanted her to go, to make use of her talents—and with her test scores, getting in shouldn't be a problem.

Once, she would have leapt at the opportunity to experience something new outside of the small town of Mayfair. But now, she wasn't even sure she wanted to go to college. And the idea of picking up her camera again…

But God, did she want to get out of here!

She decided to be evasive. "Not really…"

"You have such an eye for photography, Sara. You can't afford to waste this opportunity."

How could she tell him that she didn't want to go? How could she make him understand without disappointing him?

"I—I don't know if I really want to go."

"What are you going to do instead?"

"I don't know," Sara confessed, looking away. She didn't consider herself to be good at anything except photography.

"What are you going to do with your life, Sara?" her dad pressed.

She met his gaze. He was concerned for her. She knew he only wanted what he thought was best for her and her listlessness worried him, but he didn't understand. How could he be so calm about all of this? So okay?

"I don't know, okay?" she repeated, her voice rising slightly this time. She felt frustration welling up within. "I just want to get out of here. That's all I want. God, Dad, when are you going to accept that there's nothing here? This town is dying."

Sometimes I feel like I'm dying, too, she thought, but didn't say. It seemed too personal an admission, but she felt tears spring to her eyes, betraying her.

"I know it's hard for you," he said. "But your mom would have wanted you to go."

And that's the problem. He had played the card she'd hoped he wouldn't. Sara pushed back from the table, getting to her feet, appetite gone. She couldn't sit here and listen to this anymore and she didn't want them to get into an argument like last time.

"Mom's not here," she said softly and without waiting for a response, retreated upstairs to her bedroom.

8

The chill of Iceland clung to Damaris's bones well after she had left and didn't truly leave until she set foot in the Great Desert, once again making use of the Gates' closer proximity to each other on Earth. She inhaled deeply, filling her lungs with the hot, arid air of the desert. It brought back memories of long ago, both sweet and sorrowful. Nowhere in Wysteria made her feel at home the way the desert did.

She had grown up in a desert, though not this one, and it was as much a part of her as fire was.

The sand was warm beneath her hooves, the sun beating down overhead as she stepped out of the Golden Temple. She squinted as the sunlight glinted off its gilded surface. There were four guards posted outside, but Kadir was nowhere in sight.

Damaris felt a stab of alarm, her worst fears gathering credence. "Where's Kadir?" she snapped.

"In the city," one of the guards replied. "He's been injured."

Injured. Not dead.

Heart still hammering, Damaris wheeled around and galloped toward the city of Khae, her hooves throwing up sand behind her.

The city gates were open, as they were only closed after nightfall. Two columns stood on either side of the gates. Every gate bore carvings of a snarling wind spirit dragon, a different one for each of the four city gates, one for each direction.

Damaris had been in Khae many times before. It was a beautiful city, made to look as if it had been fashioned out of gold, but she didn't stop to take it all in. She charged through the open gates and down the central path where the city bazaar set up shop every day.

Stalls flew past, each covered by a colorful banner roof. The scent of cooking meat, exotic spices, and a crush of bodies assaulted her senses. Startled shoppers cried out and sprang out of her way as she hurtled through the bazaar. She was a familiar face in the city and if she was in such a hurry, something must have been wrong.

Taking a detour, Damaris cut through one of the city's seedier districts—occupied by taverns and gambling dens, some of which were probably illegal and yet somehow found a way to thrive. This time of day, business was slow and she passed few people.

Kadir's house was not far from the center of town and Damaris was all but out of breath by the time she arrived. The house was large enough to accommodate her as a unicorn, so she didn't bother shape-shifting, not wanting to change form unless she absolutely had to.

Her knock—rapping on the door with one hoof—was answered by one of the servants and she was shown into the living room. Colorful drapes of fabric were hanging from the ceiling and cushions were spread out on the floor amidst a few low pieces of furniture.

Kadir was reclining on a scarlet lounge. There was no visible injury that Damaris could see, but if he had already been attended to by a healer, there wouldn't be.

"I was informed you were injured," she said, only a little breathy.

He reached up, grabbed ahold of his collar, and pulled his tunic down to reveal the raised, angry scratches that ran down his chest. "I had a little trouble, to put it mildly."

Damaris let out a breath. "Galatea came through your Gate, then."

He nodded. "Yes, I saw her. Spoke to her, briefly. She wanted to go through my Gate——"

"And you refused and she attacked you for your troubles." Damaris sighed. "You're lucky. She's already killed one Guardian."

Kadir looked at her for a moment and then muttered, "There'll be no denying that it's her after this."

"No." Damaris hesitated, thinking back to the empty grave she'd found. "Did she come back with anyone, do you know?"

He spread his hands apologetically. "I'm afraid I don't know if she came back at all. She knocked me senseless before she went through."

Her jaw clenched. "This has to stop. I spoke to Lylla. She's ordered guards to be placed at every Gate."

"It'll be nice to have some help, I don't mind admitting that."

"I wish I could have been there," Damaris said vehemently. She'd have stopped Galatea from harming her friend. Whenever they inevitably clashed, she was going to show that sorceress what true vengeance was.

Kadir looked at her with something bordering on sorrow in his gaze. "So do I, *kirena.*"

"I'm just glad you're all right. I thought maybe…" She looked away. "I thought maybe she'd killed you, too."

"I'm a lot hardier than that," he assured her.

"I know. Just—be careful." How many times had she said that recently? What good did it do? She wanted to be there herself, for all of them, but she couldn't be everywhere at once. "She'll stop at nothing. I need to go speak with the queen. Keep an eye out for those guards."

***

When Damaris had gone, Kadir was left alone with his thoughts. It had been clever of Galatea to attack him before she'd left, giving him an alibi and ensuring that, for the time being, they were both safe and she could still use his Gate.

Although if she planned on confronting Professor Lawrence, she'd better cross back over before the extra guards Damaris mentioned arrived. They would complicate things, but perhaps they would also put a stop to this madness. He wouldn't have to be at her mercy any longer and no one need ever know that he had let her through the Gate at all.

But that wouldn't stop *him* from knowing.

He clenched his hand into a fist, so hard it physically hurt. *Are you really that naïve?* It would take far more than a handful of guards to make Galatea stop. She wasn't afraid of her fellow Guardians and what were ordinary elementalists in comparison?

Kadir knew he should have told Damaris what he suspected, that Galatea may pay a visit to the Professor. And yet he'd kept quiet. Letting Galatea through the Gate wasn't even the worst of what he'd done.

He had just lied to his oldest friend without batting an eye.

***

Professor Lawrence was busy sorting through boxes of relics when Felix arrived. Colin was waiting outside, with two of Lylla's other Shadows. Though the two of them may have been her personal guards, she had many others stationed around the palace at all times, always dressed in black and silver. This coloring, added to the fact that they always followed her around like her own shadow, had earned them the name.

In the past, it had irritated Felix slightly. Cassius was all too eager to make some snarky comment likening them to a guard dog. And Felix was also aware of the fact that his and Colin's proximity to the queen was less for her protection and more for their own. The Lightbringer needed protection from no one, certainly not two ordinary wood elves. The idea was laughable.

But as time went on, he'd come to see it less as patronizing and more of a position of honor. Only he and Colin had been chosen to be so close to the queen.

He had been slightly surprised, yet pleased, to learn he and Colin would be part of Lawrence's personal guard— though he doubted the old man needed much protection either.

It spoke volumes how much trust Lylla was placing in them both and he was determined not to mess this up.

The other two guards stayed stationed at the Gate itself, in the woods behind Lawrence's house. Colin remained outside, while Felix went into the house to speak with the Guardian.

He found him bent over boxes, busily sorting through them.

Lawrence answered the back door, letting him in. "Ah, Felix. Damaris told me to expect guards, but I didn't know who. Where are the others? Or is it just you?"

Felix smiled, shutting the door behind him. "I'm flattered you think I could handle guard duty all on my own, but no. Colin is at the edge of the woods and the other two are by the Gate."

"Good, good. Can I offer you anything?"

"No, thank you, Professor. I'm on duty."

Lawrence nodded. "You won't mind if I organize all this mess, would you?"

"Not at all." Felix followed him into the living room, peering down at the contents of the boxes. "Are these the artifacts from the library?"

"Yes. I thought, in light of recent events, that I should move them here. I haven't finished sorting them all yet."

"Would you like some help?" Felix reached down into the nearest box, fingers wrapping around an ornate hand mirror, drawing it out. "I know I'm supposed to be guarding you, but seeing as how we're not under any immediate threat…"

Lawrence snorted. "A Guardian, needing guarding. Thank you, my boy, but I can manage."

"What does most of this stuff even do?" Felix glanced at his reflection, eyes landing on his scars, and he quickly looked away. He put the mirror back in the box.

"Your guess is as good as mine for most of it."

"What was that?" Felix asked sharply, turning toward the front door. His acute hearing had picked up the sound of something being slammed softly. He reached for his bow, still strapped to his back.

Lawrence got to his feet and moved over to the window. "Oh, it's just Sara. She's one of my employees."

Felix hesitated. "Should I make myself scarce?"

Lawrence waved a hand. "No, no. She's harmless and you're glamoured."

Felix opened his mouth to protest, but decided against it. He could glamour himself to hide his long, pointed ears and his weapons, but his scars he could do nothing for. The darkness in the wound prevented him from concealing them with a glamour—yet another insult to injury.

But the Professor had already opened the door, struggling as it stuck, and was ushering Sara inside. "Hello, my dear."

A human. Lawrence and Hank were both humans, but they were Guardians. That was the only way a human could have magic, after all. Felix had never met an actual, magicless human before and he wasn't sure what to expect.

She was plain, as far as humans went, although even the most beautiful human paled in comparison to an elf. She didn't have the flawless skin of an elf either, but then, neither did he with scars marring half his face. Her long brown hair was plaited into a single braid and she was dressed in a pink tank top and denim shorts. There was a pair of strange shoes on her feet, blue, that looked like flat rubber slabs and made a flipping noise when she walked.

Her brown eyes turned to him questioningly.

Lawrence noticed her confusion and made the necessary introductions. "Ah, Sara, this is Felix. He's from the college."

"Hi," the girl said tentatively.

He nodded to her and her eyes flicked to the scars on the left side of his face. She didn't look horrified as some had when they'd first seen him, but her eyes still widened involuntarily.

Felix hated that it was the first thing people noticed about him, the first thing they saw when they looked—and they usually looked no further. They stared when they didn't think he'd notice, their eyes drawn to the disfigurement, thrilling at the sense of horror and morbid curiosity.

He looked away, turning his head so that only the right side of his profile faced her.

She blinked, tearing her attention away. "I'm sorry if I'm interrupting you, Professor."

"Not at all," Lawrence replied warmly.

She sat down on the floor, opposite him on the other side of the coffee table. "I wanted to ask you if the police have said any more about the robbery. Have they found anything?"

"No," he said, tone rueful. "They haven't said anything else about it. Although they did come speak to me about that murder."

That perked Felix's attention. He was slightly surprised that Lawrence was mentioning it to the girl, but then he remembered that to everyone else, the Reverend had been an ordinary human, a pillar of the community. Of course, they would have heard about it, especially in such a small town.

Sara suddenly looked as though she felt like crying, but didn't. "I don't know what's happening to our town. First a robbery and now someone killed a preacher."

"No place is perfect," Lawrence said softly.

A sudden tingling, burning sensation lanced up Felix's left cheek and he hissed in surprise. This was the last place and time he expected the sensation to happen.

Sweat broke out on his palms, adrenaline lurching through his veins. He knew what that feeling was, all too well. *Not here! It can't happen here!* His vision began to darken at the edges and Felix inhaled deeply, trying to fight the panic that had come over him. He wasn't ready. Not now!

Lawrence and Sara turned to him in alarm. Sara's eyes widened in shock and he knew his scars were glowing an angry red.

"We have company," he muttered, forcing himself to move, years of training taking over, pushing the panic aside. He hurried to the window and peered through the curtains.

Lawrence moved to join him. A tall shadow elf woman was striding across the lawn toward them, from the direction of the woods. A large fire wolf walked by her side.

"*Damn*," Lawrence murmured. He turned from the window. "Into the back bedroom. Hurry."

"Wh—what's happening?" Sara stammered.

Felix grabbed her by the arm and helped her up, escorting her after Lawrence.

"*Hurry!*" Lawrence repeated, ushering them into the bedroom ahead of him.

***

He shut the door and bolted it. Sara noticed that it had one of those old-fashioned bolts.

She had no idea what was going on, but his tone frightened her and so did the fact that they apparently needed to lock themselves in a bedroom. As a child, she'd had fears about what would happen if an intruder ever broke into her house and imagined she would retreat to her parents' bedroom and into the master bath, locking the door behind her both times.

The young man named Felix still had her by the arm, his grip strong but gentle. The left side of his face was scarred, from his forehead to just above his lips. There were five individual scars, each one jagged like a wild animal had clawed him. And they were each glowing.

He was dressed in a black sleeve-less tunic and pants, fingerless gloves that stretched to his elbows, with knee-high boots, his clothing trimmed in silver. He had a quiver full of arrows and a bow slung on his back. His ears were long and pointed. She hadn't noticed any of that before. How had she not noticed?

Professor Lawrence strode over to a large wooden wardrobe and pulled the doors open. "In here."

Sara gasped as Felix ushered her forward and the two of them stepped inside, nestling themselves amidst the clothing hanging within. Professor Lawrence stepped up after them, pulling the doors nearly completely closed.

It was dark inside the wardrobe save for the light given off by Felix's glowing scars. In such close quarters, the red light reflected off the walls and cast all their faces in a scarlet glow. The air was close and smelled heavily of mothballs. An itchy wool coat brushed against her neck, scratching her, and Sara batted it away.

The only sound was their muffled breathing, deafening in the silence.

And then, a husky female voice called out. "Oh, Professor, where are you? Come out, come out. I know you're here. What's the point of guarding an empty house, I wonder?"

Sara jumped at the sound of glass shattering, followed by a loud *thud*, as if a piece of furniture had been overturned.

"Stay here," Lawrence whispered. "I'll go."

He started to move, but Felix grabbed his arm. "What are you doing? She'll kill you."

"I'll see what she wants."

"*No*," Felix hissed. "I'm supposed to protect you."

Lawrence shook his head. "Stay here with Sara. Keep *her* safe. She's more important than any of this. Besides, I'm the Guardian. You're not."

Reluctantly, Felix released his grip on the old man's wrist. Lawrence climbed out of the wardrobe, taking care to exit through a different hallway than the one they'd come through.

Sara was shaking beside Felix, her eyes wide and frightened. "What's going on?" she asked, her voice coming out sharper than she'd intended, high with fear.

"Shh," Felix hissed, which did nothing to dispel her worry.

***

Most of the relics ferreted throughout Lawrence's house were of no interest to Galatea, but she rummaged through them while she waited for him to appear. It was in a side room that her eyes landed upon something that made her pause.

It was a sword hanging on the wall. The grip was long enough for two hands and the silver blade was straight, coming to a sharp and deadly point. But what caught her eye was the circle cut in the middle of the blade, near the hilt. She knew what this sword was, but she hadn't thought she'd ever see one in person.

Human Guardians had imbued weapons with magic during the war that led to the Exodus. Each weapon was fused with an element, giving ordinary humans the ability to wield magic through them. Otherwise, they wouldn't have stood a chance against their elementalist foes.

Galatea reached up, unhooking it from the wall. Had one of these blades ever been imbued with darkness before?

Movement down the hall interrupted her thoughts and Galatea walked back into the living room and was there waiting for Lawrence when he appeared.

She hefted the sword. "You have quite the interesting collection, Professor. Do you know what this is?"

Lawrence ignored the sword and looked at Venryk. "I see you've brought your lap dog with you."

The wolf at her side let out a low growl. "There were others here. I can smell them."

Galatea smiled at Lawrence. "Have a look around, Venryk."

***

The wolf started forward and Lawrence forced himself not to block his way to the hallway. If he did, it would only confirm the wolf's suspicions and he and Galatea would search the house until they uncovered Felix and Sara's hiding place. He had to let the wolf go and trust Felix could handle him.

And Lawrence knew he could. He *had* to.

But Galatea was a Guardian and the best intentions in the world wouldn't help Felix stop *her*.

Lawrence needed to appease Galatea as soon as possible so she would leave. "What do you want, Galatea?"

She held up the stolen grimoire in one hand. "I seem to be having a little trouble with this grimoire of yours. Some of the pages are blank and I can't read the spells that are written on them. I was hoping you could tell me how to remedy that."

Oh, dear. Lawrence stiffened, hands clenching by his sides. "I'm afraid I can't tell you that."

Galatea's eyes narrowed. "Can't or won't?"

Lawrence ground his teeth together and said nothing.

Galatea tipped her hand, letting the book fall. It landed with two blank pages facing up. She stalked toward him.

"I grow tired of your little games," she hissed, standing in front of him. She towered over him by more than a foot. "I'll ask one more time. How do I read the pages?"

Lawrence swallowed, wishing he could fight back, but for Sara and Felix's sake, he couldn't. He had to keep her busy. "You can't read it because you have not the eyes to see."

She laughed but it was mirthless. She turned and for a moment, Lawrence thought she was going to walk away and considered attacking her in that split second.

But then she whirled around, swinging the sword she had plucked from his wall. Lawrence reeled back, but not fast enough. The tip sliced into his arm and he cried out.

*****

Felix could hear Lawrence's cry of pain from inside the wardrobe and he fought the urge to run out and help him. But what could he do? He was just an ordinary elf. He had magic of his own, but it couldn't possibly compete with a Guardian's.

Where on earth was Colin? He should have come to Lawrence's aid by now. Come to think of it, where were the others? Galatea must have encountered them; she'd made the remark about why guard a house that was empty, so she knew there were guards.

An image of Colin lying at the edge of the woods, injured or dead, filled his mind and he had to try even harder to resist the urge to burst out of the wardrobe.

He was a soldier, an archer. He did not hide in wardrobes while others fought his battles for him! Not for the first time in his life, he wished Damaris were there. Or better yet, that she could somehow give him a fraction of her power even if only for a moment. But he couldn't always rely on her. Venryk had seen to that.

Felix hissed softly between his teeth as the burning in his scars intensified. Venryk was not only here, but he was getting closer.

"Are you all right?" Sara whispered. She'd been staring at his face in a mixture of bewilderment and concern ever since Lawrence had left.

She stiffened as something scratched on the bedroom door. The sound of claws on wood. Felix grimaced, baring his teeth at the noise. For him, the sound was akin to nails on a chalkboard. He could feel the claws as if they were raking over his flesh instead of the door.

He recalled the pain vividly. It had been like nothing he'd ever felt, before or since.

From the other side of the door came the unmistakable sound of something bursting into flames.

Felix muttered an oath under his breath. Trapped as they were in the wardrobe, his arrows would be of little use. He had his multitude of knives as always, but he didn't trust his luck at close combat in such a confined space, with a large animal.

He glanced at Sara. The girl had pulled a necklace out from under her shirt and was rubbing the jewel between her fingers nervously.

His eyes widened. What was this girl doing carrying an Echo Stone around her neck as if it were a common trinket? If Venryk managed to burn through the door, Felix could use the stone to amplify his own magic and maybe give them a chance at defending themselves.

He leaned close. "I need to borrow your necklace."

"What?" she exclaimed. "Why?"

"*Please.*"

She must have seen something of his desperation in his eyes, because she wordlessly slipped it over her head and passed it over.

***

A few arcing drops of blood flew through the air, landing on the blank, exposed pages of the grimoire, staining them crimson.

"Let's try this again, shall we?" Galatea growled. She held up the sword and a ball of darkness appeared in her free hand. She pressed the darkness into the circle carved into the blade, pouring her magic into it, imbuing it into the sword.

Lawrence watched in horrid fascination until the spell was complete, clutching his wounded arm. Galatea lifted the sword, the tip stained red. In the circle was darkness, flowing and swirling up and down the blade.

"Would you like to see what happens if I cut you with *this*?" she asked. "Or are you—" She broke off, staring at the grimoire.

The droplets of blood had spread and where they had landed, white text was now visible, stark against the red.

"That's it," she whispered. "All it needs is a little blood." The look on her face was exultant and she turned to him. There was a wicked glint in her eyes as she hefted her new weapon. "Would you like to volunteer?"

Glass shattered behind them and Galatea whirled as Colin smashed through the window with his sword. He ran at her, slashing with the blade. A sharp, metallic *clang* rang out as Galatea maneuvered her sword to block his.

Clenching her teeth, she shoved his blade away and countered with an attack of her own. Colin yelped as the tip of the Shadowblade sliced into his ribs. He staggered back from her, pressing one hand to the wound. Having heard the swords collide, Venryk charged back into the room.

Galatea snatched the grimoire from the floor. "We're leaving, Venryk," she called, heading for the door. "We have what we came for."

Lawrence let her go, rushing over to where Colin had collapsed to the floor. Felix and Sara ran into the room. Sara took in the destruction in awed silence. Felix darted forward to kneel beside Colin.

He was panting heavily, gasping for breath, his face pale. "Is it bad?"

The blade had slipped between his ribs and his tunic was dark and slick with blood. Felix grabbed Colin's hand, pressing it over the wound. "Keep pressure on it." He turned to Lawrence. "We have to get him to a healer. And you, too."

Lawrence glanced at the laceration on his arm. "It's nothing. Worry about Colin."

"Where's Galatea?" Colin moaned.

"Don't worry about that," Felix snapped. "We have to get to the Lightning Gate."

"Uh—my car is parked outside," Sara spoke up. "I could drive you to the hospital."

"That'd be great," Lawrence said. "He'll never make it there on foot."

Felix helped Colin to his feet and the wounded elf let out a cry of pain as he was moved.

"Should I call 911?" Sara asked.

"There's no time," Lawrence replied, moving to help Felix support Colin's weight.

She ran to open the door for them and then hurried into the driver's seat, turning the ignition. Lawrence climbed in the passenger seat and Felix helped Colin into the back.

"Head for the gas station," Lawrence instructed Sara.

"The gas station?" she repeated, incredulous.

"Yes. Trust me."

Colin cried out as they hit a pothole and Sara muttered something about bad roads. The elf had broken out into a thin sheen of sweat, still gasping in pain.

"What the hell did she slice him with?" Felix exclaimed.

"She'd fused one of the swords with darkness," Lawrence explained.

In the rearview mirror, he saw the moment Felix's face fell as he understood. Darkness in the wound. Little wonder Colin was in agony. Felix had felt how excruciating it was for himself. And he also knew, better than most, that it couldn't be healed.

Felix screwed his eyes shut. Darkness acted like a poison, slowly weakening and killing its victim. Even if Colin's wound hadn't been life-threatening by itself, he'd have died from the poison regardless.

But they still had to try.

Sara parked as close to the gas station door as she could and the four of them got out. There were people inside the store and Lawrence had the forethought to cast a glamour over them to hide their weapons and the blood.

Hank's eyes widened as they entered and made their way to the back of the store to the door that marked the restroom. Sara followed them, still likely without a clue as to what they were doing.

Colin was bleeding out and they had brought him to a gas station rather than a hospital.

Lawrence opened the restroom door and raised a hand. The back wall shimmered and disappeared, revealing a dense forest. Sara gasped.

Felix turned to her. "I almost forgot," he murmured, pressing something cool into her hand. She looked down. Her mother's necklace. In all the chaos that ensued, she'd forgotten to ask for it back.

Colin had one arm slung around Felix's shoulder and together, the two approached the opening that had been made, vanishing from sight.

Lawrence turned to her. "Stay with Hank. He's one of the good ones."

And then he turned and followed after the others. The opening disappeared and once again, the back wall was in place as though nothing had happened. Sara touched it with one hand, but it was solid.

***

The reason for not going through Professor Lawrence's Gate was twofold.

For one thing, Galatea had likely crossed through it again and it was possible that she was lying in wait for them, but Felix doubted it. The other, more important, reason was that the Wind Gate came out in the desert and Colin wouldn't have lasted long enough to make the journey from the Wind Gate to the palace.

The Lightning Gate was closest to the palace, but it still seemed ages before they had crossed beneath the Glowing Gate and struggled up the steps. By now, Colin's head hung limply, his skin deathly pale.

Serai, the head healer, had her quarters in the far west wing of the palace. She was a desert elf, with snow-white hair, bright green eyes, and very dark skin covered in white tattoos. Only healers were allowed to be tattooed. It was a symbol of their profession and ensured that even if you found yourself in an unfamiliar area and needed a healer, you need only look for the markings.

Serai went to work immediately, sitting Colin down on one of the chairs. "Help me get his shirt off," she instructed Felix.

The air in her quarters smelled heavily of herbs and several dried varieties hung from the ceiling. While Felix labored to help Colin remove his tunic, Serai turned to Professor Lawrence. She wrapped her hands around the cut on his arm. A green glow flared under her fingers and a moment later when she let go, the skin was as perfect as if it had never been broken.

She turned back to Colin, who was now shirtless, the full severity of the wound revealed. Serai didn't flinch at

136

the sight, pressing her hand against the injury. Colin hissed in pain. Once again, the green light appeared beneath her fingers but when she pulled away, the wound hadn't changed.

Serai's eyes narrowed in consternation. "It's not working."

"He was slashed with a sword infused with darkness," Felix explained.

Serai pursed her lips and took him aside, out of Colin's hearing. "This is beyond my skill. You'll have to fetch Lylla."

"But she couldn't heal me, either," Felix protested, gesturing to his face.

"I know that," Serai replied. "But it's not the same. She's the only chance he's got. Go!"

She gave him a shove toward the doorway and Felix took off at a run, calling for the queen. "Lylla!"

He met her in one of the hallways, hurrying down the marble stairs, lifting her skirts so she wouldn't trip. "What is it?"

"It's Colin," he panted. "He's hurt and Serai can't heal him."

Her face darkened but she hastened after him back to Serai's quarters. He stood to the side and watched as Lylla did as Serai had done and placed her hand over the wound. Healing required physical touch in order to work, but part of him didn't believe this would work either.

Golden light flared beneath Lylla's hand and instantly, a look of relief came over Colin, the lines of pain easing out of his face, the muscles relaxing.

Lylla stepped back to reveal perfect skin where the ugly slash had been moments before.

Felix let out a breath. "It worked."

Serai ordered Colin to rest after his ordeal and Professor Lawrence as well, even though their wounds were healed. She shooed Lylla and Felix outside.

"It worked," he murmured again, hardly daring to believe it. "Why could Colin be healed when I couldn't?"

He knew he should be grateful that Colin's life had been spared and he was, but part of him was also jealous. He hadn't been as fortunate. His wound was less severe and the darkness would move more slowly, but the end result would be the same.

Lylla looked at him, her blue eyes sad. "Because Colin wasn't marked."

Felix didn't have to ask what she meant. They'd had this conversation many years ago, after he'd first received the injury. He'd come back to the palace, hurt and bleeding and to this day, he still remembered the look on Damaris's face when she saw him.

"Marked for what?" he'd asked Lylla then, when she took him aside and explained the situation to him. Damaris had been too furious and she'd stormed off on her own.

"Death," had been the answer.

He could tell it pained Lylla to tell him, but she would never lie.

"It wasn't the same type of injury," she added, bringing him back to the present. "Whoever did this wasn't trying to mark him for a future death, they were trying to kill him now. It was Galatea, wasn't it?"

Felix swallowed his own bitterness. *You have no one to blame but yourself.* Wordlessly, he nodded.

"I thought so. You'd better fill me in while those two are recovering."

He obediently fell into step beside her and began recounting what had transpired.

You have no one to blame but yourself.

9

Hank closed early and met Sara in the house attached to the back of the store. He'd instructed her to go inside and she'd sat down at the kitchen table, too stunned to do anything else. Her mind was whirling over what had taken place at the Professor's house, trying to make sense of it and failing. None of it felt real and yet it must have been. The fact that she was sitting here now was proof of it. Just how much danger had she really been in?

She was relieved but no less confused when Hank joined her.

He sighed, shoving his hands in his jeans pockets. "Would you like some iced tea?" Tea always made everything better.

Sara nodded. "Please."

Hank opened one of the cabinets and pulled down two glasses, filling them while Sara glanced around at the metal tractor signs that adorned the walls. "I imagine you have a lot of questions."

"Just a few," she replied.

She still wasn't certain that she hadn't hallucinated the entire thing. She knew what she'd seen: Professor Lawrence, Colin, and Felix had vanished through an opening that had appeared in the back wall of the gas station restroom, but when she'd touched it, the wall had been solid.

He came back to her, handing her the tea and sitting across from her. He sighed again and began dumping sugar into his own tea.

"That robbery that happened at the library…" Sara ventured hesitantly. "That wasn't an ordinary robbery, was it?" She already knew that, but maybe Hank could explain it. The mystery that was Mrs. Miley still bothered her, but even with everything that had happened, she still hesitated to mention it.

"Nope."

Sara wrapped her hands around the glass, the condensation on the outside cooling her skin. "I watched them walk through the wall in the restroom… One minute there was a hole there and the next, just a solid wall again."

Hank pursed his lips together. "What I'm about to tell you is gonna sound crazy, but I feel like you'd rather have someone you know explain instead of a total stranger."

She nodded slowly and took a sip of tea.

"They went through what's called a Gate. There are three of them here in Mayfair and they keep the two worlds separate."

"What worlds?" Sara stared at Hank in concern, her mind reeling. If anyone else had told her this, she would have thought they were crazy. But something strange had happened in Professor Lawrence's house earlier that day and she wanted answers.

"Earth and Wysteria. That's what the other world is called. I'm sure you know a bit about mythology. Unicorns, dragons, elves. Folklore. That kind of thing?"

"A little." She thought back to when she'd noticed Felix's ears. They had been long and pointed, just like an elf's.

"They're all considered myths now, but they weren't always. A long time ago, the Gates were open and Wysterians and humans could interact freely. But eventually, the humans turned against the Wysterians and they retreated back to their own world. The Gates were sealed, intended to keep the two worlds as separate as possible."

"But why?" Sara asked. "Why would the humans do that?"

Hank took a deep breath before continuing. "All living things are born with at least some magic inside them, but most can't use it. Humans usually can't use any magic, but most Wysterians can. The humans became both jealous and fearful of their magic, of what they might do with that kind of power, and they wanted it for themselves."

"What kind of magic are we talking about?"

"Elemental, mostly. Those who have magic are known as elementalists and elementalists who can control more than one element are called Guardians. They protect the Gates, one on each side. One in Wysteria and one here on Earth. The Gate you saw used earlier is the Lightning Gate."

"And you're its Guardian," Sara guessed. She couldn't think of any other explanation as to how Hank knew all this otherwise.

"Yep. I'm the Guardian of the Lightning Gate, just like Professor Lawrence is the Guardian of the Wind Gate, which is behind his house in the woods. Reverend Pierce was the Guardian of the Ice Gate, which is in the cemetery by the small church outside of town."

Sara tried to imagine Professor Lawrence as a being with strong magical power, but couldn't reconcile the image with the elderly librarian she'd always known.

"How does this magic work?"

"As I said, it's based on the elements," Hank replied, brushing a stray crumb off the table. "Each elementalist has one element they can control and it's called their attribute. Guardians can control more than one element, but their attribute will always be the one they can control the best."

"What's your attribute?" Sara asked, leaning forward eagerly. She never would have imagined that Hank, who seemed like the most down-to-earth person ever, would have had magic either.

"Lightning," he answered, raising one hand. Sparks of electricity burst to life in his palm, dancing around his fingers, the blue bolts flashing.

Sara gaped at him, watching the dancing bolts as though mesmerized. It was real. *I'm really seeing this!* "H—how many elements are there?"

"Depends on who you ask." Hank extinguished the lightning. "Seven, officially. Eight, unofficially. The four common elements are the traditional: earth, fire, water, and air. The two uncommon elements are lightning and ice. And the last is light, which is extremely rare. The queen of Wysteria is the only light attribute currently living."

"And the unofficial element?" Sara wondered what it would be like to have control over an element like that and what one could do with it.

Hank grimaced. "That would be darkness. But it's not its own element. It's a corruption of one of the other elements—hence why it's unofficial. You only gain access to it through the study and use of dark magic, which is forbidden. And it corrupts an elementalist's attribute. So, for example, if I were to start dabbling in dark magic, I wouldn't be able to use lightning anymore. Any time I tried, it would manifest as darkness instead. But, as a Guardian, I would still be able to use all the other elements I had at my disposal."

Sara blinked, shaking her head and holding up her hands. "So what does all of this have to do with what happened with the robbery and at Professor Lawrence's earlier?"

Hank ran a hand over his face, scratching at his stubble. "Well for that, we have to go back a little ways. Crossing through the Gates and having contact with the other world is forbidden, unless Guardians are visiting each other. But, the Wysterian Earth Guardian, a shadow elf named Galatea, crossed over to Earth. She fell in love with a human named Jack and brought him back with her. Humans aren't allowed in Wysteria unless they're Guardians and Jack wasn't. Galatea refused to give him up and in the ensuing skirmish, the Earth Gate was destroyed and Jack was killed. Galatea fled to Earth and she's been here for the past fifty years until she recently stole some of Professor Lawrence's items and crossed back into Wysteria."

"Stole? But the security camera showed Mrs. Miley was the thief."

He nodded. "I'm sure that's what it looked like, but it was Galatea. She used a glamour to disguise herself."

"So Mrs. Miley really is dead?"

"You can't glamour yourself to look like someone living, so yes, in order for Galatea to disguise herself like Mrs. Miley, she'd have to kill her first."

Sara let out a shaky breath. It made a horrible kind of sense.

"But—why? What does she want?"

Hank shrugged. "We've been trying to figure that out ourselves. Damaris—she's the Flame Guardian in Wysteria—she thinks Galatea is trying to bring Jack back to life and that's why she stole that book from Professor Lawrence."

Bring someone back to life. Sara's thoughts went immediately to her mother and she pushed the memory away. She didn't want to start crying in front of Hank and she couldn't afford to think about it now. But part of her did wonder if Galatea had the power to bring someone she loved back.

No, that's wrong. That's not the way things are supposed to work. But she could understand why Galatea would want to do such a thing.

"Is that even possible?" she asked softly.

"Only with dark magic," Hank said gravely. "To tell the truth, I don't know what might be written in that book. She could be capable of doing all kinds of things. But that's why she killed Reverend Pierce. He was the Guardian of the Ice Gate and Jack was buried in that cemetery. Undoubtedly, he tried to stop her and she killed him for it."

"That's awful," Sara muttered, suddenly struck with fear at the idea that powerful beings could cross over into her world, her *town*, and murder people at will.

But Reverend Pierce was one of them. He wasn't an ordinary human without any clue of any of this. Surely normal humans are safe.

"She came back earlier to confront Lawrence over the book. He thinks that the spell to resurrect Jack didn't do as she planned and she needed a different spell, but she couldn't read the blank pages. She needs something else to bring him back as something other than a mindless zombie."

"What does she need? One of his other artifacts?"

Hank looked at her apologetically. "I'm afraid I don't know."

***

The extra guards had yet to arrive at the Wind Gate when Galatea crossed through, returning once more to Wysteria. Kadir had resumed his post, having recovered from his injuries. He'd dismissed his own soldiers, likely out of fear that she would return while he was not there and kill them. But the other guards would be coming and she knew it was only a matter of time.

"How long do you think we can keep up this charade?" he demanded. "Lylla has sent extra guards to secure the Gate. When they get here, you'll no longer be able to come and go as you please."

"Fear not, Kadir," Galatea replied. "I have what I went for and a little extra." She patted the hilt of the Shadowblade at her side.

Kadir had not been born on Earth, nor had he lived there during the war that led to the Exodus. Having spent his entire life in Wysteria, he might not know what the blade was, but he knew enough to realize it was dangerous.

"Damaris stopped by," he said, voice low even though it was only the two of them. "She seems to have bought the injuries, but how long do you think that will last? How long before she begins to wonder why you keep leaving me alive or why I don't fight to the death?"

Galatea felt like telling him that that was his problem, but she refrained, saying instead, "With any amount of luck, I have everything I require and there will be no further need of your assistance."

That seemed to mollify him, or else he realized that arguing was pointless because he made no objection as she and Venryk departed, heading back to the swamp.

As an earth attribute, Noraak had managed to reconstruct a building deep within the ruins for them to stay in and he, along with the rest of the fire wolves, Nightmares, and undead, were waiting for them when they returned.

"Was it a success?" Noraak asked eagerly. "Did he tell you what you wanted to know?"

"In a manner of speaking."

Now that she knew how to read the blank pages and reveal what was hidden on them, Galatea knew that if there was a spell that would help Jack, it was in here somewhere and she would find it. It was only a matter of time.

She retreated off on her own with her grimoire, using her stolen dagger to slice her palm, smearing the blood over the pages, one by one, until she came to the page she sought.

If she wanted to bring Jack back as he had been, she would need two Echo Stones. One was to be kept by her, as the spell caster, connecting her to the deceased. It was her life force that would keep him alive, after all. The other was to be placed in the chest of the deceased, where the heart would ordinarily be, to anchor the soul.

Galatea felt her heart skip a beat. She had one Echo Stone already, stolen from the library display case. That had been the easy part. If an amplifier was already in the possession of an elementalist, on their person, it could not be taken away. It must be given. Luckily, it had been in the case and not already claimed by another.

She frowned, looking over the other artifacts she had stolen earlier that day while waiting for Lawrence to come out of hiding. A crystal headdress and a hand mirror. She knew what the headdress was and it could prove to be very useful indeed, but she had no knowledge of what the mirror did. Perhaps the newly revealed pages of the book had an answer for that too.

But she had not found another Echo Stone among Lawrence's belongings. There had not been another among the items in the case or else she'd have taken it as well, if only to have a second amplifier.

Finding another would be difficult if not impossible. The only other place she might find one would be the palace, in that infamous library. And that was off-limits to her.

Yet another obstacle in her path. Every step forward only seemed to reveal just how much farther she had yet to go.

Galatea swore and was about to snap the grimoire shut when a sudden memory came rushing back to her. That day she had visited the library, glamoured as an old lady, she had asked the young girl behind the counter if she knew anything about the artifacts contained within the glass case.

There had been something about that girl that struck her as odd, some strange feeling, but she couldn't quite put her finger on it until now. That girl—Sara, her name was— had been fiddling with a necklace of green stone when Galatea had turned to her. It had only been for a moment before she'd hidden it back beneath her clothes, but Galatea knew what it was.

A second Echo Stone.

Galatea smiled to herself. Now she knew what that strange feeling was.

Very clever, Lawrence, very clever. But not clever enough.

She shut the grimoire and went to join Noraak and Venryk. "Venryk, I have a job for you. There's something I want you to retrieve for me…"

***

Lylla strolled along beside Professor Lawrence, Felix on her other side, as they walked through the palace courtyard. The sun was warm on her skin, but beginning to set, staining the sea red and orange. Black-clad guards watched from the palace walls and were hidden around the garden surreptitiously.

The cobblestones were still warm beneath Lylla's bare feet, her silk dress rippling as she moved. "Damaris told me that she went to Jack's grave and found it empty. If Galatea has already resurrected him, what reason would she have for confronting you at your home, Professor?"

To her, he would always be a professor, even though he'd long since retired.

"She came to me wanting to know how to read the blank pages of the grimoire, Your Highness. I refused to tell her, but she found out anyway when she cut me and blood fell onto the pages."

"For what reason would she need to be able to read the blank pages?"

"I believe that she resurrected Jack, but he was nothing like the man she remembered. You see, necromancy allows one to raise the dead, but they're mindless. Typically, this is done to acquire soldiers and, in that case, it's not a problem. But for someone like Jack, she would want him to have a will and personality of his own like he did while he was living."

"I see," Lylla said slowly. "I'm afraid I don't know much about necromancy—or sorcery for that matter—other than what I've read."

"Well, no one can blame you, my queen. It's far too sordid an affair for one of your grace and beauty."

Lylla smiled. "That's very gracious of you, Professor. But I'm afraid it is my duty to know as much about the magic being used against us as possible. Does the grimoire contain the spell that Galatea seeks?"

"I have never read what was written on the blank pages," Lawrence confessed. "But we know such a spell exists because it has been attempted before. And that grimoire is a record of all recorded spells. If it is to be found anywhere, it will be in there."

"That is alarming that Galatea can now read the spell she needs," Lylla remarked, reaching a hand out to trail it through the water of one of the fountains as they passed. "And heaven only knows what else she now has access to. Those spells were concealed for a reason."

"Yes," Lawrence said contritely. "I feel I must apologize, Your Majesty. The grimoire was in my care. I was tasked with protecting it and I have failed in my duty."

"Professor," Lylla said gently, laying a hand on his shoulder. "You are a Guardian, first and foremost, tasked with protecting both Earth and Wysteria. And you are helping do that simply by telling us all you know about Galatea's plans. What else does she need to complete this spell?"

"Rumor has it that the spell requires two Echo Stones and she's already taken one from my display case. But she doesn't know where the other is hidden."

"But you do?" she prompted.

"I saw one earlier," Felix spoke up.

Lylla turned to him, one blue eyebrow raised.

"The girl, Sara, had it around her neck. I asked to borrow it, thinking I might need it to repel Venryk if he burst through the door."

Lylla stopped walking. "And where is this stone now?"

"I gave it back to her before we left."

This is bad.

Lylla looked at Lawrence gravely. "Professor, is this the girl you told me about?"

He nodded. "Emily was her mother."

Lylla sighed. "I fear we may have made a grave mistake in leaving that girl behind."

"What do you mean?" Lawrence asked. "Galatea has no idea the girl has what she needs. And I thought it would be safer on Earth than here in Wysteria, where Galatea is."

"Normally, I would agree, but thus far we have been unable to contain her on this side of the Gates. It is too much of a risk to leave the Echo Stone there. Sara has no knowledge of what it is and does not realize its significance. It puts her in danger. No, we must bring both her and the stone here."

Felix was incredulous. "You're going to bring a human *here?*"

She turned to meet his gaze evenly. "Yes. And seeing as how you've met the girl, I'm trusting you to bring her here safely."

Realization flared within the depths of his green eyes and Lylla knew he understood.

***

Kadir had been right. They couldn't monopolize his Gate forever with extra guards on their way. They had arrived by the time Galatea reached the desert, accompanying Venryk on his errand. He would be joined in his mission by several other fire wolves, but they would need her assistance to open the Gate again so they could cross over.

There were about twenty guards posted at the Gate along with Kadir. Galatea hung back, behind one of the dunes, not wanting to be seen. She had her Shadowblade by her side if something were to go awry, but this was a task for her Nightmares and a few of her undead. She had yet to unleash them together and was counting on creating a proper distraction.

At her signal, the Nightmares rushed forward across the sand, followed more slowly by the undead. The guards were taken by surprise by the Nightmares, which they had never seen before, and summoned magical attacks as Galatea knew they would.

But she had gifted her Nightmares with magic of their own and whenever the guards fired their attacks—be it a fireball, streak of lightning, or an arrow—the Nightmares simply shifted momentarily into darkness. The attack shot right through them.

Before the guards could recover and mount another assault, the Nightmares shifted back in the blink of an eye, making good use of their fangs. By the time the undead arrived, the work was nearly all finished. Only Kadir remained standing, offering resistance, and he stopped as he realized he fought alone.

Galatea ventured out from her hiding spot, her wolves following. Kadir looked at her, horror written plain on his face. "What are these monstrosities you have created?"

"Nothing you need concern yourself with," she replied, opening the Gate. "You're safe, so long as you remember whose side you're on."

He gestured helplessly to his fallen comrades. "They'll stop you," he fumed, though she wasn't sure whom exactly he was referring to. "This can only go on so long until you meet an opponent who won't back down from you!"

"Perhaps," she said. With a wave of her hand, the fallen soldiers staggered to their feet, eyes glowing green as she added them to her growing army. "But we both know it won't be you."

The fire wolves leapt forward through the open Gate.

***

It was dusk when Felix stepped through Hank's Gate. The convenience store was empty aside from Hank, who stood behind the counter cleaning. He looked up at Felix's arrival, cocking one eyebrow.

"I need to find Sara," Felix explained. "Do you know where she is?"

Hank made a small sound between his teeth. "She was just over there." He gestured with the rag in his hand at the diner across the street. "But I saw her car leave not ten minutes ago."

"Do you know where she went?" Felix asked, fighting down rising impatience. "It's rather urgent."

"Probably she just went home." Hank set the rag down and stepped around the counter. "Here, I'll drive you."

Felix could have easily walked, but as he'd said, time was of the essence. There was only one reason Lylla would bring a human into Wysteria, especially after the disaster with Galatea and Jack, but he still found it hard to believe.

He followed Hank outside and climbed into his beat-up truck, feeling uneasy. The movement of Sara's car had been unsettling before, so different from the gait of a horse, but he was grateful for Hank's assistance. He settled back against the seat as Hank pulled out of the parking lot, thinking through everything that had happened. What would he say to Sara when he found her? Would she agree to come with him?

The poor girl was probably confused beyond belief after what had happened earlier and he couldn't blame her. It would be a lot to take in for anyone. He thought back to how frightened she'd been, shuddering beside him in the wardrobe while Venryk fought to burn through the bedroom door.

The wolf had almost succeeded. When they'd left the bedroom, they'd seen the blackened burn marks.

Felix wondered what would have happened if the wolf *had* managed to get through. Would his magic have been enough, even with the Echo Stone, to protect them? He'd never used an amplifier of any kind and he didn't know how much they actually helped.

And now Galatea wanted one and it had been in the house, under her nose, the whole time, hanging around a human girl's neck.

"We're almost there," Hank murmured.

Felix continued to stare out the window and said nothing. The roads were rutted and bumpy and just like before, the motion of the vehicle made him feel slightly sick. He shut his eyes for a moment, but that only made it worse.

He opened his eyes again and went rigid in his seat. He blinked again, leaning forward, but no, it was gone. For just a split second, he could have sworn he'd seen a flash of red among the trees…

***

Nadia and Max had wanted to go bowling, and after the day she'd had, Sara hadn't felt like joining them. But she knew how much they'd been looking forward to it and forced herself to go, hoping it might take her mind off of things. And to her surprise, it had.

But now, as she unlocked the door and stepped into her house, it all came rushing back.

Her mind was still reeling after her conversation with Hank and she desperately wanted to share her discovery with someone, but there was no way her friends would understand. Well, Max might, but he'd believe anything.

And Sara had no way of proving that what she claimed was, in fact, true.

If the Wysterians wanted the two worlds to be kept separate, they might not appreciate her spilling all their secrets. But then again, if there were powerful beings crossing between worlds and murdering people freely, shouldn't she tell her friends how much danger their town was in?

All she'd wanted was to leave Mayfair, this sleepy little town where nothing ever happened, and now too much was happening all at once. It was enough to make her want to laugh out loud. Mayfair? Here, of all places?

She suppressed a sigh as she moved into the living room. Her dad wasn't yet home from work; the house was dim with the lights off, the windows letting in fading sunlight.

The house felt stuffy, oppressive, the walls closing in around her. Irrationally, Sara felt her heart begin to pound. She moved toward the nearest light switch, stopping short at a blur of movement beyond one of the windows, too fast for her to make sense of.

A howl rang out, alarmingly loud, causing the hair on the back of her neck to stand up. It had to have been outside, and yet it was so loud, Sara couldn't be sure. She thought of the wolf she had seen with Galatea at Professor Lawrence's house and stumbled forward, grabbing the switch, her fingers slipping.

Light flooded the room and she spun around, letting out a startled shriek.

Felix, standing in front of her, flinched as though not expecting the noise.

"What are you doing here?" Sara demanded, voice suddenly hoarse. How had he gotten in here without her noticing? Her gaze drifted to the door. She hadn't locked it behind her.

"I need you to come with me," he said, eyes briefly flicking to the window.

"Why?" She took a deep breath. "Is Professor Lawrence all right? What about your friend?"

The other young man earlier had looked like he was on death's doorstep when they'd stepped through the…Gate. The backseat of her car still had some bloodstains on it that would be difficult to explain away if her dad or friends asked about it.

Had something gone wrong? Were both of them in trouble and that was why he was here? She couldn't think of any other reason why he would come to her.

"They're both fine," he said briskly. "You have to come with me."

Sara was instantly on her guard. "What? Why?"

"There's no time to explain," he said impatiently. "Now come on."

Sara opened her mouth to say she wasn't going anywhere with him when another howl rang out. Behind Felix, the door opened and Hank strode in, face grim.

"Fire wolves. They're surrounding the house. We need to go now."

Fire wolves?

Felix let out a hiss as his scars lit up an angry red. "He's here."

Sudden thoughts of a murderous elf Guardian attacking the Reverend filled Sara's mind. Felix's face had lit up like that shortly before Galatea had invaded Professor Lawrence's house.

"Who?"

"Venryk." Felix slung his bow off his back. "Get to the truck. I'll hold them off."

"Don't be a fool," Hank snapped. "There's too many of them."

"But he's out there!"

"I know," Hank said, his tone softening. "But this isn't the time for heroics. You have a duty to get Sara safely to Wysteria."

Felix looked like he wanted to argue. "Fine." As Hank reached for the door, he turned to Sara. "Stay close."

She stepped out after him, onto the porch. Hank's truck was parked in the driveway, directly ahead. Sara could have reached it in only a few short strides…if not for the large red wolves blocking their path.

Lightning sprang to life at Hank's fingertips and he hurled it at the nearest wolves, blasting them out of the way. "Hurry!"

Grabbing Sara's wrist, Felix darted toward the truck. Glancing over her shoulder, Sara saw a flash of red as more wolves rounded the corner.

Felix threw the door open and she clambered inside. Hank had moved to the driver's side, the threat of lightning holding the wolves at bay. Without turning his back, he climbed up into the truck, shutting the door behind him.

At the sight of Venryk, Felix stood frozen, one hand tightening on his bow. Sara felt the truck shudder beneath her as Hank turned the ignition. The wolves lunged forward, teeth bared, but Venryk remained motionless, his gaze never leaving the red-haired elf.

"Felix, come on!" Sara cried.

He whirled toward her, eyes wide, haunted, looking at her, but not *seeing*.

For a moment, she feared he would not listen. That he would raise his bow and hope for enough time to release the one shot that would bring the fire wolf down before the others set upon him.

Even so, it was a close-run thing. Felix blinked, jerking to life suddenly, leaping into the truck. Sara reached out, snagging the open door, yanking backward with all her strength. It slammed shut just as the first wolf reached them, the truck shuddering from the impact.

"Hold on!" Hank roared.

Sara squeezed her eyes shut, clinging to the handhold above the door, as the truck reversed and sped out of the driveway. Only after they had turned onto the paved road did she dare look.

Her heart leapt into her throat. The wolves were following, chasing after the truck with long, loping strides. She could tell from the terse silence in the truck cabin that the others already knew. Sara glanced across at the speedometer, but couldn't see it well enough to know how fast Hank was driving.

He didn't slow as they entered town. A quick glance in the mirror revealed that, impossibly, the wolves were nowhere near as far behind as they should have been. The tires squealed as Hank hit the gas station parking lot, braking hard.

"Go, go! Get to the Gate."

Sara jumped out, knees nearly buckling beneath her. Behind, the pack of wolves was less than twenty yards away, covering the distance quickly. She ran for the store entrance, moving faster than she ever had in her life and yet every movement felt as though it were unfolding in slow motion.

Felix grabbed her wrist, tugging her along behind him. At any other time, she would have been annoyed, but panic consumed everything else.

As Felix swung the door open, she saw lightning reflected behind them in the glass. And then they were inside.

"In here!"

Sara looked up to see an odd-looking girl standing in front of the restroom door, one hand outstretched, beckoning. She had long black-and-white striped hair and wore a green kimono. There were white wolf ears sticking out of her head, a white tail lashing back and forth behind her.

The girl shoved the door open. The back wall was already gaping open. Glimpses of a forest could be seen through the hole. "Hurry!"

Felix had released his hold on Sara's wrist and she stepped forward, expecting him to follow, but he turned back toward the door.

Sara hesitated. "But what about—?"

Glass shattered. Felix raised his bow. The girl pushed Sara from behind, sending her toppling through the opening.

10

Felix let an arrow fly, dropping the fire wolf that had made it into the store.

Wanderer nodded to him. "Nice shot. Now go." She nodded toward the open Gate behind them. "Hank and I will handle this."

He hesitated, staring longingly in the direction of the parking lot. Venryk was still out there. With both Lightning Guardians at his side, this was his chance to kill the wolf once and for all.

But they hadn't come here to kill. Not this time.

Forcing his disappointment aside, he turned and followed after Sara. She had to be his priority now.

***

Wanderer closed the Gate behind Felix and stepped out into the parking lot, where Hank had everything well in hand. He stood in front of the door, arms spread wide. The remaining wolves fanned out before him in a half-circle, hackles raised, tails lashing. A few had even ignited, but none were willing to step any closer and risk being electrocuted.

Summoning a concentrated blast, Wanderer hurled a bolt of lightning at the nearest wolf, tossing the creature backward.

Hank copied her, no longer content to merely hold them off, and Wanderer grinned across at him. "Just like old times, eh?"

Realizing the parameters had shifted, or perhaps admitting that they'd failed, some of the wolves began to turn, as though to run away. The two Guardians hurled bolts of electricity after them, dropping them as they ran, their fur smoking. Not a single one made it out of the parking lot.

Only one wolf remained. Venryk hadn't so much as flinched and he stood, glaring at them defiantly.

Wanderer lifted one hand, lightning arcing between her fingers. It would be so easy to cut him down and she itched to let the magic fly. But this life wasn't hers to take. That task fell to another.

For a moment, no one moved or spoke, a lone fire wolf facing down two Lightning Guardians. A flicker of fear shot through Wanderer. Surely he wouldn't attack, trusting Felix's curse to keep him safe. She stood there rigidly, all too aware that if she struck Venryk down, she would condemn Felix.

She let out a growl. "Go on. Crawl back to your master."

Unhurried, Venryk turned his back on them and walked away. Wanderer let out a shaky breath and extinguished her magic.

Hank turned to her, breathing hard. "Did the girl make it?"

She nodded, her eyes on Venryk's retreating form. "They've both crossed over."

"You go on." He inclined his head toward the door. "I'll clean up here."

Reluctantly, she turned to go, but not before giving his hand a quick squeeze.

***

Sara fell forward, her hands and knees making contact with soft mossy ground. Strands of hair had come undone from her braid, which was usually messy at the best of times, and she peered up through her hair to see she was surrounded by soldiers dressed in black uniforms.

She sucked in a sharp breath and shrank back from them, unsure if they were friend or foe. Blue-purple light flared behind her and she turned. Felix stepped through the Gate and the opening swung shut behind him, the light fading. A moment later, the Gate opened again, the wolf-eared girl following.

Sara let out a sigh of relief that they had escaped unharmed. She scrambled to her feet, even though her legs felt like they would barely support her, and she slowly turned, taking in her surroundings.

The trees towered high above their heads, the sky a deep blue, stars just visible between the thick leaves. It should have been too dark to see, but a faint green glow seemed to emanate from the plants themselves. Small golden lights were floating through the air, flickering like fireflies. Sara reached out to try and touch one and her hand passed right through it.

She recoiled. "Where am I?" she demanded, though she thought she already knew.

"Welcome to Wysteria!" the wolf-girl announced proudly, sticking out one hand. "I'm Wanderer, by the way. Lightning Guardian, at your service."

Tentatively, Sara accepted the handshake. Wanderer had a strong grip despite her diminutive frame.

161

"No doubt you're wondering why you're here. Felix will take you to the palace and Queen Lylla can explain everything. I wish I could go with you, but unfortunately, I have a Gate to guard."

"Come on," Felix said gently, slinging his bow onto his back.

"Wh—" Sara turned to him, not wanting to travel alone with him in the dark, even after everything that had just happened.

"Professor Lawrence is waiting at the palace, too."

A familiar face would make everything so much better. There must have been some mistake. Professor Lawrence would explain to these strange people and then she would be allowed to go home.

"You're safe now," Felix added when she still hesitated. "I'm not gonna hurt you."

"All right," Sara murmured. After all, he *had* put himself between her and the wolves.

The two of them left Wanderer and her guards behind, walking through the softly glowing forest side by side in silence. Sara felt like she should say something to break the quiet but she'd never been good at small talk, especially to someone she'd just met. It was all she could do just to put one foot in front of the other.

Besides, Felix didn't seem inclined toward conversation. It was hard to tell in the dark, but when she glanced at him, she thought she saw tension in the set of his shoulders and she wondered if he'd had to kill the wolf.

At last, the trees of the forest began to thin and part. Sara gasped at the scene laid out before her.

A short distance ahead lay a massive building, the many windows of which were glowing with warm light. A tall white fence surrounded the premises and in the center of their path stood a large gate, glowing with a shimmering light of many different hues, as seen through a prism.

"Welcome to the Glowing Gate," Felix said softly. "The palace of the Queen of Wysteria."

The Gate swung forth as they approached, allowing them to step inside, before swinging shut again without a sound. Vast pasture stretched out before them, interspersed with weeping willow trees, flowers—most of which Sara couldn't identity—and lots and lots of wisteria.

The grass that they walked through was not overly tall and shortened in length as they drew nearer to the palace. A sweet but subtle scent drifted on the air and a faint breeze ruffled Sara's hair. She could just make out the sound of waves in the distance.

A great, winding courtyard unfolded in front of the palace entrance, with curving paths surrounded by flora and intricate statues of mythological creatures. They had been carved with such attention to detail that they looked real, as if living creatures had been turned to stone.

A large fountain depicting a stone unicorn rose before the steps leading up to massive double doors. The palace itself was shaped roughly like a crescent moon so that as they approached, Sara felt like the building was closing in on her. She found the effect reassuring rather than alarming, in a welcoming, protective way.

Glancing around, she could see figures standing near the palace walls at various points and flanking either side of the doors, stoic and still, wearing uniforms of silver and black not unlike Felix's. They did not move as the two of them approached.

The double doors swung open from the inside and Felix led Sara into the palace. She had not a clue where she was going, but he navigated the winding hallways with ease, their footsteps echoing on the marble floors. Sara noticed that the tiles and even the baseboards had mythical creatures and various trees etched into them.

The hallways were lined with tall narrow windows, stands that held vases and other artifacts, stone busts, and tapestries hung from the walls. It was all too much to take in and then they stopped before a door. Felix knocked and when they were bid to enter, he opened the door and ushered her inside.

The interior of the room was beautiful, from the paintings and tapestries to the fountain bubbling in the corner. The back wall was open, the ceiling supported by columns and a soft breeze drifted through the room. There were lighted candles around the room in elegant silver candelabras and a chandelier hung overhead, casting everything in a soft golden glow.

But it was the two women that caught her attention. One, who was lurking in the corner, she had seen before. She instantly recognized the black braids and light brown skin. The crimson and amber eyes seemed to spear her from across the room with their strange intensity. Even with her unusual eyes, she was quite beautiful.

The other was tall and graceful, her yellow Grecian-style dress falling to her feet. Her long hair was bright blue, the same shade as her eyes, and it seemed to twinkle faintly with light as she moved. It was styled into three braids, one long plait down her back and two shorter ones hanging down on either side of her face, resting on her collarbone. Her ears were pointed like Felix's.

Professor Lawrence was sitting on a small couch on the other side of the room and he rose to his feet as he saw her.

"Professor!" she cried, resisting the urge to rush forward toward him.

Felix inclined his head toward the blue-haired woman and went to stand with his back to the wall.

"My dear girl, I'm relieved to see you are safe," Professor Lawrence said, standing up and making his way toward her.

"We ran into a little trouble along the way," Felix said. "Venryk was there, with other fire wolves. Wanderer and Hank helped us."

The woman with the strange eyes frowned, watching him, but he didn't look in her direction.

"That is most distressing," the blue-haired woman said softly, in an English accent. "I am relieved that you both escaped unharmed."

"Sara," Professor Lawrence said. "Allow me to make the introductions. Felix, you already know. But may I introduce Damaris, the Flame Guardian." He gestured to the far woman.

"So, not from the insurance agency, then," Sara remarked and Damaris's lips quirked upward in response.

The Professor turned to the blue-haired woman and gestured with a wide sweep of his arm. "And may I present Queen Lylla the Lightbringer, Queen of Wysteria."

Sara was unsure if she was expected to bow and she bobbed her head to the woman awkwardly. "Pleased to meet you, Your Majesty."

The woman smiled. "Please, call me Lylla. You are among friends." She stepped forward, studying her. "I can see the resemblance to your mother."

"You knew my mother?" Sara whispered.

"She crossed over a few times."

"She never told—" Sara broke off, realizing that wasn't quite true. She remembered her mother telling her stories when she was little of unicorns and elves and dragons, with a level of detail and a gleam in her eyes as if it were real.

But of course it hadn't been real.

Sara glanced over at Felix, at the elf ears sticking out from under his crimson hair. *Well, not until now.*

Lylla extended an arm toward the sofa and chairs. "Please, sit. Make yourself comfortable. I'm sure you have many questions."

Sara accepted a seat, sinking down onto the sofa, Professor Lawrence joining her. Lylla took a chair opposite them while Damaris and Felix remained where they were.

"Hank explained some things to me," Sara told her. "About the Gates and Guardians, magic and elements. And Galatea."

Lylla nodded. "It is for that very reason I had you brought here."

"But why? Why was Venryk after me? What was that thing, anyway? It didn't look like any wolf I'd ever seen."

"Venryk is a fire wolf, so called because they have the ability to set themselves on fire. Galatea created them, by corrupting them with dark magic. They do her bidding now."

"Hank said dark magic was forbidden."

"It is."

"But why would Galatea send fire wolves after me?"

"Because you have something she wants very desperately."

"*Me?*" Sara turned to Professor Lawrence in disbelief. "What do I have that she could possibly want?"

"You are aware, no doubt, of Reverend Pierce's murder."

"He…was the Guardian of the Ice Gate."

"Yes, he was," Lylla agreed. "But that's not why Galatea killed him, nor is that why she went to that cemetery."

"She wanted to bring Jack back to life."

The queen smiled. "Hank did tell you a lot, didn't he?"

"We think the spell didn't work," Professor Lawrence spoke up. "At least, not in the way she wanted. In order for Jack to be as he once was, she needs two Echo Stones. She stole one from the display case in the library."

"What's an Echo Stone?" Sara asked, looking from him, to the queen, and back.

"An amplifier," Lylla answered. "It allows an elementalist to use more magic while consuming less energy. All magic has a cost. Every spell requires energy. The more complex the spell is, the more energy it requires. Once your energy is depleted, you cannot use any more magic. If you attempt to do so anyway, you can die."

Damaris crossed her legs at the ankles, leaning back against the wall. "Galatea needs the Echo Stones to bring Jack back to life. She has one, but she still needs the other."

"And you have it," Lylla finished, looking at Sara, voice so quiet she almost didn't hear her.

"Me? I don't have—" Slowly, Sara reached up to touch the silver chain hanging around her neck.

The green stone necklace had been her mother's.

Lylla nodded slowly. "Galatea will stop at nothing to get her hands on that stone. But don't worry. You're safe here at the palace."

"But I can't stay here," Sara protested. "My dad will be getting home from work and wondering where I am. I have to get home."

The queen's eyes saddened and Sara noticed that, in spite of her youthful appearance, there was something very old about those eyes. "I'm sorry, but that will not be possible. Galatea has already sent her wolves after you once. They failed this time, but she may try to take the stone herself in her next attempt."

"So I'm a prisoner here?" Sara cried, voice rising beyond her control.

"No," Lylla said firmly. "You are a guest. I do not want you to think of yourself as being trapped here. But for the time being, I cannot allow you to go home, knowingly putting you in danger. Galatea is a very powerful Guardian and even if I were to send guards to protect you, I fear they may not be enough. If anything were to happen to you, I would hold myself personally accountable."

"What if I leave the Echo Stone here? It'll be safe then and I could go home."

As she said those words, the irony of her situation struck her. All she had wanted was to leave Mayfair and now she had—finding herself in a world far more exciting and dangerous than her own. And yet all she wanted was to leave. Getting caught up in some sort of magical conflict was not the kind of excitement she had signed up for.

"It will be safe, yes, but you won't be. Galatea knew you had the stone, or else she wouldn't have sent her wolves after you. She would still be after you, even if you no longer had it and she would be furious when she discovered that fact. There's no telling what she might do. At the very least, she could use you as leverage against us and get the stone that way. I'm afraid, at the moment, your return just isn't possible."

Sara looked down at her shoes unhappily. "I didn't ask for any of this."

"I know. It isn't fair to involve you in something that has nothing to do with you, but it will only be for a short time. As soon as we can secure the Gates and keep Galatea within Wysteria, you will be safe to go home. In the meantime, I will try to think of a way of getting word to your father so that he doesn't worry."

Sara glanced up. "If my mother knew about this place, does he know, too?"

"I don't know. To the best of my knowledge, no, but it's possible she may have told him something. I hope so. It would make an explanation much easier."

Sara sighed. "Why is Galatea doing this? Hank told me that she fell in love with a human, which isn't allowed, and she refused to give him up and that he was killed in a fight."

"That's not entirely true," Damaris spoke up. "Well, I mean it is, but it's not the whole truth."

Lylla took a deep breath, looking deeply unhappy. "At first, Galatea was told to take Jack back to Earth. She was expected to stay here, because she was a Guardian. She'd sworn an oath to protect Wysteria and the Gates and she had a responsibility to do so. Guardians are rare. We couldn't simply replace her. But, when it became clear she wasn't going to give Jack up, I gave her the option of going to live with him on Earth. I would allow her to stay with him, but she refused."

"Why?" Sara asked. She couldn't imagine why Galatea would refuse such an offer if she truly had loved Jack and wanted to be with him.

"Because," Damaris growled. "If Galatea were to stay permanently on Earth, her power would wane and eventually fade altogether. Earth became mostly devoid of magic after we fled here to Wysteria. The only ones who have magic on Earth are the human Guardians who are born there. She didn't want to give up her power so she brought Jack here to Wysteria, where she could not only keep her magic, but he could live forever. Humans don't age in Wysteria, but on Earth, he would eventually grow old and die, leaving her behind as an immortal elf, abandoned by both her lover and her magic. Power is hard to give up once you've had a taste and even harder when it's all you've ever known."

"Her selfishness cost Jack his life." Lylla was looking down at her hands. "My order was that he be returned to Earth, unharmed. But…" She sighed. "Two of my Guardians, Cassius and Cyren, decided to take matters into their own hands. They went to the city of Malenwar, where Galatea and Jack had fled, and confronted them. They claimed that Galatea attacked them, which is entirely possible, and that in the ensuing chaos, Jack was hit by a stray attack and killed. I do not know for certain what happened, since I was not there, nor do I know which of them dealt the fatal blow, but I believe it to have been murder. I cannot prove anything, of course."

Damaris continued the story. "Galatea flew into a rage, vowing revenge on them and all Wysterians. In her mind, their prejudice led to Jack's death, not her own actions. She attacked her own Gate and destroyed it. When a Gate is destroyed, it unleashes a powerful explosion of magic, wiping out everything in its path. It destroyed the city of Malenwar instantly, killing most of its people, and destroying the land around it. It's an inhospitable swamp now, with nothing but ruins left. Nothing lives there. In fifty years, nothing has regrown and it's possible it never will. We've had earth and water attributes try to coax the land to grow again. Lylla even tried to heal it with her light magic, but nothing has worked."

"That is why," Lylla said, rising to her feet, "we have not destroyed the Gates and completely sealed ourselves off from Earth. There are those who would have done so if it were possible, but it cannot be done. It would have destroyed our island and everything on it."

"So that's why Galatea's doing this," Sara murmured.

"Yes. Now, it's been a long evening and this is all a lot for you to take in. If you have any other questions or need anything, you can always come find me or Felix. He'll show you to your room. Feel free to explore the palace as you like."

Felix stepped forward away from the wall and Sara rose to follow him, still feeling dazed and as though what she had been told wasn't the whole story.

She followed Felix down the stairs to the second level of the palace wordlessly. The walls of the building were beautiful, but she couldn't help but think that it was nothing more than a gilded cage. *It's only for a little while,* she reminded herself. As far as prisons went, she could certainly do worse.

The hallway they turned into was lined on either side with doors and Felix stopped in front of one, pushing it open. "This is you."

"Thank you," Sara murmured, stepping inside, shutting the door once he'd gone.

She leaned against the closed door for a moment and irrationally felt like crying, her emotions threatening to overwhelm her. How could this be her life now? How could this be *real?*

Sara took a deep breath and forced herself to take in the room. It was massive. There were two ornately carved wardrobes set against the wall and Sara gave them both a lingering look, wondering if they could possibly be a secret way back home.

There was a wooden polished desk with a stag carved into one leg, and a full-length mirror, with jewels embedded into its gleaming silver frame. A large stone fireplace, currently without a fire, had two velvet chairs seated in front of it, resting on top of an intricately patterned rug.

There was a large bookshelf filled with titles she ignored and little figures of woodland creatures. The bed was canopied and quite big, with curtains on all sides that could be drawn. The sheets looked like they were made of silk. A lounge stood at the end of the bed and the otherwise flat ceiling opened up in the center to form a dome, where a chandelier hung. More velvety lounges stood by a low table, on top of which sat a small blue-leafed plant.

The door in the wall led to a private bathroom. A large bathtub made of crystal was set into an alcove in the wall, beside two white columns. A mirror hung above two sinks and what Sara assumed to be the toilet sat against the opposite wall. Yet another chandelier hung in here.

The far wall of the main room was made of two French doors, the curtains pulled back. Sara walked over to them and pulled them open to reveal an open stone balcony overlooking the courtyard below and the pasture. The courtyard was lit with lanterns and beyond the pasture, she could see cliffs and the sea she had heard earlier, the moonlight reflecting off the waves.

She stepped out onto the balcony, into the open air. A wonderful breeze was blowing, bringing with it the scents of the forest and sea. Sara leaned down, resting her arms on the rail, looking at the statues and fountains below. At the guards patrolling the palace grounds, made to look small by the distance and height. At the Glowing Gate, the swaying willow trees, and the dark sea beyond the far cliffs, where the palace grounds ended.

Sara sighed. Oh, how she could get used to a view like this. She would love to live in such a place, if only she weren't trapped here.

Her mother had crossed over into Wysteria and she had never known about it other than bedtime stories. She wished her mom had confided in her completely, but she wasn't sure she would have believed her. The only reason she had believed Hank was because she had watched

Professor Lawrence, Felix, and the other elf walk through the gas station wall.

Tears sprang unbidden to her eyes and she brushed them away. *Oh, Mom, I wish you could be here.* They were thoughts she did not allow herself to think, emotions she refused to feel. Acknowledging it only brought on the tears and that would be of no help to anyone.

She choked back a strangled laugh, aware once again of the irony of her situation and in that moment, it threatened to overwhelm her. She had wished to escape her boring little town and that wish had been granted. But this new world she found herself in, while exciting, was a dangerous one. A world where she didn't belong. A world she couldn't leave.

There was no way she could sleep right now, even though it was probably late. She realized she had no idea what time it was and fished in her pocket for her phone, clicking it on. It was nearing midnight and she had no cell service, unsurprisingly. Data wouldn't even work here.

Swallowing the lump in her throat, Sara shoved it back in her pocket and left her room, wandering the hallways aimlessly. She had nearly convinced herself that she'd gotten hopelessly lost when she passed another one of the stone balconies and spotted Felix standing there. He, apparently, hadn't gone to bed either.

Hesitant, yet not wanting to be alone, Sara slowly walked up to him. "Is this spot taken?"

He turned, startled, and then let out a slow breath. "I figured you wouldn't sleep."

"How can I?" She rested her arms on the railing, unconsciously copying him. "I want to say thank you…for what you did with the wolves earlier."

He gave her a wry, half-smile. "Don't mention it." Something in the way he said it made Sara think he really wouldn't appreciate her mentioning it.

"That one wolf…Venryk… The two of you seem to know each other," she remarked, remembering the way they had stared each other down.

"Yeah. We go way back."

She glanced at his scars, the left side of his profile facing her, at the angry lines that marred his skin like claw marks. "Um, I probably shouldn't ask, but…Venryk was the one at Professor Lawrence's house, wasn't he? Your face—it glowed just like it did when he appeared tonight."

"Mhm," Felix said tersely. "It tells me when he's nearby." He turned to face her directly, his green eyes piercing. "He gave me these scars."

Sara felt herself blush. "I'm sorry. I shouldn't have asked."

"No," he said, and she saw anger flash in his gaze. "You shouldn't have."

He turned and walked away, shoulders tense, leaving her standing there wishing she'd never left her room.

***

Galatea had been waiting on the Earth-side of the Wind Gate for her wolves to return with the stone, but all that came back was Venryk.

"I couldn't get it," he growled. "Archer was there. I could have killed him if not for those two Lightning Guardians."

Galatea hadn't planned on Lylla sending one of her pesky Shadows to get to the girl first, but she should have. Now the girl and the stone would be safely at the palace, out of reach.

She fumed silently, all the way back to Malenwar, managing somehow to keep her emotions contained until they reached it. Only then did she allow herself to seethe.

Another failure. Another setback.

She ignored Noraak, her wolves, Nightmares, and legions of undead, wandering off on her own, sinking down onto a large chunk of fallen stone. If she had been lesser, weaker somehow, she might have been tempted to give up here. But if that had been her nature, she would have remained on Earth until her magic eventually faded.

Galatea closed her eyes, reminding herself why she was doing this. She couldn't bring herself to look at Jack ever since she'd brought him back with her. But one day he would be whole again. He had been so happy here in Wysteria, happy with her, but he hadn't always been that way. The day they met was certainly not a happy one.

It had been more than fifty years ago, which was half a lifetime for a human, but to her, it felt like hardly any time had passed at all.

On a whim, she had crossed through the Wind Gate that day, under the pretext of visiting Professor Lawrence, who was much younger then and still teaching at the college. She'd wanted to see the small town where three Gates were located. All her life she'd heard about the horrors of the Exodus, the destruction that forced the Wysterians to retreat to their own world and stay there. How much had the world changed since then?

What were humans really like? The only ones she'd ever met were Guardians themselves and so they hardly counted. What was the difference between them and Wysterians other than the fact that they aged and died while Wysterians stayed the same?

She had explored, wandering the countryside, not drawing attention to herself. It wasn't at all what she had expected, but then, she hadn't known what to expect.

Galatea found Jack at the edge of some woods near a farm. He hadn't seen her and so she hung back, watching. She'd never been this close to a magic-less human before.

He had a chair with him near a large oak tree and as she watched, he threaded a rope onto one of the branches, testing its security before looping it around his own neck and climbing up onto the chair. He moved awkwardly, slowly, one of his arms hanging limp at his side.

She had no idea what he was doing when he knocked the chair away. All she knew was that he looked distressed and in pain. Without thinking, she rushed forward, burning through the rope and helping to break his fall as he tumbled to the ground.

He'd been rendered unconscious but quickly came to, gasping, looking around with wide, startled eyes. They were a dark green.

He glanced past her at the overturned chair and dangling rope. "I must be dead," he muttered.

"You're not dead," she'd insisted, still kneeling beside him.

"I want to be."

It was the strangest thing Galatea had ever heard anyone say. "Why?"

He didn't answer.

She looked over her shoulder at the chair and rope. "What were you trying to do?"

He gave her a funny look. "You really don't know?"

She shook her head, convinced humans really were the most perplexing creatures. "It looked uncomfortable so I wanted to help."

"Why did you stop me?" Now he looked mildly annoyed. "I *wanted* to kill myself." He reached up to touch his neck where it had been rubbed raw from the rope.

"Then I definitely should have stopped you," Galatea retorted, somewhat affronted. "Your life is far too precious to throw away. Why would you want to do something so daft?"

She knew that some elves eventually grew tired of living and faded away, but that was only after many, many centuries. What on earth could make a human want to cut short their already short life?

Jack had hesitated, looking at her with visible confusion. "Because of the things I've seen. Because of the things I've done. Because of the things I can no longer do." He gestured to his arm, the one she had noticed earlier, limp and motionless.

She looked down. "Your arm."

"It's paralyzed. I can't move it."

"Why?"

"The war."

"What war?" Galatea hadn't heard anyone mention a war taking place in the human world. She'd seen no sign of one on her walk around the town.

Again, he gave her a strange look. "Vietnam."

"What is…Vietnam?"

"How can you not know?"

She let out a small laugh. "I'm not from here."

"Then where are you from?"

"Wysteria."

"Wysteria," he repeated dumbly, the word sounding as foreign on his tongue as Vietnam had on hers.

"It's a world connected to yours. A land filled with magic." At his look of disbelief, she added, "Don't believe me? Where do you think all those so-called mythical beings went? The ones you humans tell stories about. What happened to them?"

"They're just stories."

"But all stories have at least some truth to them, don't they?"

Before Jack could reply, a voice called out to him, carrying on the wind. She'd learned later that it had been his father calling him.

He cursed and hastily stood. "I've got to go."

He strode a few paces away and then stopped, turning back to see if she was still there, as if expecting to find her gone, never having been real in the first place. But there she was, watching him.

Later, he told her that in that moment she had been the most beautiful woman he had ever seen, her amber eyes warm, long black hair spilling over one shoulder, flawless skin reflected in the fading light.

Jack swallowed. "I'd like to know more about this Wysteria of yours."

"I can come back tomorrow," she said, almost casually.

"I'll be here." He turned to go.

"Jack," she said, tone pensive. "What that man called you just now." She nodded in the direction the voice had come. "Is that your name?"

"Yes. What's yours?"

"Galatea."

She sighed, once again in the present, the memory fading. He had wanted to die when she'd first met him. She had brought him to Wysteria where he could be healed and live forever. Most Wysterians took their world for granted, but Jack… The wonder in his eyes had been a thing to behold.

And then, in one moment of madness, his future was taken from him, along with any future they may have had together. He'd taken a piece of her heart with him. Nothing had been able to fill it; it was still missing to this day.

She was so close to righting that wrong, to getting him back. For a moment, Galatea pushed her sadness and doubt to the side and allowed herself to imagine what it would be like when they were at last reunited. When she could again feel his arms around her.

There had to be a way. The grimoire had managed to help her so far. There had to be a way to get that stone. She refused to accept that it was gone, out of her reach, safely ensconced at the palace.

Galatea would have to weigh her options. But in the meantime…

She stood and walked over to where she had placed the headdress she had taken from Lawrence's house, running her fingers over the crystals. She would move ahead with her revenge as planned, with or without Jack.

And for that, she would need a few more allies.

11

Sara must have fallen asleep at some point because she woke up the next morning lying face down on the bed, her braid all but undone. Bright sunlight was streaming through the open French doors, landing on her face, and she groaned, rolling over. Her arms were cramped from her awkward sleeping position. There was a knock at the door and she sat up groggily, blowing strands of hair out of her face.

"Who is it?" It really was much too bright.

Instead of giving an answer, the door opened and an unfamiliar female elf stepped inside, giving her a quick bow. "Her Majesty sent me, miss, to assist you with your hair or dressing and then to escort you down to breakfast."

"Um, thanks, but I can manage. The first part, anyway. I might need your help finding my way around."

"As you wish. Let me know when you're ready and I'll take you to the dining room." The elf withdrew, shutting the door behind her.

Sara sighed and got up, walking over to the wardrobe. There were a variety of outfits contained within, but nothing remotely resembled her tank top, shorts, and flip flops.

She knew that royalty or the wealthy had often had maids to do things for them and she supposed it might be nice to have someone try and do something with her hair, but she preferred it in a simple braid and was more than comfortable with dressing herself.

She went into the bathroom, allowed herself a quick bath, using the mirror to help re-plait her braid. She also decided not to change into any of the other clothes yet, even though she'd slept in her current ones. She'd feel most comfortable in the clothes she'd come in, familiar as they were.

The elf was still waiting for her when she stepped out of her room and Sara followed her through the winding passages to a dining room that was smaller than she expected. Two columns supported the entrance, a tall window along the back wall. The table was rectangular, with only a handful of seats. An ornate chandelier hung overhead.

The table was spread with various fruits and biscuits, racks of toast, eggs, fish and what Sara thought looked like yogurt.

No one was present at the breakfast table except for the sandy-haired elf that had been wounded at Professor Lawrence's house. He was busy tucking into a plate of waffles and didn't look the least bit injured now. He smiled at Sara as she arrived.

"Where is everyone?" she asked, her voice echoing off the walls.

"Usually, it's just Her Highness, Master Colin—" here the female elf nodded at the blond elf— "And Master Felix. I do not know where Master Felix is this morning but Her Highness is out for a morning run. Please, help yourself."

"I see…thank you."

The female elf bowed and retreated, leaving Sara alone with Colin. She pulled out a chair on the other side of the table and sat down, eyeing the yogurt.

"I'm glad to see that you've recovered," she said conversationally.

Colin grinned. "Good as new. All thanks to Lylla."

"She healed you?" Hank hadn't mentioned healing when he'd explained about magic.

"Yep. She's the only one that could, being a light attribute and all. Galatea had nicked me with a blade tainted with dark magic and it acts like a poison. Normal healers can't heal it. Only a light attribute can."

Sara picked up one of the biscuits. "I've heard light attributes are incredibly rare."

Colin nodded. "Oh, they are. Lylla's the only one. We're lucky to have her." There was a pause while he chewed. "You okay? You look a little upset. Didn't sleep well? I can imagine this is all a lot to take in."

"It is," Sara agreed. "But, no, that's not it. I…had a conversation with Felix last night and it ended badly. I think I upset him and I feel bad about it."

She had thought of little else since. *Me and my big mouth.* She couldn't afford to go around making enemies when she barely knew anyone here.

"What did he say?"

Sara swallowed a spoonful of yogurt. It was surprisingly good, bursting with a flavor that reminded her of strawberry and something else she couldn't identify, sending her taste buds tingling. "Well, I remarked that he and Venryk seemed to know each other and he said they did. I—er—asked about why his face glowed—" She felt her cheeks heat at her tactlessness. "And he said that happens when Venryk is around and that the wolf gave him those scars. I told him that I was sorry and I shouldn't have asked and he agreed that I shouldn't have."

Colin grimaced. "Yes, he's really sensitive about that. He feels like people stare, that they only notice that about him and nothing else."

"I shouldn't have asked…"

"You're not wrong to be curious. Venryk did give him those scars, but that's not the first time they met. The first time was when Venryk attacked his village. Let's just say that he's got a serious bone to pick with that wolf."

"Do you know where he is? I'd like to apologize."

"He and Damaris left this morning to scout the swamp. That's where we think Galatea's hiding out. Damaris already checked it out once, but they're going to try and venture deeper into the ruins this time."

"That sounds dangerous," Sara muttered.

"It is, if Galatea's really there. But don't worry. Damaris can handle it."

"She's the Flame Guardian, right?"

"Yep and the strongest Guardian there is." Colin grinned again. "You should see her in action sometime. It's both thrilling and terrifying to behold. She fights like she's fearless."

"Nobody's fearless," Sara replied. "Everyone's afraid of something."

"Damaris is only afraid of one thing. And it's not for herself."

She pondered the remains of her yogurt. "I know Guardians are stronger than most, but is she the most powerful person in Wysteria? Stronger than Galatea?"

"*I* think she's stronger than Galatea," Colin said, then leaned forward in a conspiratorial manner, lowering his voice. "Don't tell Damaris I said this, but I think Queen Lylla might be the strongest in Wysteria. Mind you, I've never seen her fight myself, but they don't call her the Lightbringer for nothing."

"Do you know where she is? The servant that came and got me said she was out on a morning run. I'd like to talk to her."

"You'll probably find her out on the beach. That's where she normally is in the mornings."

Sara thanked him and got to her feet, heading for the main doors of the palace. They weren't difficult to find and soon she had stepped out into the sunlight, blinking and shielding her eyes with one hand.

She walked over toward the fence that bordered the cliffside, following it until she reached a place where the ground sloped down in a path that led to the beach. Sara slipped through the fence and began making her way down the somewhat steep path.

She stopped midway, movement ahead catching her attention. A unicorn was galloping along the shoreline, her coat lavender, silver hooves churning up the white sand. Her mane and tail were very long, turquoise in shade, and seemed to glimmer in the light. The long horn was the same shade of blue.

It can't be. But the blue was the exact same shade and it shimmered as the light caught it, as though tiny facets of jewels were winking back at her.

The unicorn galloped out of sight around the corner and Sara hurried to catch up. She was breathless by the time she neared the corner, following the hoofprints in the sand. As she rounded the corner, she noticed that they disappeared, replaced by footprints that looked human.

She looked up to see Lylla standing there, wearing a lavender dress this morning, standing just on the edge of the sand, allowing the waves to wash in over her feet. The water was a light green color. She turned as Sara approached, smiling.

Sara waited a moment to catch her breath before speaking. "That unicorn on the beach…that was you, wasn't it?"

Lylla turned away, looking slightly self-conscious, clasping her hands behind her back and rocking on the balls of her feet. "Yes, it was. I find few things in life as pleasing as a morning stroll—or run, as it sometimes happens—along the beach. It's nice to stretch your legs."

"Why didn't you tell me?"

"I thought it might be a little too much on top of everything else that's been dumped on you lately."

Sara danced back from an incoming wave. "So which are you really? An elf or a unicorn?"

"Elf," Lylla replied, pulling her hair back from her long, pointed ears.

"Then how—?"

"Shape-shifting. It's an ability passed down only to those directly descended from one of the original seven Guardians."

"Can Galatea shape-shift?"

"Not to my knowledge. The only other I've ever known with the ability is Damaris," Lylla replied, wading out into the water so that it came up to her knees, her dress billowing out around her legs.

Sara shifted her feet in the sand. "I wanted to talk to you about what to tell my dad. I don't want him to worry."

"Then I can put your mind to rest. It's already been taken care of. He knows you're safe and not to worry."

"Does he know where I am?"

Lylla looked at her steadily and then sighed. "I don't feel it's my place to say, but you deserve to be told. Yes, he knows. The Professor returned to his Gate this morning and offered to pass along the message."

"Professor Lawrence is gone?" Sara asked numbly. He was one of the only familiar faces in a sea of the unknown. And now he, too, was gone.

"He wanted to stay," Lylla said gently. "But he knows you'll be safe here and he cannot leave his Gate unprotected."

Quietly, Sara asked, "Does that mean my dad knew about Wysteria after all?"

"It would appear so."

Sara said nothing more, thoughts still reeling from Lylla's earlier revelation. Her dad knew about Wysteria. Her mom had actually *come* here and yet neither of them had ever breathed a word of it to her.

They were going to have a lot to talk about when she got back.

***

It had been Damaris's idea to bring Felix with her to investigate the swamp further. He wasn't sure why, but he suspected it had something to do with the encounter with Venryk last night. They hadn't spoken about the incident and he didn't want to, but he knew she could tell something had happened. And judging from the fact that his face still bore the mark of his curse, Venryk was very much still alive.

He followed behind her on Tempest, the stone path too narrow for them to walk side by side. Once upon a time, it had been wide and spacious, but they were lucky that any of the pathway had survived the Cataclysm at all.

Felix had never set foot in the swamps of Malenwar and he looked around at the bleak surroundings, eyes wide, momentarily forgetting his anger. It looked awful.

The trees were black and gnarled, their limbs bent out of shape as if an angry child had gotten ahold of them. The air was humid and hot, sticking to his skin and he had to swat away mosquitoes on more than one occasion.

Above some of the ruins, shattered stone hung suspended, frozen in time the moment the world exploded, blowing the city apart. It defied reason, the stone hovering in midair with nothing to support it. But nothing that had happened here was natural.

As he watched, one of the stones broke free, crashing into the water below, the sound echoing in the stillness.

There was more swamp water than there was land, although it was blessedly shallow in some spots. It stank of rotten eggs.

The thought of eggs reminded him that he hadn't had breakfast this morning, but he had no appetite in such an appalling place and the thought of food seemed revolting.

He had slept badly, weighed down by guilt for snapping unfairly at Sara and anger at letting Venryk slip through his fingers. He hadn't even had a chance to face Venryk last night. Not really. Not in any way that mattered.

He glanced over at Damaris, muscles rippling beneath her white coat, wishing he possessed even an ounce of her power.

For all he knew, it might already be too late. What if that was the one chance he would ever have to kill the wolf? He couldn't assume he would be given another one.

If Venryk chose to pick a fight with someone else, or encountered them in a battle, there was no telling what would happen. That person might choose self-defense, to preserve their own life, and they'd have every right to. They would kill Venryk, leaving Felix's fate sealed.

He knew he couldn't expect someone else to die for him.

He would only get so many chances and he had to make sure that he made them count. One of them had been handed to him last night and he had wasted the opportunity.

It was that thought that made him angry. Angry at Hank, angry at Sara. But mostly, if he were honest, angry with himself.

A fresh wave of red-hot shame washed over him. He'd been wrong to snap at Sara. She hadn't asked to get caught up in all this. This mess was of his own doing, not hers.

Damaris glanced at him. "I won't ask. But you can tell me if you want to."

He nodded tersely. No, he couldn't. She knew that Venryk had been there. What more was there to say? That he was weak and that's why he ultimately failed? Weakness wasn't something she understood. She never doubted herself, never been unable to act when it mattered.

And that was what bothered him most of all. When Venryk had rounded the corner of the house, Felix had found himself frozen, unable to move. Not out of indecision, torn between finishing this madness or carrying out the task Lylla had set for him.

For a moment, he hadn't been there at all, standing beside a truck, with Sara and Hank with him. He was a boy again, cowering behind the charred remains of his house, hoping that if he only stayed still and made himself as small as possible, the wolves wouldn't see him.

But they had seen him.

It had only been Sara calling to him that had broken him out of his reverie, saving him from having to find out what came next. In the time since, he had given the matter plenty of thought and hadn't much liked what he found. His reaction wasn't something he cared to think about—what it meant and what it might mean for the future.

Venryk's sudden appearance had startled him, that's all. It was one thing to know the wolf was there, his scars providing an early warning. It was another matter entirely to lay eyes on your family's killer for the first time in so many years.

At least that's what Felix kept telling himself. It was a perfectly normal reaction to have. But the whispers said differently. They said he was weak, a coward, who would never be ready no matter how much training he had.

And that was why Damaris would never understand.

She didn't say anything more and silence fell as they continued through the ruins. Felix caught glimpses of pale figures flitting between the ruins—the ghosts Damaris had spoken of in her first report—but they kept their distance.

Damaris wanted to investigate the Necropolis, which lay deeper into the swamp. For centuries, it was where the people of Malenwar had buried their dead and if she was right in her assumption that Galatea was amassing an army of undead soldiers, it would provide her with all the cannon fodder she needed.

"Look," Felix hissed.

There were rows of figures standing up ahead, on either side of the path, motionless. Carefully, the two of them crept forward until they were close enough to make out features. Their skin was pale, eyes glassy and devoid of life or intelligence. Their hair hung lank and fine, almost like cobwebs.

"They're dead," Damaris whispered as they walked past the first figures, moving down the line. "The dead of Malenwar."

"They're not moving," Felix remarked. "They're not doing anything."

It was hard not to draw back from them in revulsion. Raising the dead was a despicable act. These people should have been left to rest after the tragedy they'd endured. Not all of them had possibly been good people in life, but they didn't deserve this. Their spirits had long since departed, he knew, but to desecrate someone's resting place like this and raise their corpse to do your bidding…

He shuddered. It was unspeakable.

But they weren't doing anything. *Some soldiers they were…*

"Hey," Damaris said sharply.

Felix looked up, following her gaze. A male shadow elf was sitting among the ruins ahead and he sprang to his feet, eyes wide as saucers as he spotted them.

"*He's* not an undead."

The elf turned and fled deeper into the ruins. The shadows would soon swallow him up and he'd be out of sight.

"Stop!" Damaris called, taking a step forward.

The ground beneath her hoof collapsed and she sprang back, bumping into Tempest. All around them, the rows of undead came to life, eyes flaring with green light, jaws opening wide, hands raised like claws.

Tempest let out a scream and reared. Felix gripped with his legs and clenched the reins, desperate to hold on. A fall from here onto the cobblestones below could prove deadly.

The ranks of undead closed in, surrounding them on all sides in a circle, shuffling closer.

"We're cut off!" Felix shouted as Tempest's hooves returned to the ground.

"I guess we're not making it to the Necropolis," Damaris muttered dryly.

"What's the point?" Felix swore as the horse reared beneath him again, lashing out with his hooves, trying to keep the undead at bay. "The Necropolis is *here!*"

"As soon as you can, run back the way we came," Damaris instructed.

He looked at her and thought, for a split second, that he saw amusement written across her face. She was enjoying this. At the realization, Felix felt his fear melt away.

She whirled around, tossing her head. Fire exploded at the feet of the undead blocking the path, the force tossing them into the air and blasting a hole in the stone. The air smelled unpleasantly of singed meat and burning hair.

"Go!"

Felix nudged Tempest with his heels. The stallion needed no further encouragement, springing forward, leaping over the hole. Damaris followed after, the swarms of undead falling behind.

As a unicorn, Damaris could run faster than a horse, but she hung back, staying behind Tempest and keeping herself between Felix and the undead.

At the edge of the ruins, Felix reined Tempest to a halt, looking over his shoulder to see the undead were still coming, steadily. "You think they'll follow us out of here?"

Damaris slowed to a stop beside him, turning to face the ranks of undead. "No," she said firmly, rearing up on her hind legs.

It was all for show, Felix knew. She could summon fire at a mere thought. But as long as it was effective, he didn't care how theatrical she got.

Damaris slammed her front hooves back onto the ground and a wall of fire sprang up directly on top of the undead. One moment, it wasn't there, and the next, the air shivered with heat and light.

Felix could feel the heat from a distance and watched, unable to tear his gaze away, as their flesh was instantly seared away, down to the bone. In seconds, even that was gone, and nothing remained of the undead soldiers but ash, scattered to the wind.

The fire wall guttered and went out, plunging the swamp into darkness once more and leaving the acrid smell of burnt flesh in the air.

Felix felt a chill go through him at the display of raw power. Even knowing what Damaris was capable of, it never ceased to leave him at a loss for words.

The Flame Guardian surveyed her work with satisfaction. "Come on," she said softly, turning and heading for the trees that separated the swamp from the Briarwood.

He hesitated a moment and then urged Tempest after her.

***

While Damaris and Felix were exploring the swamp, Galatea and Venryk made their way through Iceland. The icy wind cut through Galatea's clothes and chilled her to the bone, but Venryk had conjured his flames and the warmth spiraling off of them kept her warm.

She would have considered commandeering the use of Kadir's Gate again, venturing to the cemetery on Earth and crossing through the Ice Gate, but it was far too risky. Kadir may still be compliant and malleable to her wishes, but Cyren was another matter.

They headed straight for the ice palace, armed with a bargaining chip—the stolen headdress from Professor Lawrence's house. To the average onlooker, it might appear to be an ordinary circle of crystals, but Galatea knew what it was and it had been trapped on Earth this entire time while the Icelandic dragons were locked in a vicious civil war.

The crown had been lost during the Exodus and the dragons had been fighting ever since over who the true heir was, who had the right to lead them. Without the crown, anyone could claim the title, but no one was able to prove anything and so the fighting went on.

Legend had it that the crown had the ability to reveal the true heir. When worn, the crystals glowed blue for the true heir only.

Galatea had no doubt that the dragons would be desperate to have the crown returned, to end years of war and violence. And that they would be willing to swear their allegiance in order to get it.

The ice palace was a tall, massive structure—as it would have to be to house a clan of dragons—made entirely out of ice and crystal. Reflected light from the sky gave it a blue tinge.

The dragon that had recently claimed it, along with her loyal followers, believed herself to be the true heir, like all the others before her. She had acquired something of a reputation for being incredibly shrewd and vicious when it suited her.

Galatea was stopped at the entrance by two of her supporters who were posted as guards, but once she assured them that she had something that would be of interest to Icicle, they allowed her inside.

The main room was enormous, the ceiling stretching far above their heads. It was cold inside, but the wind could not penetrate through the walls and Venryk extinguished his fire upon entering. Massive blue crystals stood on either side of the doorway and Galatea glanced at them as she passed.

Icicle was lying on a slab of ice, in the center of the room, that functioned like a dais would. She rose to her feet, movements lithe. Icelandic dragons had thin, wiry bodies, covered in a thick coat of white fur. Her long, narrow face had a rounded muzzle and two black horns protruded from the back of her head.

Her wings were black and feathered. Long, curved black claws clicked on the ice. Black spines ran from her forehead to the middle of her back, packed so closely together that they touched. From there, they continued as thinner black spines, spaced apart. Her tail ended in a black tuft of fur.

Icicle eyed Galatea with vibrant blue eyes, ignoring Venryk altogether. "Galatea. I'd heard the rumors but I did not believe them."

Galatea nodded to the dragon, who was more than twice her own height. "Icicle."

"*Empress*," the dragon snapped. "If you don't mind."

"So you believe yourself to be the heir."

"Of course I am!"

"I imagine you haven't had much time for rumors, busy as you undoubtedly are trying to defend this palace."

Icicle shifted her weight in an agitated manner. "It has been…difficult, as one might expect, but nothing we can't handle."

"How long do you expect to hold this place? You cannot hold out indefinitely. The others will not accept you as leader without the crown."

"Tell me something I don't know," Icicle muttered, lashing her tail. She sat back on her haunches, staring down at the elf imperiously. "What do you want, Galatea?"

Galatea smiled. "You assume I want something."

The dragon let out a husky, grating laugh. "How can you not? You always did want something, Galatea. Very likely something you can't have. I assume that's why you're here and not for the pleasure of my hospitality, such as it is."

"No," Galatea agreed. "That's not why I've come. I need something from you."

"How surprising!"

"And I think you need something from me."

Icicle scoffed. "What could you possibly offer me that I would want? Your eternal wisdom?"

Wordlessly, Galatea reached into her pocket and withdrew the crown, holding it up so that the crystals caught the light.

The dragon's blue eyes widened and she reared back, long neck curving gracefully, previous arrogance gone. "How did you get your hands on that?"

"It was in a dusty display case in a library in a small town on Earth, if you can believe it."

"It belongs to my people! It is an heirloom and our legacy. Give it to me!"

"Now, Empress, you of all people should know that you don't get something for nothing," Galatea chided. "I'm willing to trade you the crown if you agree to fight beside me."

Empress's black lips peeled back, revealing sharp teeth. "What sort of a choice is that? Do you think I'm stupid? Give me the crown first."

Galatea clenched her fingers into a fist around the crown. "Not without a deal."

Empress hissed. "Without the crown, I can only persuade a handful of soldiers to fight with you and you will want them all. Without it declaring me the leader the others will never follow me and it will be difficult enough as it is to convince them to leap into another war so soon after putting an end to our own.

"This is supposed to be a time of peace for us, only you would have us charge headfirst into your war. I do not want to lose any more of my peoples' lives than have already been lost. It is folly. All we have to offer you is brute force and physical strength. We have no magic of our own and you would ask us to go to war with the Guardians, knowing that we will face the Lightbringer and the Flame Guardian?" She snorted. "You are mad if you think you stand a chance against them."

"I have soldiers of my own, as well," Galatea said smoothly. "And my magic allows me to resurrect any enemies that fall in battle and turn them against their former allies."

"Terrifying, to be sure, but you still have to kill them *first*."

But Galatea knew she was merely stalling. The dragon had made her decision the moment Galatea had revealed the crown. There was no other choice she could make. She couldn't possibly hope to attack Galatea and take it by force, though she no doubt wished she could. If it were possible, she wouldn't have hesitated to do so, but without magic, she didn't stand a chance.

Empress sighed theatrically. "I have no choice. I must have the crown to put an end to this infernal war. Much as I am loath to admit it, I would rather fight in your war than continue with this one. Still, a crown is of no use upon the head of a corpse!"

"Then I suggest you try not to die while you're at it."

Empress sneered. "And you can guarantee that, can you? Give it to me."

"Do we have a bargain? You will agree to fight beside me and my soldiers?"

The dragon nodded curtly. "We have a deal." She leaned her head down so that it was level with Galatea's chest. "Now, if you'll do the honors…"

Galatea lifted the headdress, slipping it around the dragon's horns to hang down between them and over her forehead. The strands of crystals draped down the sides of her face, two on each side.

The moment Galatea let go, the crystals lit up blue.

"At last!" Empress crowed. "They can deny me no longer!"

If there was one thing a dragon hated—and Galatea knew this—it was owing a debt to someone. And Empress owed her a very large debt indeed.

***

Sara was sitting on the palace steps when Felix returned, feeling an instant prick of guilt upon seeing her. He handed Tempest's reins to a servant and approached her. Usually he would have seen to his horse himself, but he knew he wouldn't be able to relax or focus until he took care of this.

She looked up at him. "Hey."

Damaris marched right past them, heading up the stairs and disappearing into the palace to give her report. He knew she expected him to go with her, but she could wait a little bit.

Sara looked after the disappearing unicorn. "Was that…Damaris?"

Felix sat down beside her. "Yep."

"The eyes were the same." She shook her head, eyeing him warily. "You're not gonna turn into something else, are you?"

Felix let out a small laugh, barely more than a sharp exhale. "No. Although I have been known to be an ass sometimes. Especially when I haven't had breakfast."

Sara laughed. "You wouldn't be the only one."

He sighed. "In all seriousness though, I want to apologize for snapping at you last night. It wasn't your fault and I wasn't angry with you. I was angry with myself, but that's no excuse for my behavior. I'm sorry. I don't want us to get off on the wrong foot."

"I know." She shifted slightly. "Colin told me. About Venryk."

"How much did he tell you?"

"Just that you'd met before when he attacked your village and that he gave you the scars." Sara didn't look away or hesitate this time when she said it. "But I already knew that last bit."

Felix bit his lip, thankful that Colin hadn't revealed any more. "Yes, Venryk and I have something of a personal vendetta against each other." He stood. "I have to go give my report to Lylla. Thank you…for being understanding."

***

Sara sighed after he'd left, feeling like a weight had been removed from her shoulders. But something he'd said still bothered her.

How much did he tell you?

So there was more to it than that. What wasn't he telling her?

12

She spent the better part of an hour that afternoon roaming around the palace and then returned to the courtyard, deciding to explore the pasture and gardens. In the middle of the pasture, there was a wide-open space where soldiers were training. Some stood in lines, bows at the ready, taking careful aim at rows of targets. Others, behind the archers, circled each other in makeshift dueling rings.

Sara stopped, recognizing Felix's crimson hair among the crowd of archers. Colin was with him.

They stood facing a row of round targets, the flags on top flapping in the breeze. Sara settled down underneath a tree to watch. Colin seemed to be struggling, his released arrows barely finding their way onto the edge of the target.

Felix, on the other hand, seemed to have no trouble at all. He stood with his body turned to the side, feet spread even with his shoulders as he drew an arrow from his quiver, nocked it, and drew the bowstring back, his eyes never leaving the target ahead.

After only a moment's hesitation, he released the arrow. It soared forward and struck the center of the target with a soft *thwunk*.

An elf, who must have been one of the instructors, was pacing back and forth, shouting out criticisms and instructions.

"Colin! Pull the bowstring all the way back to your cheek or it'll never reach the target! How many times do I have to tell you?"

He scrambled to do as she instructed. Felix nocked a second arrow and sent it hurtling toward the target, splitting the previous arrow neatly down the middle.

"Show-off," Colin muttered.

Sara continued to watch until the instructor dismissed them. She got to her feet, about to head back inside, when Colin spotted her.

"Sara!" he called, heading in her direction, Felix following more slowly.

She stopped, allowing them to catch up. "Hi."

"You weren't watching that dismal performance, were you?" Colin groaned. "I think I might die of embarrassment."

"You did better than I ever could," she replied, then glanced at Felix. "That was impressive."

He shrugged, glancing down at his boots. "Well, archery seems to be the one thing I have an affinity for."

"It looks impressive," Colin agreed, "until you learn that he's an air attribute and he uses the wind to control his arrows so he never misses."

Felix gave him a playful shove. "Don't go giving away all my secrets. And I wasn't using the wind that time."

"Well, it's still impressive," Sara said.

"Archery's not my thing," Colin shrugged. "You wanna be impressed, you should see me with a sword. I could beat Felix any day."

"You wish," Felix muttered.

Sara watched them as they walked away, still bickering good-naturedly among themselves. Part of her was glad that she was ordinary and so wouldn't be expected to undergo rigorous training as they were.

But at the same time, the thought reminded her of how much she didn't belong in this world.

***

Lylla was understandably disturbed by the report given by Damaris and Felix, describing the horrors they'd seen in the swamp. Galatea was raising an army of the dead, utilizing necromancy as well as sorcery. The idea was acutely repellent.

She sent one of her scouts to check on all the Gates and ensure that each Guardian and the extra soldiers she had sent were all accounted for and unharmed.

Lylla didn't think Galatea would try to go through one of the Gates again. There was no reason she could think of for the sorceress to do so. Sara—or perhaps more accurately, the Echo Stone—was here in Wysteria. There was nothing left for her to cross over for. But she couldn't be certain of that.

From her quarters at the top of the palace, Lylla saw the scout return hours later, the elf dismounting from the winged horse that had carried her. The scout made her way to the top of the palace to give her report, where they wouldn't be overheard.

"All of the Guardians are accounted for and uninjured," she reported. "All of the guards are present at all Gates except for one."

"All but one?"

The scout nodded. "There are no soldiers at the Wind Gate."

That did not bode well. Galatea had been going through the Wind Gate thus far. *But if she'd gone back through, what could she possibly be after?* She knew the scout did not know what had become of the guards, having merely been sent to observe and report. Lylla would have to send someone else to get the specifics.

She supposed she could have sent the scout again, but there was someone better suited to the task. The scout had said that *all* Guardians were accounted for, which meant that whatever may have befallen the guards hadn't befallen Kadir.

If there was something untoward at that Gate, there was only one person to send.

***

The usual pleasure Kadir felt at seeing Damaris was absent, replaced by something else, far less pleasant. A mixture of apprehension and guilt. Fear about how much she knew or suspected, unease at what she wanted, and guilt that he had lied to her and would have to do so again. He could not admit the truth, especially not to her. It was too shameful.

The time for turning back had been at the beginning, when he should have refused Galatea's demands. He hadn't and now it was too late. What had been done could not now be undone.

She found him standing guard at the temple and he plastered on what he hoped looked like a pleasant smile as she approached. It felt sickly to him.

"Kadir," she called.

The desert sun gleamed on her white coat and shone on her thick, dark mane and tail. Even as a unicorn, she retained the dark beauty mark beneath her left eye.

"*Kirena,*" he replied.

As usual, Damaris wasted no time getting straight to the point. "Lylla had one of her scouts check up on all the Gates and she reported that your guards seem to be missing." Damaris stopped in front of him, casting a look about her. "It appears she was right. Where are they?"

His smile faded and he didn't have to affect the unhappiness that replaced it. "They were killed."

Damaris looked equally unhappy, but unsurprised. It was the only plausible explanation for their absence. "I don't suppose I need to ask by whom."

"Galatea," he confirmed. There was no point in denying that; she was the only one who would have done it. "Only she didn't do it herself. She sent some of her soldiers…the undead."

The Flame Guardian's eyes hardened. "Yes, I saw some of them earlier in the swamp." She looked at him directly and Kadir felt uncomfortable under her gaze. "If you don't mind my asking, how is it that all of your guards were killed, but you were unharmed?"

Kadir's heart rose to his throat, choking him. *She knows!* At least she knew something. He silently cursed Galatea and himself as well. He knew their charade could only last so long before suspicions were aroused.

But he couldn't allow his part in the treachery to be discovered, especially not by Damaris of all people. The knowledge of what he had done was painful enough. He could not bear for her to discover the truth. The way she would look at him with those flame-colored eyes would be worse than death.

"I was," he said, cringing inwardly. *Yet another lie.* How quickly one led to another. "I was healed."

The lie sounded unconvincing to his own ears, but Damaris seemed not to notice. She studied him for a few moments more and then broke the connection.

"Why your Gate?" she asked softly. "Why is Galatea always coming back here?"

Kadir felt some of the tension ease out of his body. This, at least, was a question he could answer with a semblance of truth. "It's the easiest for her. There may be Guardians on both sides, but we have to face it—Lawrence is getting old. She can't very well travel all the way through Iceland to use the Ice Gate. And the Lightning Gate is guarded on either side. Hank never leaves it. With Lawrence's house standing some distance away from the Gate, he might never know if she slips through."

"No," Damaris murmured. "I suppose you have a point. But why didn't you send word that your guards had been killed?"

"I did." He'd done no such thing. "I sent a messenger."

"No messenger ever arrived."

"Then Galatea must have anticipated that I would do such a thing and took steps to ensure that my messenger never arrived."

"She wouldn't want us finding out and sending yet more reinforcements. But don't worry. I'll make sure word gets to Lylla about your guards."

"Thank you, *kirena*. Is there anything else I can do for you?"

"No. I think you've satisfied my curiosity."

***

Damaris turned and walked away, heart heavier than it had been in a long time. Something wasn't right. What Kadir told her didn't add up. It didn't fit with the Guardian she knew.

The question was, what to do about it?

She couldn't believe her suspicions. She couldn't listen to their whispered insinuations. She needed to talk to someone, someone who wouldn't try to protect her feelings.

But that could wait until tomorrow. Today was much too soon.

***

The trip from Iceland back to Malenwar seemed to take an eternity. Galatea had left having attained what she'd come for, but it brought her no happiness. Jack was no closer to living again—really living again. He was still a mindless, shambling corpse that existed only to obey her, not love her.

Her thoughts as she traveled were filled with memories of him, memories that were both sweet and bitter, heartbreaking in their intensity. Even after all this time, she was surprised by how much she could *feel*. Only now that love was tainted with hatred, joy turned to grief, innocence corrupted.

True to his word, he had returned the very next day and found her waiting. She had enjoyed showing off for him. The smallest demonstrations of magic were enough to astound him and she had laughed at the pure expression of wonderment on his face. Even causing flowers to burst from the ground into a riot of color at his feet had amazed him.

Galatea had grown up surrounded by magic. It seemed to be in the very air that she breathed. She'd never met anyone before who had no magic of their own and Jack's awe was unlike any reaction she'd ever seen to magic.

It had taken her awhile to understand how Wysterians took their own power, their very lives in the other world, for granted. They would live forever. They had no notion of mortality, of being finite or trapped within time itself.

Jack's life, like that of all humans, had an end to it. A sense that there was only so much time, as if he could almost feel it slipping away. Even now, that was something Galatea had no notion of. Perhaps that was why she could bear to wait for fifty years before seeking revenge. Time meant nothing to her.

She watched the change in him, from the hollow-eyed young man she had first met who wanted nothing more than to die, to someone who wanted so desperately to live more than anything. She made the pond at the edge of the woods, behind his farmhouse, defy gravity. She made leaves dance on the wind, tree limbs grow until they were stretching their arms out toward the heavens.

Jack had taken it all in with wide eyes and every day he could, he came back for more.

"And everyone in Wysteria can do this?" he asked, for what must have been the thousandth time, as if he couldn't bring himself to believe it.

"Yes. Though most can only use one element."

"What else can magic do?"

She told him about shape-shifting, a rare ability granted to very few. When she talked about healing, and how even fatal wounds could be healed if the healer possessed enough skill, he became quite serious.

"Does that mean," he asked slowly, "that it's possible for my arm to be healed?"

Galatea looked at his paralyzed arm, completely intact but without motion. He'd told her that a Viet Cong bullet had caused what he called a brachial plexus injury, damaging the nerves and resulting in the loss of movement. He had told her all about the war, even though she could tell it was difficult for him, but at the same time, he seemed to want to tell someone. It didn't make a great deal of sense to her, and he didn't much understand the reasons for the war either, but it didn't surprise her to learn that humans were still causing wars even after all this time.

"Yes," she answered. Healers could even attach severed limbs, if they had enough knowledge of anatomy and the skill to do so. Jack's arm was not severed. The nerves had been damaged and they could be repaired.

"Do you think…" he said slowly, as if afraid of the answer, "you could take me there?"

Over the many hours they had spent together, she learned that his family owned a farm. It wasn't a large operation—his parents didn't have the money to hire help—but they did all right for themselves and managed well enough with the help of Jack and his two brothers.

But those brothers never returned from Vietnam and though Jack had been sent home, to safety, because of his injury, it was that very injury that prevented him from contributing on the farm.

Jack confided to Galatea that even though he thought his mother was relieved not to have lost all of her children and was merely happy that he had come back alive, his father now viewed him as another mouth to feed. One that could no longer do anything to earn his keep. It seemed inexplicably cruel to Galatea and though he never said as much, she suspected that was part of the reason Jack had attempted to take his own life the day they had met.

She knew what the restoration of his arm would mean to him. She knew why he asked. And so she'd brought him to Wysteria.

From the very beginning, the other Guardians had not been pleased. Serai had healed Jack's arm and Galatea knew that the others expected her to then return Jack to his own world. But Jack hadn't wanted to go back.

Wysteria couldn't have been further from the horrors of the war or the life he had waiting for him back home.

Here was a world of magic and wonder, where permanent, life-altering injuries could be healed. Here, he could live forever. Here, the shadow of death that had been hanging over him could not touch him.

"What about your family?" Galatea had asked, but she knew what he would say.

His family hadn't wanted him. They would have preferred if he had died rather than return only to be a burden. But more than that, more than the magic and immortality, there was something else he didn't want to leave behind.

Her.

She could not live on Earth with him. She was a Guardian, with a Gate to protect. Her magic would fade on Earth and Jack would one day die, leaving her alone. And the others did not want him to stay here in Wysteria.

But why shouldn't he? What was so very wrong about letting him stay? This broken young man that she had helped put together again, who had more appreciation for Wysteria than most Wysterians did. And all because he had no magic of his own? Because he wasn't like them?

And Galatea realized she didn't care about her Gate anymore, that inanimate object that would last for eternity. She didn't want Jack to leave. She didn't want him to die. She didn't want to live on forever, alone, with only a Gate for company. She wanted him to make her laugh. She wanted a future together where neither of them would grow old. She wanted someone who would never cease to be amazed by the world around him.

Jack had been drawn to beautiful things. Her. Wysteria. He had seen Wysteria as a place of wonder.

And it had led to his death.

Galatea was relieved to return to the swamp, able to push the thoughts away and focus on practical solutions. She took out the grimoire and began pouring over its newly revealed pages, desperate to find anything that might help her acquire the second Echo Stone. Secured as it was in the palace, it would be nearly impossible, but she hadn't come this far to be thwarted by one human girl.

It was on one of the pages that had previously been blank and hidden from her sight that she found something that made her sit up and take notice.

It read: *Faolain's Mirror.*

Galatea reached into the pocket of her skirt and withdrew the hand mirror she'd taken from Professor Lawrence. It was possible that they weren't the same, possible that Faolain's Mirror may be of no use to her whatsoever.

But she remembered something of the myth surrounding Faolain, who had lived on Earth before the Exodus. Faolain, who had supposedly used this mirror to kill her lover.

She read on:

According to legend, any who look into the mirror have their reflections captured in it, allowing the mirror's wielder to take on the guise of any who have ever peered into it. The mirror must remain on the user's person at all times in order to maintain the illusion. If the mirror is taken, lost, or shattered, the illusion will vanish, revealing the user's true form. Ironically, in order to access the mirror's power, the wielder must surrender their own reflection to the mirror's collection.

Galatea sucked in a sharp breath. Little wonder this spell had been deemed dangerous and therefore hidden. Glamours, as useful as they were, had their limitations. One could not glamour oneself to look like someone who was still alive and taking on the visage of someone who was dead had little use when everyone knew they had died.

The ability to take on the appearance of someone else could certainly assist with the acquisition of the stone. But it all depended on which reflections she had at her disposal.

She held up the mirror. The frame was ornate silver—which burned her slightly as iron would an ordinary elementalist, only in her case, because she had dabbled in sorcery, silver counteracted her magic instead of iron—with a purple gem at the base of the handle. She rubbed her thumb over the gem and the surface of the mirror shimmered, revealing a face.

It was an elf, her skin pale, face framed by long golden hair. Faolain herself, perhaps?

Galatea continued to scroll through the available guises. There were many and most of them were of no use to her, all of them being long dead. She needed someone alive, someone those at the palace would trust implicitly.

Lawrence had owned the mirror last. It was plausible—likely even—that his reflection was among the collection. Galatea could think of no one better for the girl to trust and give her stone to.

At last! Galatea froze in her scrolling, a slow smile spreading over her face. It was just as she'd hoped. At some point, Lawrence had looked into the mirror and his reflection had been captured.

She marveled again at the power of the spell. One could wreak unimaginable havoc with the ability to make oneself look like someone else.

She rose to her feet, excitement rising with every passing moment.

"Noraak!" she called. "I have a task for you."

***

Sara lay on one of the sofas in the palace's vast sitting room, her feet tucked up beside her, arms and head resting on the armrest as she stared out the window at the setting sun. Her first full day in Wysteria was coming to an end, the first of who knew how many.

She sighed, both bored and lonely, feeling as though she could drift off to sleep then and there. There was movement in the doorway and she sat up, blinking in surprise at the sight of Professor Lawrence.

"Professor." Sara got to her feet. "I'd thought you'd left."

He hesitated, as though lost in thought. "Yes, I did."

"You didn't tell me you were leaving." *I didn't get a chance to say goodbye.*

"Yes, I'm sorry about that. It was all rather rushed. I can't stay long, but I'm here now. How are you settling in?"

She shrugged. "As well as can be expected, I guess."

"You'd rather go home, I imagine."

"Well…yes. It's not as bad here as I thought it would be, but I don't really belong here, do I? I'm not a Guardian, like you."

She couldn't leave the palace for her own safety and so there was nothing much for her to do other than explore and there was only so much of that one could take.

"No, I suppose not."

Sara pulled the Echo Stone out from under her shirt, running her fingers over it as she'd developed a habit of doing whenever she found herself stressed. All of this over a little stone. "Lylla said my mother came here. Was she a Guardian?"

Or had she been more like her daughter and merely found herself wrapped up in something that didn't concern her?

"You know," Professor Lawrence remarked, completely ignoring the question. "I've been giving the matter some thought. Perhaps you could leave the Echo Stone here, where it could be safe, and then you could go home."

Sara froze, looking up at him sharply. "I already suggested that to Lylla and she said I would still be in danger, remember? You were there."

He'd been in the room when the conversation was taking place. Why would he mention an idea that had already been suggested and discarded?

He hesitated, then leaned forward eagerly. "Yes, but don't you see? There's been new developments. Galatea's been raising an army of undead and her soldiers have already attacked a fort and one of the Gates."

"How does that change anything?"

"Galatea believes everything she wants is here in Wysteria. You and the Echo Stone." He nodded to the necklace. "If we were to send you back secretly, she'd still believe you to be here. She'd have no reason to go after you, then, because she doesn't know you've been returned to Earth. But in reality, you will be safe on Earth with your family and the Echo Stone will be safe here, with people to protect it."

If they sent her back secretly, and Galatea didn't know otherwise, Sara could see how she might be safe and allowed to go back home. But something didn't feel right. Why had Lawrence said 'your family' instead of 'your dad'? He knew her mom had died. Was it just his way of trying to protect her? He knew she didn't like talking about it.

But it seemed a roundabout way of protecting her, by inadvertently drawing attention to it.

"I—I don't know," she said hesitantly, though she couldn't deny the idea was tempting. And if she could trust anyone's judgement on the matter, she could trust his.

"You can trust me to look after the stone," he said, holding out a hand, as though reading her thoughts. "I'll keep it safe, I promise. This is a burden you never should have had to bear. It's mine to look after, not yours."

Now Sara *knew* something wasn't right. Professor Lawrence might have been the keeper of the artifacts, including an Echo Stone, but he had never been the keeper of this one. It had belonged to her mother and she had given it to Sara. It had never belonged to Lawrence or fallen into his hands.

More than that, he knew how important it was to her, how she clung to it even before she knew what it really was, because it reminded her of her mother. How could he ask her to part with such a thing, even knowing its true significance?

He wouldn't do that.

Suddenly, she thought of Mrs. Miley. Or rather, Sara had believed she'd been speaking to Mrs. Miley that day in the library. In reality, it hadn't been her at all, but Galatea disguised as Mrs. Miley.

Dread coiled in her stomach. Had Professor Lawrence simply returned or was she merely speaking to someone wearing his guise? She knew that was possible now, although that would mean the Professor was dead…

He watched her as she stood there rigidly, suspicion no doubt written plainly on her face.

She shoved the stone back beneath her shirt. "You know what," she said, voice high and tight, "I think I'd better hang onto it."

He opened his mouth as if about to say something, then shut it and turned abruptly, walking out of the room. She watched him go, moving quickly and with more agility than she remembered, considering his age.

She was just beginning to wonder what had made him leave so abruptly when she heard footsteps drawing near; a moment later Lylla stepped into the room.

She looked at Sara in concern. "You look as if you've just seen a ghost."

Sara blinked, settling back down into her seat, shaking her head. "I—I was just talking to Professor Lawrence."

"The Professor was here?" Lylla's eyebrows drew together, her lips turning down in a frown. "If he intended to return, he made no mention of it to me."

Sara tensed, feeling goosebumps erupt over her skin. "I don't think it was really him," she said softly.

Lylla whirled, skirts and long blue hair flying as she stormed out of the doorway. Sara sprang to her feet, following, heart pounding.

"What did he say to you?" the queen asked over her shoulder.

"He wanted me to give him the Echo Stone—for safe keeping, he said."

"I don't think the Professor would ever ask you to do that."

"I know. I knew something didn't feel right."

"Well if there's an imposter roaming the grounds, we'll find him," Lylla assured her. "Felix! Colin!"

Never far away, her two Shadows came running within moments. "What's wrong?" Felix demanded, looking at Sara's pale face.

"There is an imposter in the palace," Lylla replied. "Someone with Professor Lawrence's guise tried to convince Sara to give him the Echo Stone. She last saw him heading out of the sitting room. Colin, I need you to put all the guards on alert. Felix, stay with Sara and keep her safe."

Colin gave a brief salute, his fist over his heart, and then he darted down one of the corridors. Felix nodded and came over, gently wrapping an arm around Sara's shoulders and guiding her away.

Lylla shifted into her unicorn form, Felix's head only coming up to her shoulder. She wheeled around and hurried down a different passageway.

"Come on," Felix said gently, leading her into one of the side rooms and over to a table. "They'll find him."

Sara nodded numbly. "Yeah." She sat down next to him, grateful for the company.

Felix sent one of the servants for tea, lingering by the doorway, his movements restless. He rejoined her once the tea arrived, but didn't take any for himself. Sara thought he would have preferred joining the search, but he made no complaint. Nor did he try to engage her in conversation, for which Sara was grateful.

She didn't feel much like talking. There was something horrifying about being tricked by someone you trusted— or at least looked like someone you trusted. *What if I had given him the stone? What if I had believed him? Galatea might have the Echo Stone right now.*

As if sensing her distress, Felix reached over, gripping her hand. His fingers were rough with calluses from years of archery, brushing against her skin. He gave a quick squeeze and then let go. Sara was surprised by the gesture, too worried to be embarrassed by it, but grateful.

Lylla returned a short time later with Colin, the clack of her hooves on the marble floor announcing her return. She reverted to her elven form as she crossed the doorway.

"I'm afraid whoever it was has escaped," she announced. "I checked with the guards at the Glowing

Gate and they said he'd taken one of the horses from the stable, telling the stable hand he was going for a ride. They let him out before we could get word to them. They had no reason to believe it was anything other than what it appeared."

Sara looked down at her hands, clasped on the table.

Lylla took a seat on her left and Colin joined her. "Don't worry, Sara. I told the guards about what happened. They know the real Lawrence has returned to Earth. The imposter can't get back in again."

She nodded. "Thank you all for trying. I didn't realize Galatea was so desperate… If the Professor wanted the Echo Stone, why didn't he just take it?"

"Once an Echo Stone is claimed by someone, as it were, it has to be given. It cannot be taken," Lylla replied. "If it is taken by force, it will not amplify the magic of the one who takes it."

"Oh." Sara reached up to touch the chain around her neck. "Lucky for me, I guess. Hank told me about glamours. How you can glamour yourself to look like someone else. But even knowing that it's just an illusion, it still looks so real."

Lylla nodded. "Illusions are meant to deceive, typical of dark magic. But I don't think darkness itself would be capable of that. I wonder if there was anything among the Professor's collection that might have given Galatea this ability."

"Do you think that was actually Galatea?" Colin asked, eyes wide. "Here, at the palace?"

"Now that I think about it, his voice didn't sound quite right," Sara said. "But it didn't sound like a woman at all."

Lylla shook her head. "I don't think Galatea is that desperate. Damaris and Felix told me they saw a young male shadow elf in the swamp earlier among the undead, but *he* was very much alive. It's not unreasonable to think that Galatea may have a helper. More likely she sent him instead. I'm quite familiar with the study of illusions and there are disadvantages to them. You can't make your voice sound like a man if you are not one, and vice versa, unless you are incredibly skilled in that area. But most of us wouldn't be able to make it sound convincing. This was too dangerous a move for Galatea herself to attempt. If we had caught her, it would have been over."

"Still," Felix muttered. "It is rather alarming that someone could come in here disguised as someone else. Someone we know and trust."

"Yes, it is," Lylla agreed. "But it's not foolproof. There will almost always be something that gives them away. After all, they are not *really* who they pretend to be and so there will be some key difference, likely something the imposter isn't even aware of."

"I thought the Glowing Gate prevented any enemies from coming through," Colin remarked.

"It does," Lylla said patiently. "But because this imposter didn't look like an enemy, but rather a friend, the guards at the Gate had no reason not to let him in."

"Galatea must be desperate to resort to doppelgangers," Felix said, leaning back in his chair and crossing his arms.

"What do we do?" Sara whispered. "She won't stop until she gets the stone."

"No," Lylla said, rising to her feet. "She won't stop until we stop her. In the meantime, all we can do is be vigilant and extra careful. Whatever the circumstances, and whoever may be asking, Sara, do not give that necklace to anyone else."

She gripped the stone beneath her shirt. "I won't."

"The threat has passed. Whoever it was cannot get back onto the palace grounds. It is late; try not to dwell on it any longer. I wish you all a goodnight."

Colin pushed up from the table and followed after the queen, leaving Sara alone with Felix.

"If you'd rather not be alone, I can stay," he offered, then quickly added, "Here. If you'd like."

She looked at him—really looked at him for the first time.

He had a longer face than average, with a smooth, defined jaw. A few crimson whiskers of facial hair covered his chin, but he was otherwise clean-shaven. The scars raked down the left side of his face, one slicing across his eyebrow, but his eye was undamaged.

His crimson hair was disheveled and a bit shaggy, but far shorter than most of the other elves she'd seen thus far. His eyes were a deep forest green and there were freckles splashed across his cheeks and the bridge of his nose.

He flushed slightly under her scrutiny, but something in his gaze softened as if he realized she was looking and seeing *him* rather than just the scars.

Sara smiled, trying to take Lylla's words to heart. "Thank you, but I'll be all right."

He returned the smile. "Goodnight, then."

"Goodnight, Felix."

13

It stormed the following day, the sky dark with gray clouds pouring down sheets of rain that rattled against the palace windows. Training was canceled for the day, due to the high winds and lightning. Sara found herself sequestered inside when she much would have preferred to be out—if it had been sunny.

But a storm couldn't keep daily necessities in Wysteria from continuing. The patrols that Lylla had ordered continued, somewhat sheltered from the fury of the storm by the thick trees of the forest.

Sara was looking out of one of the balconies, shut off now by the French doors, when Colin came up to her. It was nearly impossible to see out of the windows with the lashing rain streaking down the glass, but he stared at it as if he could see something beyond. He closed his eyes, listening to the wind howl.

"Azuma's riled up today," he remarked.

"What?" Sara asked, not at all understanding what he meant.

He turned to her and smiled. "Azuma, the spirit of the Eastern Wind. There used to be other spirits, but they're all gone now. You'll have to ask Serai, the healer, about it sometime. She's a desert elf. It's her people's culture, not mine."

"I don't think I've met her yet."

"You'll know her when you see her. White tattoos. Only healers are allowed to have them."

"Maybe I will—ask her, I mean. So you like storms, then?"

He shrugged. "They're fascinating."

"I don't like them," she admitted. "I don't like rain."

Rain reminded her of gloominess, of being sad. It was much easier to feel happy when there was warm sun outside. Even on winter days, when it looked nice out but wasn't, it was far more bearable than gray winter days.

Sara turned and left Colin there, not wanting to stare at the rain any longer. She wondered if it was raining back home.

What must her dad think of all this? Was he worried for her or relieved knowing where she was? She felt like she hardly recognized her own life at all. It had felt that way ever since her mom had died, a clear line of demarcation drawn in the sand. Her life before and her life after, never to be the same, the two worlds unable to cross over, unable to ever go back, only forward.

Sara felt like she didn't know either of her parents at all. Her mother had come here, to Wysteria, yet had never breathed a word about it. Her dad, at the very least, had known something about it, if Lylla's answer was anything to judge by. And yet he hadn't said anything either.

And even the boring, sleepy little town where nothing ever happened was home to not one but three Gates, each with its own Guardian. Mayfair had suddenly found itself the epicenter of a magical war, connected to a magical world Sara had no knowledge of.

She sighed. It would be easier to believe it was all just a dream, but she knew better. She retreated to the sitting room and settled onto one of the sofas, staring into the fire that had been lit in the hearth. Despite it being summer, the sudden storm had brought a chill with it.

She didn't know how long she'd been there, when a voice spoke from the doorway. "You look bored."

Sara looked up to see Felix standing there. "I am," she said, not wanting to admit that she'd been woolgathering. She'd never been one to get easily bored by sitting in one place. Most people preferred to play games on their phone, but she didn't have any and they wouldn't have done her any good here even if she had. "What I wouldn't give for a book. Are there any here?"

The corner of his mouth turned up in a smile. "If it's books you want, come with me."

Intrigued, Sara got up off the couch and followed him down the corridor. Lamps had been lit along the hallways, giving off small golden halos. It wasn't the same as having daylight, but they did help to cut through the gloom of the storm.

Felix led her into a part of the palace she hadn't yet been in and stopped before a plain wooden door. Without preamble, he turned the knob and pushed it open. Immediately, warm light fell upon Sara's face and she gasped, stepping inside.

The wall to her left was completely covered in bookshelves and she could just make out the one to her right, many feet in the distance. More shelves stood in the middle of the room, each filled with volumes. They were nearly triple her height and if she looked up, she could see branches extending toward the ceiling from the middle of the room, and a balcony on the second floor.

Felix shut the door quietly behind him and followed her into the room. The lush green carpet muffled their footsteps. There were lamps on the walls, emanating golden light, as there had been in the hallway, and there were lanterns hanging from the branches as well.

Sara ducked through the maze of shelves until she came to the center of the room, where a massive wooden carving of a tree sat, its branches spreading out above the shelves. There were steps that spiraled around its trunk, leading to the upper floor. Small dots of light drifted slowly throughout the room, as if weightless. There was a glass dome in the ceiling, above the top of the tree, revealing the gray sky and rain.

She stared up at the branches, vertigo making her take a step back, and felt herself smile. "What is this place?"

"Lylla's library," Felix answered. "It's my favorite room in the whole palace. I always come here when it's storming outside."

"It's beautiful."

But it was so much more than just a library, she realized. There were paintings on the walls in the rare spaces where there were breaks in the shelves. Busts of statues, candelabras, and weapons. It reminded her a bit of the eclectic nature of Professor Lawrence's house with its jumble of artifacts.

She finally made it to the far wall and spied a window seat set into the wall, the cushion a light blue. "How many of these books have you read?"

"All of them," he replied, a few feet behind her, staring up at the tree.

"Really?" Sara sat down on the window seat.

He gave a short laugh. "No, I'm teasing. I'm working on it, though. In my spare time, whenever I'm not needed for training or patrols. I've got a long way to go."

"But you're an elf," she pointed out. "You've got all the time in the world."

The smile faded from his face as Felix lowered his gaze from the tree. He wasn't looking at her, but there was something unspeakably sad about his expression. Then, just as quickly, it was gone and he met her gaze, giving her a small smile. "Yeah."

Sara wanted to ask him what was wrong, but she knew he wouldn't appreciate it and he likely wouldn't answer. If he'd wanted her to know, he'd have told her. And maybe she'd imagined it and it had nothing to do with any of this.

Instead, she glanced down at a leather-covered notebook, resting on the window seat, and picked it up. As soon as she flipped it open to the first page, she realized that it wasn't a notebook at all, but a sketchbook.

The first drawing was of Damaris, as a unicorn. Sara could tell it was her even though the sketch was monochrome. The thick lashes were the same and the beauty mark beneath her left eye. It was almost like looking at a photograph, it was so realistic.

"Did you draw these?" Sara asked, flipping to the next one.

It was of Lylla, with an unmistakable gleam of amusement in her eyes.

"Yes…" She glanced up. Felix looked uncomfortable. She thought he was blushing slightly, but it was hard to tell in this light.

Sara suddenly felt heat rush to her own cheeks as she realized she was trespassing on something private. She quickly shut the book. "I'm sorry. I didn't realize—that was rude of me, snooping like that."

"No, it's all right. I just—I'm not used to sharing my art with many people." Felix came over to join her on the window seat. It was just big enough for two people. "I probably should, though. Lylla's always saying I have so much talent, I shouldn't hide it away."

"You do," Sara said. "Have talent, I mean. I wish I could draw half as well as you."

But art hadn't been her gift. Hers had been an eye for composition, light and shadow, the ability to capture a moment forever, a split second in time worth a thousand words.

He'd said it was all right for her to look, so she opened the sketchbook again, flipping past the first two sketches that she'd already seen—and nearly leapt out of her skin upon turning to the third.

It was of a wolf—Venryk, if she had to guess—jaws spread wide to reveal sharp teeth. The wolf's fur was ablaze and it looked as though he was lunging for her throat, mere inches away.

Sara averted her gaze, glancing searchingly at the elf beside her.

He turned away, but he was to her right and her eyes roamed over the angry red scars on his face. At such close proximity, she could see the ragged edges of his skin and how the scars almost looked like they might weep blood at any moment, as though they hadn't healed at all from the moment they'd been inflicted.

"I…have dreams, sometimes," he muttered, the line of his jaw tense. "About what happened. Drawing helps."

Sara thought she knew what he meant and wished she had something that helped her deal with her own demons. It would have been photography, but that was too painful now.

She didn't know what to say and so she said nothing. Instead, she swallowed and gently shut the sketchbook. What would she want to hear, if the roles were reversed?

"You don't have to tell me if you don't want to. But I'll listen, if you want me to."

Felix smiled, but it was sad. "Where would I even start?" He rose to his feet, shaking off the gloom as if it were a raincoat. "Shall we explore the upper level?"

Sara recognized that he was trying to change the subject and she obliged. "Certainly."

***

The inclement weather did not keep Damaris from her task. She barely noticed the rain lashing her face, weighing down her mane and tail, or the wind tearing at her, her mind was in so much turmoil. She could scarcely believe what she was doing, but every step took her closer.

The storm had not yet reached the grasslands and it tapered off by the time she'd left the cover of the forest behind and stepped out into its long swath of grass.

The Water Gate, and consequently Cassius's cottage, were situated near the cliffs, undoubtedly so he could feel nearer to the sea. He wouldn't be the first Guardian to feel more at home among his element.

The cottage was smaller than Cyren's lodge, but large enough to admit her as a unicorn. Ordinarily, she would shape-shift, but she wanted to feel in control of the situation, even though she wasn't, and her true form would put her more at ease.

The cottage walls were white, the windows shuttered. The roof was black and there was no garden or flowers outside like one would expect to find at such a dwelling. But flowers weren't really Cassius's thing.

He answered her knock as she knew he would, unable to disguise the shock on his face at seeing her. "Damaris. What are you doing here? Is the world coming to an end?"

She knew why he was surprised to see her. She would have been equally incredulous if he'd come calling on her rather than the other way around.

"No," she answered, somewhat defeatedly. "I need to talk to you."

It was so unlike her usual tone of confidence or authority that Cassius looked even more taken aback and, if possible, a bit worried.

He sighed and stepped to the side, holding the door wide. "You'd better come in, then."

Wordlessly, Damaris stepped over the threshold and into the living room. The walls on the inside of the cottage, unlike the exterior, were painted a deep blue and the furniture was dark, befitting the usual taste for a shadow elf.

Cassius peered outside a moment more at the approaching dark clouds. "Looks like a storm is coming," he remarked and shut the door against the elements. The wind was coming up.

"In more ways than one," Damaris muttered. "I think one of the Guardians is a traitor."

Cassius remained standing by the door and turned to face her. He was dressed in a long dark blue robe, his black hair hanging loose.

He studied her with his yellow eyes. "I suppose you mustn't think it to be me, or else I can't fathom why you're telling me this information."

Damaris smiled wryly. "No, although I don't mind admitting I'd like it to be you."

"The feeling is mutual, I'm sure." He strode into the room, waving a hand dismissively. "But what reason do you have for believing one of the Guardians to be a traitor?"

"How else do you explain how easily Galatea was able to cross over to Earth and back on multiple occasions?"

Cassius sat in one of the chairs and reached for a wine glass on the side table he'd obviously been drinking from before she arrived. He crossed his legs. "Who do you think it is, then?"

"It can't be Wanderer," Damaris said, stalling. "I have a hard time believing she'd ever do such a thing."

"She wouldn't," Cassius said adamantly, sipping his wine.

In Damaris's opinion, one of the great mysteries of the world was how Wanderer could possibly be friends with someone like Cassius. She couldn't fathom what Wanderer saw in the Water Guardian. But then again, Wanderer was friends with nearly everyone.

"No, and besides, her Gate wouldn't be practical for Galatea to go through. Hank is always on the other side."

"I thought we *knew* which Gate she'd gone through."

"Let me *finish*." Damaris shook her head and began pacing back and forth in front of the hearth. "Initially, I thought it might be your sister. She believed Galatea was dead and that she couldn't be behind it all at first. I thought maybe she'd been careless with her security and that's how Galatea got through. Although she denied anyone going through her Gate, I wasn't sure I believed Cyren. She would say that after all, wouldn't she?"

"I'm sensing there's a 'but' coming…"

Damaris shot him a half-hearted glower. "*But* it wasn't Cyren's Gate that Galatea kept going through. It was Kadir's. It was his Gate she went through first, his guards she killed."

Cassius lowered his wine glass, expression sobering. He uncrossed his legs and leaned forward. "And you think Kadir is the traitor?"

"It's too easy for Galatea," Damaris exclaimed, her frustration coming through. "The only way she could have gone through so many times is if he *let* her through! Once, I can understand—he wasn't even there the first night those guards were killed. But it kept happening…"

"Have you spoken to him?"

"Yes, and he always manages to give me some excuse. One time he claimed he was injured and I saw the proof of it myself. All of the extra guards Lylla sent to his Gate were killed, but not him. Every time, he claims he was attacked, and yet Galatea continues to mysteriously leave him alive. Reverend Pierce was not shown such mercy!"

Cassius swirled his wine contemplatively. "He *could* be telling the truth…"

"But it doesn't add up," Damaris insisted. "The Kadir I know would have risked his life to protect that Gate. He'd have confronted her. He would have fought to the death if that's what it took. We all took an oath and we all know what it might require to uphold it. And I'd like to believe we're all willing to make that sacrifice, if it's asked of us, but now I'm not so sure!"

"So the reason Galatea kept going back to his Gate is because he was letting her through. You could be right." Cassius grimaced. "I can't believe I just said that… But what are you going to do about it?"

"I have to confront him. I have to hear what he has to say for himself." *I have to hear him deny it.*

"And if he is, in fact, a traitor?"

Damaris said nothing. She didn't want it to be true. She didn't want to have to face it if it was. She wasn't sure she could.

But wasn't that the same reaction she had despised from the others when they refused to accept that Galatea might, in fact, not be as dead as they'd all like? It was cowardice, plain and simple. Damaris drew herself up. She was the Flame Guardian. She feared nothing and no one.

"Damaris, you do realize that if he is a traitor, you have every right—and the responsibility—to drag him back to the palace. His life is forfeit."

"I know that. But I still don't know if I could, if it comes to that."

Kadir's grandfather had been her mentor, the man who had taught her everything he knew, the man who had seen her potential when she had not even seen it herself. She would not be the Flame Guardian without him. She had known Kadir all his life. He was one of her closest friends, along with Bella and Lylla. And Bella was dead.

Cassius leaned back in his chair. "Ah, now I know why you came to me. You know I have no compunction about turning him in, if necessary. You know that I will do what you cannot."

It was exactly why Damaris had come to him. If her worst fears were realized, at least she wouldn't be the one to drag her friend to the palace in shame.

"Clever of you, really. But what I can't understand is *why*. Why would Kadir aid Galatea? What is she holding over him?"

"I don't know," Damaris admitted. "I desperately wish I knew, but I don't." Maybe if she had, it would have made things easier somehow.

"I must confess, I'm curious why you didn't think the traitor was me."

"Other than the fact that your Gate is terribly inconvenient?" Damaris gave him a wry look. It, like her own, came out on the other side of the world, far away from where Galatea needed to be. "I know we don't see eye to eye on much, but there is one thing we agree on and that's the protection of Wysteria and its people. As much as I hate to admit it, you're one of the good ones. You'd never help Galatea."

And Galatea would never accept his help, after what he and Cyren had done.

Cassius crossed his legs. "Well, you've got that right. I don't envy you your task."

"Neither would I," she whispered and headed for the door.

***

Cassius opened the door for her and watched the Flame Guardian leave, galloping across the grasslands as the storm clouds above opened up. She would have a long, wet journey to the desert.

For the first time, he felt a twinge of pity for her.

***

It was not raining in the desert, but the winds were whipping, blowing sand into her eyes. Kadir was at the temple, alone, when she arrived. *So much the better.*

"*Kirena,*" he nodded to her. "Have there been more developments or is this a social visit?"

"Neither," she said shortly, fully prepared to ask for forgiveness if her suspicions turned out to be unfounded. She hoped by the end of this conversation, she would be doing just that, but she doubted it.

She looked directly at him. "It doesn't add up. None of it does."

His light blue eyes held confusion. "What doesn't?"

"What you've been telling me. About the Gate and Galatea."

"What do you mean?"

She shut her eyes. *Don't play with me, Kadir.* "Why is it that your guards are always killed and you aren't? Why would Galatea leave you alive?"

"I'm a Guardian—"

"That didn't stop her from killing the Reverend, now did it?"

Kadir said nothing, letting his hands fall to his sides.

Damaris felt her throat tighten. "Why, Kadir? Why would you *let* her go through your Gate? Why didn't you try to stop her?"

Deny it. Deny it. Tell me I'm wrong.

His shoulders slumped. Whether he was tired of lying or whether he realized she knew the truth, he didn't bother to deny it. "She threatened me. She threatened all of Khae, Damaris!"

She felt a sudden surge of anger. So he was afraid. That was it. "You are a Guardian, Kadir!" she snapped. "You swore an oath. You should have tried to stop her. Damn the consequences." *And damn you.*

"She destroyed Malenwar! By destroying a Gate, Damaris. There is a Gate right here." He flung his arm out toward the temple entrance. "What's to stop her from doing it again?"

"*You!*" Damaris shouted. "You are there to stop her. That is your job, that is why you are the Guardian of this Gate!"

"Yes, it is my job. I swore an oath to defend Wysteria and its people and if I can keep Galatea from destroying all of Khae by letting her go through my Gate, then I think I'm upholding that oath, now aren't I?"

Damaris sighed, tamping her anger down. "All right. I can understand that. But why didn't you get help? Why didn't you tell anyone? Why didn't you come to me? I would have helped you."

And that was the worst part of all. He knew she would have come to his aid, as a friend and fellow Guardian. He'd always known he could rely on her and yet he hadn't. He hadn't trusted her to help him in his time of need.

"Would you?" he muttered.

Something snapped inside of Damaris, the fire she had just tamped down bursting back to life. It was one thing to let fear get the better of him, but how *dare* he question *her* loyalty?

"I'm not afraid of her, even if you are," she snarled, taking a menacing step forward. "The Kadir I *thought* I knew would have laid down his life if that's what it took. He would have fought, not cowered and run away with his tail between his legs. No, if it was fear alone that made you capitulate, you'd have told someone, but you didn't. So what was it, Kadir? Why did you *really* help her?"

Now he looked angry as well. "You wouldn't understand."

"What wouldn't I understand? Try me."

He laughed and the sound was slightly derisive. "You don't have any pity for weakness, Damaris."

"Then I suggest you tell me, sooner rather than later."

"I felt sorry for her!" Kadir exploded. "Humans have come into Wysteria before. Jack shouldn't have been killed like that. I advised caution, but the rest of you rushed in blindly and decided that because you didn't want him here, because he wasn't like the rest of us, you were better off killing him!"

"*I* didn't kill him. Galatea knew the rules and she broke them."

"She's been gone for fifty years, Damaris! Coming back to Wysteria is not a crime."

Damaris glared at him. She could feel her vision turning red at the edges and fought to keep control of her temper. Emotions could be a powerful tool in aiding magic if used correctly, but they also could cause it to rampage out of control. And her emotions were never far beneath the surface.

"No," she ground out between her teeth. "But she destroyed all of Malenwar and killed an untold number of people. She killed your guards. She massacred a fort. *For God's sake*, Kadir, she's raising the dead!"

"I didn't think she'd go to those extremes."

"Then you're a fool as well as a liar and a coward."

"I didn't want to do it… You must believe me, Damaris."

But she didn't. There was a part of him that had wanted to help Galatea because he sympathized with her for whatever reason.

She said nothing, thinking silence might unnerve him more.

"She was my friend," he added, the fight gone out of him. Now he was reduced to pleading. "She was yours, too."

"Would a friend threaten you?" Damaris countered. "How could you do this, Kadir?" In spite of her best efforts, some of the hurt she felt at his betrayal bled through in her voice.

"I was afraid of her!"

"Who are you more afraid of? Galatea or me?"

Kadir blanched, as if only now fully realizing the situation he found himself in. "What are you going to do?"

Cassius was right. She should drag him back to the palace, where he could stand trial and be punished. But Damaris couldn't bring herself to do that. Even now, faced with what he'd done, she believed that there had to be some goodness left in him, some remnant of the Kadir she'd known.

But that didn't mean she could let it go. Something had to be done.

She looked at him. His hands were raised toward her as though she were a wild animal, unpredictable, just as likely to flee in terror as to bite.

She chose the latter.

Flames sprang to life on one of his outstretched hands and he cried out, snatching them back. Her fire burned out as quickly as it had come, leaving behind reddened, blistered flesh.

Kadir clutched the wrist of his wounded hand, trembling, breathing heavily. The fire was gone, but the pain remained. Though she could not be burned herself, Damaris knew how terrible fire could be, how horrible its wounds. He would not be able to ignore the pain and it would remind him of what he had done—or failed to do.

"Consider that a warning," Damaris told him. She could do nothing until she spoke to Lylla. "Remember your oath. If Galatea returns, I suggest you fight to the death to stop her from crossing through your Gate again. Maybe then you can redeem yourself. And if you cannot, God help you, Kadir. You'd better hope Galatea kills you before I do."

She moved past him without another glance.

He called after her. *"Kirena!" My friend.* The pain in his voice nearly made her stop.

Damaris looked over her shoulder. "Don't call me that!" she snarled. "You've no right to call me that. You forfeited our friendship the moment you threw your lot in with *her!*"

She increased her pace to a gallop, eager for the first time in her life to leave the desert behind, perhaps forever. She realized that her parting words were true and how much they hurt.

Kadir had always invited her to Khae's festivals. He had made her feel welcome. They had traveled down the city's sandy streets at dusk, walking side by side and just talking or enjoying the view.

And now they never would again.

Damaris would never admit how much his betrayal hurt, and that only served to fuel her anger. It was easier to feel angry than sad.

It felt like she had lost a part of herself. She had so few friends and now she had one less.

But anyone who sides with Galatea is no friend of mine.

***

Galatea was disappointed in Noraak for having failed to acquire the stone from the girl, but she supposed that one positive had come of it—he hadn't been stupid enough to get himself caught. He had heard someone else coming into the room and wisely fled while he had the chance. He couldn't risk being spotted by Lylla, who might see through his illusion.

And he had brought a horse from the palace stable that he'd used to escape. Galatea had been searching through the reflections some more and was determined to try again, just not today. It would be too soon and the weather wasn't ideal.

But, oh, how she hated waiting!

Ever since she had raised Jack from his grave, her patience had all but dried up. She sighed, glancing over to where he sat on a chunk of fallen stone. His glowing green eyes stared sightlessly forward. She looked away, hardly able to bear seeing him in such a state.

All she wanted was the Jack she knew and remembered back. The one she had taught to laugh again, the one she had given hope. One way or another, she was going to get her hands on that stone and bring Jack back as the man she'd known. And then, together, they were going to watch the world burn.

But they couldn't do it alone.

With the Echo Stone safe at the palace, there was nothing to lure Galatea back to Earth. It was only a matter of time before Lylla sent some of her soldiers after her and Galatea knew she would need more soldiers of her own. More than those she'd already raised. Even with their ranks, her Nightmares, and fire wolves, it wouldn't be enough.

It was time she paid the Necropolis a visit. She got up and gestured for Noraak to follow. She might need his help getting there.

The Necropolis had not been in the center of the city, but near the western edge. For centuries, the citizens of Malenwar had interred their dead here and so there would be plenty of soldiers for her to raise.

The above-ground building that stood on top of the site had been obliterated in the Cataclysm and a large stone slab had fallen partly over the entrance that led below ground. Noraak moved it out of the way, exposing a narrow staircase that spiraled down into the earth.

Galatea went first, her Shadowblade hanging at her side. She summoned flames to her palm to light the darkness around them. The blackness was complete, stretching away into the stillness. The air was musty, not having been breathed by any living creature in fifty years. It grew colder the further they descended.

Their footsteps echoed as they walked, careful to take their time. The steps were narrow and without rails. The floor was too far down to make out. It could have been twenty feet or two hundred. Either way, Galatea didn't fancy plummeting to her death.

Occasionally, they stepped out onto a slab of rock that acted as a platform for whatever level they were on. Thus far, they had passed three. The platform led to each of the niches for coffins to be placed in.

The flames weakly illuminated the walls on each platform, revealing niche upon niche and the coffins contained within, covered in cobwebs.

Galatea placed her foot on the next stone step and it fell out from under her. She cried out in surprise and felt herself begin to pitch forward, but then Noraak was there, steadying her.

A second later, there came a thud as the stone collided with the floor. Galatea nodded her thanks to Noraak and they continued on their way. She breathed a sigh of relief as they reached the bottom, solid earth beneath their feet.

She peered upward, but with the twisting staircase and the rock platforms, she could no longer see the exit. *That's fine. This will only take a moment.*

She'd memorized the spell from the grimoire by heart. She extinguished her flame and began, voice echoing in the darkness.

A moment later, the coffins began lighting up green, suffusing the Necropolis with necromantic light.

***

The rain had stopped by early afternoon and the sun peeked out from behind the clouds. Felix had left the library behind hours ago and was now outside where he felt more comfortable, being a wood elf. He took a stroll through the garden, thinking back to what Sara had said about his reading the books.

But you're an elf. You have all the time in the world.

From the moment she'd said them, the words had haunted him and he'd been unable to get them out of his head all day.

Ordinarily, what she said would be true. But Venryk had ensured that for him, it wasn't. But he couldn't tell her that.

They'd only known each other for a handful of days and he didn't have the heart to correct her. To tell her the depressing truth. What purpose would it serve other than to further dampen her spirits?

She was already stuck here, likely against her will, no matter how enchanting she might find Wysteria. She, like everyone else, had her own demons to contend with and he wouldn't add to her burden by confessing his.

But the truth was that he didn't have all the time in the world. He was slowly dying even now as he strolled through the garden. Even as he stared across the water at the fading sunset, even as he filled his lungs with air. And one day, though there was no way of knowing how far in the future it might be, one breath would be his last.

And he would die.

Unless he killed Venryk first.

Part of him felt bad for not telling Sara, as if he was keeping a secret from her. She deserved to know the truth. And he did want to tell her, to get it off his chest, even though it was no secret to any Wysterian.

What did it feel like to die, he wondered? It wasn't something he, as an elf, should ever have to think about. Was this how humans felt, knowing their days were numbered, their bodies would age and eventually give out? Of knowing you only had so much time left and every moment, another little piece of it slipped away, gone forever?

Felix sighed, feeling a familiar melancholy wash over him, the pain that was an old friend if not a welcome one.

Life was a precious gift. If only he hadn't been so careless with his.

He looked up as Damaris walked through the Glowing Gate and made her way toward the palace. Her head hung low and her tail drooped, so unlike the Flame Guardian he'd come to know.

Something was wrong.

He left the garden behind and followed after her, old worries replaced with new.

14

Cassius was already there when Damaris met Lylla in the reception hall. The shadow elf looked grim, but said nothing as she approached.

"Cassius tells me that you believe Kadir to be a traitor," Lylla said, her eyes flicking past Damaris as Felix entered behind her. "Is this true?"

"It's true," Damaris muttered. She hadn't thought she had it in her to turn Kadir in to the queen, but her anger at his betrayal had burned away any such reservations. "He admitted it."

"Why?" Lylla demanded, a rare spark of anger flashing in her eyes. "Why would he do such a thing?"

Damaris sighed and related the conversation she'd had with Kadir, then added, "I gave him a warning, but for the time being, he's still the Guardian of that Gate."

"We can't leave him there," Cassius protested. "We can't trust him to guard the Gate. He's already proven himself to be unreliable. Kadir is a traitor to crown and country. He should be stripped of his position immediately."

"I agree," Lylla murmured. "This warrants some form of punishment. We can't leave him there. But neither can we leave the Gate unguarded and seeing how we don't have another Guardian who can readily replace him, I'm afraid he will retain his position for the time being."

"If we leave him there, he'll continue to allow Galatea to slip between worlds as she sees fit!" Cassius protested.

"What would you have me do, Cassius?" Lylla asked. "We don't have any Guardians to spare and only a Guardian would have a chance at stopping her."

"I'll go," Damaris offered.

"You have your own Gate."

"My Gate is hidden, its location known only to a select few. The Wind Gate *cannot* be left unattended. It's too much of a security risk."

"I need you here," Lylla argued, but Damaris could tell the queen's resolve was crumbling.

"I can handle Galatea, if she returns to the Wind Gate," Damaris pointed out. In fact, she secretly hoped that the forsaken Guardian would come. What a surprise she'd receive when she saw the Flame Guardian and not Kadir. The look on her face would make it all almost worth it.

On the one hand, Damaris didn't like the idea of running off to the desert any more than Lylla did. If she were to commit herself to protecting the Wind Gate, she wouldn't be able to leave it. It was so very different from her experience with her own Gate, which she could leave at any time, and often did, for long periods. She wasn't used to having her freedom of movement limited.

But she would do it. To stop Galatea. To protect Wysteria and Khae, the city she loved.

She only wished she could trust Kadir to have a change of heart and do his duty, but she couldn't rely on that.

Lylla sighed. "Very well, Ris. I trust you to handle it."

"I've been thinking," Damaris added. She hadn't had time for much else during her journey back. "With the Wind Gate secured, Galatea has no path back to Earth, which means we can send Sara safely back home and Galatea would be trapped here."

"Oh, yes," Cassius mused. "I've heard about the human you brought here."

"A necessity, I assure you," Lylla said, her tone slightly chilly. "You could have a point, Damaris. Galatea has been running the show from the moment she returned. If we can trap her here in Wysteria, at least the battle can be fought on our terms. I'll talk to Sara about it."

***

The meeting broke up and Lylla went to find Sara. She found her in the dining room, speaking with Colin. The two ceased their conversation and looked up as she entered.

"I have good news," she announced. "And bad news. I suppose I should give you the bad first." She pulled out one of the chairs and sat down. "Kadir has betrayed us."

Colin paled, but Sara looked confused. "Who?"

"Oh, I'm sorry. I should have explained. He's the Wysterian Guardian of the Wind Gate, the same Gate that the Professor guards."

"How did he betray us?"

"It appears that he willingly let Galatea through his Gate more than once, which explains how she was able to cross between worlds so easily, and of course, that's forbidden."

"And the good news?"

Lylla brightened. "We have figured out a way to safely send you home."

Sara's eyes widened, her pulse quickening at the possibility. "How?"

"Damaris is going to replace Kadir at the Wind Gate. With all of the Gates secured, Galatea will be trapped here in Wysteria and unable to cross over, which means that you can go home and she won't be able to reach you."

Sara could hardly believe it. She'd expected to be stuck here for weeks, possibly longer. But Lylla was offering her a chance, a way to get back home. And she'd take it wholeheartedly.

Part of her felt a prick of guilt at the idea of going home, where it was safe, and leaving all of them to fight a sorceress. But there was nothing she could do to help. She wasn't a Guardian like Damaris or Professor Lawrence. She wasn't one of them.

"It's worth a try," Sara said quietly.

The queen nodded. "I agree. We can send you back this evening."

So soon.

Soon, she would be leaving Wysteria behind forever. One day, far enough in the future, it would seem like a dream and she might wonder if all of this had even happened. She wondered if her mother had ever felt that way.

The hours passed slowly and yet all too quickly as evening approached. Sara desperately wanted to take her mind off her imminent return home. What would she say to her dad? That was something she didn't want to think about.

But she couldn't stop thinking about it, her nerves a bundle of excitement and anxiety. She made her way to the library, hoping a book would help distract her. Even in the fading light, the room was still illuminated. She wondered what it would look like come nightfall. She would be gone before she could find out, but she could imagine it—a haven from the darkness, where it could not touch.

Despite knowing that she didn't belong here, Sara felt strangely sad knowing that she would never see this library again. *It's for the best.*

The door eased open behind her and she turned to find Felix standing there, dressed in his black uniform. "I heard you were leaving this evening."

She nodded, trying to read the emotion in his green eyes, but couldn't. "Yeah."

"Well…" He looked down at his boots.

"So…" she drawled, then laughed at herself.

He gave her a wry look. "Well, I wish you luck."

"Same to you."

For a moment, she thought Felix looked like he wanted to say more, then changed his mind. He nodded to her and left the way he'd come, closing the door behind him.

As the sun set, the light leaching out of the sky and darkness descending, Sara went out into the courtyard, roaming through the gardens, resolved to wait until someone came to fetch her and told her it was time to go.

She didn't really want to encounter anyone; it would only make the goodbyes that much harder. But she couldn't help but think of Felix and their brief encounter in the library only a few hours earlier. She would never know what it was that he was holding back. *That's his decision to make, not yours.*

Sara couldn't force him to open up if he didn't want to. It was none of her business, but at the same time, she couldn't help but be curious, perhaps morbidly so. It wasn't a very attractive realization.

She looked up. *Oh, no.* As though conjured by her thoughts, Felix was walking through the grass toward her.

For a brief moment, she considered hiding behind one of the bushes, but that was absurd! And besides, he'd very likely already seen her; he was heading straight toward her.

Sara didn't really want to avoid him. That would be ridiculous and rude. Perhaps he'd reconsidered and wanted to tell her something important, which she'd never learn by running away.

He jerked his head toward the Glowing Gate as he reached her. "Come on, there's something I want to show you."

Her pulse quickened. "Is it time?" Was Lylla waiting for her at the Lightning Gate?

He stared at her for a moment. "Yes. Come on."

Felix began walking away and Sara followed him, having to hurry slightly to keep up with his long strides. Her head only came up to his shoulder. She'd never considered herself short—average, really—but she certainly felt it compared to him.

The guards at the Glowing Gate nodded to him and the Gate swung open. Felix stepped through, heading for the forest. The dying warmth of the sun on her skin faded as they entered the forest's thick embrace.

"Is this safe?" Sara asked.

She'd never set foot outside the palace from the moment she'd arrived. She didn't know if they would have let her if she'd asked—she never had—but the answer would almost certainly have been no.

"Of course," Felix reassured her. "It's not far."

Sara remembered the day she'd set foot in Wysteria, having been pushed through the Lightning Gate. It hadn't been a far walk. She forced herself to relax and take in her surroundings. It looked almost exactly the same as it had the night she'd arrived—utterly beautiful, but she could see how one could easily get lost in its depths and she stuck close to Felix.

She had dressed in her own clothes, again the same as she had worn that night, and she soon wished she had chosen a different pair of shoes, at least for the walking bit. Flip flops were not ideal for trekking through woodland and her feet soon began to hurt.

How long have we been walking? We should have reached it by now, surely.

The realization struck her with growing dread. She had been wearing flip flops the night she'd first come here and traveled with Felix to the palace. She didn't remember her feet hurting then. *Because we didn't walk this far.*

She swallowed, feeling unease claw at her. "Where are we going?" she asked, since it clearly wasn't to the Lightning Gate like she'd thought.

"It's not far now," he replied.

Sara tried to fight down her mounting fear. Felix would have told her where they were going, surely? Unless he intended for it to be a surprise.

Still, if that were the case, she'd rather have the surprise spoiled. She'd never be able to enjoy it if she were so nervous.

"I think you'd better tell me now," she persisted.

"That'll ruin the surprise."

So it is *a surprise.*

Felix stopped suddenly and Sara nearly bumped into him. She peered around him to see what had held him up or if they had reached their destination. Her heart leapt to her throat and threatened to stop altogether.

Five fire wolves were blocking their path, Venryk in the lead. Well, that was definitely a surprise, albeit an unwanted one. Felix had his bow slung over his back and Sara turned to him, wondering what she should do. Did he want her to run or—

She froze. None of Felix's scars were glowing. Not a single one.

Her eyes flicked to Venryk and back rapidly. Yes, it was definitely him, so why weren't the scars glowing like they had before? Like Felix had said?

Sara's stomach clenched as realization hit and a memory came flooding back to her. Of Professor Lawrence's voice being wrong and the way he walked. Felix's scars would have glowed—if it had been him.

She turned to run but a hand clamped onto her wrist and she yelped. Felix—or not-Felix—had grabbed ahold of her.

"Give me the Echo Stone," he growled, pulling her closer. "And I'll let you go."

Over his shoulder, she could see the wolves approaching. "Let me go!" she shrieked, trying to twist out of his grip but he was too strong. "Help!" she screamed at the trees, hoping there was someone in the forest nearby who could hear her. "Someone help me! Lylla!"

Her cries were cut off as his other hand closed around her throat. She scrabbled at his hand, trying desperately to lessen his grasp, but it was no use.

Go for the eyes, is what people always said.

Sara flung one hand up toward his face. The light had faded from the sky, the forest plunged into darkness. It was growing darker by the minute, her vision fading.

A moment later, the world lit up white.

***

"Sara!" Lylla called, her voice echoing down the hall, but there was no answer. There'd been no response each time she'd called.

Where could the girl have gone? She knew the plan.

She turned at the sound of footsteps to see Felix striding her way. "Oh, Felix. Have you seen Sara?"

His brow furrowed. "No, why? Is she missing?"

"It appears so. I can't find her anywhere."

"You don't suppose she went ahead to the Lightning Gate, do you?"

"I can't imagine why she'd do so on her own. Do you suppose she could even find it by herself? I'd better check with the guards. You go ahead to Wanderer's Gate and see if she's there."

Lylla hurried to the doors, taking the stone steps two at a time, lifting her skirts so she didn't trip on them. She strode toward the Glowing Gate, then decided she wasn't moving fast enough and morphed into her unicorn form.

"Have you seen Sara?" she demanded, not giving the guards time to address her.

"Yes," one replied. "She came through here not that long ago with Felix."

"With Fe—But he's here at the palace. I just saw him." Her eyes widened, adrenaline shooting through her veins.

There was no doubt in her mind that Sara had indeed come through the Glowing Gate, accompanied by someone who *looked* like Felix. Galatea must have employed her illusion trick again, this time with far more success.

Even if Sara refused to hand over the stone, if her minions dragged her to Galatea, the sorceress had ways of convincing her otherwise.

Blast. She had to hand it to Galatea—this attempt had been far cleverer than her last. Rather than trying to convince the girl to part with the stone, all she needed to do was lure her outside of the Gate and its protection.

"Open the Gate!" Lylla cried. "She's in danger and we have to find her!"

There was no time to lose. It might already be too late.

***

The hand around Sara's throat let go instantly and she fell to the ground, gasping. A ragged cry of pain rang out, but the sound hadn't issued from her lips. She wasn't sure if she could make a sound even if she tried.

She blinked. Felix was gone, replaced by a dark-haired male elf lying at her feet, writhing in pain. She looked up at the wolves, who were shaking their heads in a disoriented manner.

Sara couldn't stop to ponder what had just happened. She scrambled to her feet and ran. She had no idea how far they'd come or how to find her way back. The forest really was like a maze, and the darkness didn't help, but all that mattered now was putting as much distance between her and them.

Hopefully, she'd run into someone friendly, who could help.

She'd never considered herself very athletic, but more of the bookish type and she was regretting it now. A stitch had formed in her side and her lungs were burning as she gasped for air—it never felt like enough. But she didn't dare stop.

She kept expecting to glance over her shoulder and see the wolves right behind her. They weren't, but that didn't alleviate her fear. She cast a quick glance over her shoulder again, wondering what she would do if they caught up to her. Should she climb a tree?

Sara stumbled over a fallen branch and let out a sob. Her strength was almost spent, there was no sign of the palace or any Gate, and no one had answered her pleas for help—

The sound of thundering hoofbeats made her stagger to a halt. The large black horse stopped in front of her and Felix dismounted. "Sara?"

She scrambled back away from him, arms raised. "Stay away from me!" she cried, but her voice sounded more like a croak.

He stopped, hands held out before him. "Sara, it's me."

She wanted to believe him. Wanted to believe that she was safe with him, that he would take her back to the palace, but she couldn't. She couldn't risk that the other elf had circled around, cutting her off, and regaining his disguise. She didn't know how he would have obtained the horse, but then she remembered that the last time the imposter had been at the palace, he had stolen a horse and used it to escape. Was this that horse?

"It's me," he repeated, taking another step forward.

"Prove it," she countered.

He stopped, pressing his lips together. Sara didn't know how he could prove such a thing and it was possible he didn't either.

The left side of his face lit up as his scars began to glow red. Felix hissed softly, eyes darting around.

Sara visibly wilted with relief. "Felix—" She whirled around as the fire wolves burst into view, stopping only a few feet from her. Letting out a yelp, she ran toward Felix.

"Get on the horse," Felix hissed, yanking his bow off his back and nocking it. "Ride back to the palace."

"What about you?" Sara protested. "And I can't ride a horse. He's too big for me."

"Tempest, kneel!"

Behind him, the large black horse knelt down onto his forelegs, allowing her easy access onto his back.

"But—*oh, hell,*" Sara muttered, sticking her foot in the stirrup, grabbing the saddle for support, and swinging herself up onto the horse's back. She gasped as the horse rose to his full height. "Felix, come on!"

She had no doubt that he could handle one or two. Maybe even three. But not all of them.

He hesitated, then let out a sharp whistle. Sara cried out as the horse sprang forward. Felix turned his back on the wolves and sprinted forward, looping his foot in one stirrup and using the stallion's momentum to haul himself into the saddle behind Sara.

The fire wolves sprang forward to give chase. Sara gripped the reins while Felix held on using only his legs. She wanted to squeeze her eyes shut, but that would only make it all more terrifying. She could feel the power of the horse beneath her as his strides lengthened. They were moving at a full gallop through the trees at night.

She felt Felix shift behind her, heard the *twang* of a bowstring being released and an answering yelp of pain as the arrow found its target.

Sara turned to see how close the wolves were—and how many were left—and screamed as one wolf lunged at them. Out of the corner of her eye, she saw a white streak rapidly approaching and then Damaris was there, throwing herself between them and slamming into the lunging wolf.

Felix reined Tempest to a halt. Damaris stood between them, breathing hard, teeth bared, exposing a set of fangs. At once, the wolves whirled and scattered into the trees. But Venryk paused, glancing over his shoulder, his eyes not on Sara, strangely, but Felix.

Damaris snorted, rearing up onto her hind legs and lashing out in his direction with her forelegs. The wolf turned and followed the others. Sara felt the force as the unicorn's hooves slammed back onto the ground.

A second set of hoofbeats rang out and they saw Lylla before she reached them, the light trailing around her creating a warm glow amid the darkness.

"All in order I see," she said as she reached them. "Are you all right? Are you hurt, either of you?"

Felix brusquely shook his head, removing the arrow from his bowstring.

"I'm all right," Sara said, her voice trembling in spite of herself.

"Do you still have the Echo Stone?"

Sara reached into her shirt, pulling it out so that it caught the light emanating off of Lylla, grateful that the queen had asked after her safety before ascertaining whether or not she still had the amplifier.

Lylla let out a sigh and turned to Damaris. "What are you doing here? I thought you'd left for the Wind Gate."

"I had." Damaris glanced at Sara. "I'll tell you later."

Each of them looked up as movement caught their attention. Wanderer was marching forward, her hands wrapped vise-like around the arm of a young black-haired elf. Sara gasped as she recognized him.

"Thought I heard voices," Wanderer said cheerfully. "Found him wandering around the forest, stumbling like he didn't know where he was going. Or drunk."

"Let me go," the elf pleaded, struggling futilely. His gaze was fixed straight ahead. He didn't acknowledge any of them, as though he couldn't even see them.

"Who is he?" Lylla asked.

"He's the elf Damaris and I saw in the swamp," Felix said, at the same time Sara said, "He's the elf who attacked me."

Lylla's eyes narrowed and she stepped forward. "He's been blinded."

She and Damaris shared a glance that made Sara uneasy.

"What should I do with him?" Wanderer asked.

"Take him to the palace and have him secured. If he is indeed working with Galatea, I imagine he will have much to tell us."

"Come on, you," Wanderer growled, jerking the elf away.

Damaris watched them until they were out of sight and then turned back to Lylla. The unicorn was even taller than the black stallion. "I think I'll delay my trip, if you don't mind."

Lylla nodded to her and then addressed Sara. "I think, given what's happened here, it would be best to postpone sending you through the Gate for the time being. Let's get back to the palace."

Felix slung his bow on his back. With deft fingers on the reins, he turned Tempest to follow after Wanderer, with Lylla and Damaris bringing up the rear.

Only now did Sara begin to relax, the adrenaline fading from her body, leaving her trembling. Her thoughts had shut down, leaving only survival mode, and she struggled to make sense of everything that had happened.

"You're shaking," Felix whispered.

"I'm all right," Sara insisted, though she knew she wasn't.

She was still shaken by what had happened and it was hard to convince herself that she was out of danger now. Tempest's gentle swaying gait as he walked helped to calm her a little.

But despite the warm night air, she couldn't stop shivering, her muscles releasing all the coiled energy they'd contained mere moments ago.

She was acutely aware of Felix's presence behind her. She'd never been so close to a guy before, her back occasionally bumping against his chest as the horse moved.

His arms had to reach partially around her to hold the reins, but she found she didn't mind.

She sighed, leaning back against him, and closed her eyes.

15

Upon returning to the palace, Lylla turned to Sara and said briefly, "We can discuss what has happened later. Make yourself comfortable inside. I know you must have many questions, but I must attend to other matters."

Felix helped Sara off Tempest's back and walked inside with her. Lylla reverted to her elven form and followed. It wouldn't matter what form she assumed; the captured shadow elf would be unable to see her anyway on account of his blindness. Wanderer met her in the hall.

"What have you done with the prisoner?"

"Put him in the cellar," Wanderer said proudly. "Not much chance of him escaping what with him being blind and all, but I left Damaris with him. I figured our voices would get a real nice echo down there during the interrogation and it'd rattle him a bit."

"Good," Lylla replied, following Wanderer to the trap door that led to the wine cellars beneath the palace. "I'd rather not have to use force unless he gives me no other choice."

As they went down the steps, Wanderer paused and held up a hand mirror. "I found this on him."

Lylla took it, careful not to peer into the glass. "Well, now we know how he was able to disguise himself as someone else."

Ordinarily, the cellar was dark, but there were lanterns hung on the pillars that supported the ceiling. Lylla suspected that Damaris had lit a few, the orange flames flickering behind the glass. She waved a hand and the lamps that had yet to be lit sprang to life, casting a golden glow to chase back the darkness. The flickering of the fire in the other lamps cast strange shadows. The air was faintly musty, the walls lined with casks.

The shadow elf knelt in the middle of the room, a pair of iron shackles around his wrists, the direct contact with the iron preventing him from using any magic against them. He was younger than Lylla had first assumed, his black hair chopped unevenly. But that changed nothing.

Damaris was standing over to one side and she flicked one black-tipped ear. Wanderer moved to the prisoner's left and looked to Lylla to begin the questioning.

She took a deep breath. "What is your name?"

It was a safe enough question to begin with and the shadow elf saw no reason not to answer it. "Noraak."

"Well, Noraak, care to explain why you took the guise of one of my Shadows and attempted to kidnap the human girl?"

She already knew the most likely answer, but she wanted to hear him say it. The elf hesitated and Damaris glanced in Lylla's direction, seeking permission to use force. Lylla held up one hand, forestalling her. "I advise you, Noraak, that it's in your best interest to answer our questions."

Wanderer opened her palm and lightning crackled along her fingertips, sparking menacingly. The blinded shadow elf couldn't see the electricity, but he could hear it and he cringed away from the sound.

"It was Galatea's idea! She told me to get the Echo Stone from the girl."

"Why does she want the Echo Stone?"

"She needs to it resurrect Jack. Well, to fully resurrect him. She's already done it once."

Lylla fingered the hand mirror's handle. "We found this mirror on your person. What is it and where did Galatea get it?"

"I don't know what it is," Noraak said, cringing as though he feared his less-than-satisfactory answer would bring an electric shock. "Galatea didn't tell me, she just told me what to do. She read about it in her book. She must have stolen it from the Professor; she came back from his house with it."

"Did she steal anything else from the Professor?"

He nodded. "A Shadowblade and a crown."

"A crown?" Wanderer exclaimed. "What would she need that for?"

Noraak hesitated, but Damaris didn't. The elf let out a screech as the soles of his feet began to sizzle and blister, the cellar taking on the smell of seared meat. Lylla wrinkled her nose. It was crude, but one couldn't deny that Damaris's methods got results.

"She gave it to the Icelandic dragons!" Noraak cried. "But that's all I know. I swear!"

At once, the sizzling faded. Lylla healed the singed flesh with a wave of her hand. She was dimly aware that, should Noraak have proven to be uncooperative, they could have harmed then healed him, only to repeat the process over and over. Galatea would have been fond of that method. Lylla was not.

This was alarming news. If Galatea had paid the mountain dragons a visit, it couldn't have been for anything good. *Seeking additional allies, no doubt.* It would warrant a visit to the Icelandic dragons when this was over.

"What are her plans?" Lylla asked. "What is Galatea doing in the swamp?"

"Raising an army of the dead, but that's not all. She's created Nightmares."

"Nightmares?" Damaris repeated. "What are they?"

"I don't know exactly. They were horses once, but they're terrible now." Anger suddenly appeared on Noraak's face, twisting his mouth into a sneer. "Terrible things await you in there. Horrible, unspeakable things!"

Damaris bared her teeth, fangs on full display, even though the elf couldn't see her.

"I haven't heard any reports of these creatures," Lylla said softly, meant for Damaris's ears only. "But I have heard that there seem to be an increase in the thorns around the border of the swamp."

"Undoubtedly due to Felix and I snooping around. I don't think Galatea appreciated my incinerating some of her minions."

Noraak reached up to rub at his face. "My eyes," he moaned. "I've told you what you want to know. Will you fix my eyes?"

"About your eyes," Lylla said quickly. "What happened to them?"

He hesitated once more.

She crossed her arms. "Tell us and I'll consider your request."

"I don't know," Noraak said again, only this time, his voice came out as a near wail. "One moment, I've got ahold of the girl and she's struggling and screaming for help. So I reached for her in order to shut her up and she starts clawing at my eyes. The next thing I know there's a light flaring beneath her fingers and there's this searing pain, I hear an explosion, and then I can't see anything."

Lylla could feel Wanderer's and Damaris's eyes on her. She knew what had happened, having done it before herself. It was the most common defensive tactic of a light attribute, to blind their opponent. It was equally useful in both offense and defense. If your opponent couldn't see you, they couldn't chase you, giving you the opportunity to escape. But they also couldn't see or anticipate any incoming attacks.

"That's why I came back," Damaris murmured to her. "I was on my way to the Wind Gate when I saw the explosion. I thought it was you, that something had gone wrong when you tried to send Sara back."

Lylla had seen the explosion as well. A flash of white light emerging from the forest, a shockwave accompanying it.

She frowned. This complicated things. "You've been most informative, Noraak."

She turned to leave and he must have heard the swish of her dress because he crawled forward. "No! Don't leave me here!"

Lylla ignored him, gesturing for Wanderer and Damaris to follow her. "What are we going to do with him?" Wanderer asked, glancing over her shoulder at him.

"I say we kill him," Damaris hissed. "If he had delivered Sara into Galatea's hands, she might have killed her!"

"I'll have him transferred to the cells," Lylla replied. "We'll keep him in custody for the time being. He could be useful."

"Well, destroy the mirror, at least. It's a dangerous tool and shouldn't be in anyone's hands."

"I'm inclined to agree. You can see to its shattering, if you like."

"I'll do it!" Wanderer exclaimed, snatching it out of Lylla's outstretched hand.

"Very well."

There was a slight pause as they stepped back up into the light of the palace interior and the trapdoor slammed back down, cutting off Noraak's piteous wails.

"What are we going to do about the dragons?" Wanderer asked, clutching the mirror. "You heard what he said. We can't allow them to side with Galatea. We'll have to…*convince* them otherwise."

"I would go—" Damaris offered.

"But you have a Gate to protect," Lylla finished. "And that's where you're needed. I will go."

Wanderer pointed at her with the mirror. "You?"

"Why not? It'll be good to get out of the palace for a bit, even if it is to venture into a place as unpleasant as Iceland. Besides, it might be best to handle this one sovereign to another, so to speak. Now, I must go speak to Sara about what's happened." Lylla began to walk briskly down the hall, but stopped to call over her shoulder, "And Wanderer? Make sure you shatter that mirror. I don't want it used for any pranks."

***

Sara's pulse had finally quieted once she'd stepped back inside the palace. They had apprehended the culprit, who disguised himself as others, and the threat was gone. Felix had stayed with her and so had Colin, who had fetched her a cup of tea.

She knew they probably wanted nothing more than to go to bed. It was well after dark by now. She wanted the same thing, but was still far too alert to even think that sleep would come.

Her fingers strayed to the chain around her neck, as though reassuring herself that, after everything, it was still there. Even after the first impersonation attempt, she hadn't fully appreciated the lengths Galatea was willing to go to in order to acquire the stone. Little wonder Lylla had been reluctant to send her home. The sorceress would have followed her there. She shuddered to think what would have happened if Galatea had gotten ahold of *her*.

Fortunately, she didn't have long to entertain such thoughts. Lylla entered the room and sat down on the sofa beside Sara. They had retreated to the sitting room due to its more comfortable setting. Colin sat in a chair off to one side, Felix on the sofa to her right.

"Has he said anything?" Felix asked.

Lylla nodded. "Yes. How are you feeling, Sara?"

"Better," she replied, sipping her tea. It had been too hot when she'd first been given it, but had cooled off now.

"Good. I know it may be distressing, but I'm afraid I must ask you to recount what happened earlier."

Sara sighed and began, starting with being approached by who she had believed to be Felix and being lured out of the Glowing Gate and ending with when she'd been found by the real Felix.

"How did you get away from him?"

"I…I tried fighting, but that didn't work, so I thought maybe if I went for the eyes… And then there was this flash and a scream and he let go of me. I didn't stick around to see what happened after that, I just ran."

"A wise decision," Lylla agreed. "I've spoken to the shadow elf. His name is Noraak and he is of the opinion that you caused that flash of light."

"Me?" Sara repeated, blinking at her.

"I think he's right in his assumption."

Sara gaped at her, then looked at Felix, whose expression she was unable to read, and Colin, who looked rather grave. She laughed. "But that's impossible! How could I do that?"

"The same way I can," Lylla said softly, holding up her palm. Light flared softly, nowhere near as bright as the flash that had blinded Noraak. But there was no doubt that it was emanating from her palm and not simply landing on her skin from another light source.

"But the explosion," Sara protested, "that was you."

"No, Sara. I didn't know where you were until the world lit up and I knew where to go."

Sara stared at the light in the queen's hand. "But I don't have any magic. I'm a human."

"You do if you're a Guardian," Lylla said, closing her hand into a fist. The light burned for a moment more before going out. "And you are."

"But…*how*?" Sara exclaimed, setting her cup down on the coffee table, afraid she might drop it if this conversation got any weirder. "How could I suddenly just become a Guardian?"

"You don't *become* a Guardian," Felix said quietly. He wasn't looking at her. "You're born one, even if your magic doesn't manifest at birth—and it doesn't always."

"The Professor suspected you were a Guardian all this time. We just didn't know what your attribute would be," Lylla murmured. "And now we have our answer."

Sara stared at her as if she had suddenly morphed into someone unrecognizable.

"It's not a guarantee, but given that your mother was a Guardian, there was a high chance you would be, too," the queen added.

"My mother was a Guardian?"

"Yes, but she was never assigned to a Gate. All of them already had Guardians assigned to them, so she was never called into service."

"Why didn't Professor Lawrence ever tell me?"

Lylla sighed. "I cannot say for certain, but I suspect, like your mother, he wanted you to be protected, should anything happen."

Sara gripped the sofa cushions hard, feeling like the floor was tilting beneath her. "But I didn't even know that I had magic, much less how to control it. How was I able to blind—err—Noraak?"

"Magic reacts to emotion," Lylla replied. "It was undoubtedly a frightening experience and your magic reacted to that fear."

Sara looked down at her hands, unable to look at any of them. "So what happens now?"

"You'll have to be trained to learn how to control your new powers," Lylla said, standing. "I think it would be best if you didn't return home just yet. Galatea's wolves will have seen what happened and they'll report back to her. If she wasn't after you before, she will be now, for the opportunity to sway a new, inexperienced Guardian to her side…or dispose of the threat you present. All the more reason for you to learn how to wield your element effectively. There's a pressing matter that I must see to presently, but please, if you have any questions or concerns, I want you to feel that you can come to me."

"Thank you," Sara said stiffly, for want of anything better to say. "If it's all the same to you, I think I'll go to my room now."

"Of course. It's late. You should try to get some rest."

It wasn't rest that was on Sara's mind so much as solitude. She couldn't focus on anything, so there was no point in prolonging the conversation. What she needed was time to process everything that had happened.

She stood, shaking—though from what she wasn't sure—and left the room. She knew it was unfair to blame Professor Lawrence, but it felt like a betrayal all the same. What right did he have to decide what she should or should not be told? What she should or should not know? It was making a decision for her and while she understood the sentiment, she did not agree.

She'd thought she'd known him so well and now, in the span of one evening, she felt like she didn't know him at all. But the same could be said of her own mother.

Since coming to Wysteria, she had learned more about herself and her mother and they were both alike in ways she never could have imagined. It made her feel closer to Emily Montgomery in some ways and yet further from her than ever.

Sara had thought she felt the most alone immediately after her mother's death, but if possible, she felt even more alone now. Who had her mother been, really? Had she ever even known? And now she was dead and it was too late to find out.

Her mother should have been there for her, to help her navigate this new revelation in her life, to guide her, to tell her that everything would be okay, and that no matter the challenges ahead, her faith in her daughter would be unshakable.

But Sara's faith in her mother felt like it had been shaken to pieces and faith in herself? Her self was the only thing she could trust right now, but it didn't feel like enough.

She shut the door to her room behind her and collapsed onto the bed, letting the wave of emotion wash over her, making no attempt to hold it back. Part of her half expected her magic to reveal itself again, reacting to the emotion. It was certainly strong enough—as strong as her fear had been, although different.

But nothing happened. No light flared. Her bedroom remained dark.

Her mother should have been there for her. But she wasn't. She was dead, taken too soon, taken in spite of all the doctors had tried, in spite of the best that modern medicine had to offer.

Sara raged against God, against the universe, against fate, whatever one wanted to call it. It wasn't fair! People were cured of cancer all the time. Why not her mom?

She still didn't have an answer for that.

***

That night, Wanderer slipped through her Gate. She knew it was a risk leaving it unattended for even a moment, but she was trusting in the strength of the two Guardians that protected the Lightning Gate. That their reputation would be enough to dissuade Galatea from attempting to cross over.

The gas station was dark when she stepped through, Hank having closed up for the night. Even the neon was unlit, but the man himself was still inside, sweeping the floor before heading home.

He glanced up at her and smiled. "You shouldn't be here. Someone might see you."

"And hello to you, too. Don't be silly. I can glamour myself if it'll make you feel better."

Still, with a wave of her hand, she dispersed the glamour she always wore that gave her the appearance of wolf ears and a tail. She liked being known as the eccentric Guardian—a little crazy, a little unpredictable, like lightning itself—but with Hank, she could be herself.

Hank waved the suggestion away. "We can worry about that if someone comes, though they shouldn't. I'm closed." He sighed, propping the broom up and leaning against it. "How's Sara?"

Wanderer laughed nervously. "Well, you'll never believe it, but guess whose powers manifested today?"

His green eyes widened. "How did she take it?"

She hopped up onto the counter, lying on her stomach and crossing her feet at the ankles as she related the story to him.

Hank shook his head when she'd finished. "Poor girl. I wish there was something I could do to help."

"You're too kind, Hank. You have a soft heart," Wanderer said, not unkindly at all. "She won't be needing our help for much longer. She's a light attribute."

"And a Guardian at that."

"Lucky! That's so rare. I wish I was a light Guardian."

Hank wrinkled his nose at her. "No, you don't."

She sighed dramatically. "You know me too well, Hank. No, I don't. I'm a lightning attribute to my core. And it gives off light, too, so it's practically the same thing."

That wasn't true at all and Wanderer knew it. Lightning and light might share some characteristics but they were a world apart.

"Did you come just to give me an update or were you hoping to coerce me into taking you shopping?"

Wanderer grinned. The idea of escaping to the mall for a night was appealing. She thought back fondly to those evenings that she had ridden in Hank's truck to the nearest city where the mall was. They had roamed around—her glamoured, of course—and made fun of how ugly some of the clothes were, which were precisely the ones she wanted most.

They had gone to the food court and eaten sticky cinnamon rolls until she'd felt sick. She had ridden the carousel even though she was too big for it, glamouring herself to look like a child. The attendant never had a clue. She had laughed at the unicorn ride on the carousel. Earth really had a messed up idea of unicorns.

They were everywhere—from frappes and backpacks, to stickers and little pastry cakes that looked like they ought to be the leading cause of all health problems. White coats with rainbow manes and tails and always accompanied by infernal glitter or rainbows. Or both. Wanderer thought of Damaris's fangs, a strange but terrifying characteristic.

Nope. Ordinary humans didn't have a *clue*.

Wanderer shook herself out of her daydream, reminded of the sober reason she'd come. "No. We're hoping to trap Galatea in Wysteria now that the Wind Gate is secure." She told him about Kadir betraying them and Damaris taking his place. "The plan was to send Sara back home and keep Galatea contained, but it looks like the first part's not happening. Still, security at the Gates is our topmost priority right now. I might not be able to see you for a while."

"Ah," Hank said softly. "It's a good plan. I hope it works."

"What?" Wanderer exclaimed in mock indignation. "That's all you have to say? Aren't you going to miss me?"

Hank never had been a man of many words. She said more than enough for both of them.

"No. Never."

She sat up and crossed her arms. "When did you ever get so sarcastic?"

He tilted his head, looking at her. "Hm, I wonder. Of course, I'll miss you, lassie. You know that."

"I know," she drawled. "I just wanted to hear you say it."

He shook his head again. "I wish I could come with you and help with the fight against Galatea."

"I'm sure we'll be fine," Wanderer tried to reassure him. Secretly, though she in no way doubted his abilities, she was glad that he would be staying here and that Galatea wouldn't be able to get to him.

"And now you have a second Lightbringer. Galatea had better watch out. Just as well, I'm getting too old for this kind of stuff anyway."

Wanderer rolled her eyes. "You're not *that* old."

"You're supposed to say that I'm not old, period, not that I'm not *that* old." Hank propped the broom against the counter and came to stand in front of her, arms on either side.

"I'm older than you," Wanderer pointed out, pushing her thick hair behind one of her elf ears.

She reached out to touch the gray in his beard and a stab of pain went through her. A Guardian he might be, but Hank would still age and die like any other human. Only in Wysteria could he live forever. One day he would be gone and she would still be here. Age did not touch her; her skin remained flawless while there were obvious crow's feet around his eyes, laughter lines around his mouth.

Wanderer had had many lovers over the years, but it never got any easier saying goodbye. She understood how Galatea must have felt—still felt. By now, she ought to have known better than to get her heart involved, to want something she couldn't have, but it was too late now.

"I know," Hank replied, then leaned forward to press his lips against hers, effectively distracting her.

Wanderer looped her arms around his neck, savoring the way his stubble tickled her. Yes, she could understand the way Galatea felt, falling for a human.

As always, their visits were all too brief.

She pulled back. "I should go, before someone notices I'm missing."

He helped her down off the counter. "Be careful over there, lassie. And keep an eye on Sara for me, will you?"

"I will," Wanderer promised.

After all, she's one of us now.

***

Despite Sara's best efforts, sleep refused to come. She was so tired that her eyes ached in the darkness, but the day's events and revelations proved to be too much. She could lie in bed until dawn slipped through the curtains or she could get up and at least try to do something productive with her time.

The palace halls were deserted at such a late hour, the lamps still flickering to light her way. They didn't ever seem to go out. Her steps led her back to the library, to the window seat, where she sat, legs curled up beneath her.

Had her mother ever taken one of the books down from the shelves and sat here, possibly in a similar pose? Sara would never know. There were many things about her mother she would never know. She would have to make peace with that, but she didn't know how. She'd thought, after six months, that she'd begun to accept the fact that her mom was gone, but now she wasn't so sure. All of the progress she'd made had seemingly been swept away, all in the span of one evening.

Sara stared out the window at the courtyard and the sea beyond, bathed in silvery moonlight, blinking back tears as the sight blurred before her. *I wish you could be here. I wish you could explain all of this to me.*

She turned at the sound of footsteps, quickly brushing the tears away. The tread was so quiet on the carpet that she wouldn't have heard it at all if the palace hadn't been so utterly still.

It was Felix, his uniform gone, replaced by plain trousers and a loose white shirt. His feet were bare, his crimson hair mussed.

"You couldn't sleep either," she guessed, moving over on the seat.

He shrugged, accepting the invitation to join her. "Not all that uncommon."

Sara wanted to tell him what she was doing there and she was surprised by the realization of how badly she yearned to share her story. She didn't talk about her mom. The subject was just too painful, too raw, even now. Knowing her luck, she'd start crying and be unable to finish the story, only serving to embarrass herself.

But she so desperately wanted to share some of the pain, to take it off of her chest where it sat, threatening to crush her in her most vulnerable moments. Perhaps that was selfish, but she'd been trying to be strong for so long. It was exhausting.

And there was something about the dim lighting in the library, the way it lent a certain softness to the edges of everything it touched, that seemed to invite confidence.

"I didn't know my mom was a Guardian," she said softly, not looking at him. Somehow that made it easier. "She never told me about any of this. And now it's too late. She died six months ago."

"I know."

Sara turned to him in surprise. "How did you know?"

"Well," Felix grimaced, "I don't know the specifics, but I know the look of someone grieving for one they loved."

She inhaled deeply, breathing in the scent of books, both old and new. Had her pain been that obvious? "I feel like everyone here knew her better than I did. Is that a strange thing to say?"

He shook his head. "I don't think so. That's more or less how I feel about my family."

Sara looked at him, openly, waiting to see if he would volunteer more information, but unwilling to press him.

Felix sighed. "My parents are dead. Venryk killed them."

She almost opened her mouth to offer some platitude and then thought better of it. He wasn't done speaking yet and if he felt like talking, she'd better let him.

"He attacked my village when I was just a child. Burned it to the ground and killed everyone. He'd have killed me, too, if not for Damaris." He paused. "I was so young, I barely remember them. Everyone who knew them had more time with them than I did. I remember small things…the smell of my mother's hair, for example, but not her voice. Funny. I heard it often enough, you'd think I could remember the sound of her voice." Felix trailed off, his voice thick.

His face was blank and expressionless, but there was something just visible within his gaze. She had seen something similar looking in the mirror. A hollowness. Even after all these years, he was still haunted by what happened that night.

"Is that how you got the scars?" she asked quietly. It seemed inappropriate to speak any louder.

"No," he answered, bitterness creeping into his tone. "That came later when I was older. I wanted revenge on Venryk for what he'd done, so I rode out one morning with the intention of hunting him down, only he found me first.

That's when he gave me these." Felix ran a hand over the left side of his face, tracing the scars.

"Why didn't he just kill you?"

"I wondered that myself as I made my way back to the palace. What a sight I must have made." He shook his head, as if in disgust. "I went to Serai so she could heal the wound, but she couldn't. There was darkness in it."

Sara nodded. "Only light can heal it."

"Lylla tried after that, but she couldn't heal it either."

"Why not?" Sara frowned. Had Colin told her wrong?

Felix grimaced. "It was a…different kind of wound. Venryk had marked me. It was a way of saying that my life belonged to him and that I wasn't to be killed by anyone else. He made a point of telling me that Damaris couldn't save me now."

"What did he mean?"

"Damaris has been a part of my life from the moment I was born. She made my mother a promise and Venryk knew that if she hadn't been there that night, he'd have finished me off, too. This was his way of ensuring that she couldn't shield me from him anymore." He swallowed and hesitated before continuing. "What you have to understand about darkness is that it acts like a poison. It will eventually kill unless the wound is healed."

Sara felt her throat close up. He didn't need to spell it out; the implication was enough. It reminded her of what had happened to her mom. A poison inside, a cancer that slowly spreads until it kills.

"To put it simply, I'm cursed," Felix said, giving a lightness to his words that Sara knew neither of them felt. "The only way to break the curse is to kill Venryk. But I have to be the one to do it. No one else can do it for me. If someone else kills Venryk, I'll have lost my chance and the darkness will eventually take its course. That's why

Damaris can't protect me anymore. And by marking me, Venryk also ensured his own protection from everyone else. They aren't going to kill him because they know that they risk Damaris's wrath by doing so. For better or worse, our fates are bound together, Venryk and I."

"That's…cruel," Sara whispered.

"He is cruel," Felix said, turning to face her. The moonlight turned his crimson hair silver in places. "That's why I was so angry at losing my chance the night he confronted the two of us. I don't know how many more chances, if any, I'll get."

"I don't know what to say." Sara shook her head. "I'm sorry."

"I want to live," he whispered. "There are so many things I want to do. I want to see Wysteria at peace, I want to be able to have a family of my own one day, and I want to be able to read all these books." He smiled. "But I have to kill that wolf first." He shook his head. "Sorry, I'm not usually so garrulous. It must be the way you listen."

"No, it's fine!" Sara said quickly. "I think it helps. I'm—I'm glad you told me." She paused. "Not to be a cynic or anything, but you're not telling me this now that I'm a Guardian, are you?"

He laughed softly and again it was only the slightest exhalation. She wondered what it would be like to hear him laugh, *really* laugh. "No. But before, you would have eventually left and not come back. Now you're going to stay and even when you do leave, you can come back."

She sighed. "I still can't believe it myself. I guess I'll have to be trained now?"

"Don't worry. You'll be training with Lylla—mainly, anyway."

"The queen is going to train me?"

Felix shrugged. "She's the only one who can. She is the only other light attribute, after all."

"I guess that makes sense."

"Don't worry." He bumped her shoulder with his in a comradely gesture. "You'll be fine."

There was a brief moment of silence. Sara was acutely aware of her own heartbeat. "I'm sorry I snapped at you earlier this evening," she muttered. "I just wasn't sure if it was really you."

"You were right to be wary." He looked at her. "But I'm never going to do anything to put you in danger and I'm certainly never going to ask for that stone."

"Except for when you did, in the wardrobe," Sara pointed out teasingly.

"With the exception of the wardrobe…" He sighed and stood, his leg brushing against hers. "You'd better try and get some sleep if you're going to face training tomorrow."

"Lucky me," Sara muttered under her breath.

"It could be worse. You could be training with Damaris."

She looked up, about to ask how he had heard her, but then her gaze landed on the long, pointed ears sticking out from under his crimson hair and had her answer.

16

Iceland was a land of beauty, no one could deny that, but it was also a land of cruelty, without a shred of mercy. Here, only the strong survived and it did not escape Lylla's notice that those who were strongest in Iceland, who thrived in such a place more than any other, were among the magicless species of Wysteria.

She'd left that very night, knowing that she would be expected to assist Sara, to oversee her training and guide her in the proper use of her magic. She owed the girl that much at least and probably more, but this was a visit that could not be put off. Lylla would travel all night if that was what it took, hoping to arrive back at the palace around midday, if she maintained her pace, which would be difficult but not impossible.

She decided to make the trip in her unicorn form, which could cover more ground in a shorter amount of time. It would take long enough as it was. The wind tore at her mane, lashing her eyes. It stung and she blinked back tears as it made her eyes water. The cold was so intense it physically hurt. It was a burning, but so unlike that of fire.

She had felt the wrath of both and still wasn't sure which was worse. Fire hurt worse initially and afterward was no fun to deal with either. But there was something about the cold, utterly devoid of warmth, that seemed more painful somehow. It took longer to affect you, to get under your skin and drain the warmth away, but it seemed to only grow worse the longer it went on.

Lylla was not the fire attribute Damaris was and couldn't burst into flames the way she did to ward off the chill, but she did summon a concentrated beam of light, the heat melting the snow, making a clear path for her to walk on and that allowed her to reach her destination much quicker. She wasn't going to fight through the knee-deep snow all the way to the ice palace.

She was received with no small measure of surprise by Icicle upon her arrival. The lithe white dragon walked forward to greet her and Lylla's eyes instantly went to the crown upon her head, the tear-drop crystals lit up blue.

The shadow elf hadn't lied.

Icicle grinned, flinging out one black wing. "Your Majesty! If you're here in person, it must be quite important."

"Icicle—"

"It's Empress Icicle now."

"Yes, I see you have the crown," Lylla remarked, taking her opening. "However did you come by that stroke of fortune?"

"Funny that," Empress said, walking away a few feet, her black claws clicking on the floor. "It was found on Earth. I wonder if you didn't know that it was there all this time."

"It's not my duty to keep track of the treasures of your people," Lylla replied firmly. "But I'm less concerned with the crown than how you came by it. I've been told that

Galatea gave it to you, you see, and I can't help but wonder what she wanted in return."

Empress scoffed, continuing to pace back and forth on her long, thin legs. "Is it so wrong that I've gotten it back? It is my people's legacy, after all, tragically lost in the Exodus. Our flight to Wysteria was somewhat more perilous than most, as befitting our time spent on Earth. I could have told you where it would all lead. Hunted by men for sport, although I suppose that's mildly better than some. At least we didn't consent to being trapped in cages as part of some traveling freak show. Ah, it all went to hell in the end, didn't it?"

"Consent had nothing to do with it," Lylla said placidly. She was not truly a unicorn so the barb didn't have its intended effect.

Damaris, on the other hand, would have been far less amused. It was just as well Lylla had come herself. Empress was slippery as an eel and if she could worm her way out of the conversation without giving Lylla the answers she sought, she would.

"Perhaps if I had magic of my own, I could have retrieved the crown myself," Empress mused. "Funny how the forsaken Guardian aided me but the queen did not."

"As I said, your treasures are not mine to keep track of. I hardly think Galatea returned the crown to you out of sheer goodwill. What did she ask for in return?"

The dragon lashed her tail. "A deal struck between two parties hardly concerns a third."

"It does when one of those parties is raising an army of the dead and plans to march across Wysteria." Lylla didn't know for certain that Galatea intended to do just that, but she found it likely. "She's raising the dead from Malenwar, did you know that?"

"It's hardly my business."

"She exhumed Jack and raised him. She's brought him back to Wysteria."

Empress moved her shoulder where her wing attached, the movement as close as she could come to a shrug. "Humans always were fragile creatures. It's a wonder he didn't die before he did."

Lylla took a step forward. "Does all of this mean nothing to you?"

"Why should it? The rest of you can fight amongst yourselves. It doesn't concern Iceland."

"Doesn't it, though? You're a part of this world. You can't hope to remain untouched by it all forever. Sooner or later, you're going to have to pick a side."

"Yes," Empress retorted. "I suspect I will. But after centuries of fighting, I think my people deserve some peace and I'll not be drawn into your petty squabbles all because some human died!"

"Well," Lylla said softly. "When the time comes, Empress, whose side will you choose?"

The dragon smiled, black lips peeling back from gums and sharp teeth. It was ghastly. "The side I've always been on. My own." She turned and began walking away.

It was blatant disrespect and Lylla felt a surge of anger. Diplomacy had always been her approach, whereas the threat of violence was Damaris's. She was suddenly both regretful and grateful that she hadn't decided to send the Flame Guardian. Physically attacking the dragon out of rage wouldn't accomplish anything, but a threat might.

"Then don't be surprised that when we've finished with Galatea, we turn our attention to Iceland."

"You and what army?" Empress called over her shoulder. "If what you say is true, I can't imagine there'll be many of you left."

Against a magicless species like you, I wouldn't need many, Lylla thought, but bit back the retort. She didn't want to go to war against the mountain dragons. Empress was right on one hand—after so many years of fighting amongst themselves, the Icelandic dragons deserved to enjoy a period of peace.

But they didn't have the luxury of choice, any of them. One way or another, the looming war would come for them. If they attempted to remain neutral, Galatea would still view them as being against her so long as they weren't totally in support of her, and they would become a target for her wrath as well. It wasn't pleasant for any of them to be in, the situation that the sorceress had created, but that didn't change anything.

The only way to ensure peace was to put a stop to Galatea's plans and the only way they could do that is if they worked together. *Why can't she see that?*

She's afraid. Lylla knew it with certainty. The dragons had no magic of their own, other than the ability to breathe fire. They couldn't summon or utilize any of the other elements and so it was only natural for Empress to be wary of getting involved in a conflict with either of them. Whichever side she chose, she would face powerful magic on the other end.

She had just achieved peace after centuries of war. Lylla could well understand why she would be reluctant and flat out unwilling to become involved in another so soon. After all, her newfound position as Empress was of no use if she ended up dead.

But she had no choice. None of them did. Given enough time, the conflict would land on their doorstep and they would have to decide how to respond. The only question was, on whose terms would the battle be fought?

***

When Sara woke the next morning, she half expected to be back in her own bed. Then she remembered. She hadn't been sent through the Lightning Gate and she wouldn't be going home any time soon because she was a Guardian. She sighed, pushing herself up from the bed, squinting in the bright sunlight streaming through a break in the curtains.

Her first day of training.

She got up and bathed, then opened the wardrobe, studying the outfits within. She wasn't sure what the day held for her, but she doubted that a tank top, shorts, and flip flops were the appropriate attire for a Guardian-in-training.

There was an all-black ensemble that she chose, the tunic and pants close-fitting to avoid snagging on anything. Like Felix's, the tunic was sleeveless and Sara pulled on a pair of knee-high boots and a matching pair of fingerless gloves. It was much drabber than what she normally wore, preferring colors, but in terms of stealth, she had to admit that black was much more practical than pink.

Sara decided to leave her hair in its typical braid and regarded her reflection in the mirror. *Well, at least I look like I know what I'm doing, even if I don't.*

She left her room and headed down to join the others for breakfast. This morning, it was just Colin and Felix, who stopped what he was doing and stared at her, taking in her new appearance.

"Hey!" Colin remarked. "You look just like a Shadow."

"Except I don't have any silver," Sara pointed out.

"It suits you," Felix murmured.

Nothing in his tone or expression hinted at the conversation they'd had the previous night, for which Sara was grateful. She didn't regret what she'd said, but she'd rather not dwell on it and she thought he felt the same.

Once breakfast was over and had been cleared away, Felix and Colin departed for their own session. Sara waited for Lylla to fetch her, which took longer than expected. When she did appear, Sara thought she looked slightly tired, but her smile was as warm as ever as she greeted her and led her outside, to the area of pasture behind the palace where they would have a bit of privacy.

"Initially, I thought I'd be training with the others," Sara said, feeling the sun warm on her back. It wouldn't take long for her to get hot, just standing outside, much less once they'd actually begun. "Not that I'm complaining or anything."

"Ordinarily, you would be," Lylla replied. "But no one else can teach you the basics of using light magic. And you'll need to train with the others, but only once you've got the basics down. You'll need to know how to fight against all the other attributes and how to use a weapon—sword or archery, most likely."

"Why would I need to know that if I have magic?"

"Because magic is not a limitless source of power. If you can take out an opponent with a physical weapon and save some of your energy, it's better to do so."

"Oh," Sara muttered, not looking forward to it.

No matter how bad she might be at using magic, she couldn't imagine being any better with a sword. Not with her physical strength. But she wasn't about to try and explain the limits that she'd encountered.

"So," Lylla went on. "First things first. Of all the elements, light is the strongest because it has equal defensive and offensive capability. The most common way light is utilized is by blinding your opponents, which can be both a defense and an attack."

"How do I even use magic?" Sara asked, walking alongside her. "Is there a specific spell I need to say?"

The queen shook her head. "Only dark magic uses spoken spells, though you can create a rhyme or a chant if you find it helps you focus. It's a nice place to start, but you can't rely on it during battle. No, you simply tell the magic what you want it to do by imagining it. Will it into being. You have to want it and the magic will respond, if its within your ability and you have sufficient energy. But don't worry about that last bit. Your energy threshold will increase the more practice you have and the more you get used to channeling magic. The Echo Stone will help with that."

Sara fiddled with the chain around her neck.

"There are two characteristics to light and those are the light visibly given off and heat, which make it much like lightning or fire in that respect. So, offensively, you can use it to blind and burn your opponents." Lylla waved a hand at some figures several yards away. "I took the liberty of having some training dummies set up for you to practice on."

Sara looked at them. Their bodies seemed to be a large sack stuffed with straw, a few pieces sticking out of the material. Their heads were smaller sacks, likewise stuffed, and two stick arms stuck out from either side of their bodies. Faces had been painted on.

She smiled. "They're kind of cute. It seems almost a shame to destroy them."

Lylla chuckled. "Yes, they are kind of cute, I suppose. And a bit pitiful. But for the sake of this exercise, we must pretend that they are vicious and trying to harm you. Show them no mercy."

Sara hesitated. "What should I do?"

"We'll start with some simple illuminations. That's what a skill is called when it gives off light. There are various degrees of illuminations, from just enough to light a darkened room, to bright enough to blind the world around you. Let's work on the blinding bit. I'll demonstrate."

Lylla took a step forward, her body turned slightly sideways, one foot pointed straight at the targets, the other behind her for balance. One arm was outstretched.

"You don't need an extreme amount of light to effectively blind your opponent temporarily. What you did to Noraak—permanent blindness—requires more, but it's less practical. In a battle, the goal will be to blind your enemy, thus incapacitating them, and allowing you to kill them quickly."

She flung one hand outward, toward the nearest dummy's head and a brief flash of light appeared. Sara watched, trying to copy her movements. She raised her hand and, to her surprise, the light responded, flashing briefly as the queen's had. It gave off a warm sensation, as the magic channeled through her. She could feel it, almost like heat rushing through her veins and the slightest prickling on her skin.

Lylla nodded in approval. "I'd say that's one blinded dummy."

"I can't believe I just did that." It had been so easy. Sara had pictured what Lylla had just demonstrated and her magic had responded, almost on its own, as if it were a living thing that knew what she wanted.

"The Echo Stone you carry will help a great deal. And the fact that you're a Guardian doesn't hurt either. You have the potential to access more power than most ever will."

Lylla instructed her to practice casting illuminations several more times before moving on to the next lesson.

"All right," she clapped her hands together. "Now that you've got blinding out of the way, it's time for what comes next. Dispatching your opponent."

"Do you think I'll really ever have to do this?" Sara asked, wiping a thin sheen of sweat from her forehead. "I don't think I'd be able to kill anyone…"

"And I hope you never have to," Lylla said gravely. "But that choice may not be up to you. You'd be surprised what you're capable of when lives are on the line. In battle, you may find yourself fighting to protect not only your own life, but others as well."

Sara merely nodded. She wondered if Felix had ever killed someone in a battle. She'd have to ask him later, but she wasn't sure she wanted to bring up such a subject. It didn't seem like the kind of thing one asked about.

Lylla was already moving on. "Right, then. When your opponent is blinded, now is the time to act. Unfortunately, light is not as versatile as other elements when it comes to attacking, but it more than makes up for that in other ways, which we'll get to later. So, if you are going to kill an opponent with light, your only option is to burn them. That's why most light attributes throughout history, those that were Guardians, have used secondary elements to finish their opponents off."

"Secondary elements?"

"Those are any elements that are not your attribute. Given enough time and experience, Guardians can learn to control all of the secondary elements available to them. As a light attribute, you have an advantage. You can learn to control all seven elements where other Guardians can only control six at the most."

"Why?" Sara asked. "Why can only light attributes control light? You don't have to be a fire Guardian to control fire."

Lylla shook her head. "No, that's true; you don't. It has to do with darkness. Anyone, even light attributes, can choose to turn to the dark arts. Darkness corrupts a user's attribute, meaning they cannot use it anymore, but a Guardian can still use all the secondary elements. If light were able to be used as a secondary element, that would mean a Guardian could still use both light and darkness at the same time and that just isn't possible. Light and dark are polar opposites, incompatible. Light has no fellowship with darkness."

"But what about water and fire? Aren't they opposites?"

"They can be, but not if they're working together. You have to get pretty creative with your elements. The scope of your imagination can be the most useful tool you have. It can allow you to take down an opponent who is more skilled than you are. But none of the other elements are as diametrically opposed to one another as light and dark.

"But anyway, where were we? Ah, yes, burning. Since you haven't learned any secondary elements—Damaris will probably be in charge of those—you'll have to rely on the one element you do have. It will always be the one you're best at anyway."

"Let me guess," Sara remarked. "There are varying degrees of burning, too."

"You learn fast," Lylla said approvingly. "Yes, you can decide whether to lightly singe your opponents or whether to do something more extreme…"

She shot one hand out, a beam of light surging forward to envelop the training dummy. It was over in the blink of an eye, a smoldering post all that remained of the dummy.

Sara gaped at it. "You… You vaporized it!"

"Yes." Lylla turned back to her. "But don't worry about trying to do that yet. It's not as easy as it looks. It takes a lot of energy to sustain a blast concentrated enough to turn someone into ash. I can only do it so many times in a fight before I have to stop. Otherwise, if I could, I would instantly vaporize all of them and the fight would be over immediately. But there are limits to what even light attributes can do and a cost to every move you make that must be carefully weighed and considered."

For the time being, Lylla instructed her to try and singe the practice dummy. Sara found this to be more difficult than casting a mere blinding illumination—which flared and then was gone in an instant. Maintaining a beam that was hot and would burn took much more concentration and effort.

In the end, she managed to make the sack blacken in the middle, a thin trail of steam rising into the air.

She panted. "I can see why they use secondary elements for this. Which ones would be most useful to learn?"

"Sometimes, it depends on the personality of the user as to which secondary elements they connect with best, but most light Guardians typically choose fire or lightning because both give off light and heat. It's not that far removed from what they've already learned."

"Both sound good to me."

"We'll worry about that later. That's enough for today. I don't want to overwhelm you—any more than I have already."

Free to go, Sara followed Lylla around to the front of the palace, where the other forms of training were taking place. Felix and Colin were standing in the middle of a square patch of ground, white sand beneath their feet. Their wooden practice swords clacked against each other as they sparred, lunging and parrying.

There was a sheen of sweat over Felix's skin and he was panting from the exertion. Unlike with archery, Colin seemed to have the upper hand. Felix was on the defensive, backing away. It was all he could do to keep the blond elf's attacks at bay.

He must have seen her out of the corner of his eye because he glanced over at her. Seizing his opportunity, Colin sprang. Felix flinched, barely managing to ward off the attack.

Sara turned and went back inside, leaving them to it.

***

There was another reason that Lylla had called the training to an early close and it had nothing to do with overwhelming Sara on her first day. It was far more serious than that, a problem that must be dealt with. Empress's refusal to give her a straight answer weighed heavily on her mind.

She wanted nothing more than to discuss the steps they should take moving forward with the one person whose judgement she trusted most. But Damaris had departed for the Wind Gate. It was her presence at the Gate that would allow them to do this, but that meant moving forward without her.

The other Guardians would need to step up. Lylla had sent scouts to fetch them and bring them to the palace, up to her private quarters where they would not be overheard.

She paced the floor, ill at ease and unable to relax, until they arrived.

With Kadir no longer trustworthy and Damaris gone to take his place, it was just Wanderer, Cassius, and Cyren. Lylla didn't like the odds, but she hoped that they would see reason, where before they had steadfastly refused to act.

She wasted no time with preamble. "I've called you here to address the problem of Galatea. I think the time for waiting has passed. We need to act. We know exactly where she is and with Damaris stationed at the Wind Gate, she

287

cannot flee back to Earth. I suggest we pay her a visit in the swamp."

"A full-scale offensive?" Cyren asked, shifting her weight. "Are you sure?"

At least she no longer denied Galatea's return. None of them could afford to do that and Kadir's betrayal had shattered any illusions they might have had.

"Yes," Lylla said firmly, digging her toes into the thick rug beneath her feet. "With the Wind Gate secured, now is the time to act. Furthermore, one of Galatea's minions has infiltrated the palace twice recently and threatened Sara, a blatant act of aggression and I'll not stand for it. She's also targeted the Icelandic dragons and I was unable to get a clear answer as to where their loyalties lie. She's raising an army of the dead, in clear violation of the law. The long and short of it is, something must be done."

"I agree," Wanderer said. Lylla had counted on her support and was glad that she had not miscalculated. "Damaris saw what Galatea is doing firsthand. We can't just sit back and wait for her to make the first move. This war can't be fought on her terms."

"But are you sure this is the best way to go about it?" Cassius asked. "If what you say is true, Galatea has already amassed a formidable force. You'll need the Guardians to assist in any assault if you are to have a chance at victory. And by lending our aid, we are forced to leave our Gates unattended. Hardly secure and hardly trapping Galatea here."

"The Wind Gate was where the breach in security occurred," Lylla answered. "That was Galatea's preferred Gate. It is unlikely she would choose yours, Cyren. The trek through Iceland is too long and treacherous to make it worthwhile. Cassius, your Gate is out of the question, since it comes out on the other side of Earth. And

Wanderer's Gate still has a Guardian on the other side, unlike Cyren's. Besides, what Galatea wants is here in Wysteria. She has no reason to cross through again.

"But you're right. I won't lie. Without your support, we have little hope of success in any assault."

Cyren looked at her brother. "Something has to be done. And I, for one, am tired of waiting. I'd rather any battle be fought on our terms, not Galatea's."

Cassius sighed. "Very well."

"Then we are in agreement," Lylla said. "I will begin gathering the troops, but I'll need your help."

"About that," Wanderer spoke up. "I might have an idea…"

"What is it?"

Wanderer fidgeted. "Okay, so, don't be mad, but I didn't exactly destroy that mirror…"

"Wanderer—"

"I was going to! But then I thought that it could be useful. Galatea used it against us so why shouldn't we use it against her?"

"Because it's dangerous and no one should be using it." Lylla sighed. "But I can see you're going somewhere with this, so go on."

"Well, I was flipping through the reflections trapped in it and Noraak's there, obviously. But so is Galatea!"

"And?" Cassius demanded.

"Well I thought, since you couldn't get a definitive answer out of Empress, that I could pay her a visit disguised as Galatea and order her to gather her troops or whatever and meet me somewhere. Then, if they show up, it proves where their allegiance lies, doesn't it?"

"But what purpose would it serve?" Cyren questioned.

"You know, Wanderer," Lylla said slowly. "I think the idea has merit. We'll all rendezvous at the border of the

Briarwood, where it meets the Enchanted Forest. Come; we have much to do and little time to do it in."

***

Wanderer regretted her brilliant plan, but she couldn't have had the fortune to have second thoughts the moment she set foot in Iceland. No, the doubts had waited until she stood before the ice palace, awaiting entry. The guard had disappeared to inform Empress of her—or rather Galatea's—arrival. It wasn't too late. She could hike it out of there and forget the whole thing.

But Galatea wouldn't have done that. And that's who she was now. She needed to think like the sorceress, not just act like her or else this ruse would never work. Empress must be shrewd to have wormed her way out of the conversation with Lylla and so Wanderer had to keep her wits about her.

She had known Galatea before she—as Wanderer liked to think of it—"went bad". She'd been confident even then. *Besides, if anything goes wrong, you can just blast them.* That's how Galatea would view it; confident in her skills.

The doors swung open. Wanderer took a deep breath of icy air, held her head up high, and strode inside. Empress hopped down from her dais to land lithely in front of her and Wanderer was intimidated for a moment by the dragon's size. *They don't have magic. They don't have magic.*

"Galatea," Empress drawled. "What a pleasant surprise. What is it you want this time?"

Here goes nothing. Deepening her voice closer to the sorceress's, Wanderer announced, "I've come to make good on our bargain."

Empress sighed. "Oh, yes, *that.*"

"Don't tell me you've forgotten."

"No, it's just that Lylla herself paid me a visit not long ago, wanting to know whose side I was on. Did you know that? Luckily, I managed to be noncommittal about it, as I'm sure you'll appreciate."

"Keeping your true intentions hidden from her, yes, well done," Wanderer said dismissively. "However, I need you to commit now."

Empress's bright blue eyes narrowed. "What do you want me to do?"

"I want you to gather your troops, all the soldiers loyal to you that you can muster, and meet me at the border of the Briarwood, where it meets the Enchanted Forest."

"For the purpose of…?"

"I'll enlighten you as to the details when you get there," Wanderer snapped. She turned, as though to walk away, and then added over her shoulder, "Oh, and Empress? I advise you to be there."

She walked away, keeping her pace unhurried, listening to the dragon gnash her teeth behind her, feeling quite pleased with herself.

***

Every soldier would be needed for the assault on the swamp, and that included Felix and Colin. As he saddled Tempest and checked his equipment, Felix tried not to let thoughts of the impending battle overwhelm him, but it was difficult. Venryk would be there. Fate had handed him another chance, the thing he craved most and was afraid he would be denied.

If he walked out of that swamp at the end, he was determined to do so a free man, having broken the curse that had weighed on him for years.

He wasn't as nervous as he thought he would be. Perhaps that would change when he found himself back in the swamp, but for now, there was almost a sense of eagerness lending itself to his actions.

Somehow, when you lived each day with death shadowing your steps, the prospect of facing it imminently didn't have the same effect. Felix knew death was coming for him sooner or later. If it happened to come for him today, well, he hadn't expected it to be so soon, but he'd known it was coming.

It felt strange to enter battle without the Flame Guardian, but Damaris wouldn't be coming with them. He knew that likely galled her. She was one of their most valuable soldiers, her power such that she alone could turn the tide. Her absence could very well make all the difference.

But she had her role to play, just as they all did, and it was up to the rest of them now. She had given them this opportunity. They couldn't afford to squander it.

Felix checked his equipment again, for the final time. He had a quiver full of arrows, his bow, two daggers strapped at his belt and another two hidden in his boots. And he had magic of his own, though he used it rarely enough. His armor was boiled leather, which would provide little in the way of protection but offered freedom of movement, which was just as important to an archer.

"Felix!"

He turned to see Sara jogging toward him. In the chaos of the mustering, he hadn't seen her all day. She wouldn't be coming with them. Guardian or not, her skills were still too new, untested.

"I'd worried you'd gone already," she said, reaching him.

"Soon," he told her.

She looked at him with wide eyes, looking more frightened at the coming battle than he felt, even though he was going and she was not.

"I wish I could do something to help."

"You can. Help Serai." There were herbs that would need preparing, bandages that needed to be readied for the aftermath. Not everyone would come back and those that did wouldn't necessarily be unscathed.

"I probably would just get in the way."

"She'll be grateful for the help, I promise," Felix assured her. "Trust me. She doesn't have enough apprentices for something this big."

Sara paled, but nodded.

A horn rang out, cutting their conversation short. It was time to move out.

"I have to go," he said, swinging up into the saddle.

"Make sure you come back," Sara instructed.

Felix nodded to her, hearing the unspoken word as if it hung in the air between them. *Alive.* Come back alive.

He intended to grant her wish, if it was within his power to do so, but he knew better than to make a promise he couldn't keep.

***

Reluctant as she was, Empress supposed it was worth hearing what Galatea had to say. She could show up, certainly, but that didn't mean she had to stay. Finding dragons loyal to her was harder than she would have liked. It shouldn't have been this hard.

She had gotten the crown back and had been proclaimed as ruler so they all should have been relieved to stop fighting and unite as one. But some of the challengers were surprisingly reluctant to let go of their resentment that she had succeeded and they had not. She'd had to dispose of them, believing that the dissent would cease after they were gone. But she'd been wrong.

Rumors of Galatea's and Lylla's visits had spread like wildfire and only created more problems. The Icelandic dragons were once again split, those that thought they should listen to Galatea's threats and help her to be rid of their debt—and those that thought they should remain loyal to the queen of the island on which they lived.

Whomever she chose to side with, Empress would have enemies on the other side who did not approve. With a combination of cajoling, ordering, threatening, and a little bit of physical violence, Empress managed to gather members of both sides to take with her to the rendezvous.

She didn't like being under Galatea's yoke any more than the rest of them did. In fact, she despised it. She'd sooner kill the sorceress where she stood than submit to her demands, especially so soon after getting the crown— and what should have been peace—back. But she could not.

But what Empress found waiting for her near the Briarwood angered her even further. For when they landed, descending beneath the forest canopy, they found not Galatea waiting there, but Lylla herself, backed by soldiers.

"Ah, Empress," she said, taking a step forward. "So good of you to join us."

The queen was dressed head to toe in gleaming gold and white armor, some of it inlayed with mirrors, which would catch her light and fracture it in all directions. The gold helm that framed her face caught the light as she moved, her long blue hair neatly tied back in three signature braids, two shorter in the front and one longer in the back.

In her hand, she held a sword, solid white, that gave off its own gently pulsing light.

Empress drew herself up. "What's the meaning of this?" It took an effort to keep her voice steady. She felt as though she'd been tricked and hated being made to look a fool.

"I sent Wanderer disguised as Galatea to deliver a message with the purpose of seeing what your response was, since I was unable to get one from you before. At least now we know where your allegiance lies."

Empress growled. "Well, since it was one of *your* Guardians that gave me the order instead of Galatea, how can you be certain where my allegiance truly lies?"

"I'm hoping it lies with us," Lylla replied. "Or can be persuaded to. We're about to launch an offensive into the swamp. When we go in, I'd rather it be as allies than enemies."

"Are you quite mad?" But there was no mistaking the steely determination in the queen's blue eyes.

"This has gone on long enough. I'm not going to sit around and wait for Galatea to dictate to us. This is our chance to put an end to this. Are you with us or not?"

Empress's eyes raked the crowd assembled behind Lylla. Cassius and Cyren were there, along with the aforementioned Wanderer. No Kadir, though that wasn't surprising. No Flame Guardian either. Now, that *was* a surprise.

Still, it was a formidable gathering with all but two of the Wysterian Guardians present, not to mention the Lightbringer herself. And scores of elven soldiers behind, ordinary elementalists all.

Empress couldn't deny the idea of bringing an end to Galatea and her scheming was attractive. If they succeeded, she would be free of any obligation to the sorceress. Peace could return to Wysteria and she would have regained the queen's good graces for her part in securing victory. It was a win for everyone involved—*if* they succeeded.

But in order to do that, they would need all the help they could get, and that included her and her fellow dragons. Empress cast a glance over her shoulder at those assembled behind her. Some of them thought they ought to side with Galatea, that she would win the war.

Whichever side she chose, some of her own people would turn against her. But she couldn't say that in front of everyone and admit to her own failure as a leader.

No, when they turned, they would be dealt with.

"Very well, Your Highness. I'm in."

17

Sara's hands shook as she rolled bandages or carried bundles of herbs to their proper locations on Serai's shelves. She had no knowledge of the herbs and so she wasn't tasked with chopping or sorting them, merely putting them where the head healer told her. The healer's quarters were a flurry of activity as apprentices rushed to prepare for the onslaught of wounded that would return from the swamp.

Though she knew it was ridiculous, Sara couldn't help but feel that they were marching into battle because of her rather than Galatea. She told herself that this outcome was inevitable, regardless of whether Galatea had attempted to take the stone through the use of imposters or not.

But still. How had they reached this point? And so quickly. Sara wanted nothing more than to return home and forget all of this. Pretend it had never happened. Wysteria, which had seemed so beautiful despite its foreignness, now bared its teeth as the danger it held was revealed.

She felt almost sick with worry, thinking of Lylla, Felix, and Colin walking into the swamp, putting themselves in harm's way and possibly even going to their deaths. Sara had seen what Lylla was capable of and thought the queen would likely be all right.

Damaris wasn't going to be with them, but for Sara, her power was nothing more than a rumor, something she'd heard of but not seen. Colin had confided in her that he thought Lylla might be more powerful anyway and Sara could well believe that, after witnessing her vaporizing the training dummy. She would have to hope it would be enough.

The idea that some of the people she had come to know might not return was something she couldn't think of. And yet she couldn't think of anything else. Her sense of dread made her feel physically ill.

But there was nothing she could do except wait, roll more bandages, and hope.

***

The group advanced slowly into the Briarwood, every sense on alert, taut as a bowstring. They were proceeding with caution, not knowing what to expect, but also the going was hindered by the thick thorns that Galatea had ordered Noraak to grow around the swamp borders. The thorns were so thick that they were impassable in many areas, forcing the soldiers to squeeze through in narrow gaps.

As they walked, Cassius couldn't help but feel that they were being funneled into a trap.

The thorns were particularly difficult for the dragons to navigate, snaring on their white fur until Cyren managed to coax the brambles back, widening the path.

Cassius could see Lylla in the lead, light emanating around her in the darkness. The stone path lay before them, leading deeper into the ruins. He stayed close to Cyren, unwilling to let his sister out of his sight. Felix and Colin were riding just behind the queen. Cassius couldn't see Wanderer in the crowd, but he knew she was there somewhere.

There was no sign of the ghostly figures Damaris had reported flitting about the swamp, which struck him as foreboding rather than comforting. Itching for a fight the Flame Guardian might have been, but she was not a liar. If she had seen something in the swamp, it had been real enough.

Movement came from up ahead and Cassius squinted. It was difficult to make out the wispy black steeds that came charging forward on silent hooves. Cyren raised a hand, firing a bolt of ice at one, but before the spear could land, the creature shifted into mist. The spear hurled straight through, shattering as it struck the stone beyond, and the creature reappeared to her left.

All at once, the air vibrated as magical attacks went off around Cassius, most failing to land a hit on their targets. Shouts and cries rang out and, despite the smell, Cassius sprang off the stone path, landing in the swamp water with a splash. It reached just above his knees and would make his movements a bit sluggish, but he felt better having his element close at hand.

With water already there to manipulate, he could conserve energy since he wasn't forced to conjure it from thin air. There also wasn't enough room on the stone path and others had been forced to scatter.

A Nightmare leapt into the water after Cassius, but instead of evaporating into mist, it remained solid. He summoned an ice spear of his own and plunged it into the creature's chest, easily dispatching it. The water around his legs surged, rising up and forward to slam into the next oncoming wave of Nightmares. Cyren rushed forward, freezing pools of water, allowing others to stand on it rather than in it.

A bloodcurdling howl rang out and Cassius caught glimpses of red and orange fur moving rapidly through the ruins. The fire wolves had arrived, coats bursting into flames.

Cassius stopped thinking, about the odds or whatever other horrors the ruins may have in store for them, and merely acted. He willed the swamp water to rise, slamming down into the enemy with such force the stone cracked beneath it.

Battles always were chaos and this was no exception. The swamp's dim lighting and narrow confines in the ruins meant that maneuverability was limited and it was hard to make out where the others were.

They pushed forward into where the main ruins began and that was when the undead arrived, surging forward in seemingly endless waves.

"There's so many of them!" someone screamed.

Cassius whirled, searching desperately for the queen. She wasn't hard to find, the only beacon of light in a sea of darkness. Cutting a path through the swarms of undead, he made his way toward her.

***

She's emptied the entire Necropolis, Lylla thought. There was no other explanation for it. She fought down a wave of disgust at seeing how the dead of Malenwar had been defiled.

Her sword, Pharus, was already in her hand and she struck out, lopping the head off the nearest undead soldier, plunging the blade into the chest of the next. But the first, though relieved of its head, was only down for mere moments before it rose again.

Lylla's disgust gave way to horror. Of course. They were not dead, so they couldn't be killed. The only way to stop them would be to destroy their bodies to the point where it would be impossible for them to rise again. And certain elements were better at that than others.

She waited, allowing them to close in on her. She raised her arm, her gauntlet deflecting a blow from a claymore, before swinging Pharus in a wide arc. Light flared, slicing outward, the heat carving the undead in half. Their two halves toppled to the ground, the edges of their bodies smoldering and glowing from the heat.

Lylla did not allow herself to bask in her success. She plunged forward, raising one hand to fire concentrated beams of light, and wielding the imbued light that Pharus contained to devastating effect. It would help her conserve some of her own energy—and she would need it.

The undead kept coming. Most held swords and shields, but a few had bows and arrows and one such projectile barely missed her, striking the elven soldier next to her in the forehead.

He went down instantly. It seemed no sooner had the life left him and he struck the ground than his eyes began to glow a solid green and he rose to his feet, slashing at her with his sword.

Lylla didn't hesitate to cut down the man who moments before had been her ally, but she felt a pang of loss as she did so.

She allowed herself a brief moment to look around and assess the situation. They were slowly being overrun. Their forces had been scattered among the ruins and the swamp water, effectively separating them. The ranks of undead were still streaming in from further in the ruins and seemed to be materializing out of the tree line. If they didn't do something soon, they would be overwhelmed.

Making matters worse, every soldier that they lost, that was cut down by undead, Nightmares or fire wolves, rose again only to take up arms against their former allies. Any undead that were cut down, rather than destroyed, simply got back up again.

In order to stop them, they would need to destroy the bodies completely, and for that they needed light or fire. Lots of it.

Blue flame erupted into the air as the mountain dragons engulfed swarms of undead. Lylla sighed, never more grateful than in that moment that Empress was her ally, however temporary, rather than an enemy.

She tamped down a frisson of worry that it wouldn't be enough. She knew who they needed, but Damaris was miles away, at the Wind Gate. Had it been a mistake marching into the swamp without the Flame Guardian?

Lylla ducked, parrying an oncoming sword. White sparks danced off of Pharus as the blades struck. She vaporized the undead soldier with a flash of light, eyes frantically scanning the swamp.

The ruins were crawling with Galatea's minions, but there was no sign of the sorceress herself.

Cassius appeared at her side, as though reading her thoughts. "Where is Galatea?"

Lylla shook her head. "Hiding somewhere no doubt."

She swept Pharus outward in another arc, another wave of light eliminated the rush of undead, giving them both a moment to breathe.

How much energy did it cost Galatea to keep all of these soldiers upright? Little wonder she didn't wish to engage in a fight. She couldn't afford to expend the extra energy. Not if she wanted to keep her soldiers "alive".

Cassius nodded over his shoulder. "Some of the dragons have turned on us, I see."

"Empress—" Lylla started to ask, disappointed but unsurprised that the dragon had intended to betray them all along.

"No, not her. Some of the others." Cassius turned to face forward. "I'll find Galatea, don't worry. Are you all right here?"

Lylla gripped Pharus tighter. "Of course. Are you sure? Galatea is obviously more powerful than any of us gave her credit for."

"I can handle it," Cassius replied.

Lylla thought he was speaking with more bravado than was perhaps wise, but it was too late to caution him further. He had slipped away, quickly lost among the writhing mass, and she had other things to worry about.

***

Damaris paced before the entrance to the temple, cutting swaths through the sand. Kadir stood off the side, expression the pinnacle of discomfort. She wished he wasn't there, wished she didn't have to look at him. She'd tried sending him away when she'd first arrived, but he'd insisted even though there was no need.

She had discussed the swamp offensive with Lylla before she'd left and though she had agreed to it, she was anything but pleased to be left behind. Her mood only grew all the more foul the longer she waited, wondering what on earth was taking place even now all those miles away.

They could all be dying this very moment and there was nothing she could do about it, stuck at this thrice-damned Gate because of the man who stood beside her.

Felix. Her heart ached to think of him in danger, but she could be of no help to him now. *He's a grown man, not a boy anymore. He needs to fight his own battles.*

Damaris let out a growl of frustration. Her place was in the swamp, not here, and, not for the first time, she damned Kadir to the pits of hell for putting them all in this position.

And yet, she knew her very presence at the Gate was what allowed the others to have such an opportunity in the first place. She admonished herself to be patient, but she'd never got the knack.

Though she refused to look at him directly, she knew Kadir cringed whenever she stalked past. His nervous fussing only irritated her further. She had half a mind to send him away.

He cleared his throat softly.

Damaris stopped and glared at him. "What?"

"You should go to them, *kire*—Damaris. Your place is there, not here."

"Do you think I don't know that?" she snapped. "I wouldn't be here at all if it weren't for you."

He winced and part of her hated herself. "I made a terrible mistake. I know that and I also know that there's nothing I can do to redeem myself. But please let me try."

Damaris narrowed her eyes at him.

"Trust me as you once did and go aid the others."

"I can't leave you here—"

"But you must," Kadir cried. His blue eyes were wide and he held his hands out toward her, including the one she had burned. It had not been healed and she wondered at that. For whatever reason, Kadir had refused to have a healer see to the wound. It must have caused him no small amount of pain, as she'd intended, for no physical pain could compare to that she felt within at his betrayal.

Maybe, just maybe, it was possible that he was more contrite than she'd given him credit for.

"You must," he insisted again. "Don't you see? Galatea's undead army will overwhelm them. The undead will be cut down only to rise again and again unless their bodies are destroyed. I've seen some of her abominations, Damaris. I know what our friends face in there. They *need* your fire. They need *you*. Otherwise I fear they are walking into a trap and I don't know how many will walk back out again. They'll be overrun. These soldiers cannot die, *kirena*."

Damaris turned away from him, the desert wind tugging at her mane. Was it her imagination or could she hear the sound of screams on the wind? No, definitely her imagination. The sound couldn't travel that far. But could she?

She might make it in time to make a difference, if she left now and ran hard. But how much of a difference, she had no idea. It might already be too late.

A chill came over her in spite of the heat. Kadir was right. Death lurked in that swamp but she had her orders. She'd been assigned to this Gate. She couldn't leave.

"Death is too kind," Kadir murmured. "Their fate will be worse. Galatea will raise them again and they will join her ranks. Do you want to face them on the opposite side of the battlefield? The queen? Your fellow Guardians? Felix?"

Something lurched in Damaris's chest. Damn him for using her one weakness, the only fear she knew, against her—and at this moment.

She gritted her teeth so hard she heard them scrape against each other. Desperately, she tried to chase the image from her mind but it was too late.

And just like that, her decision had been made for her, sure as anything.

She turned, regarding the man who had once been her friend. "I will go," she said softly. "Do not make me regret this trust, Kadir." It alarmed her, how badly she *wanted* to trust him. "Because if I find out this is a trick, I'll sear the flesh from your bones."

He nodded. "You will not regret it."

But Damaris barely heard him. She was already racing across the sands.

***

Felix had never been more grateful for Tempest's presence, the large stallion lifting him above the ranks of undead, where they were hard-pressed to reach him. But against an army of undead, his arrows were of little use. They neither inflicted pain nor hindered their progress.

His magic was slightly more effective, blowing them back away from him or lifting them in the air and sending them flying. But he couldn't do it for very long. He had trained to become an archer, not to learn how to launch undead soldiers through the air for extended periods of time.

When he felt himself start to tire from magic use, Felix returned to his bow, focusing on picking off the fire wolves. At least they were alive. They could be killed.

It felt more satisfying, anyway, whenever one of his arrows sank into the flaming creatures and brought down one more. A bit of revenge for what they'd done. Venryk may have been their leader, but they'd all played a part.

But none of the wolves he shot down were the one that really mattered.

Felix flinched, Tempest shying nervously beneath him as part of the ruins exploded behind him, chunks of rock hurling through the air to squash or bury undead. Earth attributes, working their magic.

The ground trembled as the massive chunks of stone slammed back down to earth, causing cracks to spiderweb outward from the impact site. Some completely broke through the stone floor, leaving gaping holes that seemed more hazardous than in any way helpful.

Tempest tossed his head and backed away from the crumbling walls while Felix gazed around, looking for Venryk. Surely the wolf wouldn't miss the chance to confront him here? It was the perfect opportunity.

Neither of them could afford to miss it. Even though the others were aware of the stipulation regarding who could kill the fire wolf, there was no guarantee that someone else wouldn't do so in order to save their own life in the heat of the moment. Especially in battle.

Things happened so quickly and one fire wolf looked much like another. *Perhaps he was already dead.* No, that couldn't be. Felix refused to accept it. He couldn't—wouldn't—accept it until he came across Venryk's dead body.

One of the undead rose up on Tempest's left, sword raised to slash at Felix. The stallion wheeled, trampling the corpse with his hooves. It wouldn't stay down for long.

The familiar sensation that was somewhere between an itch and a painful burn lanced up the left side of Felix's face. The hair rose on the back of his neck. Venryk was here, somewhere nearby. He twisted in the saddle, trying to locate him amidst all the chaos.

And then he saw him, a fraction of a second too late.

The wolf had climbed up one of the ruined walls, making him even with Felix's height in the saddle. Their eyes met for the briefest of moments. Before he had the chance to raise his bow, Venryk snarled and sprang at him, claws outstretched and fangs bared.

Felix gasped as the wolf slammed into him, knocking him from the saddle. He grunted as he collided with the stone floor, pain shooting through his ribs, the air forced from his lungs. His bow lay beyond his grasp.

And then the wolf was standing over him.

The din of battle around him seemed to fade, and all Felix could hear was his own breathing, each inhale ragged, the blood rushing in his ears. His hand went to the dagger at his belt. The wolf was faster.

Venryk's jaws parted and with a snarl, he lunged for Felix's throat. Desperately, acting on instinct, Felix flung his arm up to shield his neck and the wolf's jaws clamped down on his forearm instead.

His armguard shielded him from Venryk's teeth, but not the force of the bite. Amidst the chaos of the skirmish around them, Felix heard a sickening crack and screamed in pain as he felt the bone shatter.

Venryk's ears flattened, eyes narrowing. He flung Felix's arm away from his neck and the elf let it lay to the side, limp and useless. Gritting his teeth against the pain, Felix brought the dagger up, sinking it into the wolf's neck. Venryk let out a yelp, but the blow had lacked the strength to penetrate deep enough through the wolf's thick red fur.

But it bought Felix a few precious seconds. He shoved his hand against the wolf, summoning the wind to knock him off, even though it physically pained him to do so. His vision swam at the edges. He was coming dangerously close to his limit.

Venryk landed on his shoulder several feet away and scrambled to his paws, growling. Felix managed to get to his feet, pushing himself up with his uninjured arm and stood facing the wolf.

The fire wolf lunged and Felix staggered back, away from him. The stones beneath his boots fell away and for an instant, he found himself suspended in the air before falling through the opening. There was no time to scramble for purchase, but at least Venryk could not reach him.

Felix cried out as his bruised body collided with a pile of rubble, landing painfully on his broken arm, and rolled down to lay motionless on the stone floor beneath. For several long heartbeats, he lay there, dazed, fighting unconsciousness. It was all he could do just to draw breath, every nerve ending on fire.

He peered up through his eyelashes at the hole he'd fallen through, some twenty feet above his head and the pile of stones that had broken his fall. There was no chance he could climb back up with his arm broken.

Wincing, he sat up and peered around at the darkness. The only source of light was coming through the opening at the top and he could dimly make out a few skeletons. There didn't seem to be any immediate threats.

Strangely, the sound of the battle raging above didn't penetrate down here.

Felix gritted his teeth and stood. There was no other way out, but corridors receded into the darkness, no light piercing the utter blackness. Lylla would have had no trouble illuminating the way, but he had to make do with shuffling forward, his good arm outstretched, hand trailing against the stone wall he could feel but not see.

Cradling his injured arm close to his side, Felix set off limping down one of the passages, his footsteps echoing in the dark. The darkness was absolute; he could not see his hand in front of his face and his eyes soon ached from straining to see.

The passage was quite narrow, like a hallway, the stone walls pressing in on either side, the air close and stale. Felix had never considered himself to be claustrophobic, but there was something about being trapped in an unfamiliar tunnel, not knowing if there was even a way out, and helpless to defend himself against any threats that might be lurking down here, that set him on edge.

The tunnel went on for what felt like forever, until it finally opened out into an even larger space than the one he'd fallen into. The wall beneath his hand fell away and his stumbling footsteps echoed louder in the larger space.

"Who's there?" a voice called out.

Blinking, Felix walked in the direction the voice had come from, his pace agonizingly slow. He'd thought the voice sounded familiar, but it was difficult to tell with the echo.

His boot connected with something soft, which let out a cry of protest: "Hey, watch it!"

Felix stopped and knelt down. "Wanderer?"

Blue light flared as lightning crackled to life over her fingertips. Felix winced at the sudden brightness. She had one hand pressed against her side, but her glamoured ears perked up as she recognized him. "Oh, Felix. You fell down, too."

He squinted at her. "How do we get out of here?"

"We'll have to go down one of these passages. I was stopping to catch my breath." He leaned closer and saw the dark blood on her kimono, beneath her fingers.

"You're hurt."

"One of those zombies got me with a sword. It's nothing serious." She forced a grin, reaching out to gingerly touch his brow. "You don't look so hot yourself."

He reached up as well, fingers coming away red. He must have struck his head when he fell from Tempest. His head hurt, but so did the rest of him. "Venryk," he sighed, by way of explanation.

"Here, help me up. You might have to let me lean on you."

Awkwardly, he helped her stand. "You'll have to lean on this side. My arm's broken. And you'll have to keep the light going."

She looped one arm around his neck. "That I can do." The blue sparks of electricity made their shadows flicker erratically, but it was better than nothing.

Together, half shuffling, half limping, they made slow progress down the corridor.

"Where do you think we are?" Felix murmured.

"Catacombs of some kind, I think," Wanderer replied. "For when there was no more room in the Necropolis. Not sure they were ever used though."

"Or else it's empty thanks to Galatea." *And the occupants are upstairs.*

"I wonder if we've won yet. I hope there's stairs in this place. Oh, and don't tell anyone about my being stuck down here. It's rather less than heroic."

"I won't tell if you don't."

An explosion came from above, causing the earth to tremble beneath and Felix and Wanderer to stumble.

Slowly, they turned to look at each other. "What was that?" Wanderer asked.

Felix had an idea and he desperately hoped he was right.

***

It had not escaped Cyren's notice that Galatea was absent from the fray. *Hiding like the coward she is, no doubt.* And even though there were too many undead to count, she hadn't spied Jack's body among them either, which stood to reason.

Galatea had yet to acquire the second Echo Stone. She wasn't going to send Jack out into battle, where his body could be permanently destroyed by fire. There would be nothing to resurrect then.

Perhaps that would be for the best.

Cyren clenched her hand into a fist. She'd killed him once. He should have stayed dead.

Cassius reappeared at her side. "Any sign of Galatea?"

"Nothing yet," she growled, spearing the advancing undead on icicles that rose from the ground. "We need to find Jack's body. If we can destroy him, it will put an end to this madness. You can't resurrect someone when there's nothing left."

She could tell from the gleam in Cassius's eyes that he understood. "There aren't many places to hide in Malenwar, are there? I think we should try the Necropolis."

"Good idea. I'd expect it to be otherwise unoccupied, judging by the amount of undead out here. You circle around to the left. I'll take the right."

He nodded. "Just like old times, eh?"

Cyren darted forward, slipping through the fray. Some of the undead broke away and gave chase, but she froze the ground beneath their feet to slow them or froze them in blocks of ice to halt them altogether. Yes, it would be just like old times.

The two of them had slipped into Malenwar once before and dealt with Jack. The human had refused to leave and Galatea had refused to see reason and give him up. Cyren had realized that Galatea would not be persuaded and that the only way to put an end to it all would be to dispose of the human.

It had been her icicle, a spear of ice, that had dealt the killing blow.

The fighting had not yet reached the Necropolis, nor was it likely to if the tide was anything to go by. The undead had no magic of their own, save for the Nightmares, who were tricky to deal with. They were vulnerable in water, but on solid ground, one had to get the timing just right. It was a war of attrition. The sheer number of undead was overwhelming.

Magic could handle quite a few, but not when there were dozens swarming you. One could only last so long before one ran out of energy. Even the strongest Guardian couldn't keep that up forever.

Cyren had spent enough time in Malenwar prior to the Cataclysm to know precisely where the Necropolis had been. The building that had been built above the crypts had long since been destroyed, but the entrance—a dark opening leading down into the earth—was clear.

And there was Jack, standing motionless by the entrance. Death had not been kind to the human, his features withered and decayed. Cyren approached slowly, both repulsed and fascinated by his appearance. Well, she had killed him once, she could do it again.

Summoning a spear of ice to her hand, she hefted it, debating with herself how she should go about destroying him.

Cyren gasped as pain pierced her back, the tip of a sword protruding from her stomach. The ice spear slipped from her grasp, shattering as it struck the ground.

"A life for a life," a voice hissed in her ear.

Galatea pulled the Shadowblade free and stepped back. Cyren fell to her knees. She hadn't even seen the sorceress. *Fool. She wouldn't leave him out in the open like that.*

For the first time in her life, Cyren felt cold. *That shouldn't be possible.* But there was a silky feeling, not exactly slimy or wet, that could only be described as cold slithering through her. She knew it was the darkness; there was nothing else it could be. A tearing sensation followed the cold, almost as if her insides were being twisted and slowly pulled apart.

Was this what it felt like to die, feeling the life draining from your body, knowing you had only moments left? Was this how Jack had felt?

For the first time, Cyren began to comprehend the magnitude of what she had done. But it was too late.

Too late…

***

"Cyren!" Cassius ran to his fallen sister, Galatea entirely forgotten. There was no sign of the sorceress or Jack, just the yawning chasm that led down into the crypts.

Fear twisted his stomach into knots and his throat felt like it was trying to close in on itself. He knelt beside Cyren, cradling her in his arms as she gasped for air, her yellow eyes wide.

Only Lylla could heal the wound, he knew, but the queen was back in the center of the ruins. There was no way he could reach her in time. By the time the Lightbringer reached her, his sister would be dead.

Cassius touched her cheeks, tears blurring his vision as he watched her life ebb away, knowing he was powerless to stop it.

He knew the instant she died, when the awareness faded from her eyes and her gasps for air ceased. He sat back, silently cursing himself. He shouldn't have left her side, even for a moment.

Cassius looked down at her body. She'd have to be given the proper rites, of course, as a fallen Guardian in defense of her country. It seemed wrong, knowing that he would have to go on without her. She was his sister. He'd always been there to protect her, only to fail now.

He'd rather he were dead alongside her.

He swallowed back a sob, reaching out to touch her, but her eyes flared green and she sat up, her movements jerky like a marionette's. It was the same look he'd seen earlier in all the undead.

"No," he whimpered, scrambling back, but he couldn't seem to find purchase on the smooth stone. "No!" She reached for him, hand outstretched.

Cassius froze in horror. If he hadn't been so completely overwhelmed with shock and revulsion, he might have summoned some anger at Galatea for what she had done. Killing his sister was bad enough, but now she was to be one of her puppets! And she would be his own downfall.

He sobbed, unable to raise a hand against his own sister, as she put her hands around his neck. It was only fitting after all, that they die together.

And then there was a blur of white and Cyren was being shoved away from him. He blinked through his tears and saw, impossibly, Damaris standing over him and Cyren's body in flames.

He screamed at her not to hurt her, even though he knew she was beyond hurting now. The Cyren he had known was gone, leaving behind an empty shell. Cassius got to his feet and tried to go to her, but Damaris blocked his path with her body. He pounded on her with his fists, but to no avail.

Within moments, there was nothing of Cyren left.

Damaris reverted to her human form and Cassius felt her arms go around him, gently pulling him away. He could hear her murmuring something to him, though he paid no heed to the words. Only one sentence broke through to him.

"Lylla's given the order to retreat."

The fight went out of him and he let her lead him away.

****

Kadir had been right. The battle was just as horrible as Damaris had feared when she arrived, her body exhausted

315

from the run. She had pushed herself to the limit, afraid she didn't have anything more to give when she arrived. But she had to. She would, or else it was all for nothing.

The ruins were crawling with undead when she arrived. There were no dead bodies; they'd all been raised again. Those who were still alive found themselves facing more undead than they could handle.

End it, as fast and brutally as possible.

Her fiery explosions rocked the very foundations of the fallen city, burning the undead to ash, and nearly bringing her to her knees. But she was the Flame Guardian. She bared her teeth and refused to fall.

She had cleared a path, making retreat possible before any more were lost. She wasn't too late to save those that remained, but for many, she had been.

What remained of Lylla's bedraggled army had regrouped in the Briarwood. Wounded were carried on makeshift stretchers formed of spears or branches and cloaks. The air was filled with the sounds of quiet weeping and moans of pain.

Damaris stayed in her human form, helping Cassius along. She could see no physical injury, but he moved as though his legs would barely support him. She'd never seen the shadow elf look so haunted when he was usually so sure of himself. But she supposed that watching one's sibling die and rise again would be enough to shake anyone to the core.

In spite of their past disagreements, she felt unspeakably sorry for the Water Guardian. She knew how close he and Cyren had been and had envied them that closeness on more than one occasion, wishing she'd had a sibling with which to share life's pain and joy.

But Damaris did know how it felt to lose someone close and she vowed to help Cassius in any way she could, past differences be damned. Such things mattered little in the face of so much suffering. Life was too short to waste time on petty squabbles. That was what most people didn't realize until it was too late.

Lylla looked relieved to see them, likely having feared they'd both been lost. "Where is Cyren?"

Damaris wordlessly shook her head.

Lylla's shoulders slumped marginally. There would be time for questions and mourning later. She sighed, drawing herself up again. "I've sent those who were badly wounded back to the palace."

Damaris nodded, glancing around the assembled group of survivors. Colin stood beside the queen, an arrow shaft sticking out of his shoulder. Empress sat off with the other Icelandic dragons, watching the queen. The dragon's left wing looked a bit ragged and bloody where feathers had been ripped out. Damaris expected Empress to make some scathing remark about how poorly it had all gone, but she stayed silent, looking as tired as everyone else felt.

But no matter how much she scanned the crowd, Damaris did not find the familiar crimson hair she was looking for.

She tensed. "Where's Felix?" And for that matter, where was Wanderer?

Lylla opened her mouth but had no answer to give.

Damaris handed Cassius over to Colin and morphed back into a unicorn, adrenaline flooding her veins, shoving aside exhaustion.

"Damaris, wait—"

She ignored Lylla and whirled around, charging back into the swamp, heart shuddering against her chest so hard it physically hurt. She knew that there were still some of Galatea's minions left, even though there weren't nearly as many as there had been. It didn't matter. She didn't care how dangerous it might be. She would use up her magic until the last ounce of energy she possessed if that's what it took.

Felix couldn't be dead. She refused to believe it. She had made his mother a promise! How could she have been so careless as to let something happen to him?

No, she wouldn't believe it until she found his body. Until then, there was always hope.

If anything had happened to him because she hadn't been there—because she couldn't be there… This was all Kadir's fault. Blindly, Damaris ran through the gnarled trees as she had never run before, frantically scanning the ruins, rage and fear threatening to overwhelm her, each warring with the other.

She skidded to a halt. Suddenly, Felix and Wanderer were both there, the Lightning Guardian holding off a few undead with her lightning.

Damaris lunged forward, blasting the undead apart with the force of a fireball. Adrenaline still racing, she turned to them, unable to relax until she'd assured herself that they were all right.

They were both filthy, covered in a thin layer of dust. Felix was holding his left arm protectively close to his ribs as though it were injured. Dried blood had crusted at his brow but he otherwise appeared unharmed. Wanderer had a hand pressed against her side, but she was grinning.

"Boy, am I glad to see you!"

"What happened?" Damaris demanded, more sharply than she'd intended. "Didn't you hear the order to retreat?"

Wanderer shook her head. "The ruins collapsed and we fell into a series of passages beneath. We just found the way out a few minutes ago."

Damaris sighed. At least she had found them. If they'd taken any longer to find their way out, they might have been left behind in the swamp.

She looked at Felix, at the scars still marring the left side of his face, unable to read his expression. "At least you're all right. Come on."

***

It was late in the afternoon by the time Felix's arm could be seen to. Serai had been busy working with those who were far more seriously injured than he was. She'd wanted to heal his minor wounds as well, but he refused, saying they could heal naturally. He could tell she was exhausted and didn't need to spend any more energy on something superficial.

Sara had approached him, wanting to know how things had gone, but he put her off, promising to talk to her that evening. What he wanted most right now was a warm bath and a long nap to soothe his disappointment.

He retreated to his room, pulling his tunic over his head, throwing it to the bathroom floor. The leather armor was already gone, having been removed in the infirmary. It hadn't shielded him from the beating he'd taken falling off Tempest or when he'd fallen through the stone floor and into the hidden passage beneath.

Felix grimaced at the bruises that were already forming along his ribs and back, though he had to glance over his shoulder to see those. They would be ugly and tender for a while, but they would heal. Serai likely had some sort of poultice he could smear on them to make them heal faster.

The scars, on the other hand, would never heal.

A servant had already come and gone, drawing the bath. Felix finished undressing and slid into the warm water, sighing as it soothed his bruises and washed the dust off his skin. But it did little to ease his inner turmoil.

He'd had another chance to kill Venryk and that had gone even more poorly than before, even though he hadn't frozen in fear. He'd had no time to react and had barely escaped with his life. Painful as it had been, it was fortunate that the ground had opened up and swallowed him. He knew he was lucky to be alive, but he didn't feel particularly lucky.

Still, no one else had killed the wolf either. *Better to live to fight another day,* as Damaris always said, though he doubted she'd be impressed with the way he'd handled the confrontation.

Felix sighed, too tired to dwell on it, but he couldn't help but wonder if he truly ever would be ready to face Venryk. It was the doubt that kept him up at night, the doubt he could never confide to anyone.

Certainly not Damaris. She wouldn't understand.

Craving sleep, Felix climbed out of the tub and dried himself off, throwing his trousers back on and collapsed face down on the bed, hoping the nightmares wouldn't follow him.

They didn't, for once, and within moments he was asleep.

Sara met him in the library later that evening. He found her perched on the window seat, staring out the glass at the courtyard beyond, but she sat up straighter upon seeing him. "How did it go?"

Felix sighed, coming to join her. She scooted over to make more room for him. "Not well." There was no point in sugar coating it. Rumors had probably circulated all over the palace by now and she had likely seen the wounded streaming in earlier for herself.

"What happened?"

"We were just outnumbered. Galatea seems to have raised the entire city of Malenwar against us. Not only that, but any of our soldiers that we lost she was able to raise again to fight against us."

Her eyebrows drew together in concern. "That's awful."

"We lost Cyren, the Ice Guardian."

"I'm glad you're all right." She regarded him. "There's a cut on your forehead."

"I know."

She reached out as if she were going to touch it. Felix didn't shrink back and her fingertips gently alighted on his skin. "Why didn't you have it healed?"

He shrugged. "Serai had enough to deal with."

Sara made as though to pull away, her fingers slipping slightly, brushing against one of his scars. She flinched as though she'd been burned, eyes darting around wildly.

Felix knew what she'd seen. She hadn't been the first. Serai had been the first unfortunate recipient of the vision, when she'd laid a hand on his cheek to try and heal him all those years ago. It was only a memory, but the terror connected with it was real enough.

Sara took a deep breath, steadying herself. "Did you see him earlier? Venryk?"

"Yes," he answered softly. "I saw him." He didn't want to say anything more and admit to failure. The scars spoke of that well enough on their own.

"You never did tell me how your training went," he said instead, changing the subject. There hadn't been time with the chaos of the mustering and the battle that followed.

Her eyes visibly lit up in excitement and, he thought, not a little bit of pride as she settled back and began to describe and demonstrate all she'd learned.

***

Cassius hadn't moved from his seat on the sofa in the sitting room since returning to the palace. He simply sat there, staring into the hearth as if the flames held the secrets of the universe within.

Damaris wordlessly set a steaming cup of tea on the table in front of him. She'd asked Serai to mix some herbs into it to create a mild sedative. He made no move for it, nor even glanced at it to acknowledge it. Damaris didn't mind; he would reach for it if he wanted to.

She should have been on her way to the Wind Gate, leaving as soon as her presence was no longer needed, but instead she took the seat next to Cassius, folding her hands in her lap as she too watched the flickering flames.

There was something inherently calming about staring into fire, both deadly and beautiful in its hypnotic dance. But then again, she was the Flame Guardian. Of course she would find comfort in such a thing.

Cassius stirred beside her. "You shouldn't have interfered."

She glanced at him. "If I witness someone attacking another and stand back and do nothing, that makes me no better than they are, now doesn't it? I'm not going to sit idly by and let her kill you, Cassius. You know better than that. I am no murderer."

"Some would argue otherwise."

"Of course they would, but war is different. You know that."

"You should have let her kill me," he said again.

"Is that what Cyren would want?" Damaris said, perhaps a bit harsher than she should have. But she was no good at offering comfort and empathy. That was what Lylla excelled at, not her. "I doubt she'd want you to lie down and give up, not after everything she sacrificed. She'd want you to avenge her."

"Like you're trying to avenge Bella?" There was no rancor in the words, but Damaris felt a sharp stab of pain all the same.

"Yes," she replied, making no effort to deny it. "Like I'm trying to avenge Bella."

The name of her friend brought to mind images of a beautiful elf with strawberry blonde hair, her eyes a vibrant forest green. She was sitting outside in a white wicker chair, a young boy balanced on her lap. He had the same green eyes as his mother, but his hair was an unruly crimson, from his father, William. There was a splash of freckles across his nose and he squirmed, refusing to sit still, wanting to get down and go off to explore.

Damaris remembered a time when Bella had been too busy cleaning the house to take him out to play, so she had offered to do it. Bella had been immensely grateful and had allowed the rambunctious youngster to wander off into the forest, trusting in the knowledge that he was safe with the Flame Guardian by his side.

"Is that what she would have wanted?" Cassius asked, scattering her thoughts like mist.

"I know what she wanted," Damaris murmured, recalling her friend's last words. "She wanted me to protect her son and had me swear an oath to that effect. Avenging her was just a little extra, of my own choosing. But it's not up to me to avenge her anymore, is it? Somehow, I suppose it's more fitting that way. Her son will be the one to avenge her."

"Do you think he'll be able to?"

"Yes," she said, without hesitation. "He may doubt himself, but I don't." She realized, thinking of the night Bella and William had been killed, that perhaps she knew more about how Cassius was feeling than she thought.

Lowering her voice, she added, "Galatea will pay for *every* life she's taken."

Something changed in Cassius's gaze, a hardening and hint of determination. The line of his jaw clenched even though he still did not look at her. "You're right. She'll pay."

He'll be all right, she decided.

"If there's anything I can do, just say the word."

He turned to her then, eyes glistening in the firelight. "Why are you being so kind?"

"Because there's enough cruelty in the world." And Cassius was not her enemy.

Damaris left him there, giving him some privacy, and went to find Lylla. The queen was in her personal chambers, her armor gone, her white sword hanging on the wall in its customary place when not in use. She stood before one of the open walls, staring out at nothing, arms wrapped around herself as if she were cold. The light that always shimmered in her hair seemed subdued.

"I never should have given the order to attack," she said softly.

"You couldn't have known how it would turn out," Damaris insisted.

"But I should have suspected. It's my duty to weigh and consider every possibility. If I had known, I never would have done it."

"Not every battle ends in victory. She hasn't won the war yet."

"All those lives…their blood is on my hands."

"No, it's not," Damaris said firmly, striding toward her friend, taking her hands in her own. "It's on Galatea's."

Lylla sighed. "But such is the way of leadership. If it's a good plan, you're a genius. If it's a disaster, it comes down on your head."

"We'll get her next time. I wasn't there. I should have been."

"It's a good thing you came when you did. I never should have sent you away."

"*I* insisted on going, if you recall."

Lylla smiled. "Yes, I suppose you did."

Damaris released her and stepped back. "I was just talking to Cassius."

"How is he? I worry he may do something…foolish."

"He won't. He has too much pride for that."

Lylla nodded and looked at her. "What should I do now? You always have all the answers, Ris. Tell me what I should do."

The queen wasn't usually so unsure of herself, but Damaris knew that she was mourning for those lost in her own way. Their deaths had not been by her hand, but still she blamed herself. They followed her with blind loyalty and she felt that she had led them to their deaths.

Neither of them were strangers to losing soldiers. It was unavoidable in any conflict and Lylla had been through it before. But it never got any easier. It would always be a case of *I should have thought it through more. If only I had done this…*

Damaris would not have wished the role of ruler on anyone. It was an inevitable reality that the needs of the kingdom as a whole came before those of the individual. That was why they had marched into the swamp earlier, hoping that some deaths would prevent more in the future.

"I'll think about it," Damaris replied. "And give you my answer in the morning. It's too late tonight." She doubted she could have made the journey to the Wind Gate that night regardless, exhausted as she was.

"Fair enough. I shall have to plan a ceremony for Cyren, even though we don't have a body."

Damaris nodded and took her leave.

18

Damaris spent the night at the palace, unable to completely banish her worry over whether or not Kadir could be trusted. But even if he couldn't, she had made her decision and she was too far away to do anything about it. And even if she had been, her body needed rest or else she'd be of no use to anyone.

She didn't bother worrying over her own Gate, safely nestled deep within the Enchanted Forest. True to her word, she made her way up to Lylla's personal chambers the next morning, having thought long and hard about the best path to take moving forward.

Lylla was waiting for her, wearing a dress of gold, the color of her element. Her blue hair was divided into its signature three plaits, silver bands interwoven throughout the strands.

"You asked me what I thought we should do," Damaris began. "I've given the matter plenty of thought and I think we ought to send the girl back after all, like we originally planned."

"But she's a Guardian," Lylla protested. "She needs to be trained how to use her powers."

"I agree, but not right now. It's too dangerous to keep her here, to have the Echo Stone and Galatea in the same world."

Lylla turned to look out the open wall. The morning had dawned overcast, with a chill in the air, befitting the mood that had fallen over the palace since the previous day's defeat. "Isn't that exactly why we *should* have her here? We've no guarantee that we can keep Galatea here. She's clearly more powerful than we thought."

Damaris shook her head. "I don't know how we can say that for certain. We didn't see her in the swamp, only her minions."

"That's what I mean," Lylla said patiently, walking over to the fountain. The windchimes outside clinked together. "She maintained all those undead at the cost of her own energy. Each time one fell, or one of our soldiers was felled, she had to expend more of her own strength to raise them back up. Little wonder, given the fact, that she didn't show herself during the battle. Apart from the fact that it would pose a danger to herself, I'm not sure she wanted to expend even more energy by confronting us directly."

"Of course not. Why would she? But we don't know if she can make it back to Earth again and I don't intend to give her the chance."

"But as soon as we send Sara back and Galatea learns of it, she will try."

Damaris smirked. "Not if Galatea doesn't know Sara has already been sent back and she believes she's still here."

Lylla's eyes widened. "You mean to use the mirror."

"Precisely. If we have Sara look into it, we can use it to have someone impersonate her, making it seem as though she's still in Wysteria, while the real Sara has been safely returned to Earth."

"You intend to use the fake Sara to lure Galatea out."

"We need a win after yesterday," Damaris confirmed. "It would give us the advantage. If we can get her out of her swamp and away from her horde of undead."

"It could work...but it'll be dangerous. In any case, I think we should ask Sara. She's one of us and she should have a say in this."

"Fine." Damaris wasn't sure she approved, but she'd take it.

***

Sara had just settled down to breakfast when a servant came and fetched her, saying she was needed in the queen's personal chambers. She looked up, sharing a glance with Colin and Felix, but they looked as equally perplexed as she and offered no answers.

The servant delivered her to the appropriate door and then departed. Sara stepped inside as she was bidden to enter. The room was empty except for Damaris and Lylla herself. "You wanted to see me?"

"Yes," Lylla replied. "I am considering sending you back to Earth for your own safety, and for the added purpose of luring Galatea to us." Sara listened as the queen explained the plan with the mirror and how it would be used. "I wanted to consult you first and offer you the choice. We don't have to do this; we can find another way. You are a Guardian and I offered to train you. The decision to return at this time is yours."

Damaris's eyes narrowed and Sara could tell she didn't approve of her being offered a choice. And she hadn't been given much of a choice before she'd officially become a Guardian. But still, Sara knew there was only one decision to make.

She hadn't been there herself, but she knew the battle in the swamp yesterday had gone poorly. She'd seen the evidence of that with her own eyes. It had been fought on

329

Galatea's turf, to her advantage. If they could lure her out of the swamp, they should do everything in their power to make it so. If she had thought of such a thing, she would have suggested it herself.

And while a part of her was still relieved at the idea of going back home at last, another part of her felt disappointed. It didn't seem right or fair to leave them to face Galatea alone. Her thoughts strayed back to the line of wounded she had seen the previous day, each more bruised and battered than the last. And Felix, with the image of Venryk her touch had conjured up. She didn't want to leave them, any of them.

But it would be easier now, she told herself. She was a Guardian and that meant she could always come back. It wouldn't be saying goodbye forever, the way she had previously thought. That, coupled with the obvious and badly needed advantage it provided, made the choice easy to make.

"I'll go," Sara said, hoping she sounded confident.

Lylla nodded. "Then I'll give you one last lesson before you leave. And of course, you'll be welcome to come back and continue once this mess has been dealt with."

"We'll have to make it convincing," Damaris warned. "Sara hasn't left the palace yet, except for that one instance she was lured out by Noraak. If we're going to use her illusion to lure Galatea out of the swamp, we have to make it believable. There has to be a good reason for Sara to have left the palace or Galatea will sense the trap."

"As to that," Lylla said slowly. "I think I have an idea…"

***

After the meeting was over, Sara accompanied Lylla outside as she had her first day of training. Once more, the pasture to the rear of the palace was relatively empty, giving them privacy away from prying eyes.

"What would you like me to teach you this time?" Lylla asked. "We've covered some of the offensive basics, but I think defensive uses of light are too advanced to be of much use at this stage. Have you given any thought to a secondary element?"

She had. She and Felix had discussed it in the library and she had asked him which secondary element he thought would be most useful. His answer had, perhaps unsurprisingly, been fire.

"I've decided on fire."

"An excellent choice," Lylla said, then chuckled. "I should turn you over to Damaris then. There's no one better to teach you the basics of fire."

"Is she really the most powerful Guardian?" Sara inquired, finding the idea of training with her daunting. Felix's words came back to her. *It could be worse. You could be training with Damaris.*

"Yes. That kind of mastery over an element takes centuries of practice."

Sara's eyes widened. "Centuries? How old is she?"

"Very," Lylla answered. "Older than both you and I. But don't tell her I said that."

"I don't think I have that long to learn."

"Of course you do. Humans don't age in Wysteria, remember? Wait here. I'll go fetch her." Lylla's eyes seemed to sparkle with mischief as she glanced back at her. "Good luck."

Sara swallowed nervously as she watched the queen walk back to the palace. Surely Damaris wouldn't be too hard on her. This was just to demonstrate the basics of fire. She glanced at the line of training dummies, her eyes landing on the gap between where Lylla had vaporized one. She wouldn't have wanted to be that dummy.

A few minutes later, Damaris emerged, in human form. She stood several inches taller than Sara, but not quite as tall as Lylla. The clothes she had previously worn were gone, replaced by a crimson tunic and skirt—short in the front and long in the back—with gold embroidery and black leggings. Golden armor covered her legs up to mid-thigh, vambraces shielded her arms and pauldrons on her shoulders. Sara noticed with some alarm that the armor covering her fingers ended in sharp points more akin to claws.

Her unsettling eyes landed on Sara. "So. You've chosen fire as your first secondary element."

Sara didn't think it was a question, but she nodded anyway.

"I can't say I'm surprised, nor do I think you'll be disappointed. Though I must warn you, you won't find this as easy as manipulating light."

"No. Fire isn't my attribute."

Damaris grunted, but Sara thought it was with approval. "Fire, along with lightning, is one of the most aggressive elements. Unlike some of the others, fire has little defensive applications. You can't make a wall to hide behind, like you can with ice or earth. Are you sure you don't want to learn one of those instead?"

Sara shook her head, refusing to be deterred. "Lylla said lightning or fire would be easiest to start with because they're closest to my attribute."

Damaris nodded. "They are. Fire won't provide you with much defense, but in my opinion, the best offense is good defense. The goal is to burn your opponents before they can get to you. You've learned about illuminations?"

Sara nodded.

"Fireballs are the flame equivalent and the simplest attack." Damaris raised one hand, palm side up, and fire burst to life. "You don't need to summon much, just enough to throw."

Sara opened her palm as the Flame Guardian had and tried to do as she instructed. She pictured the fire appearing in her hand and it obeyed, though it didn't burst into existence so much as slowly grow. She turned back to her instructor, ready to continue.

Damaris turned to face the training dummies. "You can do one of two things. You can throw it like you would a baseball, trust in your aim, and hope it hits your target. This method uses no extra energy. Or you can will the fire to hit your target after you've thrown it, and it will unless it's blocked."

"I don't have very good aim," Sara confessed. *Or much strength to put behind the throw.*

At school, whenever dodgeball was played, Sara never attempted to throw at the other team. The balls were an awkward size and made of foam, making them hard for her to throw with much force. They always seemed to float in the air, allowing someone on the other team to catch it, getting her out and everyone else on their team back in.

So Sara had never thrown. She had always hung back, waiting, and inevitably was usually the last one standing. It was up to her to catch one of the other team's balls and get the rest of her team back in. That was what she had excelled at. Catching.

That had all changed, of course, once they'd reached high school. Since the balls were foam, they'd theoretically hurt less, but that didn't matter. The boys had all beefed up and threw them like bullets so that they stung if they hit you.

They were harder to catch and harder to dodge. Sara could remember the loud *smack* as the balls collided with the wall at her back. She didn't have a chance to shine anymore, either, once they were in high school. The new teacher always called an end to the game before she could catch a ball, presumably to avoid her getting hurt.

Sara resented that. She might not be able to bench-press more than the bar itself, but by God, she could catch a ball.

It was strange to think of the boys hurling dodgeballs at her now. What would they say if they could see her now? What would they think if she threw fireballs at them instead of dodgeballs? Oddly comical, the thought made her smile.

"Still with us?" Damaris's voice rang loudly in her ear, making her jump.

"Y—yes." Sara felt her cheeks heat at being caught daydreaming.

"If you can't throw, you'd better guide it, then."

Now that she had her attention again, Damaris demonstrated what she wanted her to do. The Guardian flung the fireball in her hands at the nearest dummy. Rather than striking the target, it landed at its feet and exploded, a wall of flame rearing up to engulf it. The ground shook as the fireball struck and the air whooshed with the heat.

Sara flinched as the sudden heat made her skin feel tight. The dummy had effectively been reduced to ash. She reached up, surreptitiously checking to make sure she still had eyebrows. They probably needed a trim anyway.

Damaris nodded at the smoldering patch of ground. "Now you try."

Well there's no way I can replicate that. And she doubted Damaris expected her to. The Guardian probably just wanted to show off a bit. Sara would too if she were capable of such a thing.

She threw her fireball at one of the other targets, willing it to connect. It smacked into the dummy's chest, the flames catching on the burlap sack and spreading, devouring the straw filling. Sara realized she didn't have to use any energy to encourage the flames once they caught hold. Like a normal fire, it spread on its own, using what it had been given as fuel rather than feeding off her own strength.

"Not bad," Damaris remarked. "If he's not dead, I'd say he's in a lot of pain and that's enough to allow you to get away."

Sara grinned, standing up a little taller at the Guardian's praise.

"*But*," Damaris added, causing her to tense. "It's all very well and good to attack a target that can neither move nor fight back." The crimson irises of her eyes began to glow slightly, suddenly more scarlet than crimson. "But how well do you fare in a real fight?"

What? Before Sara could reply, the Guardian had rounded on her, her fists bursting into flames. She sent one hurtling toward Sara, the fire surging toward her face.

Sara didn't think; she merely acted. With a cry of surprise, she dove to the side, hoping to execute a graceful summersault and land on her feet, tensed and ready for the next attack. In reality, she landed awkwardly on her shoulder and flopped, landing on her stomach with strands of grass tickling her face.

She whipped her head around to see Damaris still standing where she had been, pulling her arm back to throw the next fireball. Sara flung one arm up, casting an illumination as Lylla had taught her—to blind, not kill.

Damaris flinched, her eyes closed protectively, and she took a step back, her free hand raised to shield her face.

Sara scrambled to her feet and took off running for the palace.

This wasn't part of the plan! What sort of madness had come over the Flame Guardian? Sara glanced up at the windows of the palace, wondering if anyone was watching and might come to her aid.

She staggered to a halt, jamming her toes in the ends of her boots, as a wall of fire rose up in front of her, spanning the length of the pasture and cutting off her escape. The palace was inaccessible and there was no hope of leaping over. The wall was as tall as she was.

Sara whirled to see Damaris stalking toward her, flames licking up over her body. She'd set herself on fire and yet she didn't so much as flinch.

"Turn and fight, Guardian!" she growled, eyes glowing red as she called upon her power.

Now Sara thought she understood what Felix had meant. The ground suddenly felt hot beneath the soles of her shoes and she jumped to the side as a column of flame erupted where she had stood only moments before.

But there was no time to stop and catch her breath. No sooner had her feet landed back on the ground than it felt hot again and she was forced to keep moving, running and leaping in a rough semi-circle around Damaris.

Sara clenched her teeth and flashed another illumination in Damaris's direction and then another. She couldn't allow the Guardian to see where to cast her attacks.

Her momentary feeling of success faded as flames sprang up around her in a circle, completely surrounding her and leaving only a few feet on either side in which to move. She glanced around desperately, searching for a gap in the flames, but the circle was complete. Sara looked up to find Damaris standing over her and she gasped.

The flames winked out of existence with a sudden *whoosh*.

Damaris's lips parted in a sudden grin, revealing bright white teeth and canines that were longer than they should have been. "You did well."

Sara exhaled a long breath. "Wh—what was all that? Are you crazy? You could have killed me."

"Yes," Damaris said seriously. "I could have killed you instantly if I'd wanted to, but I didn't. I wanted to see how you would react and handle yourself in a fight and you fared better than I expected. You didn't let fear overwhelm you."

"But why?" Sara demanded, still trying to catch her breath and still her racing heart. "I'm going back to Earth." *I'll be safe there…right?*

She suddenly wondered if the Flame Guardian knew something she didn't.

"I know," Damaris said, her eyes no longer glowing that creepy red. "But it never hurts to be prepared. That's good enough for the time being." She began to walk away, but she called over her shoulder, a wicked grin on her face. "Oh, and don't worry. You won't be facing me in a real fight."

The thought was immensely comforting, but Sara almost felt sorry for any who *would*.

With that, the Flame Guardian continued on her way, having thoroughly terrified her pupil.

***

Damaris walked back toward the palace, leaving the girl standing in the middle of the pasture, strands of hair coming undone from her braid. She had been both pleased and surprised by Sara's effort. There were those who panicked, froze in fear, and were incapable of acting at all.

Sara was not one of those, but Damaris knew it wouldn't be enough against Galatea.

Perhaps she should have taken a gentler approach, but she was no teacher. Her own mentor, Shazar, hadn't coddled her. She'd hated it at the time, but found herself grateful for it years down the line. His instruction had forged her into what she was now, had made the Flame Guardian he'd seen in her a reality. And so Damaris knew how important having a teacher was.

But still. She'd gone easy on Sara, something she would never do in a real fight and certainly not something Galatea was likely to do either. She supposed the only good thing was that Galatea couldn't kill her—not if the Echo Stone had to be given.

What might the sorceress do to that girl in order to convince her to hand over the stone? That was what worried Damaris more. *But she's going back to Earth. Galatea can't reach her there.* They would have to make sure of it.

Damaris walked into the palace to find Lylla standing in the hall. "You have a guest waiting for you in the reception hall. It's Kadir."

Kadir? What the hell was he doing here, so far from the Gate?

Without wasting time asking pointless questions that Kadir could answer himself, Damaris strode into the reception hall. Kadir stood alone, hands clasped behind his back.

He turned and spoke before she could. "Before you ask, I didn't leave the Gate unattended."

Damaris huffed. What was that supposed to mean? *He* was the Guardian. Who knew how many guards it would take to equal him alone.

"Why are you here?"

"I wanted to know the outcome of the battle. Was it a success?"

Damaris let out a bitter laugh. "If by success you mean not *everyone* died, then yes, it was a success."

Kadir bowed his head. "I'm sorry."

She sighed. "You were right. About me being needed. It was the right decision to make." She owed him for that much at least.

"You should have been there for the whole battle. You would have been, if not for me."

It was nothing Damaris hadn't thought for herself, but somehow hearing him say it took some of the fight out of her. "You needn't have come all this way. I'd have told you when I returned to the Wind Gate."

"Will you be returning? I have been informed that you are taking Sara back to Earth and I would like to assist—"

"Are you out of your mind?" Damaris demanded. How did he even know about this? The only explanation she could think of was that Lylla must have told him, though why she didn't know.

"All I ask is that you hear me out," Kadir replied. He looked as though he had aged decades since she had last seen him, the lines around his eyes and mouth more pronounced. And elves did not age beyond a certain point, unless they wished to.

"Let's hear it, then," said Damaris, gathering her patience.

Kadir wrung his weathered hands, suddenly appearing more like a man than an elf. "I didn't know who Sara was before, you must believe me, or I never would have agreed to help Galatea. No matter what she threatened. Not if I'd known."

"Why should that make a difference?" Why should it change anything?

"I knew her mother," he said simply.

"We all did."

Emily had been a Guardian, but there had been no Gate for her protect. She hadn't stayed in Wysteria very long before returning to her own world and the life that waited for her there. Damaris hadn't thought about Emily in years, not until recently, when she'd received word she had died.

"Yes, but…I knew her in a different way. I cared for her, you understand. I…loved her. But whatever her feelings toward me, they were not the same as my feelings for her. She didn't love me; not in that way. So I let her go. Her happiness meant the world to me and if that meant she loved another, then…" He trailed off. "After my wife died, I never thought I could love again, only to find myself in love with a human. Of all things." Kadir shook his head.

"That is why you helped Galatea," Damaris muttered.

"Yes. I knew what she felt for Jack. I understand what drove her to do the things she did. If Emily had loved me, everything would have been all right. She would have been allowed to stay and we could be together because she was a Guardian. Jack was not. They were both human. That was the only difference. But for a twist of fate, Jack's fate could have been Emily's."

"Why didn't you tell me?"

"Would that have changed what I have done? I don't expect you to understand, but I am sorry. I deeply regret my actions. I would never knowingly put Emily's daughter in danger. And the elf she has become is not the Galatea I knew…"

Damaris believed him and not merely because she wanted to.

"No," she said softly. "She's not the Galatea any of us knew. She killed Cyren in the swamp and reanimated her dead body and nearly used it to strangle Cassius to death. *That* is who she has become."

Kadir paled. "I didn't know. She must be stopped. I see that now. I will *not* allow her to harm Sara. I swear on my life, I will do all I can to protect her."

It was eerily similar to the vow Damaris had made to Bella, on that fiery night in the village in the forest, while a little boy clung to her.

When he next spoke, Kadir's voice was ragged, eyes brimming with unshed tears. "I have hurt you, Damaris, far more than I have anyone else. I know our friendship can never be what it once was, but I ask that, if you can, you find it in your heart to forgive me."

Damaris lowered her gaze to stare at the blue and white floor tiles. And she knew what she must say. "When I left after confronting you about the truth, I was sure I would never forgive you."

Kadir flinched.

"But what I saw in that swamp changed my perspective. I witnessed what happens when you hold on to anger and bitterness and it becomes hate. Hate made Galatea kill one of her fellow Guardians and resurrect Cyren's dead body to turn it against her brother. Galatea has nurtured her hatred and look what has become of her." She looked up at him and met his gaze. "I will not become like her. I don't want to be angry anymore."

And it was true. She could feel her anger slipping away, like a robe that had been shed.

"Revenge isn't worth it. It is willing to destroy everything and everyone in its path and then, if and when it finally gets what it thinks it wants, it is still unhappy and can't understand why. Galatea may not realize that or care, but I do. I forgive you, Kadir."

She stepped forward, closing the distance between them, and wrapped her arms around her friend.

Kadir stiffened in surprise before returning the gesture. "I don't deserve such mercy."

"I'm not sure any of us do."

"I cannot take back what I have done. I cannot make things the way they used to be."

"No," Damaris agreed, releasing him. "But you can strive to be better than you were before. And sometimes that has to be enough."

Kadir let out a choking laugh. "When did you get to be so wise, *kirena?*"

It was almost as if his grandfather, Shazar, had uttered those words.

***

Sara was sent back without ceremony or fanfare, accompanied to the Lightning Gate, where Wanderer stood sentinel, by Lylla and Felix. While Wanderer opened the Gate, Sara turned to Felix.

"I hope this plan works," she remarked, suddenly feeling at a loss for words. She felt like she should say something to him, but unsure what. Nothing seemed adequate, given what they had gone through together.

She had always been awkward at goodbyes as it was, even if she was just leaving a friend's house. She would stall and loiter by the door or in the kitchen, carrying on a conversation about something inconsequential, unsure what to say or do.

"So do I," he replied, giving her a small half-smile that struck her as somehow nervous.

A brief flash of light flared behind her and Wanderer stepped back. "Gate's open."

"Be careful, okay?" Sara said, suddenly fearful for Felix. If the trap went wrong… He had been one of the lucky ones to survive the encounter in the swamp, but one could never take things for granted or assume luck would be on their side again.

"You, too."

There was something sad about his green eyes. Later Sara would wonder what had come over her, but perhaps it was just that, that made her step forward and wrap her arms around him in a hug.

She felt him tense in surprise and then put his arms around her tentatively. It lasted only a moment and then she let go and stepped back, her face burning as hot as Damaris's fire.

Wanderer looked at her hesitantly. "Will you miss it here? I'll miss having you around."

Sara nodded. "I will." When she had first stepped through the Gate, all she'd wanted was to go home. But now that she was getting her wish, it was bittersweet. *Funny how that happens.*

"It's only temporary," Lylla assured her. "But I wish you well, until we meet again. Be safe."

Wanderer patted her on the shoulder. "Take care, kid. If you find yourself in any trouble, you know where to find Hank."

That she did.

Sara took a deep breath and stepped forward toward the waiting Gate, glancing over her shoulder even as she stepped through. The forest around her vanished, replaced by the white tiles of the gas station bathroom walls.

She could still see the three of them, standing in another world. And then the Gate swung shut, the tiles shifting back into place, and she found herself looking at a plain wall.

***

Lylla instructed Felix and Colin to remove Noraak from his cell and bring him to Serai's quarters. She was glad that she had chosen to spare Noraak's life, in the event he might prove useful. It was her hope that he would soon prove very useful indeed.

Right now, all she wanted was for Noraak to stop thanking her profusely for her generosity in allowing his sight to be restored. Lylla sighed to herself as Serai sat Noraak down on one of the cots and set to work.

Lylla stepped outside the room, where Damaris waited, lowering her voice as though in confidence, but loud enough for anyone within the room to hear.

"We'll send the girl back through the Lightning Gate at dusk."

"Are you sure that's wise?" Damaris asked, playing her role of devil's advocate.

"She's not a prisoner here," Lylla replied. "I can't keep her forever and she wants to go home. She thinks it's too dangerous here and besides, it's better this way. Galatea will be unable to get to her once she's through."

"Very well. Dusk then."

Lylla glanced at the doorway, confident that Noraak had heard every word.

∗∗∗

Noraak blinked, hardly daring to believe that he could see again. He looked at the desert elf kneeling before him, marked as the healer by her white tattoos. "Thank you!" he cried, then saw a taller figure standing in the doorway.

He knew it was the queen. He'd heard tales about her long turquoise hair that sparkled in the light. Noraak moved forward, willing to fall on his knees at her feet and thank her for the mercy she had shown him if that was what it took to get back in her good graces.

"Thank you, Your Majesty," he began. "How can I ever repay you—"

Lylla ignored him, turning to her two guards, dressed in black. One of them had tanned skin and blond hair with light blue eyes. The other was pale, with hair a rare shade of crimson, and green eyes. The left side of his face was marred with scars and it made Noraak cringe to lay eyes on him.

The queen gestured to Noraak, speaking to her guards. "Take him outside the palace walls, to the cliffs, and kill him." Her voice was like shards of ice, cold and sharp. "Throw the body in the sea when you're done."

Noraak's eyes widened. "What? No! Your Majesty, I beg of you, have mercy!" Each of the guards seized one of his arms, hauling him to his feet and began to drag him away.

Lylla's blue eyes were flinty. "You are a traitor and will die a traitor's death."

"Then why bother healing me?" he cried.

She leaned so close her face nearly touched his. "So you can see your death coming." She turned, her long yellow dress swirling about her feet, and strode down the hall without a backward glance.

Too shocked to struggle, Noraak stared after her as the soldiers dragged him away. He had heard tales of Queen Lylla the Lightbringer and her mercy and kindness but it would seem that they were lies, nothing more than propaganda to benefit her reputation. For he had seen neither in her gaze.

He knew struggling was pointless. Both of the guards were stronger and taller than he was, their muscles honed and hardened by the relentless training they received at the palace to become one of the queen's Shadows.

They led him out of the fenced area that designated the palace grounds, over toward one of the cliffs that overlooked the Green Sea beyond. Noraak felt bile rise in his throat. He knew what happened to traitors and it was just as the queen had said.

Killed at the cliffs, in one way or another throughout history. Sometimes they were killed first and thrown in. Others, they were weighed down with enormous stones and tossed into the water alive to drown.

Seeing as how the two Shadows had no stones with them, he suspected it would be the former. Hardly any better. Death awaited regardless, the body consigned to the depths for the sea serpents and sirens to eat.

No, it couldn't end like this! He had survived too much to die. Not here, not now.

In fact, he might be able to get a little revenge on all of them for treating him this way, if only he could get away. They were going to take the girl through the Lightning Gate at dusk. Noraak wasn't sure that Galatea would be pleased to see him after he'd been gone so long—and having failed her again.

But she would be interested in what he had to tell her.

Noraak had conserved his energy the entire trip, refusing to waste it by struggling, and he chose his moment with care.

He slammed his foot down on the blond Shadow's instep, eliciting an oath and the grip on his right arm weakened. Noraak jammed his elbow into the scarred elf's stomach and was rewarded with a satisfying gasp of pain.

Noraak broke free of their hold and ran for the forest. The crimson-haired elf had a bow, which could put a quick end to his flight and for a moment, he imagined them dragging his lifeless body back toward the cliffs. But if he could just make it to the tree line, he'd be safe…

An arrow whizzed past his ear, narrowly missing, but a miss all the same. Noraak's lungs felt like they might burst and he waited for the next arrow to come flying and find its mark.

But it never did and he vanished into the shade of the Enchanted Forest.

***

Felix lowered his bow with a sigh, grimacing and rubbing his ribs.

Colin grinned up at him from his place on the ground, where he sat massaging the toes that had been trod upon. "He got you good."

"He caught me on one of my bruises." Felix gingerly returned the bow to his back. "Pity I missed him." There was a lightness to his tone as he made the remark.

Colin's grin widened. Noraak might have been fooled, but he knew the truth.

Felix never missed unless he wanted to.

***

Noraak wasted little time returning to the swamp. He stumbled to a halt at the entrance to the ruins, surprised by how visibly the landscape had been changed. The gnarled trees, already dark in color, had been singed by fire. Where there had once been pools of swamp water, there were now empty pits in some places. The ruins themselves had been changed the most.

If possible, they looked even more damaged than before, lying in crumbled heaps of stone. As Noraak walked along the path, he took care to avoid more than one gaping hole, cracks spiderwebbing outward. He misplaced his step once and the ground gave way beneath him, nearly sending him plummeting.

Where were all of Galatea's undead? The last time he had been there, they had been lined up and were standing in plain sight, impossible to miss. Now there was no sign of them. Or anything or anyone else.

He considered calling out to his mistress, to announce his presence, thinking it a good idea since he had been gone for some time. If there were still undead lurking here, he didn't want to startle them into attacking.

Noraak nearly leapt out of his skin as Venryk sprang from behind one of the piles of rubble.

"Oh," the wolf growled. "It's you."

The elf clapped a hand to his chest. "Where's Galatea?"

Venryk jerked his head in the direction leading further into the swamp. "This way."

After a brief hesitation, Noraak followed him. "Where are all the undead?"

"Further on, with her. We lost more than intended in the skirmish."

"What skirmish?" Noraak hadn't heard anything about any battle, but he supposed he couldn't really be expected to, locked away as he'd been.

Venryk let out a derisive growl. "Lylla and her forces invaded the swamp. If you'd been here, you'd have known that."

If I'd been here, I'd probably be dead right now, Noraak thought but did not say. "I'd have thought Galatea would reanimate any of the fallen undead."

"She would have, but the reason we lost them is because, thanks mostly to the Flame Guardian, there was nothing left to reanimate."

The building that Noraak had raised for Galatea to stay in had been destroyed in the battle. Venryk took him to the entrance of the Necropolis, where Galatea was sitting on the ground, surrounded by her creatures.

The sorceress rose to her feet. Her Shadowblade was drawn, gripped in one hand. He couldn't read the emotion in her black irises, but her lips were turned down in a scowl and Noraak didn't think she was as pleased to see him as he would have liked.

"Where have you been?" she demanded. "My wolves informed me that you failed to capture the girl and that you'd been blinded in the process."

He fidgeted. "True, but the blindness, I'm happy to say, has worn off."

Noraak refused to further wound his pride by admitting that he'd had to be healed by his captors.

"Then why," Galatea asked, "have you taken so long in returning to me?"

"I was captured," he confessed. There was no way to impart the news he had heard without mentioning how he had come by it. "But don't worry—I told them nothing, though they interrogated me. Because I refused to talk, they took me to the cliffside in order to kill me and toss my body into the sea."

"And yet here you stand."

"I managed to break free of the guards and escape. I came directly here to tell you. While in the palace, I overheard a vital piece of information that I think you'll be most eager to hear."

Galatea still had not put the sword away. "Enlighten me."

This was it. Noraak took a deep breath. "Lylla plans to send the human girl back to Earth through the Lightning Gate at dusk. She will be out of the palace and I thought you could use the opportunity to get the Echo Stone before they send her through and it's too late."

He had Galatea's full attention now.

"Well done, Noraak. You can come with me, as a way of making up for your past failures. There's just one more thing. Do you have my mirror?"

He grimaced. "I'm afraid not. I heard the queen give the Lightning Guardian permission to destroy it."

Galatea *tsked* softly. "Well. It doesn't much matter now."

*****

As dusk approached that evening, Galatea set out from the swamp, accompanied by Noraak, Venryk, the remainder of her Nightmares, and only a few undead. It was a risk not to bring more, but a larger force would be difficult to conceal and would also require more of her energy during the battle, which was better used as fuel for her own powers.

Galatea didn't know if she would be able to cross through a Gate again, which she'd have to do in order to reach the girl once she had been sent back. If this succeeded, she could capture the girl before she was out of her reach and retreat with her to the swamp. Once there, Galatea was confident she could convince the girl to give her the stone.

This was an opportunity she could not afford to pass up.

Even if she suspected it to be a trap.

Allowing Noraak to hear such information was far more careless than Galatea took Lylla for. Which meant it was deliberate, from him overhearing the information to his miraculous escape.

But it was a far riskier move on Lylla's part than it would be for her. After being routed in the swamp, Lylla was willing to risk the girl's life in order to lure Galatea away from her advantage. That would be her mistake.

The loss of the mirror was disappointing but Galatea doubted she'd have used it again anyway. Another illusion wouldn't have fooled them all a third time. That was the problem with Lylla, though. She saw some of the more devious artifacts as dangerous, better to be destroyed than utilized, as though she were afraid of them.

Their small group halted before reaching the Lightning Gate and observed through the trees. She could see Lylla's assembly making their way toward the Gate, Wanderer standing guard. The queen had come herself, of course, along with her two personal Shadows and the human girl.

That gave Galatea pause. *So few.* If this was a trap, Lylla hadn't brought many with her. Suddenly she wondered if she'd been wrong, if paranoia was getting the better of her. Perhaps this was nothing more than it appeared to be.

The small procession had nearly reached the Gate. It was time.

Galatea signaled to her troops and Venryk sprang forward with the Nightmares, leading them out of the cover of the trees and charged directly for the Gate.

Wanderer whirled around in alarm and blasted lightning at the nearest Nightmare. The creature merely shifted into mist to avoid the attack and reformed elsewhere.

Galatea gripped her Shadowblade, already having once tasted Guardian blood and hungry for more. She darted forward, sticking to the shadows, hoping to get close to the girl, Sara. Lylla spotted her and sent a beam of light surging her way. Galatea lifted a hand, darkness pooling in front of her, absorbing the light before it could reach her.

The sorceress retaliated with an attack of her own, but the queen merely blocked it with an illumination, burning the darkness away. They were evenly matched, it seemed, as Galatea had predicted. Light and dark canceled each other out. In a weaker light attribute, such as the girl, Galatea would have little trouble overwhelming her, but Lylla was as strong as any Guardian. In a direct confrontation, it would come down to the use of Galatea's secondary elements and whoever made a mistake first.

But Galatea didn't have time to indulge in a fight with Lylla and she broke away, a Nightmare momentarily demanding the queen's attention. Lightning crackled from Wanderer's fingertips, but unless she called upon her secondary element of fire, she could not destroy the corpses and prevent them from rising again.

A feral yelp caused Galatea to turn toward Venryk, an arrow protruding from his shoulder. Felix drew another arrow to finish the wolf off and Galatea felt a surge of anger. If the scarred wood elf was not Venryk's to finish, she'd have struck him dead on the spot.

But that didn't mean she couldn't offer a little assistance. She flung one hand up and darkness surged forward like a black wave, blinding the archer. His horse neighed in alarm and backpedaled.

With that threat taken care of, Galatea turned her attention back on Sara and took a step toward her.

The girl's eyes widened and she backed away, the chain hanging around her neck clearly visible. Galatea reached out toward her and in that moment, the girl's appearance changed.

Her eyes, which had been brown, became crimson and yellow. Galatea stared at her in horror, recognizing her mistake a second too late. This was why Lylla had felt confident traveling with so few.

She yanked her hand back as Sara vanished, replaced by Damaris, the mirror hanging around her neck.

Flames sprang up from the ground and Galatea cried out as they seared her arm. She swung the Shadowblade, the sword connecting with the mirror hanging around the unicorn's neck. The glass shattered but the Guardian was otherwise unhurt. Damaris bared her teeth and sprang forward with a snarl, jaws parted, flames engulfing her.

Galatea staggered back, swinging up her sword as she did so. It whistled past Damaris's nose, but it forced the Guardian to come to a stop.

The sorceress threw an orb of darkness at her feet. It exploded into black smoke, the world thrown into pitch blackness. Galatea turned and fled, giving the order to retreat, heading back toward the swamp.

It had been a trap, just as she'd expected. But what she hadn't expected was for the girl not to be a girl at all. She should have suspected something when she hadn't spotted Damaris among the group! Lylla would never attempt such a thing without her most powerful Guardian.

She had underestimated the queen. Lylla hadn't destroyed the mirror at all, but had instead used it against her. Galatea had made a grave mistake and nearly paid the price for it. She didn't stand a chance against Damaris when she had the advantage of surprise.

By the time the darkness cleared, Galatea was out of sight, clenching her teeth against the pain in her arm. She dared not look at it, afraid of what she would see, knowing she had been lucky. Venryk limped beside her as they reached the ruins, the arrow still stuck in his shoulder.

Noraak, for his part, had survived without a mark on him.

That little detail nearly undid Galatea.

With a growl, she turned on Noraak. "This is your fault! Your information led us into a trap!"

She had been so sure she would get her hands on the stone this evening and finally be able to resurrect Jack. But all she had managed was to make a fool of herself, suffer a serious burn—if the pain was anything to judge by—and lose more of her soldiers.

She should have known better. And the fact that she hadn't, that she'd fallen for it anyway, only added fuel to the fire of her anger.

Noraak quailed beneath her fury. "How was I to know?"

"Oh, don't play coy with me!" Galatea hissed, teeth bared. "Did you really think you had managed to escape from the palace on your own? You were helped. They *let* you go."

"That's hardly fair—" Noraak began.

Galatea swung her Shadowblade in an arc as though it weighed nothing. The blade slashed from Noraak's collarbone to his ribs, silencing his words.

His yellow eyes stared at her in shock and pain. His throat moved, but only a choked gurgle came out as blood spilled over his tunic. Noraak's knees buckled beneath him and he collapsed onto the cobblestones.

Galatea stood, trembling with unsated rage, and watched him bleed out, unable to conjure a shred of sympathy for the shadow elf who had outlived his usefulness. She did not turn away until the last of the light faded from his eyes.

Killing him had done nothing to assuage her anger. She would not rest until she held that Echo Stone in her hand. She had waited for it long enough.

The Shadowblade still thirsted for the blood of a Guardian and Galatea was eager to comply.

19

ank kindly offered to drive Sara home. She walked up the steps to her house to find the door unlocked.

Her dad wasn't home yet from work so for now, she had the house all to herself. Sara pulled her phone out of her pocket and hooked it up to its charger. It had gone completely dead during its time in Wysteria. A quick glance at the date revealed that time passed in Wysteria the same as it did on Earth.

Sara knew she should find some way of letting Nadia and Max know she was back. They deserved that much at least. But she didn't feel ready to face them. She didn't know what they'd been told or where they thought she'd been. They would ask her questions that she wasn't prepared to answer.

She would have to lie, a fact that she knew was necessary but hated all the same. As much as she might want to, there was no chance she could confide what had really happened.

Just as well her dad wasn't home. She had questions for him that she wasn't sure she wanted to ask, much less know the answer to.

Sara made her way to the kitchen, taking down one of the instant meals in the cabinet and popped it in the microwave. Minutes later, she was sitting on the couch, eating Szechuan chicken and watching the evening news, even though she had no interest in it.

It never covered anything that happened in her small town, but she somehow felt the need to reassure herself that the world wasn't coming to an end. That nothing drastic had happened during the time she was gone.

It appeared not.

Her dad arrived before she'd finished her chicken, looking tired as he always did, having to commute an hour each way to his job because there were none nearby that paid decently.

He froze as he saw her, then smiled. "You're back."

"Yeah…for now. You know, don't you?"

"I knew about it," he sighed, setting his briefcase down. "I just thought that was the end of it. After your mother…I didn't expect it to come back into our lives again."

Sara reached over, turning the TV down. "Mom was a Guardian. That's how you knew."

Her dad sank down into one of the armchairs. "She didn't tell me at first, but I knew something was up. It's a bit difficult to live with someone for so many years and not wonder where it is they sneak off to. You know, there was a time your mother visited Lawrence so often that I suspected she might be having an affair."

Sara stared at him, speechless, searching for something to say.

"I confronted her about it. She seemed to think it was funny and then apologized for keeping me in the dark. She realized it wasn't possible any longer and so she offered to take me to Lawrence, saying he would explain. I went along with it and they both proceeded to tell me. I thought they were having a laugh at my expense, but Lawrence took me to his Gate and I crossed over for a few seconds." He shrugged. "It's a bit difficult to disbelieve when one moment, you're in the woods, and the next, you're standing in the middle of the desert with the sun blinding you."

"Then, if you knew, why didn't you tell me?" Sara asked, her heart giving a little twinge. "Why didn't either of you tell me?"

"I barely knew anything myself. I knew enough of the truth, to know where my wife went and how she was involved and I left it at that. It was good enough for me. We didn't know if you would ever display powers of your own. And then with your mother gone, I saw no reason to mention it. It seemed…better somehow. Easier to move on. I'm sorry if that doesn't make sense. I hardly understand it myself."

But Sara did understand it. It would have been a memory of Emily Montgomery, now dead and gone and never to return. She had memories of her own that she'd tried to bury because just thinking of them was enough to make Sara feel like she was breaking apart all over again.

"Well I do have powers," Sara said, holding up both hands and willing light to flare briefly. "And I'm a Guardian, just like she was."

She hadn't tried to summon magic since she'd left Wysteria. Part of her wondered if the magic would come at all or if she'd somehow imagined it. But the light did come. It was harder than it had been in Wysteria, where you could almost feel magic in the very air you breathed, but the magic was there.

Her magic.

"I can see that. I take it you'll be going back?"

"Yes. I don't know when."

Her dad nodded, looking slightly unhappy about something, but Sara had no idea what.

Suddenly, she wondered how much he knew about the danger she'd been in. "You did know where I was, didn't you?"

"Lawrence told me. He said you'd be staying there, but he didn't say for how long."

So he didn't know then. Sara decided not to tell him. He would only try to keep her from returning and besides, he and her mom weren't the only ones who could keep secrets.

He stood, looking as though he wanted to say something more, and then decided against it. "We can talk more about it later, if you'd like."

"Yeah," Sara said, her voice sounding strangely flat to her own ears.

He nodded, then retreated down the hall, likely to take a shower.

Sara sighed, watching him go, and then looked down at her hands. Golden light flared briefly once more, reassuring her that this *was* real.

All of it.

The following day, she met up with Nadia and Max at the park at noon. Nadia had stopped at McDonald's and ordered food for all three of them. Sara munched on some of the salty fries, but all she could think was that they certainly didn't have anything like this in Wysteria.

What was happening there right now? Were her friends fighting Galatea even now? Had they won or lost? Had anyone been killed? Sara hated not knowing. That was the worst part of all, even worse than the dread she'd felt while waiting for the others to return from the swamp.

In the end, having little appetite, she tossed most of her fries to the squirrels, who seemed to like them.

"Hello?" Nadia said loudly. "Earth to Sara!"

Sara blinked and turned to her. "What?"

"I was just saying, you don't seem yourself. Ever since you got back from that internship."

She had explained away her absence by saying that she had taken a brief internship out of town. It had been a last minute decision and she'd barely made it and so that's why she'd rushed off without saying anything. She told them that the internship hadn't gone well and that she didn't want to talk about it, to avoid having to answer unwanted questions.

Her lack of communication she blamed on her phone being dead, which was partly true. It might have seemed a lame excuse, but her friends knew she had a cheap phone that had been having battery problems for months. She really needed to replace it, but couldn't be bothered.

Sara wasn't sure if her friends believed her story, but it was the best she could come up with. They certainly wouldn't believe the truth.

And the truth was that she didn't feel like herself. Not since she'd returned from Wysteria. How could she? She didn't even know who she was anymore. Or, as her dad always wanted to know, what she planned on doing with the rest of her life. Whatever she may have considered, Wysteria had thrown another factor into the mix that couldn't be discounted.

Whatever else she may have been and whatever she wanted to be, she was a Guardian. There was no denying that.

But more than that, she felt like she didn't even know who her own family members were. Her dad, mom, Hank, Lawrence…all of them had turned out to be different than what she'd thought.

Even this small town, that she'd long yearned to be free of, was more than it appeared. Her life had been derailed, turned upside down first by her mother's death and now this.

And she couldn't share it with any of them.

"Just tired, I guess," she said to Nadia and threw another fry to the squirrels.

***

The ceremony for Cyren was held the day after Sara had been sent back. There was no body to gather around, but that didn't stop everyone from assembling. Cassius was there, naturally, dressed entirely in black, the first time Felix had ever seen him wear the color.

Wanderer and Damaris were also present to show their support for a fellow Guardian. Kadir, unsurprisingly, remained absent, his recent actions likely still too raw.

Lylla presided over the service, saying a few words about Cyren's character and how she had died faithfully serving her kingdom. Cassius did not give a speech, but he, as a relative of the deceased, was the first to toss a handful of silver roses—symbolizing mourning—over the cliffside and into the sea. The others followed suit, starting down the ranks with Lylla next as the queen and then the other Guardians.

Words were offered for those who perished in the assault on the swamp and moments of silence observed.

Various dishes had been provided for after the service, but no one seemed particularly hungry. The Icelandic dragons had agreed to remain at the palace, following the failed attack on the swamp, until after the ceremony was over.

"She doesn't look happy," Colin whispered, nodding to Empress.

Felix glanced at the dragon and silently concurred, but he found it hard to concentrate. All he could think of was the failed trap they'd set for Galatea. She had come and she had escaped.

Immediately after the service had concluded, the Guardians made their way back to their Gates. With the trap having failed, they would have to ensure that the sorceress did not cross back over to Earth. Having escaped the trap, Galatea might assume that Sara had returned to Earth and attempt to get to her.

They couldn't afford to have any of the Gates unguarded. Even coming here to this briefest of ceremonies had been a risk, but Cassius had insisted. He would not be denied.

Felix knew that Damaris felt ill at ease at letting Galatea slip through their fingers, but it wasn't her escape that irritated him so much as Venryk's.

He had managed to land a hit on the wolf and had the chance to finish him off. And he would have! But Galatea intervened.

"I suppose we shouldn't have been surprised," Damaris had growled afterward. "I'd have done the same had the roles been reversed."

Felix knew the truth of her words, and while he would have been grateful for her intervention, it was only a temporary reprieve. Until that wolf breathed his last by his hand, Felix continued to face down a death sentence.

And if that wasn't enough to worry about, Galatea's escape was far more dangerous, not for him, but for Sara. The Guardians were the only thing standing in the sorceress's way now and they had lost one. With Cyren gone, no one guarded the Ice Gate.

Felix found himself worrying about what was happening on the other side of the Gates. Was Sara safe? Was she as worried for her own safety as he was? Or was she worried for his?

What if it was already too late?

***

Empress remained where she was, watching the proceedings for a time, and then rose to her feet, making her way over to where Lylla stood, set back a little from the crowd, alone.

The queen looked up as she approached. "I expect you'll be wanting to head back to Iceland now."

"Yes," Empress replied. "But I wanted to talk to you about something first." She glanced over toward the cliffside, where people were still tossing roses. In time, a statue of Cyren would be made in her honor and join those already within the courtyard and gardens. "With Cyren gone, and the Reverend having preceded her, there are no Guardians at the Ice Gate, on either side."

"Yes, I'm painfully aware of that."

Empress tilted her head slightly, frowning. "Well since Galatea escaped the trap you set, you know what will happen next. She knows the girl was a fake and you lost the mirror in the process. She'll be after the real Sara now and that means she has to get through one of the Gates. With the Ice Gate completely unprotected, it isn't hard to imagine which one she'll pick."

"No," Lylla murmured. "And we don't have any Ice Guardians to spare."

"You don't have *any* extra Guardians period," Empress pointed out.

362

"No. Empress, could you assign some of your people to that Gate?"

The dragon pulled a face. "I suppose so. Though I fail to see what good it'll do against a Guardian."

"You're dragons. Just put as many as you can spare on the Gate."

"Personally, I'm a little surprised you asked me," Empress admitted. "Since I had…questionable loyalties at best."

"You fought alongside us at the swamp," Lylla replied.

"Yes, and I'm hardly likely to change sides now, am I? Given how publicly I announced my intentions by siding with you during that fight, I doubt Galatea would welcome us back if I came crawling to her and begged."

"I find the idea unlikely," Lylla murmured, meaning it in both senses.

Galatea would never forgive Empress that betrayal.

And Empress would never beg.

***

After leaving the park, Sara drove herself to Professor Lawrence's house and walked up to the door, thinking back to the day she'd first been dragged into this mess. He was at home, as she expected, and let her in.

"So you've come back. I expected you would, before long," he said, shutting the door behind her. "Would you like some lemonade?"

"No, thank you. I just wanted to talk to you."

"I imagine there's much on your mind." The two of them moved into the living room where they could talk comfortably.

"Yes." Sara sat heavily in the ugly floral chair. "You knew I was a Guardian, didn't you?"

"Suspected. We can't know for sure until the magic reveals itself."

"Still…why didn't you tell me?"

Professor Lawrence grimaced, but his gaze was steady. "Would you have believed me if I had?"

Sara would have liked to say yes, but despite all she had seen and learned since stepping through that first Gate, she still wasn't sure she'd have believed that *she* was a Guardian herself. She looked down, picking at the fabric on the armrest.

"I'm really very sorry I wasn't able to be there for you myself," he added. "But I have a duty to protect my Gate and so that's where I need to be."

"How can you stand it?" Sara said suddenly, looking up.

"Stand what?" Professor Lawrence repeated. "That chair? It is rather ugly, isn't it? But it's an antique, been in the family for years."

"No, not the chair," Sara said, fighting a smile in spite of herself. "I mean, how do you, as a Guardian, sit on this side not knowing what's going on? Doesn't it bother you?"

"Of course it does. Especially given the recent circumstances. Although I must say, it's been rather quiet for the past fifty years. Still, I have to remember that the Guardians in Wysteria are stronger than I am and I have to trust them. That's what being a Guardian is about. You each trust the other, on the other side of the Gate, and that you'll each do your job when the time comes."

"But I don't have a Gate," Sara muttered.

"No, but you're also a Light Guardian. Given enough time, you might become more powerful than the others."

But I'm not powerful now! Sara wanted to scream. What good was any of that if she didn't have the power to help now, when it mattered?

"I can always cross over and check on things, if you'd like," he offered.

Sara rose to her feet. "No, that's all right. I'm just being impatient."

"You miss it," Professor Lawrence said softly. "You miss *them*."

"Yes," Sara admitted. "I do."

And she did, far more than she'd have thought possible.

Sara bid the Professor goodbye and walked back to her car. His words came back to her. *Given enough time, you might become more powerful than the others.* And something Damaris had said about it not hurting to be prepared.

Maybe she was never meant to go back. Maybe that was just something she'd been told to make leaving easier. Maybe it would be better if she just forgot about the whole thing and moved on with her life instead of wanting something she couldn't have.

But there would be no forgetting. No moving on. Not from this.

***

Galatea departed the swamp that evening, with her sword at her side and Jack seated behind her on the horse Noraak had stolen from the palace. All of the Gates were guarded, save for one, but still she had to think long and hard about which she would choose.

The Ice Gate was vulnerable, both of its Guardians dead by her hand, making it the most obvious choice. For that reason, she passed it by. If she recognized that fact, she could be sure Lylla would also. After Lylla's clever utilization of the mirror for her own purposes, Galatea vowed not to underestimate her again.

In the fading light, she rode toward the desert and the Wind Gate. She would pay Kadir one last visit and see if she found him once more amenable to her will.

Her bandaged arm throbbed, the burn raw and angry. She ignored it, nothing more than an inconvenience she would pay Damaris back for. She could see to it once she had finally resurrected Jack. That took precedence over all else.

She encountered no one among the desolate dunes until she neared the temple. She found Kadir alone, almost as if he knew to expect her.

"What do you want?" he called as she reined her horse to a halt. "I won't assist you anymore."

His words came as no surprise. Somehow, Galatea had suspected he wouldn't help her. She'd pushed her luck—pushed him—one too many times.

She dismounted, approaching slowly, leaving Jack with the horse. "Why not? I thought we had a deal, you and I."

He shook his head. "That was before. Now turn around unless you're looking for a fight."

Galatea sighed. "Have it your way, then."

She summoned the darkness to cloak herself and darted forward. Unlike Kadir, she could see in pitch darkness, though it was not the same as normal vision. Inanimate objects glowed softly, enough to make out their outlines, while living beings glowed red and blue, the light pulsing in the center of their chests where the heart would be.

Galatea drew her Shadowblade back, slicing it downward toward Kadir's chest. The blade never completed its arc. At last, Kadir made good on his oath and called upon the desert winds.

Thrown back by the force, Galatea's focus slipped. The darkness faded. Kadir summoned lightning and sent it toward her, but the darkness absorbed it before it reached her.

The wind sprang up again, throwing sand into her eyes and Galatea winced, staggering back. The gale was too strong for her to reach him and she could scarcely see from all the sand being stirred up. Panic momentarily stabbed her. She needed to do something and fast.

"Stand aside!" she screamed, unsure if he could even hear her over the wind. She didn't want to hurt him, but she would if he gave her no other choice.

"I won't let you hurt her!" he shouted back, his voice carrying perfectly on the wind.

Galatea pushed back with a tempest of her own, though not as strong as his, lamenting the fact that she no longer had control over the earth and could not simply cause the ground to open up beneath him. It would have served as a wonderful distraction.

Her conjured windstorm did not cancel his out, but it bought her enough time. She could see shadows within the temple, beneath the large pillars at the entrance, cast by the dying rays of the setting sun.

She called them forward, engulfing Kadir. Galatea threw herself to the side, summoning an ice spear behind the Wind Guardian as she did so. The howling wind dispersed the darkness like fog and then immediately died, revealing in stark detail what Galatea had hoped for.

The shard of ice had speared upward from the ground behind Kadir, piercing him through the back. His face contorted in pain, and Galatea knew she had a few seconds, maybe less, before he rallied and the winds would come again.

Gripping her Shadowblade, she strode forward. The sword sang as it whipped through the air, slicing into his neck.

Galatea heard two impacts behind her, the first as Kadir's body fell to the ground and the second a moment later as his head joined the rest of him.

She glanced back, lowering the sword, breathing heavily. The sand, stained red, was already beginning to soak up the blood. Like Noraak, Kadir had simply outlived his usefulness.

Galatea fetched Jack and then headed for the Gate in the back of the temple.

20

Damaris knew something was wrong the moment the temple came into view. It was too quiet, too motionless, not a sound traveling on the desert wind. Bracing herself, she strode forward.

She froze, breath hitching, at the sight before her. Her instinct urged her to rush forward and kneel beside her friend, but she knew there was no need. Not now. Kadir was dead and she had been too late to save him.

If only she hadn't attended the ceremony for Cyren. If only she'd left for the Wind Gate immediately after the trap had failed. She could have prevented this!

For a moment, she saw Bella's body lying there instead of Kadir, mutilated beyond recognition. She had seen the smoke, heard the cries, but still she'd come too late. She was always too late.

Damaris squeezed her eyes shut, but the image was seared in her memory, imprinted on her eyelids.

And the worst part was, she had wanted this. How she had berated Kadir for breaking his oath rather than upholding it. Hadn't she been the one to tell him that he should die in defense of his Gate if that was what it took?

Her shock faded, melting away before the force of something stronger. Her anger spread over her slowly, heat creeping over her skin. She knew better than to let the wave carry her away, but she let it deepen, harden, turning into rage. She buried it deep within herself, to be unleashed later. Right now, she had to think. She had to act.

It might already be too late.

"I'm sorry, my friend."

Lifting her head, trembling with fury, her every muscle coiled, Damaris stepped past Kadir's body and over the threshold of the temple's entrance.

***

The pang of something striking her window screen distracted Sara from the doodle she was absentmindedly working on. Figuring a bird had run into the screen, she ignored it, but when it came again a second later, she got up and went over to the window, peering out.

Felix stood below, looking up at her. He lifted one hand and waved. He was dressed in his Shadow uniform, his bow and a quiver full of arrows on his back.

Sara opened the window and called down to him. "Felix! What are you doing here?"

"I came to check on you."

"Stay there. I'll come down."

She closed her window and hurried downstairs and out into the yard where he was waiting. "If my dad sees you here, he'll flip."

Felix raised an eyebrow. "Really?"

She thought back to her conversation with her dad and that he had, in fact, been aware of Wysteria's existence all this time. She smiled. "Well, maybe not." Still, he hadn't believed Wysteria would be a part of his family's life any longer. What would he think to find it, here in his back yard? "But why are you here?"

"I told you. Lylla sent me to check on you."

"Why? Has something happened since I left?"

He frowned. "The trap we set for Galatea failed. She came, as expected, but fled when she realized it wasn't really you. Damaris claims she got a hit on her, though, if that's any consolation."

It wasn't, really. Sara crossed her arms. "So that's it. The plain failed and Lylla's worried Galatea might try something."

"Aren't you? Worried, I mean?"

"Of course, but—" Sara broke off as her phone rang. "Hold on a sec."

She pulled the phone out of her pocket and glanced at it. "It's Professor Lawrence. Here, I'll put him on speaker. Hello?"

"Sara? Something's come up. I need you to meet me at my house as soon as you can. Come through the back door. You know how the front sticks. See you soon."

Before Sara had a chance to say anything, he hung up, severing the connection.

She put her phone back in her pocket. "I'd better go."

Felix held out an arm to stop her. "Wait. I'll go with you."

"I'm just going to Professor Lawrence's."

There was something in his green eyes she didn't like. "I know, but…well, don't you think it's odd that he didn't say what this thing was that's come up. He didn't mention that, but he made sure to mention you should come through the back door."

Sara shrugged, hoping it masked her growing unease. Felix was making her nervous. "The front door sticks."

"Has that ever stopped you from using it before?"

"Well, no. He usually opens it, though."

"It's settled. I'm going with you."

"Suit yourself," Sara replied, walking toward her car. Felix climbed into the passenger seat and two minutes later, they pulled up outside Professor Lawrence's house. The sun was beginning to set, bringing an end to the long summer evening. The fading light illuminated the house's white siding, the windows dark within.

"No lights on," Felix observed, staring at the darkened house. "I don't like it."

"Maybe the power went out," Sara suggested. "He's on a different line than I am in town."

Still, she took the possible warning to heart and crept around to the back of the house, Felix on her tail, where the back door was located. It was unlocked and she eased it open, stepping inside. The interior of the house was dark, without a single light on. *Too dark, perhaps?*

Heart in her throat, Sara groped along the wall for a light switch. She was tempted to summon light of her own, but every instinct screamed at her not to. Her fingers found the switch and she flicked it. Nothing happened. She flipped the switch several more times and then gave up.

Sara couldn't see Felix in the dark, but she felt his presence beside her, heard his breathing. She summoned a gentle illumination, a small sphere of light.

"Professor Lawrence?" she whispered. It seemed wrong to speak any louder.

"So good of you to join us," a voice replied, but it didn't belong to Professor Lawrence.

All at once, the darkness that permeated the house vanished and the lights were on once more, no longer cloaked, flooding the room with light. Sara yelped, her illumination fading. Professor Lawrence stood in the middle of the living room.

Behind him stood a very tall woman, with long black hair and a black dress. Her irises were black, so dark Sara couldn't make out the pupils. Her skin had an unhealthy gray tinge to it and two curved, pointed ears marked her as an elf. She held a sword to Professor Lawrence's throat.

In a flash, Felix's bow was in his hand, an arrow nocked and ready. "Galatea!" he hissed, confirming what Sara had been thinking. He stepped between her and the sorceress.

Sara inhaled sharply, unable to form any words. She could only stare at the woman in stunned silence. At last, she could put a face to the name. At last, she stood face to face with the sorceress she'd heard so much about—and feared more than she cared to admit.

Galatea smiled, both beautiful and terrible at once. "Felix. I'm surprised to find your Guardian is nowhere to be found."

"She's never far away," he replied, but Sara heard the uncertainty in his voice. He held the bowstring at the ready, but neither of them dared make a move so long as the sorceress held the sword at Professor Lawrence's neck.

Galatea's eyes flicked to Sara. "Hand over the stone and his head stays attached to his body. There's a good girl."

Sara looked at Professor Lawrence, whose face was white despite his set jaw. He was bleeding from a gash on his temple and she noticed with alarm that the shoulder of his shirt was wet with blood.

He said nothing, but she thought she saw him give a slight, nearly imperceptible shake of the head. She found herself slowly reaching up for the chain around her neck, as though moving in a trance, her eyes never leaving his face.

"Don't," Felix whispered. "You can't give it to her."

"I have to!" Sara choked out, finding her voice. "Or she'll kill him."

"And as soon as she has the stone, what's to stop her from killing *all* of us?" Felix demanded. He turned back to face the sorceress and her prisoner, helpless to do anything.

Sara slipped the necklace over her head, the chain dangling from her hand. She stared at the green gem hanging at the end of it.

The stone that had belonged to her mother, one of the few pieces of her Sara had left. Her heart ached to part with it, to part with what had become a part of herself. But in the end, the Echo Stone was just a trinket. It wasn't worth forfeiting someone's life in order to foolishly hold onto it.

Not when it was within her power to save him.

It seemed strange to think that this was what Galatea had wanted all this time and fought so hard to get her hands on. She had sent two imposters to try and coerce it from her and later kidnap her for it. Both attempts had failed. Sara had done all she could to ensure the sorceress never acquired the Echo Stone.

And here she was, about to hand it over to her.

Galatea held out one hand, still keeping the sword firmly in place. "There's a good girl," she repeated softly.

Sara stepped around Felix, ignoring his protests, and slowly approached the sorceress. She took a deep breath and draped the stone into Galatea's open palm. As soon as the stone touched her skin, her fingers wrapped around it like a vise and she yanked it away. Sara stumbled back away from her.

"At last," Galatea murmured.

"Now let him go," Felix ordered.

She smiled. "I think not."

"No!" Sara screamed as Galatea's Shadowblade opened the Professor's throat.

Blood poured forth, staining his shirt red. Sara rushed forward as he fell, kneeling beside him, her hands trembling uselessly. There was too much blood. It was everywhere, and she choked on its coppery tang.

Felix loosed his arrow. Galatea knocked it aside with a blast of wind. Lightning sprang from her fingers. Felix cried out, falling to his knees.

"Jack!" Galatea called out, yanking the stone off the chain and hissing softly as the silver burned her. "Come here!"

Professor Lawrence reached out, taking one of Sara's shaking hands in his own. "I'm sorry," she sobbed, helpless to do anything as the life bled out of him. "I'm sorry."

Another figure came shuffling down the hall and into the living room. Sara looked up and recoiled in horror at the sight of Galatea's dead lover. His skin had decayed, his clothing tattered, shirt riddled with holes, including a particularly large one over the center of his chest. His eyes glowed a solid green and the stench of the grave rolled across the room, mingling with the blood. Sara felt like retching.

Galatea turned to him, lifting the stone with a sort of tenderness that Sara found both endearing and revolting.

"At last, my dear," the sorceress whispered. "You may live again."

Her fingers slipped into the hole in his chest, placing the stone in his ribcage. She stepped back, surveying her handiwork and waited. Sara watched, her breath coming in ragged gasps, expecting Jack to speak at any moment.

Slowly, before her eyes, his skin began to mend itself, the color returning to his face. The green glow faded from his eyes and he blinked, his gaze focusing on Galatea. His eyes had been a deep green in life and now they shone with awareness for the first time.

Galatea stared at him as if in awe. She whispered his name and slowly reached up to touch his face.

Jack's eyes met hers. "Galatea?" he whispered.

"Yes," she breathed.

Slowly, his gaze traveled around the room, taking in the scene before him. Felix, on his hands and knees, struggling to rise. Lawrence, his throat torn open, the blood covering his neck and chest. Sara, kneeling beside him, sobbing quietly, the blood having managed to cover her as well.

Jack's gaze returned to Galatea. "What have you done?" he asked, voice soft but full of horror.

Galatea's exultant expression faded. "What do you mean? I did it for you. For us. At last, we can be together again!" Her voice took on a desperate note, aching to make him understand, and then dropped to almost a whisper. "I thought you'd be happy to see me…"

But Jack was backing away from her, recoiling in revulsion, shaking his head. "This isn't right."

Behind Galatea, Felix staggered to his feet. He raised his bow. With a growl, Galatea whirled on him, lightning blasting out from her fingertips once more, sending him back to the ground. He cried out, writhing in pain, as the electricity continued to course through his body.

She'll kill him, Sara thought, *if I don't do something.* But what could she do against a Guardian as powerful as Galatea? She began to rise to her feet when the large window along the back of the wall exploded in a shower of glass.

Galatea's lightning ceased. Felix's cries cut off. Damaris sprang into the room, in her unicorn form, eyes blazing. She surveyed the scene, eyes locking on Jack, teeth bared. Flames sprang to life at his feet and an acrid smell filled the air as his flesh began to sear away.

"That's for Kadir," the Flame Guardian growled.

"*No!*" Galatea cried, scrambling toward Jack.

Strangely, he made no sound, though the flames must have caused unbearable pain. He made no attempt to move away from the fire or to put it out. Sara watched him, transfixed by the odd reaction. He retreated from Galatea, further into the flames, as though he welcomed death, for he never should have been given life in such a manner.

"Get out!" Damaris yelled at her and Felix, but she barely heard the Flame Guardian.

Gritting his teeth, Felix got to his feet, hurrying over to where Sara still knelt beside Professor Lawrence. Darkness rose up around Galatea, lightning crackling within its depths, and the whites of her eyes darkened as she turned toward Damaris.

The flames spread from Jack to the curtains and up the walls, licking across the ceiling. The ugly floral chair was engulfed and all Sara could think was how Professor Lawrence had said it was a family antique. The heat made her skin hurt and her eyes water even more than they already were. She could hardly see, everything blurred impressions of what she knew them to be.

Damaris shouted at them again. Felix tugged at Sara. "Come on, we have to go."

"No!" she cried. "I won't leave him!"

"He's already gone, Sara. We have to go."

She looked at the Professor and saw the truth of Felix's words. With a muffled sob, she let him pull her to her feet and bundle her out the back door, into the night air. She followed him, her tears blurring the world around her. The outside air felt cold after the searing heat inside the house.

Sara choked in sobbing gasps as she ran, lungs burning, side aching. They were halfway across the yard when the house exploded behind them. Sara yelped, a wave of sound and heat washing over her. The force threw them both to the ground. Sara felt something whizz through the air above her head. The air was partially knocked out of her as she fell, Felix's body breaking her fall as she landed on top of him.

Blinking, she quickly scrambled off of him and together, they turned and stared at what remained of Professor Lawrence's house. The roof had been blown off by the force of the explosion, the walls leveled. A fireball was still rising into the air as though a bomb had gone off, debris raining from the sky.

A brick had landed a few feet away, among others that had been scattered by the force, and Sara realized dimly that that was what had narrowly missed her. The wreckage of the house was completely engulfed in flames.

She wanted to run forward and find Professor Lawrence and drag him outside to safety, but she knew it was pointless. He was dead, and even if he hadn't been before, he was now. She didn't know how anyone could survive such an explosion.

She and Felix merely sat there in the grass, watching the flames. Sara could still feel the heat from where they were, the night lit up orange and yellow.

Sara gasped as Damaris pushed her way out of the wreckage and ambled toward them, limping slightly, though there was not a burn on her. She was panting softly by the time she reached them, turning to solemnly regard the flames.

"Galatea?" Felix asked softly.

Damaris shook her head. "I don't know."

"Professor Lawrence?" Sara asked, even though she knew what the Flame Guardian would say. It just couldn't be true. It couldn't be.

Damaris shook her head again, this time the meaning clear.

A ragged sob was torn from Sara's chest. She had given Galatea the Echo Stone and the sorceress had still killed Professor Lawrence. Everything that had happened here tonight was her fault. Galatea might have left the Professor alone if Sara hadn't come.

She hoped Galatea perished in the fire. Her and Jack both.

Sara felt Felix's arms slip around her, which only made her cry harder, and she turned to bury her face in his shoulder, unable and unwilling to watch the fire burn any longer. He smelled faintly of leather, horses, and sweat, chasing away the scent of blood and death that had clung to her.

She didn't know how long she stayed like that, but she heard him ask, "How did you know where to find us?"

"I had returned to the Wind Gate, but I arrived too late," Damaris replied, a hint of bitterness in her voice. "Galatea had gotten there first."

"Go on back. I'll take Sara home."

"I'll wait here at the Gate for you."

Sara didn't know how, but she managed to drive herself and Felix back to her house, the road passing by in a blur. She didn't even remember climbing into the car, but the next thing she knew, she was back home, standing out on the porch with him. The tears had stopped, but her nose was stuffy and her eyes red and swollen.

"Are you going to be all right?" Felix asked softly.

Wordlessly, Sara nodded. Her throat felt too tight to speak and she didn't trust herself not to start crying again. Part of her wanted to beg him not to leave her alone, but she knew that was impossible. He had a job to do.

"Come find me if you need me."

She nodded again and stepped inside, closing the door on the endless summer night.

***

Felix watched Sara until she was out of sight. He knew what she felt—how they all felt, and that there was nothing he could do to help. It was not a physical wound that could be healed with medicine or bandages. It would heal, but more slowly. Not all scars were visible.

He sighed. News of the house explosion would spread like wildfire throughout a town like this and they would need to be gone by then. The house still burned when he returned to Damaris, standing vigil beside the lonely red Gate.

He wondered if she thought of the same thing he did. The sound of crackling flames and falling timber reminded him of the night his village burned. An entirely different situation, but two things were the same. Someone had died. And she had come for him, as she always would.

"Let's go," she murmured, opening the Gate for him.

There was no sign of Kadir when they exited the Golden Temple, but the sand was still stained with blood where the fallen Guardian had lain. Desert elves had come from Khae to kneel outside the temple, mourning the loss of their chieftain and Wind Guardian.

Two Guardians in one night.

Felix glanced at Damaris and could see the sorrow visible in her gaze, but he knew she would not weep. She never did. She had expended the anger at Kadir's death by causing the house to explode with Galatea in it, knowing she would be immune to the flames.

He reached up, touching her thick mane and wrapping his fingers in it. He hadn't been tall enough to reach it the night she'd saved him.

"Come on." She began walking away and he followed.

"What happened in the house?"

"Does it matter?"

Felix thought for a moment. "No." He waited a few heartbeats before asking, "Do you think she's dead?"

"I intend to go back and find out," she replied.

"You don't think she's dead."

Damaris sighed. "I'd very much like for her to be. But after what happened with Malenwar and everyone assuming she was, I can't allow myself to believe it without seeing the proof with my own eyes."

"Well, Jack and the Professor are both dead."

"Destroyed, along with the Echo Stone."

"Yes," Felix said. Then, with a sudden anger, "What a waste."

The loss of life was senseless and all because Galatea couldn't let go of the past, of a grudge she had nurtured for the past fifty years.

They had all lost something because of the sorceress, but Felix was beginning to think that Sara had lost more than any of them.

21

Galatea waited in the darkness until Damaris, Felix, and the girl had left. No sooner were they out of sight than she wanted to rush forward to the burning wreckage that had been Lawrence's home. But she forced herself to wait. It could be a trap, the others waiting just out of sight, to see if she would come back into the light.

But they did not return. Galatea realized she was being ridiculous. No doubt Damaris believed her dead. And she should have been. The darkness that she'd gathered around herself had absorbed most of the blast, but not all.

A small sound of pain escaped her lips. She didn't need a mirror to know it was bad. Burns lanced up her left arm, over her shoulder, neck, and the left side of her face, all the way to the scalp. She could feel where the hair had been and now was no longer. Her left eye must have been damaged as well, for she couldn't see out of it. She had no way of knowing if the loss was permanent but thought it very likely was.

What would Jack think if he could see her now, no longer flawless as elves were meant to be? Galatea wanted to weep to think of him now. The horror on his face as he'd looked at her had come as an utter shock. It could not have been further from the way she'd expected him to look at her.

After everything she had sacrificed, all the years she had waited… Didn't he understand what she had done for him so that he might live again? Wasn't that what he had wanted? To live?

Wincing, Galatea got to her feet and limped over toward the remains of the house. It was still burning, the scattered timbers glowing red hot, but she ignored them. The ash burned the soles of her feet as she stepped across them, but she ignored that too.

Nothing could compare with the torment raging inside her.

She had known. Of course she had known. But still she searched for Jack's body, among the wreckage, among the ash. She found only Lawrence's blackened corpse and he had been dead before the fire took him.

There was no place for a body to hide. Her Jack was gone. Forever this time.

A body she could resurrect. Ash she could do nothing with.

With a wail, Galatea sank to her knees, sparks and embers floating around her, fire crackling among the timbers. There was no one to hear her and even if there were, she didn't care. There was no one to witness her pain.

Desolation swept over her, unlike that which she had felt at Jack's first death. Somehow, she'd known even then that he wasn't truly gone. There was still hope of a second chance, of a future together. And now there would be no future. She would continue on alone.

Galatea reached out and grabbed her Shadowblade from where it had fallen, half-buried in the ash. For one mad moment, she considered ending it all there and now. She could bring an end to her pain. The afterlife was the only way she could hope to be reunited with Jack now.

Letting out another cry of frustration, the blade fell from her hands. She couldn't. She wouldn't.

Galatea let her wave of grief carry her away, losing herself in it, letting handfuls of ash slip through her fingers.

***

Damaris returned to the scene of Professor Lawrence's house the following morning, in her human guise. The collapsed debris still smoked and smoldered and a fire truck was parked nearby, along with the sheriff's car. She circled around them, sticking to the trees, and then approached on the road so that they wouldn't see her coming out of the woods and wonder why.

Her sandals crunching on the rock driveway, Damaris walked up to where the sheriff stood, surveying the mess.

"Good morning," she called out. "I'm from the newspaper. I was wondering if you could tell me anything about what happened here."

"Gas explosion," he replied. "Mr. Lawrence was home at the time. Died in the fire."

Damaris did not have to affect sadness, even though the news was no news to her at all. "Was he home alone?"

"It appears so. There have been no other bodies found."

She let out a quiet breath. That was both good and bad. They wouldn't have found Jack's body among the wreckage. She had incinerated him so that Galatea would have no hope of attempting to reanimate him again.

But there was no female corpse that could have been Galatea. That didn't mean she had survived, of course, but if the fire had been hot enough to incinerate her completely, why had they been able to find Lawrence? There should have been nothing left at all.

Seeing her expression, the sheriff went on. "We haven't quite gone through everything, but we're pretty sure it was him."

She nodded. "I see. Thank you."

Damaris turned and walked away. There was nothing else she could do here except return to Lylla and give her report. Once she no longer felt the sheriff's eyes on her, Damaris headed back into the trees and entered through the Gate.

***

Lylla looked up from the shoreline at the sound of steps nearing, crunching on the sand. Damaris headed in her direction. Lylla stepped back, pulling her feet out of the ocean.

"Any news?" she called.

"The house completely burned to the ground and anything inside was destroyed. The police have found a body. Lawrence."

Lylla regarded her steadily. "Only him?"

Damaris nodded. "Yes. No sign of Jack, as expected. But also no sign of Galatea."

"Are you surprised?"

The Flame Guardian made a wry face. "I'd be lying if I said I was. No. Just disappointed."

"She could be dead," Lylla acknowledged. "But we must assume she's still alive. Everyone believed she was dead after Malenwar and look what that cost us."

"Too many Guardians dead…Cyren, Reverend Pierce, Kadir, and now Lawrence. Not to mention all the other soldiers she's responsible for." Damaris tilted her head. "If she doesn't end up dying of her wounds, do you think she'll dare show her face again?"

"If she's alive, I can't see her giving up on vengeance now."

Damaris shook her head. "She should have died with Jack in Malenwar."

Lylla said nothing, staring out over the waves at the endless Green Sea, the wind stirring her dress around her legs.

Galatea had caused so much pain, all because she had been made to hurt. *How could you do that to someone else, when you know what it feels like?*

She thought of Damaris and the loss of Kadir, one of her dearest friends despite his betrayal. The desert elves had lost their chieftain. She thought of Cassius having his own dead sister attack him, of Reverend Pierce being cut down in his own churchyard, and Lawrence being killed in front of a family friend who was powerless to save him.

Lylla wondered how Sara was taking it. She would give the girl time to mourn her loss and then training would have to resume. Sara needed to learn to control her powers and successfully defend herself in a fight.

Lylla had the sickening feeling that it would be needed.

***

After Felix had returned her to her house, Sara refused to come out, except for the funeral. She didn't want to go, but she felt that she owed Professor Lawrence that much. In the crowd—practically everyone in the town attended— she saw Lylla, her turquoise hair pinned up in a bun and mostly hidden beneath an enormous black hat. It was the first time Sara had ever seen Lylla dressed in black. Damaris was also there, likewise in human form, standing beside Felix.

They stood out, even with glamours, but everyone else must have assumed they had something to do with the college where Professor Lawrence had once worked.

386

Sara avoided their eyes. She didn't want to be near them and stayed close beside Nadia and Max, who had come, more to offer her moral support than anything else. They hadn't known Professor Lawrence personally, but Sara was grateful for the gesture all the same.

Her dad stood close behind, a clear line drawn between the two sides. One side belonged to Earth, the other to Wysteria. It was strange to see the two brought together, here, in her hometown. But Professor Lawrence had been a part of both.

More than once, out of the corner of her eye, Sara saw Felix glance over at her. She wasn't the only one to notice the concerned looks he was giving her.

"Who's the redhead?" Nadia whispered.

Sara shrugged, didn't look up. "Someone from the college, I guess."

"I wonder where he got those scars," Nadia added, her voice too low to carry. "It looks like he was mauled."

Sara winced inwardly. The darkness in the wound ensured the scars could not be concealed with a glamour. It must have made Felix uncomfortable, knowing everyone was staring, but his only concern seemed to be for her. That only made her feel worse, ignoring him and all the others as she was.

When the service concluded, she saw Lylla begin to make her way through the crowd toward her, but Sara turned and left, not wanting to talk and once again sequestered herself in the safety of her room, where no one could reach her.

Even her father's prodding couldn't convince her to leave her room for anything other than what was essential. Her food was brought to her and then taken away, often untouched. He talked about taking time off work to be with her, but he didn't. They couldn't afford that. She had not the desire or the energy to do more than lay on her bed, staring at the muted light trying to come through the blinds on her window.

She couldn't help but feel that Professor Lawrence's death was somehow her fault. She had been the one foolish enough to give Galatea the Echo Stone after all. How could she have been so stupid as to think that it would help anything? Why would Galatea release Professor Lawrence unharmed once Sara gave her the stone? She had everything she wanted in that moment and all of them at her mercy.

Sara sometimes heard something small pinging against her screen toward the evening hours or when her father was at work. Out of curiosity, she'd pushed back the blinds and peered out to see Felix standing there, as he had on that fateful evening.

She ignored him and went back to bed. Eventually he stopped coming. She wanted nothing to do with any of them. They were part of the reason Professor Lawrence was gone. Damaris was the most powerful Guardian and there had been nothing she could have done to save him. She had arrived too late.

Sara knew that wasn't fair. Professor Lawrence would still have been part of Wysteria, even if she herself wasn't a Guardian and had never learned about it or become involved in any way. He still might have been confronted by Galatea at some point and the end result would have been the same, only Sara would have known nothing of it. Not the cause or the reasons why.

But mostly she was angry at herself. She was a Guardian and yet she had been utterly helpless. All the power she was supposed to possess was nowhere to be found when she needed it most. What good was having such abilities if she couldn't use them when it mattered?

She tried to forget, to pretend that Wysteria didn't exist, that she wasn't a Guardian, that none of it had ever happened, and that she could go back to living a normal—if somewhat boring—life in a small town. Give up her aspirations of wanting something more. But Professor Lawrence was still gone. No amount of pretending would change that.

And all she had to do was lift a hand and conjure light into her palm to painfully remind her of the truth. That was one fact she couldn't deny hiding away in her room.

Gradually, the pain dulled sufficiently for Sara to leave her house again. By then, summer was beginning to come to a close. In just a few weeks, she would be starting her senior year of high school. It felt much too soon, but it would, like everything else, have to be faced.

She couldn't hide in her room forever. She owed it to Professor Lawrence to show more courage.

Thankfully, by the time she emerged, talk of the house fire and explosion had died down to almost nothing. It was old news and people were on to speaking of other things. Her friends did not question her about it; there seemed to be some unspoken understanding between them not to mention it and she felt a rush of warmth toward them.

Just before the start of school, someone from Wysteria finally tried to contact her again. She had chosen to wait, rather than go to them, figuring they would try again sooner or later. And she'd been right.

Sara went to her window as a familiar pang struck the screen and looked down to see Felix standing there, looking up expectantly. To her surprise, she was far happier at seeing him than she'd anticipated, her heart feeling lighter than it had in months. She gestured that she'd meet him around front and hurried downstairs, stepping out onto the porch. The concrete was still warm on her bare feet from the day's sun.

She sat down on the edge of the porch, dangling her legs over. The bare patch of earth beneath had once held bulbs, but she couldn't remember which kinds. She'd never been very good at keeping plants alive and left the gardening to other people.

Felix came around the side of the house and joined her on the porch. His legs nearly reached the ground beneath, he was so much taller than her.

He broke the silence first. "How are you doing?" If he was hurt that she had ignored him previously, he gave no sign of it.

"Better," she replied. "What's been going on in Wysteria?" Part of her dreaded the answer, but she craved it at the same time. Perhaps he hadn't merely come to check on her. Maybe something had happened.

"The usual. Still no sign of Galatea, so either she's dead or gone into hiding."

"Which do you think?"

Felix stared across the lawn at the street beyond, the setting sun falling on his face. She could see every freckle on the left side of his profile, and of course the scars.

"I think she's out there somewhere," he said finally. "We'll have to be ready. Jack may be gone for good now, but I don't think she'll let this rest. Have you…given any thought to coming back?" He turned to her then, his deep green eyes slightly imploring.

Sara swallowed. She had come to a decision during her months of seclusion, but she had yet to share it with anyone. It terrified and excited her at the same time and if she spoke it aloud, then it would be real. "I've decided that I want to train to take Professor Lawrence's place as Guardian."

It seemed only right somehow. She couldn't save him from Galatea, but she could try to make sure the same fate didn't befall anyone else.

"I—I think it's what he would have wanted," she added, suddenly feeling self-conscious.

Felix's eyebrows rose. "It's an ambitious goal, to be sure, but I think you can do it. It won't be easy, though."

Sara quoted one of her mom's favorite sayings, "If it were easy, everyone would do it."

Felix laughed then, really laughed, more than a mere chuckle. It was still too brief and left Sara wanting more. "Well, that's the truth."

"What about you? Now that Galatea's gone, what's going to happen with you and Venryk?"

His smile faded. "I don't know. All those years Galatea was gone, the fire wolves were reclusive. I don't know how long Galatea will stay away, if she's alive. If she isn't, I don't know if the wolves will show themselves at all ever again."

Impulsively, Sara reached over and laid her hand on his. If Galatea had been killed in the fire, Wysteria had won. It would be a great victory for them. But Felix's battle was far from over. She didn't want him to become yet another casualty. She didn't want him to lose. *She* didn't want to lose him.

He squeezed her hand gently. "Don't worry about me. I'm still going to hunt that wolf down, if it's the last thing I do."

It very well might be. But Sara couldn't say that. He didn't want her to doubt him. The task would be hard enough as it was.

"Are you here to guard me?" she asked instead, changing the subject. "Or are you just here to visit?" She kept her tone light, teasing.

Felix smiled, his gaze leaving her eyes for a brief moment. "Maybe I'm just here to visit."

Sara felt her pulse spike. Had he just leaned closer to her?

"I was instructed to give you a message. Lylla says to take all the time you need, but when you're ready to continue with your training, she'll be waiting."

"I look forward to it," Sara replied. She didn't add that it may have to wait until she was out of school. *If Galatea gives us that long.*

"So do I," Felix said, sliding off the porch to stand on the grass. "I have to get back. With the Gates so heavily guarded, I don't know how often I'll be able to come back. But when you're ready to return to Wysteria, I'll be waiting for you."

"Be careful."

He regarded her for a moment. "You too." He hesitated, and then added softly, "If Galatea does come back, we'll be ready for her."

She watched him walk away until he had rounded the corner of the house and disappeared from sight.

Sara sat there on the porch, looking after him, thinking over his last words to her. *If Galatea does come back, we'll be ready for her.*

She lifted one hand and the light flared to life.

Yes, she thought. *We will.*

Thank you for reading!

Thirteen years ago, I wrote the very first words in the very first sentence of the very first draft of what would become this story.

Thirteen years ago, I decided that my dream was to become a published author. I have since achieved that dream, but an author is nothing without their readers. So thank you, reader, for giving this book a chance.

If you enjoyed this book, it would mean the world to me if you would consider leaving a review. Reviews are essential for authors. They help our books get seen, they help our book get promoted, and they can be the difference between whether or not another reader decides to take a chance on a book.

While it may sound cheesy, you are literally helping make my dream come true. So thank you again for your support and happy reading!

ACKNOWLEDGEMENTS

And now we come to what is arguably the most daunting part of the book to write, but which will hopefully be only the first of many.

Finding where to begin is not difficult—first, thank you to Mom, who has always stood by me and encouraged me, believing in me even when I did not. Thank you to Maw Maw for proofreading countless drafts and offering unwavering support.

Thank you to Coco, for the absolutely stunning cover art and Rena for the phenomenal cover design. These two ladies are incredibly talented and I could not be more grateful for their help in bringing my stories to life.

Thanks must also be extended to all of the friends and family members for offering support. Even the little things, though they may seem simple, mean more than you can know. So thank you.

Thank you, reader, for taking a chance on this book and for helping to make a dream come true. It means the world to me.

And last, but certainly far from least, all glory to God, for giving me this gift and setting me on this path.

ABOUT THE AUTHOR

Rachel Terry grew up in a small town where nothing much ever happened, dreaming of grand adventures and far-away places, which she found between the pages of books. When not writing, she can be found reading, making YouTube videos, gaming with friends, or indulging in her love of history. She currently resides in the Midwest with her family and a cat named Crinkles. *Lightbringer* is her first novel.

Visit her online at: rachel-terry.com

YouTube: RachelTerryAuthor

Instagram: rterrywriter

Facebook: rachelterryauthor